"We are hard-pressed
on every side,
yet not crushed;

we are perplexed,
but not in despair;

persecuted,
but not forsaken;

struck down,
but not destroyed."

**2 CORINTHIANS 4:8,
NKJV**

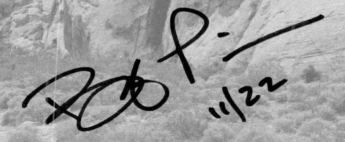

THE ATOMIC DELI
a dangerous love story

BOB PIERCE

Published by Bob Pierce
Milton, Vermont 05468
BobsAwesomeBooks@gmail.com
www.BobsAwesomeBooks.com

Printed in the still-relatively-free United States of America.

Kindle printed edition
ISBN: 9798444951170
Independently published

Back Cover Background photos by: Pexels Adam Kontor and Alex Andres, props and models by the author.
Front Cover Photo by the author

Interior photos by: Pexels Pixabay, public domain and/or by the author.

Models and props constructed by the author.

DEDICATIONS

To the Lord who has given me the inspiration, story and characters in this book and the wherewithal to express them. Who showed me that there is value in telling an impactful tale that may inspire and move others.

To my wife, Stephanie, who has been beside me all these years on this meandering road and added her ideas, inspirations and occasional proofreading.

To long-time married couples and those just beginning their own meandering journey together who will face challenges and intrusions that would conspire to pull them apart. To take heart and find the strength that is sometimes needed to perservere. May this story be an encouragement.

To those who have endured the government-imposed mandates and constrictions of the pandemic years, not sure whom to believe, continually hoping for an imminent and decisive ending. Hopefully this story will inspire some level of strength through the coming times.

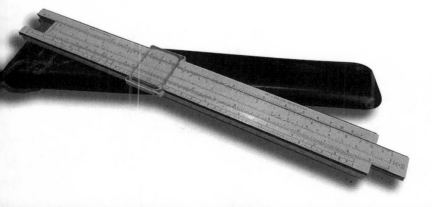

Table of Contents

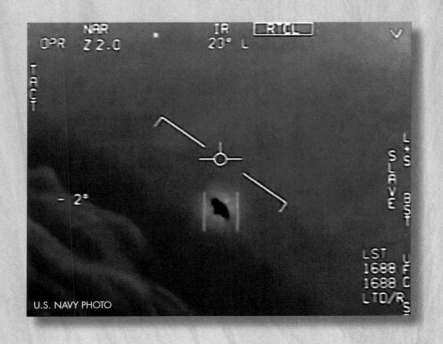

BOB PIERCE

Introduction

Recently declassified videos released by the Pentagon and filmed by American Navy F-18 fighter pilots over the course of several years showing the undeniable images of unidentified flying aircraft performing inexplicable aerial maneuvers fueled the argument for a long-lobbied-for investigation by the Senate, the White House's National Security Council, the Pentagon, Homeland Security, the Department of Defense and various intelligence agencies. Fascinating as they might have been to the UFO faithful and the passively curious minds of some Americans, the testimony of one of the Navy pilots on an NBC television news program where some of the videos were shown to the public added an element of undeniable reality to the story. No longer could they simply be disregarded as the stuff of science fiction novels, movies and wild imaginations.

The government, who had been studying these aerial phenomena for decades at various levels of security and sincerity, was finally convinced from within that these craft — because they *cannot* be identified or explained — may actually pose a legitimate threat to national security.

Funding for the Unidentified Aerial Phenomena Task Force and the Advanced Aviation Threat Identification Program was finally secured after years of insistence by Senator Harry Reid of Nevada and later shepherded by Florida Senator Marco Rubio after Reid's subsequent retirement.

The inquiry had been promoted by Senator John Chow of Hawaii. His constituents routinely reported strange lights in the sky around the islands. Home to the Pearl Harbor naval base, the largest and most capable in the Pacific, and the Joint Base Pearl Harbor-Hickam Air Base along with assorted radar, satellite listening facilities and tracking stations (many of which highly classified), the islands are strategically vital for national defense and intelligence. Frustrated by seemingly dismissive, official explanations and stonewalling, Chow called for a Senate hearing to interview witnesses both official and civilian, technical and anecdotal. He and others in both the House and Senate insisted on these hearings to happen before the Task Force would finally be launched and before it could issue its final report to hopefully add perspective from various credible sources.

Joining Chow in this quest was Senator Emily Stone of Nevada, the state that had been the site of nuclear testing in the desert and home of the Nellis Air Force Base where the infamous Area Fifty-One is located — the state that Reid had previously represented. Stone, the chairperson of the Senate Judiciary Committee, insisted in public comments that such an investigation was a critical matter of national security. In widely heralded speeches, she stressed that we as a nation needed to know just what those lights in the sky — and other unexplained sightings — actually were. Did they pose a threat? Were they from hostile nations like Russia, North Korea or China? Were members of the opposing political party somehow in collusion with them and perpetuating a cover-up?

Senator William McDermott of Rhode Island added his endorsement as well. As chairman of the Senate Intelligence Committee, he insisted that all of the evidences and reports — both those classified and unclassified — dating from the Roswell crash in 1947 to present day, be reexamined. All of the Air Force's Project Blue Book files were to be opened and reviewed as well as the findings of the Robertson Panel. Reported crash sites in the sóuthwest as well as Ohio, Pennsylvania, Florida and throughout the rest of the country needed to be revisited and studied anew. Police reports of sightings from every state and every municipality and county were to be given the same new scrutiny. Abduction reports such as the sensationalistic story of Betty and Barney Hill of New Hampshire, were to be given fresh eyes and closer, open-minded examination to separate legend from fact.

The three senators, with the endorsement of the White House and support of the Pentagon, were finally able to launch their investigation, including public hearings and the media circus that would undoubtedly accompany it. Such comprehensive coverage would assure the public that their government was taking the issue seriously and doing all that it could to get to the bottom of it all.

It would all culminate in a comprehensive report which, with the exception of any sensitive materials that had to remain classified, would be released to the public. It would, hopefully, satisfy the military, intelligence community and federal government with the answers they needed to make informed judgements about national security and, too, quell the curiosity of the general public, particularly the UFO conspiracy-theory faithful who insist upon perpetuating anything and everything relating to flying saucers and little green (or gray) men and insisting that any official denials were certain proof that it was all true.

Previous attempts by the Air Force to release reports reputably, decisively, explaining all that had happened at Roswell in 1947 were filled with details and photos and met with only luke warm responses. Mostly, the UFO conspiracy community dismissed them as being misinformation intended to put the public off of the trail. The reports ended up actually fanning the flames rather than extinguishing them, giving rise to innumerable cable-television, streaming, blog and internet programs about aliens and UFOs as civilian communication technologies entertainment outlets would evolve in the ensuing years.

The hearing would be convened to hear from and question a long list of witnesses which would include scientists, people from NASA, various military, intelligence and security agencies within the government, prominent UFO conspiracy theorists and one Dennis Foster, a physicist who claimed to have been employed at a secret laboratory at Area Fifty-One.

He, along with his wife, Olivia — Livvy, had been subpoenaed at their Boston bakery to appear and give his testimony about his alleged time at the secret government facility deep inside Papoose Mountain in the desert. A facility where he'd claimed alien technologies were being reverse-engineered, alien spacecraft were being studied and flown and the aliens themselves were being dissected and studied. The ultra-secret Facility R-Four-Seven.

No one else had ever come forward to talk about the lab. Security was so tight that the lab's very existence was just little more than a persistent rumor, even to nearly every member of government, but nevertheless popular amongst conspiracy theorists. Members of Congress knew that the Air Force, the CIA and other agencies, along with support from other shadowy groups like M-7, spent billions of black dollars on secretive projects in the desert. Few questions were ever asked as results from Lockheed's Skunkworks kept producing breakthrough spy and stealth aircraft that were built, tested and developed at the Groom Lake air base within Area Fifty-One.

The U-2 spy plane that showed President Kennedy the Russian missiles being amassed in Cuba. The SR-71 spy plane that showed General Westmorland details of North Vietnam and China during the war and would later give NASA a platform for high speed, high altitude atmospheric studies. Even the strangely-faceted F-117 stealth fighter and the B-2 Spirit stealth bomber — their existence kept entirely shrouded until their deployment during the first Gulf War — were all developed and tested there under a thick veil of secrecy.

But what about the UFO questions related to the base? It has nagged at the government for over seventy years. Could a Senate investigation finally answer questions that had persisted, unanswered, for all that time? Questions often addressed with official denials or by fanciful inventions of critics and self-proclaimed experts on radio shows, podcasts and popular websites.

The hearings would be a media event. Senate hearings were routinely shown on television via CSPAN, as any other legislative procedures, and largely ignored by a disinterested public. For this one, however, the press would be ponderously present. Even the odds makers in Las Vegas were taking bets on various aspects of the testimony and the likely outcome as far as what the Senators' report might actually admit to — or not.

Dennis and Livvy Foster, with their pro-bono lawyer Saul Rabinowitz, flew into Washington the previous afternoon after the couple had left their shop in the capable hands of two trusted, long-time employees. That evening, in the hotel's restaurant, Rabinowitz went over some last minute preparations with them — but mostly he gave a coach's pep-talk before the big game — dinner, encouragement and a bit of strategy.

They met the morning of the hearing's first day in the hotel's lobby and boarded a town car that had been sent for them. They rode up Constitution Avenue to the Dirksen Senate Office Building to be on time for their appointed appearance at the inquest.

They were issued visitor passes to wear as they entered the building, walked through the metal detectors, and then directed to the hearing chambers in room 226. A gathering of people in office attire loitered in the hallway outside along with a few Secret Service agents who stood close by the doors and a handful of reporters who were waiting to interview any witnesses out in the lobby as they'd leave after having given their testimony. The trio stopped and stood in the hallway just beyond the velvet ropes at the periphery of the motley gathering.

"Nervous?" Rabinowitz asked of the two Fosters.

"Yeah," Livvy responded. "I'd much rather be making scones right now."

"Me too," Foster added. "But maybe this will finally be the end of it. It's been a long, frustrating ride. Maybe this will be where we can finally get off."

"Well, let's hope so," Rabinowitz encouraged. "Now remember, when you get in there, just tell the truth. Answer their questions and tell your story — don't leave anything out — America needs to hear this. We all know that these politicians couldn't care less about either of you but you're not here for them."

"As someone once said to me, 'if they can do all of this to a bona-fide rocket scientist, they can do it to anyone.' He was right. Believe me, I won't leave out a thing."

"And, Livvy..." the lawyer began.

"Don't worry about me, Saul. I've stood by Denny through the worst of it so far. I'll be there for him in there, today. Don't forget, what they did to him, they did to me, too."

"Good," he looked up and saw one of the Secret Service agents waving to them. "Looks like it's time."

The Fosters followed their attorney as they wove through the crowd who, not knowing who they were or what to expect from their testimoeny, paid no mind to them and spread apart to let the innocuous looking, septuagenerian couple pass. One of the agents pulled the door open for them. Waiting for them on the inside was another agent who then escorted them to the front of the room to a long witness table, directing them to sit down in the three chairs that had been set up for them near its center — the proceedings would begin momentarily.

As they walked down the long, center aisle between hundreds of people seated in the gallery to either side, Foster looked around. The space seemed a lot smaller than he'd expected, even kind of cramped. The room was appointed with wood paneling from the floor to its towering ceiling with bronze, art-deco light fixtures and ornate, carved wooden details.

The dais was a semi-circular desk made of mahogany in the same ornate style as the paneling on the walls. It arced across nearly the entire width of the room at the outside ends and was elevated just enough to allow those seated at it to look down on the witnesses sitting at the long table before them. Spaced all along the circumference of the dais were a couple dozen empty chairs for the senators, military officers and other interrogators to sit facing into the center where their witnesses would be seated at the table. Each of the stations were outfitted with microphones on desk-top stands and small engraved name signs to identify those who would be seated there for both the witnesses and the media.

Behind the senators' seats was a shallow gallery of a row of seats along the back wall in which were already seated various advisors, lawyers and aides. Several intern/gophers prepared to dash out of the room at a moment's notice to retrieve documents, coffee or snacks as the senators might direct, stood at the ready in the periphery.

Foster studied the faces of those seated behind the dais and noticed a few that were quite familiar, two of which he knew all too well and others that he'd seen around during his dubious adventure that he was about to testify about. They were older than he'd remembered, a bit more gray hair (and less of it) and a few more wrinkles — like him — but unmistakable nevertheless. It seemed to him even before he sat down at the witness table that the fix was in — but then, what more could they do to him? And on national television, no less? If their presence was intended to be an intimidation tactic, it would only serve to steel Foster's resolve as he'd testify.

The Fosters and their lawyer sat down at the long, rectangular table with Dennis in the center, Livvy to his left and Rabinowitz to his right. Each place had its own microphone on a stand and interns quickly set name signs in front of each of them once they were seated. A pitcher of water on a shallow tray was on the table with an empty glass in front of each position. Interns would tend the table, refilling the pitcher as needed and to help with anything else that the witnesses might need.

One of the marshals standing in the periphery would shuttle any exhibits or other documents back and forth between the witness table and the dais.

In the open, hemispherical space between the dais and the witness table were a pair of small, matching desks where a pair of stenographers sat. One was at about ten o'clock to their left and the other at two o'clock and both angled to face toward the witness table and much lower than the dais behind them. On the desk to their left was perched a glowing red lava lamp conspicuously set up at its front corner. A detail not lost on Foster as he surveyed the room.

Crouched in the space between them were several photographers from magazines, newspapers and various news agencies with their press passes dangling on lanyards from their necks. On tripods behind the witness table were a quartet of CSPAN's television cameras with their lenses trained on the line of senators on the dais and four others were set up behind the senators and their own gallery of advisors with their lenses trained back toward the witnesses at the table.

Rabinowitz set his briefcase down on the table off to his right and opened it to remove a few folders, a couple of note pads and pens that he passed along to the Fosters. Then, finally, the announcement was called out for all to stand as the Senators then filed into the room from a side door and began taking their seats at the dais.

Senator Chow was the hearing's chairman and sat in the center seat on the dais with Senators Stone and McDermott to his immediate left and right, respectively. Beyond them sat General Richard Quinn from the Department of Defense and Air Force Colonel Mark Cibrian. The rest of the seats at the dais were filled with other senators, military officers and assorted and sundry members of the intelligence community. Once all were in their seats, the rest of the people in the room were allowed to sit again and Chow banged his gavel to call the proceedings to order.

One of the marshals stepped up to the witness table with a Bible in his left hand. He held it out flat and reached it out for Foster and his wife to lay their left hands on it and all three then raised their right hands to take the oath promising to tell the truth, the whole truth and nothing but the truth — so help them God.

Chow put on a pair of reading glasses to quickly scan a sheet of paper in front of him and then removed them again as he looked up at the Fosters and said, "Would the witnesses please identify themselves for the record."

Rabinowitz stood up and answered, "Your honor, these are the Fosters, Dennis and Olivia, here to answer your subpoena."

"And you, sir. Who are you?"

"I'm their counsel, Attorney Saul Rabinowitz."

"This isn't a trial, Mr. Rabinowitz. And you don't have to refer to me or anyone else on this panel as 'your honor,' just 'senator' or 'general' or whatever might be appropriate."

"Thank you, Senator."

"You may have a seat, sir," Chow turned his attention to the Fosters. "Mr. Foster, we on this panel have all seen your television interview and read the transcripts of the your radio interviews as 'John Smith'."

Foster leaned in to the microphone, "You have? Why then, Senator, are we here?"

"Frankly, sir, your story is rather unbelievable although it has gained wide acceptance in certain circles. We want to hear your story from you in person, on the record — your sworn statement under penalty of perjury — and to ask questions as we might see fit."

"The 'official' version, eh?"

"You could call it that — yes"

Foster picked up the water pitcher and poured himself a glass of water. Then, as he reached for his wife's empty glass to fill it, too, he asked, "Where would you like me to start?"

"Why, at the beginning of course."

"The beginning? Alright then, from the beginning."   ■

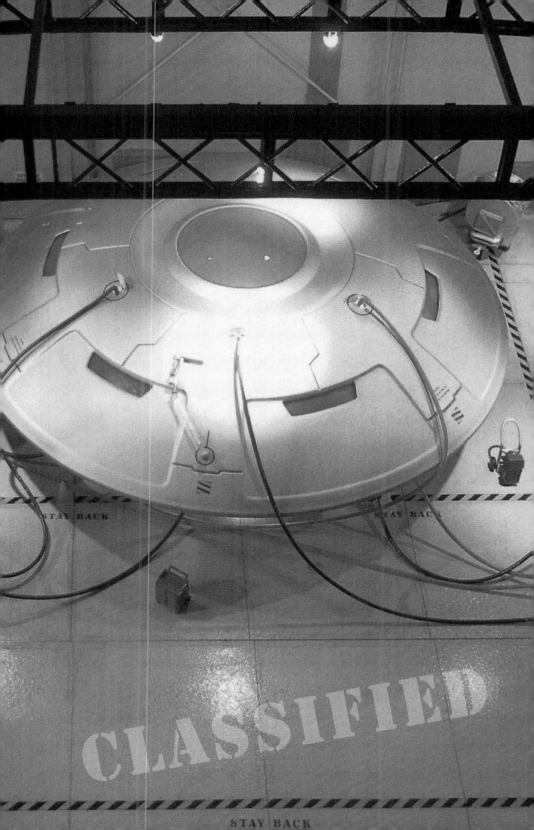

STAY BACK

STAY BACK

CLASSIFIED

STAY BACK

PHASE 1
THE PLAN

CHAPTER ONE

Underground New York

Benny Taffin and Max Garner stood on the platform at New York City's Grand Central subway station waiting for the special train that would come along and take them northbound to a clandestine meeting site at an undisclosed location somewhere beneath the city. They had just flown in from Los Angeles the previous afternoon and checked into the Trump Plaza downtown where they'd spent the previous night in a luxury room reserved for them by their hosts complete with room service, dinner and open bar. The instructions they'd received said to be there at the station by ten o'clock that morning. The special, an express train, would bring them directly to their destination.

"This is creepy," Garner grumbled as he adjusted his wire-framed glasses. Standing in the midst of the thronging crowd on the long platform, the pair patiently watched each regularly scheduled train successively arrive, exchange passengers, and depart.

"Kind of exciting, though," Taffin enthusiastically retorted. "You gotta admit."

"I've worked on a lot of spy flicks, Benny, and they usually don't end well for the peripheral characters."

"Like the red-shirts on *Star Trek?* Somehow I don't think that we're all that peripheral in this particular case. C'mon, why would the government want to have a couple of guys from Hollywood come all the way across the country to some secret meeting in New York? Put us up in a fancy — and I might add, expensive — hotel and treat us like kings? Guys who specialize in special effects, especially sci-fi flicks, no less? Naw, there's something goin' on and I'm pretty psyched to be a part of it — even if I don't know what it is yet — and even if you're not."

"Okay, I have to admit, part of me is intrigued by the whole thing.

But I just don't like not knowing what's coming."

"You're a plotter, Max, I know. You like to have all your ducks aligned before you do anything and know precisely where they're waddling off to."

"I do — and there's nothing wrong with that."

"Of course not. But this time we're dealing with somebody else's ducks."

"Yeah, that's the part that worries me. Tell me, Benny, are you thinking what I'm thinking?"

"I think so, Max. But where we gonna find a llama down here at this hour?"

"What? Oh, never mind."

A familiar roaring sound grew out from the tunnel to their left and a gentle breeze blew stronger and stronger as another subway train rolled into the station, pushing the air out ahead of it. The placard on the front of it said "Woodlawn," When it slowed and finally stopped, the doors opened on each of the four connected cars, disgorging a stream of anonymous commuters, some in business attire, others in casual looking clothing, while an equally large, similarly looking mass simultaneously pushed past them to get onto the train as quickly as they could.

"Not our train," Taffin commented.

"I can see that. The letter said that it would specifically say 'special' on it." Garner glanced at his watch. "Five minutes, then it's late."

"You're so OCD, Max. Relax, man. Relax."

The doors on the train shut and, with a loud hiss of air from the brakes, the train moaned and slowly rolled out of the station, quickly picking up speed until its red tail lights disappeared into the tunnel to their right.

"This may be a big deal but, really, it could be a huge and expensive waste of time," Garner grumbled. "You know Lucas is working on another Star Wars and asked me to bid on building some of the sets for it. If we miss out on that contract because we've been dinkin' around here in New York with a bunch of government spooks, I'm gonna be really pissed."

"Well, that hasn't happened yet — now has it?"

"Hmph, no. Not yet anyway."

Another rumbling sound of an approaching subway train from the tunnel at the left pushed that same familiar breeze across the platform again and within a minute a single, unmarked silver car rolled into the station. It was an older style car, longer than the ones in regular service at that time and meticulously clean and polished. Except for the motorman's windows at either end, all of the rest were darkly tinted. They could only see a few backlit silhouettes inside, but nothing more. It rolled to a gentle stop at the center of the platform.

"That's it," Taffin announced. "Says 'special'."

"I can see that, Benny. C'mon, let's go."

Garner, with a briefcase in his hand and Taffin carrying a canvas courier bag slung over his shoulder, began to wend their way through the crowd on the platform toward the train just as the one pair of doors at its center parted and two men with stern expressions on their faces dressed in black military fatigues stepped off onto the platform carrying MP-5 submachine guns. They positioned themselves a few feet to either side of the open door, menacingly facing the throng gathered behind the yellow line. The crowd backed off a little allowing a semi-circular void just beyond where they stood.

The duo from Hollywood stopped abruptly in their tracks at the sight while much of the rest of the the people on the platform receded around them.

Following immediately behind the two armed guards, a man in a black suit, white shirt and narrow black tie stepped off the train carrying an aluminum clipboard. He wore a pair of mirrored aviator-style sunglasses. A coiled wire protruded from the earbud that he wore in his left ear and disappeared into his collar. He was followed by a second man similarly dressed in black who remained standing by the door.

The ambient sound of voices and clatter amongst those crowded on the platform was suddenly hushed with all eyes fixed on them.

Garner and Taffin were both immediately intimidated by the scene but not entirely surprised. They'd seen this sort of thing in several of the movies they'd worked on. The imagery was familiar but what they were witnessing wasn't a movie; what they were seeing was real. They also noticed that there were a few other people that were approaching the train with them, a few men in suits and a couple of women in sharp office attire.

The two from Hollywood realized that they were seriously underdressed in their button-down shirts devoid of neckwear, in California-casual blue jeans and spring jackets. It was too late to go back to the hotel to change. They were from the west coast after all. Surely the stiff east-coast government-types would understand their less-than-formal appearance.

They'd just have to.

A meticulously-groomed older man in a gray suit approached the man in black holding the clipboard. He was accompanied by a woman in a dark pants-suit and told him who they were. The man in black looked down the list in his hand and checked off their two names, then nodded and waved them onto the train. The other man in the black suit smiled and directed them inside to find seats.

Another man in a frayed green army jacket scattered with embroidered patches including a circular peace symbol and an inverted American flag. His hair was long and unruly. He stepped up with his girlfriend, a shapely young woman wearing a white, embroidered peasant blouse and a beaded Cherokee headband across her forehead restraining her long, blonde hair. He asked, "Where's this train goin', man?"

"Not anywhere that you are, sir," The man in black replied, looking up at him with disdainful regard.

"Hey, man, we paid our fares, you gotta let us on."

"No, sir, I don't. If you're not on the list, you don't board this train."

"That's bullshit!"

"Alright, sir, you two may board this train but you will never reach its destination. Perhaps in the not-too-distant future, the authorities will come across your remains in one of those abandoned tunnels out there — whatever the rats haven't consumed first, that is. Perhaps they'll never find you, which is just as well." The man with the clipboard then just grimly leered at the hippie and his girlfriend over the top of his mirrored sunglasses.

The shaggy young man surveyed the armed pair in black uniforms for a moment and then turned to his girlfriend and snapped, "C'mon, Cindy, let's go!" He grabbed her hand and the two began to march toward the open door, presuming that the man in black wouldn't dare follow through with his threat, especially with such a crowd of witnesses. He was going to make a point, stand up to the "establishment," and ride that train to wherever it was going.

As soon as they took their first few steps toward the train, the two guards quickly moved into their path and leveled their rifles at them.

With the muzzles of a pair of MP-5s staring them in the face and red laser dots glowing in the centers of their respective chests, the couple froze in their tracks. The young man held his hands up, showing his open palms to the two guards and called out, "Alright! Alright! Don't shoot! It's cool, man! It's cool! *Don't shoot!*"

He turned to his girlfriend and slowly the pair stepped backward until they finally turned and quickly disappeared into the receding crowd. The two guards returned to their posts resuming their ready postures. Apparently the show of force motivated the rest of the impatient, waiting passengers to back off and keep even greater distance if they hadn't received a specific invitation to be on the list.

"That was *so cool!*" Taffin quipped to his friend.

"Disturbing, actually." Garner gruffly replied. "Come on Benny, I believe we'll be on that list."

"Right."

They walked up to the man with the clipboard who grimly looked up at them without saying anything and then, before the pair could announce themselves, grunted, "Garner and Taffin?"

"Yeah," Benny replied a little surprised. "How did you know?"

The man looked them over quickly and just answered, "Lucky guess." He checked their names off on the list and then waved them onto the train.

"C'mon, Benny."

As they walked up to the open door, the second man in the black suit waved them inside and told them to find a couple of seats anywhere and not to talk with anyone else inside. They'd be leaving momentarily.

The interior of the car was stark. None of the customary subway car advertising signs or graffiti anywhere. The walls were gleaming, polished aluminum and the seats were a dark blue vinyl with a little bit of padding underneath — a bit more comfortable than the typical IRT cars in service then and infinitely cleaner, lacking the usual blackish-brown crud creeping out from every crease and crevice and the ever-present aroma of rotting urine.

Near the back of the car, the couple who had boarded just before them were seated together. They looked over at the two Hollywood men as if they were from another planet. The woman judgementally shook her head.

Taffin smiled at her and waved.

Standing at the very end of the car was another armed guard in a black uniform brandishing a machine gun. The whole atmosphere was like something out of a movie that either of them might have worked on over the course of their respective careers. They observed every detail, both of them taking mental notes for ideas that might one day be incorporated into a future production. It was almost imagination overload for both of them — and they hadn't even left the station yet.

Another distinguished looking man wearing a substantial, mostly-gray beard and wearing a tweed suit boarded the train and sat down and then a young black man in a conservative brown suit came on board by himself followed by a handsome, middle-aged woman in a black polyester jacket a moment later who sat down next to the older man with the beard.

No one spoke.

Finally, the two men in the black suits and sunglasses got back on board followed by the two guards who posted themselves, one at the center of the car and the other at the front by the motorman's door.

The doors closed. The brakes released.

The car slowly rumbled forward and left the Grand Central subway station headed north into the dark tunnels.

Once they were underway, the man with the clipboard stood up bracing himself against one of the upright poles at the front end of the car. "Good morning, ladies and gentlemen," he began. "My name is Mr. Dwayne Steele. I am here to conduct you to your meeting uptown. I'm sorry if our security measures have been at all disconcerting but, I assure you, once you find out the details of this operation, you'll understand the need." He looked at his watch, "The ride should take about twenty-five minutes."

Taffin raised his hand like a schoolboy looking to ask a question.

"Yes, what is it?"

"Are there rest rooms where we're going?"

"Yes, of course."

"And snacks?"

"Snacks?"

"Shut up, Benny," Garner snapped.

As the train continued along through the tunnels, they could darkly see the lights of passing stations through the tinted windows. The train only paused inside the tunnels a couple of times for a few brief moments to allow for the city's IRT trains in regular service to make way for one another into each of the stations. Everyone on board just sat quietly, patiently, occasionally checking their watches.

After a while, the train didn't take any sort of pauses any more and they didn't see any more passing lights. A curious thing to the two obsessively observant Californians who weren't sure that anyone else on board had noticed. The pair noticed everything. Perhaps by their experiences they were more attuned to things that may appear out of the norm and the concept of government conspiracies, especially Taffin.

The train they were riding had, in fact, left the rails of the regularly used tunnels and switched onto a line that veered slightly easterly, under the river. A tunnel that had been abandoned years ago and restored by the government to be used as access to the shadowy facility to which they were headed. If they'd looked closely through the tinted windows at the passing, dimly-lit platforms, they might have seen a few more of the armed security guards in black uniforms just like those on board with them who stood vigil to keep vagrants and the dangerously curious from venturing beyond.

Still, no one spoke.

Finally, they could feel the car slowing and a glow up ahead grew brighter as they approached what appeared to be a fully-illuminated station platform much like those they had previously passed on the IRT's main line.

They slowed more and more until finally, with the subway car centered under the lights of the station's platform, it came to a stop.

The brakes hissed. The doors parted.

Steele, the man in black, stood up with his clipboard in hand and stepped off of the train with one of the guards. The other man in the black suit waved to everyone and called out, "This is our stop. Everyone please get off the train and stay together on the platform."

One of the armed guards got off first and walked to position himself with a second guard about halfway across the platform, facing the train to keep the passengers corralled as they would begin detraining and gathering into a small group. The third guard who stood at the back of the train, remained on board until everyone had left and then followed after them.

Garner and Taffin stood up and filed off of the train with the others. They stepped out onto a platform that was obviously quite old but as clean and sterile looking as the subway car they'd just walked out of. They stood on a floor of smooth concrete, the walls and the columns were covered with glossy, ceramic tiles in a dark gray color from the floor to a narrow maroon belt line and then changing to an off-white from there to the arched ceiling over their heads. Across from where they stood was a pair of polished stainless steel doors looking like those of an elevator and, on the wall to the right of it, spelled out in a mosaic of small, maroon tiles that matched the band below it, was the name of the subway station, North Brother Island.

Taffin recognized the name instantly. He had done some research on the island and the abandoned facilities on the surface above them for a Wes Craven horror film. He swallowed hard, suddenly gripped with an irrational pang of fear that perhaps the two of them had gotten themselves into something far more dangerous than they had imagined.

It was all suddenly becoming starkly real. He kept it all to himself and didn't say anything to his companion.

The three guards and the second man in black stood around the group of passengers gathered at the center of the platform when the steel doors in the center of the tiled wall parted and a mature, brown-skinned woman in a black suit with her auburn hair pulled up in a bun stepped out and met with Steele who waited for her just outside the door. He handed her the clipboard and they talked quietly with one another for a moment, too softly and too far distant for any of the others to make out any of their words.

Occasionally, as the two spoke, they'd look over in the direction of the clustered passengers standing on the platform, and particularly at the pair from Hollywood. Finally, they turned together and walked up to the waiting group and Steele introduced her, "Gentlemen, ladies, this is Elsa Kendrick," his voice reverberated profusely in the tile-lined cavern. "She is the director of this facility."

"Welcome," Kendrick greeted with a professional smile. "As you may have gathered, this is a highly compartmentalized facility — very high security."

"Black ops," Taffin whispered to his comrade, "CIA?"

"Mr. Taffin," Kendrick called out.

He quickly turned his face toward her, "Ma'am?" he sheepishly replied.

"Are you going to be a problem, Mr. Taffin?"

"Uh, no, ma'am. I'll be good. I promise."

"Glad to hear it. I would really hate to have anything, um, *unfortunate* happen here today."

"Unfortunate?"

"Use your imagination, Mr. Taffin."

He swallowed hard. His vivid imagination could envision all sorts of unfortunate, official horrors.

"Yes, ma'am."

Garner elbowed him in the arm and shot him a stern look like a scolding parent trying to silently keep a precocious child in check.

"In a moment, we'll enter the facility. We will be using a couple of the conference rooms on this level. I ask that you not wander off anywhere else alone, the signs warning of deadly force are not for decoration. If you need to use the rest rooms, a guard will accompany you. You will be asked to sign papers to assure your silence about this facility and anything that you might discuss here. Does everyone understand?"

Murmuring voices replied that indeed they did. Apparently none had come without some sense of the gravity and need for secrecy and accepted any of the restrictions willingly.

Taffin raised his hand again.

Kendrick rolled her eyes and impatiently responded, "Yes, Mr. Taffin?"

"Will there be a lunch?"

"Yes, Mr. Taffin. That's what the second conference room is for." She sighed. "Anything else?"

"No, ma'am. Thanks."

His west coast enthusiasm was quite annoying to her institutional sensibilities.

She then just shook her head and turned toward the open doors. The two men in black waved the group on to follow. Steele led them into the large room just inside the doors whose walls were covered in tiles just as the walls around the platform were with linoleum tiles on the floor instead of bare concrete. It was, for all intents and purposes, a lobby. He guided the group to a table where each of them had to sign in, had a bright red plastic security bracelet fixed around their left wrists and issued a visitors' badge to clip onto their lapels or, in the case of the two from California, their shirt pockets.

At another table, they were each to surrender anything they were carrying in their pockets to be inspected. Some innocuous items were returned to them like money, writing implements, etc., while others like jack knives, keys and other potential weapons or tools were sealed in large envelopes, labeled with their names and stored in a large bin behind the table to be returned upon their leaving the facility later.

Finally, anything they might have been carrying — briefcases, purses, Taffin's courier bag — were inspected. Papers, folders, pens, pencils, calculators and other things that might be needed in the meetings were allowed through while other things were bagged and left out front with the guards.

Once processed, Kendrick led them to another door with a keypad beside it. She quickly punched in a four-digit code and the door unlatched with a loud, echoing click. She pushed the lever and swung the door open, leading them into a long hallway. To the left were a pair of doors about fifteen feet apart from one another and to the right were another pair of doors separated by only a few feet from one another.

Just beyond that immediate area was a desk that partly blocked the hallway. A soldier in black fatigues like those on the train they'd come in on stood behind it and two others were respectively posted beside the two doors to their left. None of them carried machine guns but were each armed with sidearms in holsters and other sinister looking pouches hung on a harness fixed to a utility belt at their waists.

It seemed pretty obvious that nobody in the group were allowed beyond that desk.

"Ladies and gentlemen, the doors to your right are the restrooms, each one labeled for your particular gender. These men in the hallway will escort you from the conference rooms to the restrooms and back again one at a time as needed. The first door to the left is the conference room where lunch will be provided later — for those who've asked —

and this door..." she stepped up to the second door, pushed the handle down and swung it open for them, "...this is the conference room that you will be meeting in. Please come in."

The group walked into the room to find a number of other people already inside standing around the periphery of the room talking quietly among themselves in groups of three or four. There was a long table in the center of the room that extended from where they'd just entered across nearly to the opposite wall. It was rimmed along both of its long sides with chairs, seven on each side. On the table in front of each chair was a folder with a name printed on it, a couple of pens, a yellow legal pad and an empty glass. A few pitchers of ice water were set down the center of the table on small trays.

At the head of the table were a couple more chairs, a chalk board and a projector on a stand pointed at a screen set up in front of the chalk board.

A gruff-looking, bulky man with graying temples in a dark suit and wearing a brightly-colored Jerry Garcia necktie stood at the front of the room talking with two other men, one of which in a military officer's uniform. Taffin presumed that the man in the loud tie was the one in charge of what was happening, he just sort of came off to him like a boss.

Steele followed into the room behind the last of the group and closed the door. "Alright, people, seats have been assigned. Please find the folder with your name on it and sit down. Do not open the folders until you've been instructed to."

The people who had just come in from the train looked for their assigned seats and began to sit down in their places. The others who were already in the room when they'd walked in, knew their assigned places. They broke up their conversations and got to their seats. When everyone was seated, only the bulky man at the head of the table, Steele, Kendrick and a couple of other men in suits remained standing, scattered around at the head end of the table.

Kendrick stepped up in front of the blank screen which was, essentially, center-stage, and explained, "The folders in front of you contain a document that you will need to fill out and sign before we get started. Your signature will swear you to secrecy and explains some of the possible consequences should you divulge anything about this facility, this meeting, or the details of the operation that will be discussed here. When you are finished, close the form back into the folder and someone will come by and collect them up. Does everyone understand?"

Those around the table each quietly nodded their agreement.

"Alright, then. Open your folders now and complete the forms."

The room was filled with the sound of rustling papers as the folders were opened up and the security forms inside were filled out. For some, the form was a matter of routine, nothing they'd not seen or signed before, but for others — civilians like Garner and Taffin — it was a little intimidating as it explained about surveillance, tracking, telephone taps, attaching bank accounts and even prison. Garner could hear Taffin quietly chuckle to himself as he read parts of it.

Finally, everyone had finished, signed the forms, and closed them back up in the folders. Two men in black suits walked around the room and took up each folder, quickly glancing inside to be sure the forms had been completed and signed as they moved from one chair to the next. They stacked them up on the corner at the head end of the table.

Kendrick then stood up again and began, "I know you are all anxious to find out what this is all about. Now that we have your assurance of silence, let me introduce you to Mr. George Weisz. He is the director of this operation."

The big man in the loud tie stepped out from beside the projector and up to the head of the table. "Good morning," he greeted. "I am pleased that you all were willing to come out for this meeting. You've all been deeply vetted and I can assure each of you that your colleagues are some of the very best in their particular fields. I think we should begin with some introductions. You've already met my associate, Mr. Steele, and those of you who just came in on the train also met Mr. DeSantis of the Central Intelligence Agency. Seated to my left, are Mr. Duwan Freeman, security specialist, technical advisor Dr. Harrison Kimber and his secretary Miss Beverly Stone. Beside Miss Stone is Major Luke Albertson, director of the high-security facility that we'll be utilizing at the Nellis Air Force base in Nevada. Finally, at the end of the table are Mr. Max Garner and his partner Mr. Benjamin Taffin of the Fantasy Factory in Hollywood.

"Across the table from Mr. Taffin are Drs. Damon Tryst and Brooke Hidleman, Central Intelligence Psychological Operations and Colonel

Raymond Baker, Army Corps of Engineers. Beside Colonel Baker, General Bradley Sangster, Air Force Special Operations, Mr. Scott Desaultus of the National Security Agency and, finally, Mr. Peter Hunt of Lockheed Aviation's special projects division.

"And standing up front with me and Miss Kendrick is Mr. Donald Pittman of the White House's National Security Council. He's here to observe and report back to the president."

"Some of you may know one another or, at least, know *of* one another already," Steele injected. "As we work together, you will come to know one other better, especially those that you will be working most closely with."

Taffin smiled and just nodded his head.

Garner leaned over and whispered to him, "You know one of these people? Who?"

"Weisz. A couple of the others I've heard of, too."

"You know him? Weisz?"

"I've never met him but I know who he is."

"Why are you smiling?"

"He's M7."

"M7? Are you *kidding me?* That's just an urban legend — isn't it?"

"Gentlemen," Steele interrupted, addressing the pair at the end of the table. "Is there something you want to bring up?"

"Who is that? Who blurted that out?" Weisz impatiently asked.

"Those two from Hollywood, sir."

"Oh? Do you have a question, gentlemen?"

"I'm sorry, sir. Benny believes he knows you, Mr. Weisz."

"He does? I can't recall ever meeting you, Mr. Taffin. I'm certain that if I had, I'd remember someone like you. How do you think you know me?"

"I do a lot of research for the movies that we work on — sci-fi, spy flicks, that sort of thing. I'd come across your name on a few occasions."

"You have? How so?"

"You're the head of M7."

The room suddenly filled with murmuring whispers.

"Again, I'm sorry, sir, I told him that's just an urban legend," Garner explained. "He's into all this conspiracy theory and UFO stuff."

Weisz just looked down the table at the two of them. "Hmph —
Mr. Taffin."

"Yes?"

Weisz smiled. "That is exactly why you are here." ■

CHAPTER TWO

Luncheon at the Asylum

At the meeting in the secret government installation beneath North Brother Island in New York City, the revelation that the project they had signed on for was an operation being run by the secretive, quasi-government organization known as M7 was a shock to those who didn't already know. For those who had actually ever heard of it, the organization was thought of as just a legend, something made up in the imaginations of the UFO conspiracy community and just a peripheral part of their doctrine of aliens and government cover-ups.

George Weisz, the organization's director, stood at the head of the conference table and didn't appear to be upset by Benny Taffin's revelation nor his surmising that the Air Force base in the desert that he'd mentioned was, in fact, the legendary Groom Lake air field at Area Fifty-One. Perhaps it may have just been bad timing, perhaps Weisz had planned to eventually reveal all of that in his presentation. One way or another, however, it was not ultimately intended to be kept secret. Those working on the project needed to have as full a disclosure as possible to be able to perform their respective parts. If they were to think for a moment that they were being lied to or manipulated in any way, the entire operation could collapse and utterly fail.

Weisz had a technician put up an image of a formation of black, World War II fighter planes on the screen and then then began his talk.

"In 1945, a squadron of U.S. Army Air Force night-fighters were flying over parts of Germany and saw some lights in the sky. The lights flew around them and between them with maneuverability and speed they'd never seen before. Suddenly, the lights just flew off and disappeared. They were amazed but they assumed that they had just seen some sort of experimental German aircraft. Stories were circulating at the end of the war about rocket planes and some of the first jet fighters, infinitely faster than their propeller-driven planes. But, in fact, they had no idea what it was they had actually seen so they nicknamed them 'foo-fighters' after a popular comic strip of the day.

"After that, several other sightings of so-called foo-fighters took place across Europe until shortly after the war ended. Almost immediately after that, sightings began to be reported here in the United States. Some of the first were reported on a clear day over the mountains of Utah. The pilots who saw them described them as silvery, cigar-shaped craft that were moving at incredible speeds. They flew off and disappeared just like the ones in that first sighting over Germany.

"Then, in 1947, something crashed in the desert outside of Roswell, New Mexico. The rancher who found the wreckage described it as a flying disc. The local sheriff also described it as a flying disc and a press release issued by the public information officer at the Roswell Army Air Force base reported that they had recovered a flying disc that had crashed in the desert. Instantly, people jumped to the conclusion that what they had found in the desert was, in fact, a craft from another world.

"Witnesses came forward who said they had seen something on fire streak across the sky the night before. There had been a wild lightning storm that night and the assumption was made that the craft had been struck which disabled it and caused it to crash. They described some of the wreckage that had been collected by the rancher and brought into town. The UFO craze quickly blossomed and Roswell became a Mecca for the UFO faithful.

"The AAF retracted their story the very next day and insisted that the wreckage that was found in the desert was actually a crashed weather balloon — scraps of aluminum foil and sticks of balsa wood. The Air Force would continue to maintain that explanation to this day."

"What about the bodies?" Taffin interjected. "The alien autopsy?"

"That's the damnedable thing of it all, Mr. Taffin — none of that ever happened. It was a complete hoax but the more the government denied it, the more the UFO community insisted that we were hiding something, that it was all strategic misinformation. We learned quickly, however, that it could all work to our advantage. The Air Force launched Project Blue Book to investigate the sudden influx of sightings and unidentified aerial phenomena. Other countries like England,

France and even Russia formed their own similar agencies. Project Blue Book investigated thousands of reports. Some were obviously and easily explained but we made sure that some were explained with preposterous rationales like swamp gas, moonlight reflecting off of a passing mist, St. Elmo's fire, that sort of thing. That just helped to convince believers that we were trying to cover up the truth.

"But the thing that poured gasoline on the fire was that Project Blue Book admitted that, on occasion, they just couldn't come up with an explanation — perfectly reasonable or completely outrageous. Some incidents remained unexplained. Of course, to some people, that just confirmed that they'd seen an alien spacecraft and Blue Book was just charged with covering it all up."

"All the while, you're secretly building and flying spy planes around in the desert? People see these things in the sky, things they'd never seen before, and jump to the only logical conclusion — flying saucers."

"Exactly, Mr. Taffin. You catch on quickly. It's almost impossible to test-fly any sort of aircraft anywhere in this country — even in the remote Nevada desert — without running a real risk of some civilian getting a glimpse of it. In fact, you can almost count on it — especially when they come out looking for it. But if those people see an unconventional aircraft and think that they're actually seeing a flying saucer — and of course we deny it and they presume we're coving something up — then the secret remains safe. The witnesses are written off by anyone in the intelligence community and much of the public at large as crackpots. It's really been a boon for our aircraft development, especially experimental and stealth projects."

"So, to tell the truth, Mr. Weisz, what *really* crashed outside of Roswell in '47?"

"A weather balloon, Mr. Taffin."

"A weather balloon? You're still going with that?"

"A weather balloon."

"Right."

The respectable looking man in the conservative, tweed suit raised his hand, "Yes, Dr. Kimber?"

"I'm sorry, sir, but I'm not really clear what we are here for. If you have such a successful ruse in place, are we then here to work on the next stealth aircraft project? To my knowledge, most of us are not aeronautical engineers of any sort. I know that I am certainly not."

"Yeah," Duwan Freeman stood up to add his own question. "We're not rocket scientists here or aircraft engineers. Why are we all here, sir?"

Before Weisz could respond, Taffin chuckled and blurted out, "The next ruse, of course!"

"The next ruse?" Freeman asked. "What are you talking about?"

Taffin stood up with a Cheshire Cat grin on his face, placed his palms on the table and leaned in to address everyone else at the table, "Simple: They've been lucky so far. They didn't start this thing but they've been milking it for thirty years now. It's been working great for them till now, but fads and sensationalistic rumors tend to peter out after a while. They need to recharge the UFO machine, probably have a new aircraft project that they'll be testing in the desert soon and they need to make sure that the public is primed to see flying saucers in the sky again when they do." He turned to Weisz, "Am I close?"

Stunned by the scruffy man from Hollywood's insights, Weisz admitted, "I'm afraid you're pretty damned close, Mr. Taffin."

"Those of you who don't read the credits at the end of movies — it's okay, nobody ever really does — but Max and I build sets and movie props. We've done some pretty elaborate installations like the bridge for space ships, the laboratories for mad scientists, that sort of thing. Why are we here with all of you — psychologists, technicians, military and spies? Don't you get it? *It all makes sense.* This is an elaborate, super-secret, gaslight *con.*"

"I'm not sure I'd call it a 'con,' Mr. Taffin."

"Then what?"

"Alright," Steele interjected. "I think it would be fair to call it that, but we'd like to use the word 'operation' if it's all the same to you."

"A sting?" Freeman commented. "Like in the movie?"

"We build some sort of facility where a mark can see first-hand behind the curtain — space ships, bodies, cabinets full of files, laboratories full of supposed alien technologies. We build him up, convince him that it's all real and he's a part of the whole operation."

"And then we cut him loose." Steele added.

"Piss him off. Make his life miserable," Freeman continued. "Make him so angry that he goes public and blows the whistle on it all."

"When he does, he'll be believed, even by 'mom and pop' America because he's the genuine article."

"He'd have to be someone with credentials," Dr. Tryst explained. "He'd have to be someone who has a reputation right now for being unassailably credible, esteemed in his field. Perhaps someone in a field that would somehow engage with these supposed alien technologies."

"A nuclear scientist. Particle physicist," Dr. Kimber replied. "I might know of just the man for the job."

"The mark," Taffin quipped.

"The mark," Kimber repeated with a grin. "I think so."

"It seems that you all have this thing figured out," Weisz commented with a sly grin on his face. "Would you like me to continue or do you think you're okay without me?"

"Apologies, Mr. Weisz," Freeman said, lowering himself back into his seat. "I guess we just kind of got caught up."

"I appreciate your enthusiasm. Indeed, Mr. Taffin and Mr. Garner are here to apply their Hollywood movie expertise in setting this up for us. Like the movie — and, yes, I've seen it — we'll build an apparently operational facility. In this case, an underground laboratory. On the Nellis Air Force Base, there's an unused underground space that was built into the Papoose Mountains. It was hollowed out of the rock to be used as a nuclear waste dump. It's about twice the size of a football field and three stories high. But the Nuclear Regulatory Commission changed some of its storage guidelines before it was completed and we were unable to adapt the space so it was never used. It's now just a big, open hole with a level concrete floor, electricity and plumbing. We just need to build the walls inside and fill it with furniture and laboratory equipment. It's perfect and, more than that, it's real."

Colonel Baker then stood up and introduced himself, "I'm with the Army Corps of Engineers. Once the plans are finalized, we'll build whatever infrastructure that's needed. We'll build the facility inside the mountain and access roads to it from the airbase."

"The facility already has a secure entrance and a blast door on the exterior," Major Albertson added. "An interior space with loading docks large enough for trailer trucks to turn around in that's sealed for handling nuclear waste — it's pretty impressive looking, especially to a civilian. We could add some signs, a parking area outside, chain-link fencing, razor wire, make it look really official and secure."

"This is *so cool!*" Taffin could barely contain himself.

"Mr. Garner, can I get you and your giddy companion to stay on for another day?" Weisz asked. "I'd like to have a sit-down with you two to talk about some of the specific things we're looking to have built."

"We have no plans, sir. Didn't know what to expect so we cleared our calendar for a few days."

"Fine," he looked at his watch, "I believe lunch is set up next door?" he glanced over at Kendrick who nodded her confirmation. "Alright, let's break and then meet back here again afterwards."

As the group retired to the adjoining conference room for sandwiches, potato salad and coffee, they talked among themselves, sharing all sorts of ideas from the perspectives of their own, personal specialties.

Garner and Taffin eaves dropped as much as they could without being too conspicuous to absorb as much of each conversation they'd overheard as possible like a pair of sponges. Ideas for the project just blossomed in each of their fertile imaginations. This was their sandbox and they were reveling in it.

After lunch, the table was being cleared and everyone began returning to the first conference room except for Weisz and DeSantis who asked Garner and Taffin to stay behind with Major Albertson and Dr. Kimber.

"Grab a couple of coffees, gentlemen, and have a seat. We need to talk."

Not sure what was actually going on, they each made themselves a mug of coffee and then pulled up a chair to the table.

First off, Weisz introduced DeSantis, "CIA Special Ops."

"I figured — well, something like that, anyway," Taffin said.

"Mr. Taffin," DeSantis addressed, "you seem to know a lot about this whole UFO scene, a lot of the background — both the official things and the 'other' things. I'm curious, how is it that you are so well informed?"

"Ha, ha, nothing sinister, I assure you," he replied. "Our company has done special effects for a lot of science fiction films. It's important to have a handle on what the public may or may not be believing or understanding at the time. Perceptions shift and fads come and go. You want the audience to invest themselves in the story and the characters. They need to relate to what they see from their own perspectives, in their own time, when the films are released. Our job is to make everything look as real as possible so we have to do our homework and keep up to date.

"The best special effects are those that don't look like special effects so they don't distract from the story. I've read a lot of books and papers, government reports, and whatever I can get my hands on from Project Blue Book and the various publications from the UFO fringe. I've seen documentaries on TV and even climbed Freedom Ridge with a bunch of MUFON believers with telescopes, binoculars and cameras with lenses as long as my arm to look down at the Groom Lake airbase. When the Fantasy Factory builds something for a movie, people think they're seeing the real thing — even if it doesn't actually exist."

"And he's a bit of a conspiracy junkie," Garner added.

"Yeah, I got that." DeSantis replied.

"But, as I said," Weisz injected, "that's precisely why you're here."

"So what's the plan? What do you need us to do?"

"Much of what we do is dependent upon what you two can provide for us," Weisz explained. "We need to create a whole world inside of this mountain. Major Albertson is the director of the Area Fifty-One facility and the Groom Lake airbase. He'll be working with Colonel Baker to build and outfit this facility. But first we have to work out with you just what that needs to look like."

"That's kind of backwards from what we're used to. Normally we get a call from a producer or director who contracts us to produce certain things for their films, they hand us a script, storyboards, even blueprints and sketches sometimes — everything's already planned. We don't get a lot of our own input."

"We need to sell this to our subject and none of us have the expertise or, for that matter, the imagination that you two have to make this work. So if we're doing this backwards then, fine, we'll do it backwards. Whatever works."

"Do you have anything already in mind? A starting place?"

"I've been talking with Dr. Kimber about some technical specifics and Dr. Tryst about various scenarios that we'll need to sort of steer the subject through."

"So what have you got so far?" Garner asked.

"Well, I have a list for you," Weisz handed Garner a folder with a few typed sheets inside.

"Hmmm, you need a radioactive element unknown on this planet and machines to study it with. You need four full-size flying saucers?"

"A couple to be seen up close, lots of believable details, one that's wrecked like it's crashed in the desert and one that flies."

"You need one that *flies?*"

"You can't do that?"

"I didn't say that. I just don't know how yet — but we can do it. Two beauty saucers and one pile of wreckage — those won't be any problem. The radioactive element isn't really a problem either but if the mark is experienced in this field, he's going to be familiar with the machines that he'll be using to study it. We won't be able to manufacture anything that will make them react the way they'd have to. Whatever we build will be totally inert, just machined out of aluminum or something, so we need to rig the equipment and computers. We'll need someone to show us how these machines work so we can hot-wire them and write software to operate them from off-set."

"I can give you a list of all the things you'll need to outfit the lab," Dr. Kimber explained.

"Can you come out to LA and show us how it all works? Show us how they should react so we can rig them?"

"Uh, sure, I could do that. I can get you the service manuals and schematics, too. Would that help?"

"That would be great," Taffin injected. "We can wire them without accidently blowing up our workshop."

Garner quickly glanced down the list. As he did, Weisz asked, "Any other problems you see on that list?"

"No, no problems, but I do have one question: Who's paying for all of this? I'm sure that the equipment for that lab and all the other specialty stuff — let alone the construction materials — are going to have a pretty big price tag attached to them."

"Not to worry, Mr. Garner. M7 is picking up that tab and other parts of this operation are being funded by various black ops budgets. There will be more than enough to cover all of the expenses including salaries."

"A blank check!" Taffin quipped to his partner. "Isn't that just refreshing?"

"And no unions," Garner smiled and then set the list down on the table, "Do you have any sort of a layout or floor plan of what you're envisioning for this lab?"

Albertson lifted a briefcase up from beside his chair and set it on the table. When he flipped it open, he pulled out a folded blueprint and handed it across the table to Taffin. "This is what we were thinking. Right now it's just a big, open space. Kind of a blank canvas, if you will."

Taffin unfolded the paper and smoothed it out across the table so that both he and Garner could get a good look at it. As they studied it, they looked over at one another and pointed at different places on it to discuss various elements between themselves. Finally, Taffin looked up at Albertson and asked, "No morgue?"

"Morgue? No, why on Earth would we need a morgue?"

"One of the most persistent legends in the UFO community is the fact that, when the ship crashed in Roswell, three alien bodies were recovered." Taffin explained. "There are grainy, fuzzy photos circulating around of an autopsy — they're probably fake — but if you really want to sell this, a wall of shiny stainless steel refrigerator doors and a couple of matching autopsy tables in a locked room with a window would really help flesh out the whole thing. He'd only have to be able to get a quick, accidental glimpse."

"That's a marvelous idea," Weisz commented with a spark of enthusiasm.

"Can we take this?" Garner asked.

"Certainly. We want you to work up whatever it is that you think you'll need to do. The Corps of Engineers can take it from there and build it for us."

"There's one major thing missing in this floor plan," Taffin noted, "back spaces."

"Back spaces?"

"When we shoot a movie, we build a set which can stand alone on a soundstage. Technicians who work lights, cameras and other effects can be in the periphery, out of view of the cameras. Sometimes hiding in cavities built into the set itself. In a layout like yours, there is no soundstage, everything is just out there and interconnected. You need spaces behind the sets for technicians to move around unseen."

"We hadn't thought of that," Albertson admitted.

"Do you have a scenario? A plot line you plan to follow?"

"A plot?," Weisz replied. "You mean like in a movie?"

"Oh, sure — we need to tell this guy a story. It has to have a beginning, a climax and an end," Taffin explained. "Even in that movie, they gathered their team, set up the gambling room and then followed a plan from hooking the mark, playing him up and then the so-called 'sting' at the end. You have a lot of ideas of isolated things you want to show him, but no plan. Give us a few weeks?"

"What can you do in a few weeks?"

"We'll have the whole package worked out for you. A plot, a story, all the effects, floor plans, the works. We'll sit down with your psyche people and tech experts to work out the details and then give you a shopping list — make sure we have everyone's phone numbers before we leave today so we can confab long distance while we put this together. How does that sound?"

Weisz looked around at Albertson, Baker and DeSantis who mostly either nodded or shrugged their shoulders — or both — and then turned to Garner and Taffin, "Alright, gentlemen, three weeks? We can do that. Your place or ours?"

"Oh, I think it's pretty clear that your people need to come out and see Hollywood for yourselves."

"Yeah," Taffin chimed in, "and you can leave your suits and ties back here."

Weisz glanced down at his brightly-colored Jerry Garcia tie and just smiled. ∎

CHAPTER THREE

Welcome to Hollyweird

Three weeks later, a commercial flight from Washington, DC landed at Los Angeles International Airport. Along with hundreds of other passengers simultaneously arriving on several airplanes from cities around the world at that time, George Weisz, Dr. Harrison Kimber, Felix DeSantis and Colonel Raymond Baker disembarked together. They followed the flow of humanity from the gates to the baggage claim carrousels and then descended the escalators with their luggage in hand to the lobby to get a cab to finally take them to their ultimate destination, the Fantasy Factory.

They had each taken Garner and Taffin's advice — though it may have been offered somewhat with tongue in cheek — to dress more casually to fit in better on the left coast. Each wore either a button-down shirt or a polo shirt under a much less formal sport coat. Kimber even dared to don blue jeans as he'd seen the two from Hollywood appear at the meetings in New York.

When they reached the terminal's street level, there was a gathering of people standing off to one side of the lobby behind a red velvet rope. Many were holding up signs with names on them trying to catch the attention of those descending the escalator. Friends and relatives who were waiting to pick up newly arrived travelers along with a number of people in black suits and chauffeurs' caps, drivers for various livery services who had been contracted to pick up movie executives, wealthy captains of industry and celebrities. Cab drivers were not allowed inside the building.

Weisz and his companions paid little attention to the gauntlet. Their intention was on the large, glass doors ahead of them and across the crowded spans and the sidewalk beyond to hail a couple of cabs to take them to the Northfield section of the city where Garner and Taffin's offices were located.

Standing about halfway between the end of the escalators and the glass exit doors, along the velvet rope at the forefront of the gathered group of welcoming faces, was a shapely young woman with long blonde hair wearing black heels, black fishnet stockings, a tight black miniskirt that protruded only a couple of inches beyond the bottom hem of a tailored, black suit jacket that she wore over a white dress shirt and black tie all topped off with a black chauffeur's cap. She held up a white sign with large bold, black letters that spelled out the word "FANTASY" across it.

DeSantis noticed her — in truth, none of the men hadn't not noticed her — and commented, "Sure, this is Hollywood. She's obviously *somebody's* fantasy in that get-up."

But as they were just about to walk past her with total disregard, Weisz stopped in his tracks. He turned to the woman and asked, "Fantasy *Factory?*"

"Yes!" She enthusiastically replied with a broad smile of perfect, glistening white teeth behind brilliantly red, pouting lips. "Are you the producers from the east coast?"

"We're not movie producers," DeSantis indignantly replied.

"Actually," Baker interrupted, "if you think about it, we sort of are."

"Ha, ha, yeah," Kimber added, "that's true, we sort of are. I guess this young lady is *our* 'fantasy'."

"Alright," Weisz said, disregarding the banter of his companions. "Are you our driver?"

"I am," she lowered the sign and waved to a Red Cap to come and gather the men's luggage. "Your limo is right out here."

"Limo?" DeSantis whispered.

"Like you said," Kimber quipped, "this is Hollywood."

They piled their suitcases up on the Red Cap's cart keeping their briefcases with them and then followed the young chauffeur's undulating runway gait out through the glass doors to the sidewalk where a black stretch Cadillac limousine was parked. Another curvaceous young blonde woman in an outfit matching that of the chauffeur (sans the driver's cap) stood waiting at the curb. She greeted them with a smile and opened the door as the Red Cap loaded the bags into the trunk.

As they climbed into the car, a third blonde woman in a black suit and fishnet stockings was waiting inside and welcomed them to Los Angeles. When all of the men were seated, the woman who had held the door for them followed them in and took a seat between Weisz and Kimber.

They heard the trunk close and then the driver's door. In a moment, the car gently rolled out from the curb and into the flow of traffic headed for the freeway.

"Champagne?" The third woman asked as she opened the lid on a cooler beside where she sat. A rack of tall champaign glasses hung by their stems just above.

DeSantis was visibly annoyed. "Are these two movie characters toying with us? I don't think they're taking this whole thing very seriously."

"No," Baker replied. "It may be a bit excessive, but I think they're trying to give us a taste of Hollywood hospitality. Get us to loosen up and 'go with the flow,' as they say."

"Hmph — I don't like this 'flow'." DeSantis complained.

"Fine," Weisz interrupted, "then you don't get any champaign." He looked up at the woman and smiled, "I believe I would enjoy a glass, my dear."

She smiled and poured him a glass, reached across and handed it to the woman sitting next to him who then gracefully handed it to him. They repeated the process for Kimber and Baker and then made one last attempt to offer a glass to DeSantis. "I think our designated stick-in-the-mud will still pass," Kimber chuckled.

The two hostesses seated in the back of the limo with the four stodgy government men made them feel comfortable for the long ride north out of the city. They played soft music on the car's stereo system, poured them drinks, fed them pastries and chatted them up with giggles and bright smiles. In the end, the long ride seemed to pass all too quickly. Before they knew it, the limo pulled up to the front doors of the Fantasy Factory's sprawling warehouse workshops.

The chauffeur pulled the door open and the young woman who had escorted them into the car at the airport climbed out first. One by one the men got out of the car as the woman took each one by the hand to assist them with a smile and made sure they didn't bump their heads on the way out.

"Welcome to Hollywood, gentlemen!" Garner called out from the building's entrance as he and Taffin walked out across the sidewalk to greet them. Another man followed them out with a dolly to gather up their luggage from the trunk and bring them inside.

"Mr. Garner," Weisz said as he shook his hand and then turned to Taffin, "A stretch limousine with supermodels as attendants?"

"This is Hollywood, Mr. Weisz. What did you expect? A black Chevy Suburban?"

"Well, actually…"

"Did you enjoy your ride from the airport? Were the ladies attentive and friendly?"

"Yes, they were all of that."

"Then relax, enjoy your time out here. We have plenty of real work to do so enjoy the lighter moments as they might come along."

Taffin handed three envelopes to the chauffeur, "Thank you Kimberly for taking good care of them. These guys are kinda big shots. A little extra for you and your crew."

She smiled as she took the envelopes from him, "That's very kind of you, Benny. It's been a pleasure — as usual. Call us when you need us again."

"You know we will."

As the man with the luggage began to push the cart back toward the building, Garner rubbed his hands together and announced to his guests, "Well gentlemen, time to get to work."

The three women got back into the limousine and drove off as Garner and Taffin led their guests into the lobby of the Fantasy Factory. As they stepped inside they were greeted with a wide counter facing them and some comfortable looking chairs for people to wait on. On the walls all around them were framed movie posters from films that the Fantasy Factory had worked on with a few glass cases filled with examples of props they'd created for many of them. Some were familiar, others they'd never heard of.

"Welcome to the Fantasy Factory," Garner announced as the group stood in the lobby, not giving them too much time to ogle their surroundings. "We'll head upstairs where we you can look down from the balcony and see the facility on the workshop's main floor. We have a planning room up there where we can spread out and get busy. Right this way."

He led them to a stairwell and up to the second floor. When they stepped out onto the balcony, they could look out across the expanse of the cavernous warehouse. The open floor was populated with large work tables and machine tools. Cabinets and shelving lined the perimeter of the space, reaching from the floor to the underside of the balcony, filled with hundreds of storage bins all labeled with their contents. It was all neat, well ordered and obviously ready to work.

"We're between projects right now — actually gearing up for you guys — so the place is pretty empty, not a lot going on down there at the moment. A few of our core staff are keeping busy working on some smalls of our own, spec pieces for your project. We went shopping at a couple of electronic and aircraft salvage yards and now we're putting together what will look like components pulled from your flying saucers. Props, window dressing as it were." He turned and walked around the corner, "This way, gentlemen."

The group followed him into a large, rather industrial looking conference room. There was a broad table in the center as one would expect to find in any conference room but instead of it being built of finely-finished exotic woods intended to impress clients, it was topped with simple sheets of plywood sanded smooth and coated with glossy polyurethane. It was obviously large enough to be able to spread out large blueprints and other elements for various projects.

There were pedestrian-looking office chairs all around the table and a large-screen television on a rolling stand parked against the wall near the head end of the table with a VCR player on a shelf just below it. Bookshelves filled with all sorts of reference materials, binders and samples rimmed three sides of the room and one low bookcase in the corner of the room was topped with a Mr. Coffee machine and a tray of cups, powdered creamer and sugar packets. And, just to make sure that any visitors didn't forget that they were in Hollywood, posters of well-known classic films like "Casablanca," "War of the Worlds," and "Gone with the Wind" decorated the walls.

In its own way, the room made a distinct impression on their clients. It showed that, even in so-called Tinseltown, these guys were all business and all about the job.

There were folders, wire-bound booklets and rolled up plans waiting for them on the table. A third man in a Hawaiian shirt followed them in as Garner closed the door behind them.

"Before we get started," Garner explained, "I need to introduce you to our foreman, Ray Costello."

The man in the Hawaiian shirt reached out his hand and shook with Weisz and the others.

Weisz looked at the man with suspicion and then waved Garner and Taffin over to the far end of the room, "We need to talk, gentlemen."

When they'd gathered away, out of earshot of the others, he began with a stern, lowered voice, "You two each signed a document promising your complete silence on this project. You are not to share any of the details of this with *anyone* — there are some very specific consequences."

"Yes, we know," Taffin explained with an uncharacteristically serious tone. "Right now, Ray thinks that he's meeting a group of producers who are here to pitch a movie. This sort of meeting happens here all the time and, in fact, if he wasn't included, *that* would seem strange."

"I think you need to read him in," Garner added.

"Why? I've given you two a lot of latitude so far. Right now I think you're taking liberties with my patience — pushing the limits here."

"Look, with all due respect, Mr. Weisz, a project of this scale, the two of us are not going to be able to deliver all by ourselves. We'll need to bring in our entire staff and hire out specialists and temps for parts of it. This space, as big as it is, isn't going to be near large enough. We're going to have to lease out even more room to build some of the sets and those flying saucers."

"If he knows what's going on," Garner continued, "he can better coordinate everything."

"I had no idea that this was going to be such a project for you. Maybe we should shop around for someone else."

"There is no one else," Taffin answered. "Nobody else is big enough or connected enough in the industry to pull this off."

"That's right," Garner added. "You have to trust us, Mr. Weisz, we have a plan and we'll explain all of it shortly. Give us this, you won't regret it, I promise."

Weisz stood and pondered silently for a moment, looking past Taffin and Garner at Costello at the opposite end of the room pouring coffee for the others in the group and chatting them up about movie stars and special effects. "Alright," he said. "But you know the consequences for breaking that trust. All of this," he waved his hands around the room, "could go away in the blink of an eye."

"We understand. But believe me, Ray is the consummate professional, he's been with us for years. You have nothing to worry about."

"I certainly hope not." Weisz looked back at the others gathered around the coffee machine. "Alright, let's get this show on the road."

Garner, Taffin and Weisz returned to the group who were talking movies with Costello who regaled them with some of the well-known projects they'd worked on and some of the particular special effects challenges that they'd built for each one. Weisz addressed the Fantasy Factory foreman as they approached, "Mr. Costello, allow me to introduce us. This is Felix DeSantis of the Central Intelligence Agency, Dr. Harrison Kimber, physicist, senior fellow at MIT and technical advisor for this operation, Colonel Raymond Baker, Army Corp of Engineers — and I'm George Weisz, director of M7. My group is coordinating and funding this entire operation."

Costello stood glassy-eyed for a moment, looked at the four men and then quickly glanced over at his employers and then back at Weisz, "Right!"

"No, *really*," Taffin injected.

"It's not April Fool's Day, Benny. C'mon, CIA, M7? Seriously?"

"No, it's true," Garner confirmed. "*Seriously.*"

"Have a seat, Mr. Costello," Weisz directed. "I'll fill you in on the operation, get you up to speed."

With a bit of astonishment — and initial disbelief — he did as Weisz had told him to and sat through a short but relatively detailed explanation of the operation and how the Fantasy Factory was involved. Afterwards, he sat just staring forward at the four government men standing across the table from him.

He looked over at Taffin and whispered with a big, stupid grin, "No, it's not April Fool's Day, *it's my birthdaaay!* This is *sooo cool!*"

"I know — *right?*"

"You're doing all this to gaslight just *one* guy?"

"Just one guy," Kimber replied. "But the *right* guy, the guy that the world will believe when he goes public."

"You know what really sucks about all of this?" Costello soberly asked.

"What's that?" Taffin replied.

"We'll do some of our best work on this and we won't be able to tell anyone about it!"

"Well, yeah, there's that."

"Alright, alright," DeSantis interrupted, trying to get Garner and Taffin back on track. "You told us in New York that you'd have the whole package ready for us to look at. We're here now — so show us."

"Okay, have a seat," Garner took charge of the meeting. He picked up one of the large rolls of paper and began spreading it out across the table, placing small, palm-sized sandbags at each corner to keep it flat. "To begin with, we took a look at the floor plan that you had made up and made some modifications to it."

Baker looked over what was displayed in front of him and commented, "'A few modifications?' You carved it up like a Thanksgiving turkey!"

"Okay, here's the thing," Taffin stood up to explain. "You had no plan, no scenario for this thing whatsoever. You were going to bring the mark in and show him some amazing stuff and them cut him loose to blab it to all the world. Good concept, but there's no structure to it. Like we said in New York, you need to have a story to tell him. From the time you first contact this guy, it all needs to be scripted — it all has to tie together. He's a rocket scientist, a genius, you've gotta make it all make sense to him."

"Scripted? I don't understand," Weisz commented.

"We have to tell the mark a story," Taffin interjected. "We need to have the introduction, the build-up, the climax, the big reveal, and then the surprise ending. We need to lay out the story and build each part of it on the last — follow the plot — and lead him to that climax. Any gaps and he might see right through it."

"So, basically, we need to prosecute this as though we're making a movie," Garner added.

"What?" DeSantis interrupted. "Making a movie? What the hell are you talking about?"

"The movie industry is just that, an industry. Hollywood is geared to build motion pictures from screenplays with lighting, cameras, sets, props, actors, directors — and the gears of this industry are greased with money. Lots of it. So far, all we've got is the money. There is no way that the Fantasy Factory is going to be able to pull this off without a lot of people in this town seeing what we're doing. As much as we have a culture of keeping secrets out here, there's also a rabid culture of people snooping around. They report and speculate about rumored projects on television talk shows, in supermarket tabloids and trade papers about whatever they think is going on — and they're not afraid to make wild, unsubstantiated speculations and report them as facts."

"The first part of our plan for this sting operation," Taffin continued, "is to gaslight the media. Here's what we've got in mind," He passed out folders to the four government men and their foreman. "You are the producers, associate producers, and so on. The money men. There are hundreds of scripts floating around this town and we've selected one. Now we have to announce that we're — *you're* — going to make it into a movie. You'll pay the writer his usual fee with the contingency of royalties and what-not, a typical, boiler-plate contract which our lawyers have already drafted for us. Then we fire up the press and the rumor mill with flagrant misinformation."

"Won't people get suspicious when the movie doesn't actually get made?"

"Naw, that happens all the time. When it does, we'll just leak to the media that the producers have pulled their backing for reasons unexplained. Directors, actors and other people are released to move onto other projects and the props that we'd built disappear into a warehouse somewhere — in this case, into the Nevada desert."

"And what about all these people that you say will need to come in and work on this? How are you going to keep the secret from them, keep them from talking about it to their friends and relatives out there?"

"Everyone that we hire has worked on numerous films before — for us or for other companies like us. Each one works on a particular task that we assign them to. Nobody really knows anything about any other parts of the whole. We'll need to bring in carpenters, welders, electricians and some electronics experts to pull this off. A lot of them are union and all very professional. They work under contract and move from one project to another. We also hire on some extra people as temps for all of the other labor. Some interns, film students and some on-again, off-again employees of the Fantasy Factory. We have a list of people that we call whenever a new contract comes along. For a project of this size, it will be all-hands-on-deck."

Garner continued. "The big stuff like the sets and the saucers will need to be built out here in our shops, broken down to be transported to the site, and then reassembled there. We'll have a small crew of your people working here alongside ours to sort of train them up. They'll just come off as more temp workers so no one will suspect anything. When the movie project falls apart and the props go into 'storage,' they'll go with them back to the facility with us and Ray to set it all up inside the mountain."

"So nobody from Hollywood aside from you three would ever have to come out to Groom Lake?" DeSantis asked.

"No. As far as anyone back here would be concerned, it will be business as usual. Their contracts will end, they'll go home and when the next project comes along — with us or someone else — they'll get another call."

"As adept as you and your various organizations are at keeping secrets," Taffin interjected, "Hollywood's culture of secret-keeping is probably just as good — maybe more so."

"Hmmm," Weisz mused, then asked Major Baker, "What do you think, Raymond?"

"I think it can work. We'll have to work out the logistics, of course, and keep it under complete cover, but I think we can make it work."

"Well, so far, so good, gentlemen," Weisz commented. "What else have you got?"

"Wait," Dr. Kimber interrupted. "I have a question."

"Yes, what is it, sir?" Garner asked.

"We told you that we needed one of the saucers to fly. Back in New York you seemed unsure about that. You said that you were confident that you could do it but didn't know how. We believe this is a critically important element going toward credibility but you haven't mentioned anything about it yet. Have you figured that out?"

"Ha, ha, ha!" Taffin replied. "Oh, yeah, we've got it all worked out. We took a page from the Dick Tracy tech manual."

"Dick Tracy?"

"Magnetic air cars!"

"I don't get it," DeSantis grouched.

"I think I do," Kimber grinned. "Please, go on."

"We figure, to be believable, the saucer doesn't have to actually fly around the desert. We can keep it contained inside a hangar. They're supposedly trying to reverse-engineer these craft so we'll set one up without any landing legs and as devoid of details as possible to save weight. It'll be sitting in a really high tech-looking stand with yellow and black safety stripes on the floor and lots of umbilical cables. Because of the assumed risk of radiation, witnesses are kept at a distance."

"So they can't get too close a look."

"Right. This saucer will be built with really lightweight materials, as much of an empty shell as we can get away with. We'll build a big magnetic coil into the base of it and another in the the stand underneath. When we do the 'flight test,' they'll power up the two magnets which will repel one another and the saucer will rise up from its stand. No wires, no visible means of support. Totally believable."

"I like it," Weisz commented. "This will work?"

"Have you seen the Air Jordan displays in the malls? A mannequin hand with an open palm and a basketball floating over it?"

"Yeah, I've seen those. Never took too close a look at it, though."

"We've done this sort of thing on a smaller scale for another movie," Costello explained. "We'll call in the same whiz-kid who worked on that to come in and work out the details for us — same concept, just scale it up — way up. It'll take a lot of juice to work, though."

"Not a problem," Baker said. "We can give you all the power you need for this. Just give us the specs and we'll build it."

"That's great." Taffin said. "Once our guy works out the details, we'll send you all the info."

"Now that brings us back to an even bigger point," Garner said as he leaned over the floor plan spread out on the table in front of them. "If you look at our layout, as you've noticed, it's quite different from what you had worked up. Two factors drove this design. First of all, the need for back spaces to have stage hands and effects people moving around unseen to operate various gags throughout the facility — like the flying saucer. And, secondly, to follow the plot."

"Plot?" DeSantis asked.

Garner looked over his shoulder at his partner, "Benny?"

Taffin took a loose-leaf binder off of the shelf behind him and set it down on the table. He opened the cover to reveal the first leaf inside, "This is our script, of sorts. Like we said, we selected a script to work with, but that's just a front for the media. We'll be following our own scenario on site. This is more of an outline of scenes so far, one that logically follows another and relate to one another as this story that we're telling unfolds just to keep us on track. We reveal a little more and a little more and build up the mark to the crashing climax when he gets in trouble with a coworker and gets fired."

"A coworker?" Baker asked.

"A woman, to be specific. The notorious 'honeytrap.' It's a classic Hollywood gimmick, totally believable."

"And you've got this whole thing planned out?" Weisz asked.

"We still need to work out some of the technical details and the logistics of it all, but, yeah, we do."

"Look at the floor plan," Garner directed. "You can see that we have the particle lab where he'll be working situated right here in a highly restricted area with the very private employees' lounge across the hall. The administration and director's offices are all located in the lowest security area, accessible to anybody. But he can't venture beyond the area where his assigned laboratory is unless we either take him or we get him to explore on his own. That's where the hangars and the morgue are located."

"Or make him *think* he's exploring on his own."

"Exactly. Dr. Tryst will be on set the whole time to study the mark and his reactions to things as we go along and help us to plan ways on the fly to manipulate him."

"What if he breaks from any of that? What if he really does go off and explore on his own?"

"Look at the floor plan. There are passageways for cast members and crew to move around unseen, to head him off with some sort of contingency. There will be armed guards in the hallways. He won't be able to see behind that curtain so, even if he does wander off somehow, he'll only see what we want him to see."

"In a sting operation like this," Taffin added, "there is always the possibility that a mark can do something unpredictable. We try to anticipate anything but it's important to have contingencies that won't blow it all up, it's important to be as flexible as possible."

"You mention 'the cast,' what do you mean by that?"

"People — we need to fill this place with people — scientists, office workers, guards, technicians. Because of the secret nature of this whole thing, we can't just advertise for extras in *Variety* like we normally would."

"So where do we get these people?"

"They'll be people from your various agencies, from M7, CIA, Lockheed, Air Force from the Groom Lake air base. Anyone who has the clearance to be involved with this, we can use them."

"How many will you need?"

"A couple of hundred — we could get away with a hundred and fifty."

Weisz looked around the room at his colleagues, "Well, gentlemen, do you think we can round up enough people for this? A hundred and fifty of them or so?"

They looked across the table at each other and began to shrug their shoulders, "Yeah," Baker said, "I could probably come up with that many just from the Corps of Engineers."

"I think we'll need to have some more variety," DeSantis injected. "I know I can probably get twenty or thirty Agency people. We can recruit some of our office and technical people to make that part of it more real."

"That's great," Garner said. "One thing, though, we need someone on site to manage the mark and his immediate environment. The film's director, of sorts. I'm thinking that Tryst's colleague who was at the meeting in New York, Dr. Hidleman, might be perfect. She'd work closely with us and Dr. Tryst to direct the cast throughout the facility and handle the mark as we move from one phase to the next. Do you think that she'd have the balls to get into arguments with the mark, be a real hard-ass and fire him in a really heated, ugly but professional kinda way?"

"Oh, yeah," DeSantis smiled. "She'd be perfect."

"We'll also need a couple of technicians to work closely with the mark. They'll need some training to sound legitimate to him, and one has to be our 'lady in red' to seduce him at the end."

"I have just the person for that," Weisz said with a smirk. "She's M7 and a real black widow in a tight skirt. Tie her hair back, put her in a white lab coat and add a pair of nerdy eyeglasses and I think you've got it."

"Do you think she could pick up on all this physicist stuff?"

"She's frighteningly smart. I don't think she'll have any trouble at all. Dr. Kimber and Miss Stone will train our lab workers between now and then and be on hand as advisors. They can coach her along the way if she needs it."

"And she'd do just about anything for an operation," Weisz soberly added.

"Anything?" Garner asked.

"Anything."

"I think this is coming together nicely, gentlemen," Taffin said with a smile. "Now all we need is a screenplay."

"I thought that's what was in the notebook," DeSantis said.

"That's the plan for our sting operation. Like we said in New York, we're kind of coming at this backwards. We need to look like we're making a real movie here," Garner explained. "We've optioned that script we mentioned, a sci-fi flick called 'The Creature from Alpha Centauri'."

"It's awful," Taffin added with a snicker. "Nobody in their right minds would ever touch this one with a ten foot pole — or even a ten foot Lithuanian."

The government men just looked at him for a moment. The joke was obviously lost on them. Costello couldn't help but chuckle quietly to himself.

"Uh, okay. M7 is our producer," Garner continued. "We'll use whatever names you would like. For a dog like this, it's not unusual to have several producers involved so we figure at least four names and a couple of actual faces for the public to see. We'll create a fake production company, whip up a logo, rent a small office somewhere with a phone and a secretary to answer it. We'll hire a screenwriter to work up this screenplay and put a director on retainer. Again, this isn't the scenario that our gaslight will follow. This is all for show, to keep the

Hollywood news hounds at bay. It should give us enough credibility to be able to build all of what we need without blowing our cover."

"Sounds expensive," DeSantis grumbled.

"Movie making is an expensive business," Garner explained. "This is the barest minimum that we think we can get away with. More importantly, it gives us a legitimate looking reason to hire on all of the hands and peripheral services we'll need."

"And when you, the producers, pull your financial backing out from under it all — which nobody in the industry would blame you for doing," Taffin continued, "we pack up everything that's still here and ship it off to the desert. The Hollywood attention span is so short that 'The Creature from Alpha Centauri' will be forgotten in the blink of an eye as the buzz shifts to the next rumored blockbuster in town."

"Alright," Weisz agreed, standing and looking around the table at his colleagues. "I think that covers everything. I like it."

"Good," Garner said, picking up a small stack of papers stapled together and reached across the table to hand it to Weisz, "here's our shopping list."

Weisz glanced at the list, quickly flipping up the first couple of pages to scan through the whole stack. and then looked up at Garner, "Materials, office equipment, furniture — whatever you need, gentlemen. This is a matter of national security. Consider that you have a blank check for this project."

"Just one more thing," Taffin interrupted.

"What's that?"

"The name of the lab. It has to have a name for the UFO people to talk about — something catchy, memorable. We're calling it 'Facility R-Four-Seven'. Has a nice ring to it."

"And once this new world wide web thing starts catching on — and, believe me, it will — it will be a complete game-changer. This will spread like wildfire."

Weisz crossed his arms over his chest and smiled broadly, "Seems you boys have thought about just about everything. I *really* like it." ■

PHASE 2
THE MARK

CLASSIFIED

EYES ONLY

CHAPTER FOUR

A Day at the Races

Dr. Harrison Kimber parked his rental car in the Desert Raceway's infield parking lot outside of Los Angeles. It was a particularly warm day in May with a welcomed cooling breeze drifting in from the Pacific Ocean. He could hear the sounds of racing engines circling around him out on the track. He looked at his watch, it was about ten-thirty in the morning. He was dressed in a white polo shirt with a navy blue polyester sport coat and gray slacks — pretty casual compared to his customary tweed and professional looking neckwear — a new consideration complements of his newfound Hollywood colleagues.

He paused as he considered leaving the blazer in the car but, no, something in him would not allow the concept of "casual" to quite that extreme. He smiled to himself, realizing how foolish that attitude was, but nevertheless, he left the coat on. He locked the car, slipped on a pair of sunglasses and turned for the pathway that led down the hill to the paddocks.

At the bottom of the hill, he walked out into an area just behind a wire fence that separated the space that was open to spectators on the one side from that which was behind the pit wall and along the main straightaway on the other side where only racers and their teams were typically allowed to venture. Through the fence, he could see racing cars flash past out on the track, their engines wailing at full-chat as they did, grabbing all the speed they could on the long straightaway before having to brake hard at the end and dive into a sharp right-hand turn.

He could feel the sun beating down on his balding scalp so when he came upon a souvenir trailer, he bought himself a ball cap to shade himself. He wasn't a racing fan. The various logos on the hats in the vendor's display didn't really have any significance to him. He selected the hat with a BMW logo on the prow just because it was blue and sort of matched the color of his blazer.

He turned and looked out past the wire fence at the people standing with their backs to him along the inside of the pit wall. He saw a man with a clipboard clutching a stopwatch in his right hand as he very intently watched the passing cars. The man was wearing an open, short-sleeved blue uniform shirt over a colored t-shirt. When he saw what was printed across the shirt's back he just smiled, realizing that he had most likely found whom he had come looking for.

The races that day were local amateur events sanctioned by the Sports Car Club of America and far less stringent in their rules regarding spectator access, unlike some of the other national sanctioning organizations like IMSA and NASCAR. Many of the amateur drivers had friends and family working as their crews or just there to watch and cheer them on. They were allowed to go pretty much anywhere they liked within certain practical limitations. Kimber found an opening in the fence which, during those big, national events, would be guarded by someone checking credentials, was left unattended. He walked in and did his best to stay out of the way as he made his way to the man he had spied through the wire.

"Doctor Dennis Foster?!" Kimber called out in a loud voice to be heard over the sound of the passing race cars on the track just a few feet beyond.

Without taking his eyes off of the action out on the track, the man replied, shouting to be heard over the noise, "Denny's out there in the car today!" Just then a pack of race cars flew past where they were standing and he stabbed at the button on his stopwatch, studied what it showed on the dial and then recorded it on a form on his clipboard. He then began to turn toward the man standing next to him to explain, "I'm his friend, Luke Robbins…" He immediately recognized the man in the blue sport coat. "Holy cow — Dr. Kimber? What are *you* doing here?"

"You know me?"

"I've read your books, sat in on a few of your lectures at Pacific Tech. Denny and I went to your seminar in Las Vegas a few years ago. Sure, I recognize you," he dropped the stopwatch to let it dangle by its lanyard from his neck and then thrust his hand out, "You're a rock star in our field!"

Kimber shook his hand and smiled, "I'm flattered," he replied, "maybe a bit embarrassed, frankly."

"Oh, I'm sorry, Doctor."

"It's alright, really. I'm just here looking for your friend, Dennis. Is he out there right now?"

"Yes, he is. The blue and green car with 'Quantum Racing' on the sides."

"'Quantum Racing,' of course. Is he winning? It's hard to tell."

"This is just a practice session. Every class gets a practice session in the morning, there are a bunch of them. The actual races start right after lunch. Denny's a pretty good driver — he's usually up in the lead pack. He's won a few times, too."

"I saw your shirt from the other side of the fence. The name of your racing team. I knew it couldn't be just a coincidence."

"Hey, this practice session will be over in a few minutes. Denny'll bring the car back to the trailer and we were going to do an early lunch. Wanna join us? Just hot dogs and potato salad. I know he'd love to meet you."

"Well, that's actually what I came for — thanks."

As the checkered flag wove from the flagstand at the start/finish line signaling the end of the session, Robbins led Kimber back out from the pit row and through the paddock area along the maze of dusty, narrow roads lined with trucks, car trailers and motorhomes to their own encampment. As they walked, he warned Kimber to stay close to the edge of the roadway as the racing cars coming off the track would be coming through while those headed for their assigned practice session would be making their way out to line up on the false grid.

When they reached the trailer, Foster was already there and had parked the car in the shade underneath a tent fly attached to its side. His helmet and gloves were perched on the car just in front of the cockpit with the tethered steering wheel lying beside them. He was unzipping his driving suit as the pair walked up. "Denny!" Robbins called out, "We have a guest for lunch."

Foster looked up and saw Kimber approaching with his friend. He was dumbfounded for a moment, "Dr. Kimber? Dr. *Harrison* Kimber?" He shook the man's hand like a schoolboy who'd just met his television idol. "This is a real surprise, sir — an honor. What are you doing here? Are you a race fan?"

"Fan? No. This is actually the first time that I've ever been to the races. I can see how it can be quite exciting, though. I wish I had more time to stay and watch. But, no, I'm actually here hoping to talk with you for a few minutes. I called your office yesterday afternoon but your secretary said you were out. She told me I could find you here this weekend. I thought at the time that was pretty strange but I reckoned that, since I'd only be in town for a day, I'd drive out here and at least take the chance and see if I could catch up with you."

"And so you did, sir. We were about to have lunch. Can you stay for that? We don't have a lot of time, we could talk for a bit while we eat."

"That would be marvelous, thank you."

"I'll get the grill fired up," Robbins announced, "You two just sit."

"I need a cold drink — can I grab one for you, Doctor?" Foster flipped open the lid of a cooler just inside the side door of the trailer.

"Thank you. Sure is a hot one today. I'm not used to this southern California heat."

Foster handed him a dripping wet, ice cold can of Coca-Cola, pulled out a second one for his friend, then grabbed one more for himself. "Please, Doctor, have a seat," he waved toward a lawn chair next to the car in the shade beneath the tent fly and then sat himself down in the open trailer doorway.

"This is quite a hobby you have here, Dr. Foster. Not the sort of sedate hobby I'd expect a scientist of your ilk to be involved in."

"Like collecting stamps or something?"

"Exactly."

"Ha, ha! We're really in this together. Luke works with me at Cyberdyne Technologies. We got into this a few years ago. We take turns driving at each race. This is our second car, we moved up from Formula Ford to Formula Atlantic this year. It's our first season with this car and we're having a blast."

"What does your wife think?"

"Well, she'd love to have the second bay in our garage free, but she loves showing off the row of trophies in our living room whenever guests come over."

"Maybe her rocket-scientist husband isn't such a dweeb," Robbins chimed in with a chuckle.

"Yeah," Foster chuckled, "something like that."

"You have a lot of them? Trophies? Won a lot of races?"

"This is amateur racing — SCCA — there's no prize money unless you make it to the national Run-Offs in the fall so everyone in the top ten gets a trophy and everybody who shows up gets a dash-plaque for participating in each event. You'll see them inside the lids of open toolboxes everywhere. It's all about having fun and, if you do well at it, some bragging rights."

Foster took a sip of his Coke and then leaned forward, resting his elbows on his thighs, "I love talking racing with you, Doctor, but I'm sure that's not why you're here. What can we do for you, sir?"

Kimber smiled, "Perceptive. Well, Dr. Foster, my organization as you probably know, is a sort of think-tank for the highest levels of technology. But Kimber Associates is also a head-hunting service for the industry. Tech companies and government agencies — even NASA — come to us to help find the crém-de-la-crém of candidates for very specialized positions."

"And you've come all the way out here to recruit Denny?" Robbins asked as he approached with a styrofoam plate stacked with grilled hot dogs.

"Not to put too fine a point to it, but — yes. I have a particular government contract to find someone with Dennis' particular qualifications."

Robbins chuckled and turned to his friend, "Looks like you've been flagged as 'creamy,' my man."

"Is that right, Doctor?" Foster asked, "Are you here looking to hire me for a job?"

"I am."

"Do you just need me to help on a particular project? I couldn't commit to anything full-time."

"It's actually full-time, but a temporary contract."

"For you, Doctor, I suppose I could take a leave of absence. How long would this project take?"

"Well, I'm afraid a leave probably wouldn't be long enough. This would be a commitment of at least a couple of years."

"I'd have to quit my job at Cyberdyne to do that. I'm sorry, Doctor, but I'm very happy there. I could never do that. I've been there a long time and they've been really good to me and my family."

"Naturally, I'm disappointed but, truthfully, I understand. I'm not here to pressure you and, frankly, I'm a lousy salesman so I'm not going to try and pitch you." Kimber reached into his jacket pocket and pulled out a business card. He handed it out to Foster. "But please do keep me in mind. With the Apollo project finished and NASA cutting way back, I'm sure you've seen the ripple effect through the entire aerospace industry. So far, you're one of the fortunate ones but my door will always be open. A man with your credentials I know I would be able to place in a heartbeat. Keep this — give me a call if you ever need to. Or if, perhaps, you've thought about my offer today and reconsidered."

Foster smiled and took the card while he chewed on a bite of his hot dog. He looked at it briefly and saw the words "Kimber Associates" in the largest letters with the address at the bottom. "You're in St. Louis," he observed.

"My office is, yes, but depending on the assignment I can connect you with, you could be working just about anywhere."

"So we'd have to relocate. Not sure how Livvy would feel about that."

"Livvy — that's your wife?"

"She is."

"Well, depending on the project, you may not have to. I could try and keep you somewhere within the Los Angeles area. There's still a lot of high-tech industry around here."

"Well, Doctor, I'll hold on to this — I will — and I'll think about your offer. I promise."

"You'll call me? Whichever way you decide?"

"I will."

"I'm grateful. I'll look forward to hearing from you then."

"Alright. Well then, we need to finish up lunch and then get the car ready for our race. You're welcome to hang out here with us."

"Thank you, I wish I could but I have a plane to catch." Kimber looked at his watch, "I was just in town for a meeting yesterday and now I need to get to LAX to fly back to St. Louis this afternoon." He looked over his shoulder at the race car parked behind him. "I'll have to admit, however, I have become unexpectedly fascinated by this sport. I wish you the best of luck out there."

"Thank you, Doctor. You have a safe flight back. And thanks again for coming out here today. I'm flattered that you would think that I'm worthy of such an offer."

"Take me up on it, Dr. Foster, you won't regret it and I'll be the one thanking you!"

"Potato salad?" Robbins interrupted holding out a plastic container from the deli.

Kimber looked up at him and smiled, holding up his paper plate, "Oh, alright. I believe I have just enough time for potato salad — thank you." ■

CHAPTER FIVE

Ted

Sunday afternoon and the two friends pulled up in front of Dennis Foster's Burbank home in suburban Los Angeles in his diesel powered Ford pickup truck towing their enclosed racing car trailer. Foster pulled up just past the driveway. Robbins got out and directed him as he backed the rig up to the open garage door, all the while being careful not to scrape against his wife's car parked in the driveway alongside.

It was a very precisely calculated and oft-practiced routine the pair had executed after every weekend racing excursion — deftly performed by a pair of actual rocket scientists.

Once in position, Foster set the truck's brake, stuffed wedge-shaped chocks in front of each of the trailer's tires and Robbins lowered the ramp door at the back. The pair then rolled their racing car out and pushed it into its place inside the garage. They then unloaded their tool boxes and carried out coolers, soiled rags and various garments and anything else that needed to either be attended to, laundered or kept on hand in the garage to prepare for the next racing weekend.

The door from the house opened up and a woman's voice called out as she stepped down into the garage, "I thought I heard a noise out here!"

"Hi, Sweetie!" Foster called out to her.

"Hi, Livvy." Robbins added from the far side of the garage as Foster stepped up and gave his wife a kiss, avoiding any hugs or other contact for the moment to prevent transferring any grease and dirt from his hands and clothing.

"Is Betty here, too?"

"She is. She's in the kitchen — we're getting dinner ready. You're a little early so you have plenty of time to clean up. Are you almost done out here?"

"We just finished unloading the trailer. I just need to park it around the side and we'll be in."

"I'll tell Betty. Oh, and how did you boys do?"

Robbins reached into a cardboard box that he'd set down on the floor next to the car and pulled up a trophy, "Your husband brought home a second!"

"Well, congratulations to the both of you! For a second place," she smiled, "we'll make some space on the living room shelf!"

She went back into the house to help her friend, Robbins' wife Betty, finish getting dinner ready. It was part of their home-from-the-races routine for all four of them. Nothing fancy, just a tuna-noodle casserole, a tossed salad, beer for the guys and wine for the wives. All set out buffet-style on the kitchen's breakfast bar for the very best of friends to partake.

Foster and Robbins each took turns taking quick showers and changing into clean clothes before appearing in the kitchen. By then, the meal was ready and Betty was setting the hot-from-the-oven casserole dish out on a trivet. Livvy lifted up the lid and impressed a serving spoon into it for everyone to help themselves.

"That smells great!" Robbins commented as he walked into the kitchen.

"It's just tuna casserole," Betty dismissed with a grin.

"Nobody makes tuna-noodle casserole like you do, my dear," He hugged her and gave her a kiss and then picked up a plate to start gathering up some food and make his way to the kitchen table to sit and eat with his wife and their friends.

Foster pulled open the refrigerator and grabbed a couple of bottles of beer and brought them with him to the table, handing one to his friend. Livvy poured two wine glasses of rosé and put the bottle back into the refrigerator. She carried the glasses to the table and the four friends sat down and began enjoying a pleasant and relaxed evening meal together.

The men told tales of their racing experience that weekend. The sights they'd seen, the excitement and the competition. Their wives always enjoyed hearing their animated stories. Being intellectual types, both men tended to have introverted, almost intense personalities. Their racing adventures seemed cause for them to step out of their shells and brought out a side of them that was fun and exhilerating. The wives laughed at the funny parts, asked questions and made comments as they were regaled. Eventually, the conversation came around to the unexpected visitor who had come by the track to talk with Foster.

"It was the strangest thing," he explained. "Out of the blue, Dr. Harrison Kimber showed up in the pits yesterday morning and found Luke while I was out for a practice run. He stuck around and had lunch with us. Said he'd never been to a race before — found it exciting."

"But he had to leave," Robbins continued. "He had to catch a plane back to St. Louis so he couldn't stay for the actual race."

"Didn't you two go to a conference or something to see him a little while ago? I've heard you mention the name before."

"I've got his books on the shelf and read everything he's ever published. He's an inspiration to everyone in our field."

"We want to be just like him when we grow up," Robbins chuckled as he picked up his beer.

Before the conversation could continue, the doorbell rang.

Foster looked out from the kitchen and through the living room to the front door beyond, "Are we expecting someone?"

"Not that I know of," Livvy answered.

The bell rang again.

"Guess you'd better go see who it is," Robbins quipped, "they seem pretty persistent."

"Probably just some salesman."

"On a Sunday evening?" Betty asked.

"A real go-getter, I guess," Foster quipped as he stood up from his chair, wiping his mouth with his napkin one last time. "I'll get rid of him — be right back."

He walked through the living room to the front door. When he pulled the inside door open he found, standing on the other side of the screen, a devastatingly handsome man, apparently close to his own age, with a tanned, chiseled face, trim athletic physique, and perfectly trimmed and coiffed, wavy hair. When he smiled, his perfect, white teeth nearly glittered in the late afternoon sun. Foster instantly pegged him to be a movie star since, living in Burbank, the area was generally infested with them — although he didn't recognize him.

"Hello?" He said to the man. "Can I help you?"

"Hi," the man said with a deep baritone voice, "I hope I'm not intruding — I just bought the house across the street. The phone company won't be hooking up my phone until next week and I don't have any hot water. I need to call a plumber."

"On a Sunday evening? Good luck with that — it'll cost you a fortune."

"I know, but I can't bear the thought of a cold shower in the morning. I've got an important meeting I have to be at and really don't want to start off on a downer. If I can get someone out tonight, it'll be worth it."

Livvy walked up behind her husband and asked, "Is everything alright out here?"

"Good evening, ma'am," the man said with a beaming smile through the screen as she approached.

"This is our new neighbor from across the street," Foster explained, then turned to him and added, "I didn't get your name."

"I'm sorry, it's Ted," he looked into Livvy's eyes, smiled alluringly and added, "Ted White."

She smiled and softly repeated, "Ted."

"His water heater's not working and he needs to call a plumber. His phone's not connected yet."

"And you need to use ours?"

"If it's no trouble, ma'am."

"Certainly not," she said with a slight giggle as she invited him in. "Please — you can use the extension here in the living room."

Foster, holder of two doctorates and a Ph.D., was clueless to the flirtatious air of their new neighbor and the spontaneous schoolgirl responses that his wife was cooing in response as he pushed the screen door open and allowed the man inside, pointing out the phone on the end table beside the sofa.

"Do you have someone to call?"

"The people that I bought the house from left me a list of numbers of some of the people that they'd used and were happy with," He pulled a slip of paper from his shirt pocket and glanced at it, "Peterson Pluming, Jerry Peterson — you know him?"

"I've heard the name. I know some people who use him and they've always said good things about him."

"Great — now if he'll only come out on a Sunday evening."

Hearing the voices in the next room, Robbins and his wife realized that the doorbell hadn't actually announced a pesky salesperson at the door and so got up to peek into the living room and see what was happening. Betty saw the look in her best friend's eyes as she was looking at the dashing man dialing the phone. "Uh-oh," she whispered.

"What? You know him?"

"No, but I know Livvy. Can't you see that look on her face?"

"What are you talking about?"

"For a couple of rocket scientists, you two can be pretty stupid sometimes."

"Oh, for crying out loud. Livvy is the second most devoted wife that I know. I think you're just seeing things that aren't there."

"*Second* most?"

"Why, sure," he said as he looked over at her with a grin, "I'm married to the first."

"Awww. Thanks, honey," she reached up and gave him a peck on the cheek. "Come on, we shouldn't spy. Besides, the casserole is getting cold."

"And the beer is getting warm." ∎

CHAPTER SIX

Nothing Personal

In the Cyberdyne Technologies cafeteria, among dozens of other employees on their respective lunch breaks, sat co-workers Dennis Foster and his friend Luke Robbins, just finishing up theirs together at one of the tables. Robbins took a last sip from a small carton of milk as Foster commented, "I can't believe it's Friday already. On Monday, I didn't think it could get here fast enough. I had a mountain of work on my desk. But, in the blink of an eye, here it is."

"I guess when we're busy like that, the time really flies. Got any plans for the weekend?"

"Well, some yard work. Gotta mow the lawn and do the hedges. They're getting pretty ragged looking. If I can get all of that done on Saturday, maybe Livvy and I will take a drive up into the hills on Sunday. There's a neat little hot dog stand up there we like to go to with with some picnic tables. You can see the ocean from up there on a clear day."

"That sounds nice. Looks like my plans for Saturday are pretty much the same. The joys of suburban homeownership, I suppose."

"Yeah, I guess."

Robbins looked up at the clock on the wall and noted, "Looks like time to get back to it."

Foster pushed his glasses up with his index finger and glanced at the clock, "I suppose, but five o'clock will be here before we know it."

They each gathered up their trash from the table and got to their feet. They deposited it all in the bins near the door and then headed out to the hallway, Foster turning to the left and his friend turning to the right to return to their respective offices and the work that awaited them on their desks.

When Foster walked back into his office, he could see the red light on his phone lit up signifying that he had a message waiting for him. He sat down at his desk and reached for a note pad and snatched a pen from his ever-present pocket-protector to jot down any message or phone numbers that he might have to call back and then, when he was ready, he pushed the button to play the message.

"Mr. Foster," It was the voice of Mary Shea, his supervisor's secretary, "Mr. Esposito would like you to come up to his office when you get back from lunch, please."

That was the whole of the message. Shea was efficient if not lacking a little in social tact. Still, it was not unusual for his supervisor to call on him or any of his colleagues in the department to come up to his office for any number of reasons such as passing on new assignments, getting updates from his crew or discussing new company policies and handing out pages to be added to the company handbook. Esposito rarely ventured out from his own office.

Foster got up from his chair with a groan — he'd just gotten back from lunch with his mind already fixed on the work waiting for him on his desk and was settling in to get to it. He hoped that the meeting with Esposito would be quick so he could return and get right back at it. He grabbed the pad and took it with him as he headed for the door just in case he might need to take any notes.

He climbed the stairs to the second floor offices and headed down the hallway to John Esposito's office near the end. He walked into the open door of Mary Shea's outer office. She looked up and said, "You can go right in, Denny. He's waiting for you."

"Thanks, Mary." Still, observing a certain professional propriety, he knocked on the door before opening it, not bothering to wait for a response, and walked into his supervisor's office.

"Ah, Denny," Esposito said as he rose from his chair. "Please, have a seat."

His demeanor seemed uncharacteristically hospitable, lacking his customary gruffness. Nevertheless, Foster walked around in front of the chair that faced the desk and sat down.

Esposito sat down.

They looked across the desk at one another.

A silent, uncomfortable pause.

"I, uh, have a lot of work on my desk, John. Can you tell me what you called me up here for?"

"I'm sorry, Denny. It's just that this sort of thing is really difficult for me."

"Difficult?" He felt an unexpected pang in the pit of his stomach.

"Uh, as you know, NASA has been cutting back on its programs for a while now. Since the Apollo program ended and the shuttles began their service lives, contracts for companies like ours have been drying up. Not much left but some satellites, deep-space probes and the damned space station. We're scratchin' and clawin' to get whatever contracts we can. Just crumbs, compared to the old days. The bean-counters have been looking to cut costs and asked each department head to come up with a list of employees who could be considered for — ya'know — layoffs."

"And you picked me?"

"If there is any sort of respite for me in this, no, they specifically named you. Frankly, Denny, we just don't have much call for a particle physicist anymore. And, to be completely truthful — and please keep this to yourself for the time being — they're eliminating the entire freakin' department. You're just the first to go. Some of the administrative staff, secretaries, lab assistants, they'll be reassigned somewhere else, maybe at one of our other locations. I'll be the last one out the door in the end — right after we've liquidated and mothballed all of the equipment down there."

"But the work you've been passing down to me — a ton of it. Haven't I been doing a good job with it? Can't I be relocated somewhere, too?"

"Your work has been exemplary, to be fair. But it's so far beneath your qualifications. Call it 'busy work' if you like. This has nothing to do with your job performance, Denny. In fact, I'd have to say that you're one of my best and brightest but, to be painfully honest, you're just too damned expensive to be doing that sort of work here. It just *kills* me to have to do this."

"I've been working here for eight years, John. It stinks, to be 'painfully honest' — but I guess I understand."

Esposito reached across the desk and handed him a large envelope. "I wrote you a really positive letter of endorsement. There's one from the CEO and a couple from your co-workers, too."

"I appreciate that," Foster reached across the desk and took the envelope.

"I went to bat for you, too, and got you a really generous severance package. We'll keep your major-medical for a year or until you find something else. I thought it was the very least we could do for you."

"Thanks."

"You're taking this pretty damned well, Denny. I don't know what I was expecting, but I appreciate your understanding."

"It's not that I could actually do anything about it."

"Well, true."

"Why get wound up about it? You've been a good boss, John, thanks."

Esposito rose to his feet and reached out his hand to Foster, "There's a security guard out in Mary's office who will escort you to your office so you can gather your personal stuff. I know it's kind of cold, but it's company policy, protocol. Hope you understand."

"Yeah, I get it."

"Good luck out there, Denny. And don't hesitate to use me as a reference, please."

"Thanks, I'll keep that in mind." He reached out to shake hands with his soon-to-be former boss. Then, without another word, he turned and walked out of the office.

In the secretary's outer office stood a uniformed security guard holding an empty copy paper carton, "Hi, Denny."

"Hi, Fred."

"I'm sorry about this. Company policy — nothing personal."

"I know. Let's get this over with." He turned to the secretary, "Bye, Mary."

"Bye, Denny. Good luck."

He turned to the guard and started walking toward the door to the hall, "Come on, Fred."

The guard followed him downstairs to his office, the office he had just left a few minutes before. He flipped on the light and then just stood inside the doorway for a moment and looked around. The room had been his home-away-from-home for eight years. He took a deep breath and sighed.

Taking the box from the guard, he walked over to his desk, pulled the chair out and set it down onto the seat. He began with the diplomas, certificates and photos on the walls. A photo of him posing with Apollo astronaut Michael Collins when he had come to visit Cyberdyne during the heyday of the space-race caused him a moment to pause. The pinnacle of his career, he thought. He'd only been there for a couple of years when the photo was taken. He took it down from the nail and studied it for a few seconds and then carefully set it into the box. He collected his various mementos and personal nic-nacs from the shelves. His personal reference books. The items on his desk like the pen set that his wife had given him — too gaudy and impractical to actually use, but it looked really good on the desk next to his nameplate. He took that, too.

When he had finally packed up the last of it, he gathered up the box, put the lid on it, then laid his briefcase over the top of it. He picked up the box by its handles and walked toward the door.

"Here, let me take that," the guard offered.

Foster handed him the box, reached over and flipped off the light switch and closed the door behind him.

They walked down the hall past all of the doors and offices that he'd passed time and again each day for the previous eight years. In his mind he thought about how that was all going to change in his life and, too, how would he explain it to his wife when he got home?

At the very end of the hall was the door that led out to the parking lot. The guard pushed the latch bar with his hip and shoved the door open. He stood holding it open with his shoulder as Denny walked past. "This is as far as I go, Denny."

Foster stopped and then turned and took the box from him, awkwardly holding it up with his left arm wrapped under it and balanced on his knee so that he could shake the guard's hand, "I'll miss this place, Fred. Thanks."

"Good luck out there, man. I'm sure you'll do just fine."

"I hope you're right. Well, good-bye, Fred."

"Just one more thing."

"What's that?"

"Your badge. I need to take that now that you're, you know, out of the building."

Denny looked down at the plastic card clipped to the pocket protector protruding above his shirt pocket. The card that displayed the company's logo, his name and photo had allowed him access to the building and anywhere else within the campus that he might ever have needed to go. It had been a part of his life for all those years. Reluctantly, he twisted his torso around so that the guard could grab hold of it and unclip it from the place where it had resided for so long.

"Thanks, man."

"Bye, Fred."

"Good-bye, Denny. And again, good luck."

Foster wrapped both arms around the box and turned to walk out into the vast parking lot to his pickup truck. After a few steps, he heard the door shut behind him. He closed his eyes for a moment and groaned to himself when he heard the sound but just kept walking to his assigned parking space.

He put the box on the floor in front of the passenger seat and then climbed in behind the wheel. He just sat there for a moment. Part of him was angry, but a bigger part was just sad and fearful for the future. He barked out a primal shout as loud as his voice was able as he slammed his palm on the edge of the dashboard four or five times.

Then he sat for a little while longer. Silent, pensive. His stinging hand rested on the edge of the padded dashboard.

Finally, he heaved a deep sigh, put the key into the ignition, started the truck and slowly drove out through the gated driveway and turned down the road toward home that he had done so many times before — for one last time.

He drove to a park in the foothills not too far from home. He had to get out, take a walk, clear his head, and figure out a way to break the news to his wife. They both knew that this sort of thing could happen to him one day. The entire industry was shrinking and almost anyone could be pared away at any time. It was just his turn.

Though that thought didn't really do much to console him.

It was early, not quite two o'clock. He still felt that he couldn't go home just yet. If he were to show up at home at that hour, Livvy would immediately know that something was wrong. Stories of aerospace workers being laid off across the country had been fodder for the evening news and daily papers for the past few years. She would probably presume the worst — and she'd be right.

In his mind, he reeled over all the things in his life that would

— and could — change if he couldn't find a new job relatively soon and at about the same salary as the one he'd just been let go from. What would he have to give up? Sell? Could he go back to school? Get another degree? Would they have to move to a less expensive house? What about his friends?

It was almost more than his stratospheric IQ could handle in the moment. It was a human problem, the sort of thing that he wasn't particularly good with. His analytical mind was approaching overload.

After an hour or so of pointless self immolation, he decided to just drive home and face Livvy. Once they could get past the initial jolt of it, they could start working on figuring out a new normalcy. They could do that together.

Sure, it would all be alright in the end.

Somehow.

He got back into the truck and drove across town to the suburban neighborhood where he and Livvy had lived for the previous five years and turned up into the driveway.

Parked in the driveway, he just thought for a moment, trying to think of things to say to her. He'd just spent the last couple of hours pondering that very same thing. He realized that a few more minutes thinking about it wouldn't make any real difference.

He'd leave the box behind for the time being.

He slipped the keys into his pocket, took a deep breath and walked up to the front door.

As he walked in, she was in the kitchen and saw him through the living room when she heard the front door open. "Denny! You're home early." She put down her dish towel on the breakfast bar and walked to the archway to the living room as he came up to meet her there. She could tell by the way he was walking that something wasn't right. As he got closer, she noticed his ever-present ID badge was missing. He'd misplaced it often enough in the past so in and of itself it wasn't cause for concern. But that time, considering the hour of the day and the look on his face, she feared what they'd half-expected for some time had finally befallen them. Nevertheless, hoping she was wrong in her presumptions, she trepidously asked, "Is anything wrong, dear?"

He just stepped up to her and silently hugged her. He wasn't a very romantic sort. He rarely showed his feelings openly. The very act confirmed to her that her intuitions were probably right, "Did they let you go, Denny?"

He just held her for a moment while she wrapped her arms around him and tried to comfort him. He pulled away after a short while and looked her in the face with a dejected countenance, "The company is shutting down our entire department. Even John."

"I'm so sorry, dear. So sorry."

"They gave me a pretty good severance package. We should be alright for a little while."

"We'll make it work. Don't worry."

"Not a lot of call for particle physicists these days."

"It's okay, dear, we'll figure it out. I can get a job — we can make it stretch. Please, don't worry."

"Thanks for that, Livvy, but I wouldn't ask you to do that."

"We'll both do what we have to. I saw that Alma at the dress shop is looking for someone. I'm sure I can find something. It's just temporary."

"Temporary, right. I sure hope so."

"For better or for worse, richer or poorer — we're in this together — right?"

Foster mustered a faint smile, "Right." ∎

CHAPTER SEVEN

Bambi

Friday morning and Dennis Foster was camped out in his home office at his desk surrounded by neat stacks of folders and papers strategically spread across it in his own special OCD sort of order for quick and ready reference. His IBM computer was on, the monitor glowing green with an open document, his curriculum vitae — his resume — displayed before him. He'd been at his job at Cyberdyne for so long that he had never bothered to update it in over eight years.

He had been happy there. It was stimulating and rewarding work. He felt like he was a part of something so much bigger and every time he'd watch Walter Cronkite host a launch of the next successive Apollo or shuttle mission, he swelled with pride knowing that he had had a hand in the technology that made it all possible.

He never thought he'd need a CV ever again. But all good things, it would appear, ultimately come to an end.

He had been hard at it for a few hours when Livvy walked in with a glass of iced lemonade and asked, "How's it going, dear?"

He leaned back in his chair. "Oh, it's going — albeit, *slow* going."

"I brought you something to drink. Thought you'd be pretty dry by now."

"Thank you, sweetie. I keep reminding myself to go and refill my coffee but then I get involved again and forget. That is, until I think about how thirsty I am and decide it's time to go get another cup — again — and then something else comes to mind and I get sidelined. Again."

She set the glass down on a coaster to his left. "I was downtown yesterday afternoon and stopped in to see Alma."

"Alma?"

"Alma — you know. The dress shop?"

"Oh, yeah."

"She hasn't filled the job yet, so I applied. She said that she likes the idea of having a more mature person working for her."

"Did she call you 'old'?"

"I think she just meant that she gets a lot of high school and college girls applying. They don't take the job as seriously and just aren't as reliable as she'd like. They don't last very long, either. I think she likes the idea of a married, settled woman working there, someone she can count on. Besides, I'm not old, I'm only thirty...*something*."

Foster smiled. In his eyes, she was still the same twenty-something as when he'd first met her while they were both still in college. "Well, sweetie, I know she can count on you. You'd be the perfect choice. I hope she calls you."

"Thanks. She said she'd make a decision by the end of the week sometime — by today. Fingers crossed!"

"Yes, fingers crossed. I hope I have equally good luck in my own search."

"Oh, I'm sure you will," she looked across the surface of the desk at the sea of papers, certificates and letters in neat, squared-up piles. "You've had quite a career so far."

"It's had some real moments, that's for sure. Hard to take your whole life, though, and boil it down to just a couple of pages."

"I've never had to do it, myself. Looking at all of this I can only imagine. Pretty intimidating."

"Not the most difficult problem I've ever had to solve. I'll get it together — it's just gonna take a little time."

"Hey," she paused for a moment and picked up a business card she spotted lying on the desk just beyond the perimeter of all the other papers. "What's this? Isn't this the man who came to see you at the race track last summer?" She reached out and handed him the card.

"It is. He had come out to recruit me for his consulting firm in St. Louis."

"Do you think he still wants you?"

"I don't know. Probably."

"You gonna call him?"

"He's sort of 'plan B' for the time being. I'm hoping I can find something closer to home. Most of the aerospace industry is still around here. I think I'll have a better chance at places like Lockheed and McDonnell Douglas."

"I hate to break it to you, dear, but the aerospace industry is just a shell of what it was. There are way less jobs to be had than there used to be."

"I don't want to start talking about pulling up stakes and dragging you off to some other part of the country until I've exhausted every opportunity here first."

"I appreciate that, but like I told you, I don't really mind. I'll miss our friends, sure, but I'm totally okay with it. We'll send Christmas cards to each other and keep in touch. I think you should call him."

He smiled, "You do, huh?"

She grabbed the arm of his chair and spun him around and then dropped herself into his lap. She wrapped her arms around his neck and smiled at him, "Yes, I do." She gave him a long, lingering, encouraging kiss, her tongue sending an electric tingle through his whole body.

She got up from his lap and walked around the desk, deliberately wiggling her hips seductively as she walked across the room to the door where she paused, leaned up against the jamb and looked seductively back at him, "Call him, sweetheart. It's okay. Call him."

He shook his head with a broad grin on his face, "Alright, alright — since you put it that way," he chuckled. "I'll give him a call."

After his wife had left him to his task, he got back to work at composing and editing his resume. The time slipped by in his busyness without notice and a few hours later, as his stomach was beginning to remind him that it was just about lunch time, Livvy returned to his office, "You ready to take a break, dear?"

He looked up from his keyboard, "A break?" He took a quick glance at his watch. "Oh, wow — I totally lost track of the time. Lunch?"

"Yeah. Ted came by. He saw your truck in the driveway and asked if we'd like to come over for lunch. Nothing fancy, just hot dogs and burgers on the grill. Thought you'd like some human interaction for a little while before getting back to all this."

"Human interaction can be greatly overrated, sweetie — depending on the humans involved, of course."

"What's the matter — you don't like Ted?"

"The guy's just another Hollywood phony. He's alright, I guess, but really not my sort."

"I know, but he's trying to be neighborly. He knows you're out of work right now. He just wants to reach out."

"Did you tell him?"

"No, he just knew. I don't know how he heard. But it doesn't matter, he's just trying to be nice. We should be neighborly, too. Come on."

"Alright, alright. Let me just save my work here and shut things down. I'll be along in a few minutes."

Livvy walked back out to the kitchen while he saved and closed his CV document and shut down his computer. He picked up the empty lemonade glass with a few half-melted ice cubes at the bottom, took a slug of the ice cold water pooled around them, and then got up and brought it out to the kitchen to leave in the sink.

Livvy had pulled a bottle of wine out of the refrigerator to bring with them. She felt uncomfortable going to visit a neighbor empty handed — especially for the first time.

"I called that guy in St. Louis," he told her as they began walking toward the front door.

"What did he say?"

"Well, he wasn't in. He's in San Diego right now doing one of his seminars. His secretary said he'd be flying back on Sunday and she'd give him my message on Monday morning when he'd be back in the office. She sounded like she was expecting my call. It was weird."

"Oh, don't be so suspicious, dear. You said that he came out looking for you at the race track. Maybe he told her about you, hoping you'd change your mind and call him."

"Maybe."

They walked across the suburban street together and up the steps to Ted White's porch. They knocked on the door. After a moment or two, the inside door swung open wide and a bare footed young woman greeted them with a broad smile.

She was petite and shapely, wearing a tight, dark blue tube top which displayed every detail beneath it in clear, protruding relief and left her flat middle exposed all the way down to the wide belt around the top of her hip-hugging, embroidered bell bottom jeans. Her long, black hair was parted down the center and wrapped with a tie-dyed headband around her forehead and a yellow flower was poised over one ear.

Her face was almost devoid of makeup save for a liberal application of light blue eye shadow, black mascara and long, prosthetic eye lashes. Her long hair parted like a pair of curtains that draped around her dark brown eyes which, in turn, floated above a constellation of freckles that spread from the bridge of her nose and out across her cheekbones to either side.

Momentarily dumb-struck, Foster awkwardly asked, "Is this Ted White's home? Are we in the right place?"

"You must be the Fosters!" she said with almost annoying enthusiasm, bouncing on the balls of her feet. "Yeah, hon, you're in the right place! C'mon in! Teddie's in the back."

"Teddie?" he whispered to Livvy.

As they walked in, the woman closed the door behind them. Livvy handed her the wine bottle and she took it with her fingers adorned with long, glossy red stick-on nails, "Why, thanks, hon!"

"I didn't know that Ted was married," Foster commented.

"Married? Naaah, me an' Teddie are just friends, y'know, *really good* friends..." she gave an exaggerated wink, "...know what I mean?"

"I'm afraid I do. Are we interrupting anything?"

"Nah, we was expectin' you! C'mon back, he's got burgers on the grill. How d'you like yours?"

The Fosters followed the effervescent, oversexed young woman through the living room and into the kitchen at the back of the house to a large pair of sliding glass patio doors. She grabbed the handle and slid it open, "Hey, babe! They're here!" she called out as she stepped down from the house to the slate-paved patio.

Ted stood behind a black barbecue grill wearing an apron with the words "Kiss The Cook" emblazoned across his chest. He looked up with the long spatula in hand and saw the young woman stepping down onto the patio with the Fosters right behind her. "Oh, wonderful! Thanks for coming over!"

"Thanks for inviting us," Foster replied, trying his best to sound as neighborly as he could.

"Well, I know what it's like to be out of work. In my business, it's feast or famine." He reached down with the spatula and flipped over a few burgers. "But one thing I've learned is that, after every famine comes another feast. Just a matter of time."

"I hope you're right," Foster commented.

The young woman stood next to Ted at the grill and showed him the bottle of wine. "You brought this? Thanks, it's perfect. But, really, you didn't have to."

"It's alright," Livvy replied, "I thought it would go with the hot dogs and burgers. Besides, I couldn't come empty handed."

"Oh, that's okay, hon," The young woman replied. "We're all friends here."

"I didn't get your girlfriend's name," Foster inquired.

"Girlfriend? Well, she is a friend and, well, obviously a girl. 'Bambi', her name is Bambi," he reached out and wrapped his arm around her bare midriff and pulled her up to himself, she smiled and looked up at him giggling. "She's very talented — an actress."

"Oh? An actress, eh? What movies might I have seen you in, Bambi?"

"Well, you ever seen 'All The Way Down'? Or 'Slippery When Wet'?"

"Uh, no, I'm afraid we must have missed those."

"They're on VHS now — you can rent 'em!"

"I'll, uh, keep that in mind."

"They're in the back, hon. All the stores put 'em in the back."

"Of course they do."

"Do you two swing?" Ted brazenly interrupted.

"Swing?"

"Yeah, you know — *swing?*"

"Uh, no, we don't 'swing', Ted."

"Too bad, Denny, you don't know what you're missing," he slapped Bambi on the butt. She giggled as she walked away back into the kitchen to put the bottle of wine on ice. "Acting isn't her only talent — she's quite the contortionist."

"Maybe so, but I've got the real thing. Not interested, thanks." He turned to Livvy, "Maybe this was a bad idea."

"Oh, no, don't leave — you just got here! We won't talk about that stuff anymore. I only just moved in, just getting to know the folks in the neighborhood. I didn't know where you were at with that sort of thing," Ted was overtly apologetic as he tried to convince his guests to stay. "It's cool, forget it." He grabbed a plate and began taking burgers off the grill and stacked them up to bring to the table. Wanting to change the subject, he asked, "So, Denny, how's the job hunt going?"

Foster took a breath and hesitated as his mind shifted gears, "Well, it's only been a couple of weeks."

"Need any help with your resume? I know a guy. He helps a lot of people in the movie business — we're always updating ours."

"Thanks, Ted, but I think I've got it handled. It's a lot of work but the way I look at it, for the time being anyway, *finding* a job *is* my job."

"A good way to look at it, Denny, I like that." He reached the plate of burgers across the table to him. "Anything else you need, you just come knock on my door…" he turned and looked directly at Livvy and smiled, "…anything at all."

"Yeah, uh, thanks — duly noted."

Livvy's cheeks subconsciously blushed at her neighbor's suggestive offer and then broke her attention away when Bambi handed her a bowl of macaroni salad. She looked at her smiling face and just said, "Thanks," as she took it from her.

"So, Denny," Ted continued the conversation, "Livvy tells me that you have a race car. That's really cool, but I'd never peg you as a race car driver."

"Oh? Foster replied with an edge of annoyance, "What *would* you peg me as — Ted?"

"Hey, no offense, man. I didn't mean anything by it. It's just that you're such a serious sort of guy, an intellectual type, a rocket scientist, you know, uh…"

"Nerd!" Bambi offered with a sparkle in her eye, "A *nerd!*"

"A nerd?"

"In a *good* way, hon," she added as she spooned out some macaroni salad onto her plate.

"Well, Denny, you look to be about as straight-laced as they come. The pocket protector, the glasses. Ya' gotta admit, man, you certainly *look* the part."

"I helped put men on the moon, Ted. What have you accomplished in your lifetime so far? Besides Bambi, I mean."

Livvy, sitting beside him, patted him on the leg under the table to get him to dial it back a bit. Their friendly neighborhood lunch was starting to take an ugly turn.

"Ha, ha!" Ted guffawed. "I mean, just *look* at her, Denny — 'doing' Bambi would be a real accomplishment in *any* man's life. Too bad I can't put *her* on my resume."

Bambi giggled and slapped him playfully on the arm, "Oh, Teddie!"

Denny raised his hamburger up to his face, hiding his mouth for a moment as he quietly grumbled, "Oh, *please...*"

"What was that, dear?" Livvy asked, having heard his muffled voice.

"Oh, nothing," he said as he took a bite of his burger.

"I'd love to see your race car someday, Denny," Ted cheerfully continued. "Never seen one up close."

"Not sure how long I'm going to have it. If I don't get a new job soon, this hobby is going to become too expensive to keep up."

"Oh, that's a shame. I can only imagine how much fun it must be. The competition, the strategies, the adrenaline — must be a real rush."

"It can be." Racing was Foster's favorite secular subject. The change in the conversation's direction turned his attitude on a dime.

"Do you win a lot?"

"Once in a while, a few podiums, too. We've got a small collection of hardware on the shelf."

"Hardware?"

"Trophies, Ted. We nerds have got a bunch of trophies."

"That's great, Denny. You'll have to show me sometime," He turned and looked at Livvy, "Livvy must be proud of you."

"I am," she quipped.

"Maybe sometime I could come by and you can show me." He suggested to her with a grin.

"Maybe," she said. "Sometime maybe."

Tense but congenial, the conversations continued through lunch. There were plenty of light moments, too. Plenty of laughs. It was a bumpy road for very different sorts of strangers trying to get to know one another and build some kind of neighborly relationships. The wine definitely helped.

After a few hours had slipped by, Ted looked at his watch and commented that he had a conference call he had to get ready for. Foster saw it as a perfect cue to excuse himself and Livvy and head back across the street for home.

"It was great to have you come by, Denny," Ted said as the two women gathered up the plates and empty glasses and carried them inside to the kitchen.

"Thanks for inviting us."

"It's good to get to know your neighbors. We live so close to one another, you never know when you might have to be there for them — you know what I mean?"

"I think I do."

"You know, Denny, I'm convinced you're going to be alright in all of this. Something will come along, I'm sure of it. In the meantime, look at what you've got," he nodded his head toward the kitchen inside the house, "She's a wonderful woman, man. Sexy, devoted, she obviously loves you to death. You're a lucky man, my friend. A very lucky man."

"Thanks, I sincerely think so."

Ted shook his hand and then slapped him on the shoulder as the pair walked back into the house and out to the front door. Foster and Livvy stepped out onto the porch and paused to thank their hosts. Ted stood with his arm around Bambi's taught midriff, "You remember what I said, if you need anything at all, you just come on over."

"Yeah..." Bambi added with a giggle, "...you just 'cum' — *anytime.*"

He barked out a guffaw and then slapped her on her denim-clad butt. She giggled louder and cackled, "Oh, Teddie!"

Foster just rolled his eyes and gave a half-hearted wave before he turned and led Livvy down the driveway toward home, quietly commenting, "Let's get out of here — I think I'm gonna be ill." ■

CHAPTER EIGHT

Waiting for the Phone to Ring

Monday morning, Dennis Foster was once again hard at work at his desk in his home office massaging his CV trying desperately to get all of the most important and pertinent information distilled down to just two pages. That's what all the experts in the how-to-write-a-resume books said was optimal. With his multiple degrees from MIT and CalTech, it was difficult to get even just the portion describing his education brief enough and still make him feel that it did him justice.

And then there were the seminars, technical residencies, publications — all before he even began to tackle his job experiences and references.

The task seemed impossible.

He had to take a break. He got up and walked out to the kitchen to refresh his coffee. As he poured from the pot into his cup, the phone on the kitchen wall rang. He set the pot back down in its stand to keep it hot and set down his mug as he turned around. He walked around the table and answered the phone.

"Hello?"

"Hello? Is this Doctor Dennis Foster?"

"It is. How can I help you?"

"Dennis, this is Doctor Kimber. Do you remember me? I came out to see you at the race track a while ago."

"Oh, certainly I remember you, Doctor." He tried to contain his excitement at having the man call him after having left his message on the previous Friday. He didn't want to get his hopes up too much though, just in case it was just a courtesy call just to tell him that he didn't have any openings at the time.

But he was pleasantly surprised by what he heard next.

"I got your message. Your timing is perfect. While I was at the seminar this weekend, a man from the Pentagon came up to me after I spoke and told me about a very specialized position he was hoping I could help him fill. I immediately thought of you. Tell me, Dennis, have you changed your mind about moving on from Cyberdyne?"

"Well, to be honest, that decision was sort of made for me already."

"Oh, no. They laid you off?"

"Yeah, they did."

"There's a lot of that going around these days. I suppose one can't work in aerospace and not expect it could happen to you someday."

"No, I suppose not."

"I guess, then, that the timing of your call has turned out to be fortuitous for both of us."

"It would appear so." Foster paused for a moment and then asked, "Tell me, Doctor, what is this specialized opportunity?"

"It's highly compartmentalized. I can't tell you too much until you've been cleared and read into the program. But what I can tell you is that it's a contract job expected to last for up to three years, maybe longer. The pay is about half again what you were making at Cyberdyne with some, uh, unusual perks."

"Unusual perks? What do you mean?"

"I can't really say much more than that right now except that your advanced skills in particle physics and isotope analysis are precisely what they are looking for. You can see why I thought of you right away."

"Sounds intriguing."

"So you *are* interested? You want me to put you in for this?"

"Oh, certainly. Nothing ventured, nothing gained, as they say. But I'd like to know more about it before I commit to anything."

"Getting hired onto this sort of position is an involved process, Dennis. I've placed several people into high-security government jobs like this. It will take a little time and, as more and more is revealed to you, you'll be able to back out any time that you feel uncomfortable — but I just know you're going to love it the more you find out about it."

"Just one question, if you can answer me this much — will I need to relocate for this?"

"The job is at a remote facility. So remote, you can't even drive to it. They shuttle all of their employees out to it with daily flights back and forth. You live in Burbank, right? You can stay where you are and catch the flights out of the airport there. You won't have to relocate."

"Oh, that's good news. Any decision I make, of course, my wife has to rubber stamp. She keeps telling me that she's okay with relocating but, when it gets down to it, I'm not sure how she'll really feel. I know she'd really rather stay put right here. She'll be happy to hear that."

"Then you're in?"

"Yeah, I'm in."

"Great. Do you have a resume that you can fax to me?"

"I'm working on it. It's not ready yet."

"That's alright, send me whatever you have right now. The fax number is on the business card. Can you get that off to me today?"

"Sure. There's a copy shop in the plaza down the street. I can fax it from there."

"Oh, that will be just perfect. I'll pass it on with my recommendations and see what sort of response we get. I have a feeling I'll be flying you out here to St. Louis shortly to get the ball rolling. How's that sound?"

"It sounds great. I'll look forward to hearing from you."

"Thanks again, Dennis. I have a good feeling about this. Give my best to your wife."

"I will, thanks."

He hung the phone up and stood in the kitchen for a long moment just looking at it on the wall. He could feel an involuntary grin spreading across his face. He pulled off his glasses and wiped his face with his palm from his forehead down to his chin, "Wow," he whispered to himself as he replaced the spectacles. "This is incredible — what an opportunity."

He shook his head and turned back to his just-filled coffee cup still on the counter across the room and quickly reminded himself, "Gotta keep things grounded, though. Yeah, it *sounds* great, but nothing's etched in stone yet. One step at a time."

He walked back into his office and sat down again at the computer. He scrolled through the five pages that he had been working so hard to edit down to just two and shrugged his shoulders. So much more work he needed to do, but everything was there. Too much, actually. But there wasn't time to work on it just then.

He rolled the mouse around to put the curser on the word "print" at the top of the screen, clicked the button and heard his printer come to life.

While he waited for the pages to print out, he picked up Dr. Kimber's card and slipped it into his shirt pocket and thought out loud, "I should leave Livvy a note!"

His wife was out at the grocery store at the time and probably wouldn't be back for an hour or so. He couldn't wait for her, he had to rush out as soon as his CV was finished printing. He quickly jotted down a few short words on a note pad saying where he'd be and that he'd be right back when he was done without including any details about the phone call. He'd fill her in when he got home.

When the last page finally dropped out of the printer, he grabbed an empty manila folder from the desk drawer and dropped the CV into it then shut down his computer. He rushed back out to the kitchen, left the note pad on the table, dumped what was left of his cup of coffee into the sink and left it with a little water in the bottom of it. He snatched the keys to his truck from the hook as he continued through the living room and out the front door.

* * * * *

Foster returned home from the copy shop to find his wife's car in the driveway. She'd no doubt found his note on the kitchen table by then. He couldn't wait to break the news to her.

He grabbed up the folder from the passenger seat and hopped out of the truck and then walked briskly up the walkway to the door. As he walked inside, she saw him from the kitchen. Her first instinct was to ask if anything was wrong but she could see by his expression that he was excited by something.

He rushed through the living room and said, "Livvy, you'll never guess!"

"Guess — what? We hit the lottery?"

"No, no...well, at least I don't *think* so. No, Dr. Kimber called me while you were out. He wanted me to fax him my CV as soon as possible. I just came from the copy shop to send it to him. He has a job opening with the Pentagon and he thinks I'd be the perfect candidate for it!"

"Really? That's wonderful, dear!"

"And we won't have to move, either."

"It's right here in LA?"

"No, not exactly. I'm not clear on the details yet, but he tells me the company has airplanes that fly their people in every day. I'd fly to work from Burbank."

"Fly? What kind of company is this?"

"It's the government, sweetie."

"The government?" She was beginning to feel a little apprehensive.

"The job is at a high-security facility. Dr. Kimber says it's about a forty-five minute flight from Burbank. That's about the same as my commute to Cyberdyne was. But it's a job for a particle physicist — a specialty that only a few people in the whole country are qualified for."

"And you're one of them."

"That's right."

"That's exciting, it really is!"

"And it pays more than my old job at Cyberdyne — *a lot* more."

"Gee, Denny, it sounds like a dream job for you. When do you start?"

"Well, truthfully, I haven't actually gotten it yet. So far, after talking with Dr. Kimber on the phone, I've just sent in my CV. He said he'll forward it to his contact at the Pentagon and, if they want to proceed, we'll move into the next phase — whatever that might be."

"One step at a time, I suppose," she leaned over and kissed him on the cheek. "If nothing else, this is encouraging. It makes me think that there may be more opportunity for you out there than we thought. I hope it works out."

"Me, too."

* * * * *

Waiting for the phone to ring is a demoralizing experience, especially when you're unemployed and hoping to hear back from a prospective new employer. One's future is in someone else's hands. Every time it does ring, your heart leaps and then, when you find out it's someone else — *anyone* else — it sinks again. Each time it does, it sinks just a little bit lower.

But, being the pragmatist that he was, Dennis continued work on editing his CV down to a more manageable length while he waited. Finally, after a week of concerted work, he felt it was ready. He saved the document file to a floppy disk and then shut down his computer. The clock on the bookshelf showed that it was already fairly late in the afternoon so he set the disk down next to the computer keyboard on the desk and made mental note to take it to the copy shop in the morning to get it set up and printed on fancy paper with matching envelopes and some letterheads for cover letters. Progress, he thought — another step forward. Even if he would never hear back from Dr. Kimber, at least he was making some progress and he'd have the tools to go and start knocking on other doors and lining up interviews.

After dinner, he sat down in the living room with his wife, sipping on a glass of wine, and watched a re-run of "Star Trek" on television before turning in for the night.

In the morning, Livvy got ready to go off to work at her friend's dress shop. She had to be there by the time it would open at ten o'clock. Dennis tried his best to stay out of her way. Since his only real plan for that day was to get to the copy shop, he could leave the house at any time so he just grabbed a cup of coffee and sat down in the living room with a technical journal that had recently come in the mail. He wanted to keep updated on the latest technical advancements and news to stay fresh while he was between jobs.

After Livvy kissed him goodbye and left, he went upstairs and showered, shaved and got himself dressed for the day. Even though most days he didn't leave the house, he insisted to himself that he would not skip his daily routine. Every day he'd get up at the same time that he would if he were going off to work, he'd get dressed, comb his hair, make some coffee and engage himself in something mind-stimulating. He refused to let himself go and just hang around like a bum in his pajamas all day and committed himself to not even turning on the television until evening.

He got thinking about what he might involve himself in that day once he got back home from the copy shop. He wandered out to the kitchen and to the door to the garage and just reached around to flip on the light switch. There, parked in the flickering fluorescent light, was his green and blue, open-wheeled, Formula Atlantic racing car. Still wearing the dust and grime from its last outing and surrounded by the tool boxes, plastic tubs and cardboard boxes filled with other gear that he and his friend, Luke, had unloaded from the trailer when they'd first gotten home. They just left it all there to attend to on some other day.

Since he'd lost his job, they hadn't ventured out for another race. They talked about it on the phone and Luke had come over with his wife, Betty, a few times. They kept talking about 'someday' — soon, hopefully. He thought he'd recalled a local race on the calendar coming up in a few weeks. Maybe it was time. For the moment, he was still able to afford it, still had his truck, the trailer and all the equipment they'd need. A concerted weekend to get the car ready and they could get back out there. Who knew when they'd be able to again — maybe not until his life got to be settled again. Whenever that might be.

He turned off the light and went back inside, "Maybe I'll work on the car when I get back," he said quietly to himself. "Clean it up, put all the stuff away, sweep out the trailer..." He looked at his watch, it was time to get going to the copy shop. He went into his office, picked up the disk from his obsessively orderly desk and slipped it into his pocket, then headed for the door.

While he was in town, he stopped by Alma's Dress Shop to say hello to Livvy. Business was slow at that hour of the day so the two of them and Alma had a little time to chat and then he left to pick up a sandwich at the deli to bring home for lunch.

When he got in, he hung up his keys and put his sandwich in the refrigerator and then turned to go up to the bedroom to change into something more work-on-the-race-car appropriate when the phone rang.

He turned and grabbed the receiver off the kitchen wall, "Hello?"

"Dennis? It's Doctor Kimber."

"Doctor Kimber — hello. I've been anxious for your call. Any news?"

"I sent your resume to General Sangster at the US Space Command at the Pentagon. He's the one who's directing this project that they need me to find people for."

"And...what did he say?"

"He wants to meet you, Dennis."

"An interview?"

"A first meeting — yes — sort of a 'get acquainted' meet. He said he liked what he read. As I said before, I have a good feeling about this."

"Well, if nothing else, that's encouraging. When, uh, where?"

"He'd like to meet next Tuesday here in my offices. Can you fly out this weekend for Monday morning?"

"I suppose — sure. I'll have to call the airline and make reservations — and a hotel in St. Louis…"

"Don't worry about any of that. I'll have a boarding pass waiting for you at the counter at the Burbank airport and my firm keeps a few rooms at the Hilton for clients who come to town, I'll set you up there. Just go to the desk and give them your name when you get here."

"Really? Uh, alright, I'll pack a bag and have Livvy drive me to the airport on Sunday."

"That's great, Dennis, I'll have my secretary call you with the particulars. I'll see you here in my office at ten on Monday morning — we have some prep to go over before we meet with the general on Tuesday."

"I look forward to seeing you, then — Monday morning."

"Thanks, Dennis — be seeing you."

He hung up the phone and stood in the kitchen for a moment. The first thought that came to him was how excited he was to tell Livvy. He couldn't wait for her to get home. He snatched the phone back up again to call her at the dress shop and give her the good news. ∎

PHASE 3
THE RUN-UP

CHAPTER NINE

Vaguely Familiar

On Sunday morning, Livvy Foster drove her husband to the Hollywood-Burbank Airport just a few miles from their suburban home and he boarded a commercial flight to St. Louis. As Dr. Kimber had promised on the phone, a round-trip boarding pass was waiting for him at the counter.

From the time he boarded, the flight was pretty routine and he landed in St. Louis, got a cab to the Hilton, checked in and called his wife to tell her that he had arrived and all was well.

By then, it was mid-afternoon and his meeting with Kimber wasn't until the next morning so he had a little time to kill. He'd never been to St. Louis before so he decided to take a walk — not too far from the hotel, he didn't want to get lost in a strange city. He could see the famous arch down by the river and with the wind blowing in just the right direction, there was the prominent smell of licorice in the air. He watched as a few barges ambled down the Mississippi River being pushed by boats seemingly far too small to move such mass with any sort of control, the sight fascinated him.

Finally, as it was getting dusky, he returned to the hotel. He had dinner in the restaurant and then went up to his room for the evening.

Monday morning, he got a pre-arranged wake-up call at six o'clock from the front desk. He rose to get ready for the day, showered, shaved, and put on a white dress shirt and gray slacks — something professional-looking for a formal meeting.

When he came back from having breakfast in the restaurant, he added a simple maroon tie to his ensemble and instinctively reached for his pocket protector but then paused before grabbing it off of the dresser. Not for a meeting like that. Still he felt incomplete, almost naked without it — his pens, his slide-rule. He tossed it into his briefcase. He'd at least have it with him like a security blanket, just in case.

Finally, he slipped on a charcoal gray sport coat that complemented his slacks, scooped up the handle of his briefcase, and went down to the lobby to catch a cab to the building where Dr. Kimber's office was located. He was early but he had no idea how far away the office was and how long it might take to get there. He didn't want to blow the opportunity by being late.

The driver was skilled and just daring enough to get through the thick morning city traffic and get him to his destination in about fifteen minutes. After paying the cabbie, he went into the lobby of a towering, glass and steel office building. He followed a flow of people passing through the large, revolving doors who were just then arriving for work at offices located elsewhere in the building on various floors. When he emerged from the rotating portal, he found himself in an expansive space with a shining aggregate floor — the building's lobby.

In the center of the opposite wall in front of him was a long reception desk with a couple of uniformed security guards sitting behind it. The address of the building was spelled out in polished stainless steel letters and numerals high on the wall behind the desk. To either end of the desk were openings leading to two wide hallways that extended back into the building. He could see the doors to several elevators just a short way down each hall.

On the wall to the left was a large, black display board with the directory of all of the offices in the building showing which floor they were on and their respective office numbers. He knew from Dr. Kimber's directions which floor and which office he was looking for so just continued to walk toward the banks of elevators.

He rode up to the twelfth floor with a small clutch of people who packed into the elevator car, trying hard not to make eye-contact with one another or actually speak to anyone. The only sounds were the whirring noise of the elevator's mechanisms and Muzak coming through the speakers overhead playing a familiar Neil Diamond tune in its own soft, unique, instrumental style.

When he exited on the twelfth floor, he saw a sign showing that the odd numbered offices were to his right and those with even numbers were to his left. He turned to the right, found office number 1247, and walked through the glass door into the outer office where Dr. Kimber's secretary, Beverly Stone, was seated at her desk. She was a matronly-looking, middle-aged woman in classic office attire and reading glasses with half-lenses that hung from her neck on a beaded, silver chain. Her brown and gray streaked hair was pulled back into a bun.

She smiled at him as she looked up from her desk and asked, "You must be Mr. Foster?"

He was glad for the welcoming and confirmed that he was, in fact, whom she'd presumed.

"Wonderful," she got up from her chair. "Right this way, sir. He's expecting you."

She led him to a dark wooden door, knocked on it gently, and then opened it just enough to announce him.

He could hear Kimber's voice call out from inside, "Marvelous — send him right in!"

She pushed the door open wide and allowed Foster to pass by her into the office.

Kimber stood up behind the desk, leaned forward and reached out his hand to shake with him, "Thank you so much for coming, Dennis. It's so great to see you again."

"I'm happy to be here," he stood in front of the desk with his brief-case clutched in his left hand.

"Can I get you some coffee, sir?" the secretary asked.

Foster turned and looked back at her, "Yes, please."

"I'll be right back," she walked out, closing the door behind her.

"Have a seat, Dennis, please."

Foster pulled back one of the chairs that faced the desk and sat down, setting his briefcase on the floor beside him.

"I'm glad you were able to send me your CV, even though it was a work-in-progress. It filled in a lot of gaps in what I already knew about you."

"It did?"

"Well, for example, I didn't know that you had been published so many times. I was only aware of the one in *The Journal*."

"I brought copies."

"That won't be necessary. The people who will do the background checks would prefer to get their own from some independent sources.

Don't worry, they'll read them," he chuckled, "They won't understand any of it, but they *will* read them."

"They don't trust me?"

"They don't trust *anyone*. Don't take it personally, it's their job to be suspicious. This is the Pentagon we're dealing with."

"Alright, I guess."

"Dennis, you're about to step into the dark world of 'national security.' These people chant that phrase like some kind of mantra and use it as an excuse to justify all sorts of intrusions into our lives as well as other dubious activities."

"Other activities? Like what?"

"Thankfully things that we won't ever be privy to — and just as well — trust me on that."

"You're making me nervous."

"Oh, don't be. Everyone who works for these people goes through this process. It can be intimidating, I know. Lots of questions, lots of paperwork, but I've been through it with a number of my clients and I just know you won't have any trouble. I and my associates will coach you through it. I wouldn't put you through it if I didn't think it was worth it."

"Have you been through it yourself?"

"We all have, that's how we have such insight into the process."

At that moment there was a quiet rap on the door and Beverly walked in with a mug of coffee for Foster. "You looked like a 'one cream, two sugars' kind of man."

"That's right. Thank you."

She smiled and then left the office, again closing the door behind herself as she did.

"I swear she's the last of a dying breed," Kimber mused as she walked out of the office. "I'm so lucky to have her here working for me."

"Knows where all the bodies are buried?" Foster quipped.

"Something like that," Kimber chuckled. "Sometimes I think the woman is psychic."

"As long as she uses her powers for good."

"Ha, ha! Precisely."

"I had a pretty good secretary at Cyberdyne. She served our whole department, very efficient but kind of a snob."

"Yes, since you've brought it up. Let's talk about Cyberdyne for a moment. When I met you at the race track, you told me that you were happy there and couldn't imagine ever leaving. Tell me about that — what happened?"

"Well, I like solving problems. I love rolling up my sleeves and digging in to find answers. At Cyberdyne, working on all sorts of projects for the space program, I kept getting assigned a variety of things to analyze, calculate. Sometimes I'd even design systems and procedures to deal with things like gamma rays, radiation, cosmic particles, all the sorts of things that the astronauts would encounter out in open space. A big part of it was being challenged with some brand new unknown, a problem that needed solving, and finding solutions. Incredibly rewarding work and no two days were quite the same."

"For people like you and me, that sounds pretty exciting."

"I know people call me a nerd — and to be fair, I suppose I am — but without nerds like me, we would never have reached the moon. We would never have beaten the Russians."

"I like your attitude."

Once again, there was a knock on the door and Beverly stepped inside to announce that Dr. Melissa Lopez, Kimber's associate, was ready for them in the conference room.

"That's good, thank you, Beverly." Kimber stood up again and said, "Let's move this into the conference room and start our prep for tomorrow's interview," he waved his hand toward the door. "Shall we?"

Foster got up and grabbed his briefcase still holding his cup of coffee in his other hand. Kimber told him that he could bring it with him and then the two followed the secretary across the reception area to another door that opened up onto a walnut-paneled conference room with a window at one end overlooking the city.

A long table in the center of the room was surrounded with soft leather uholstered chairs and a few oil paintings hung on the walls for a bit of classic decor. Along with rows and rows of books on the bookcases built into the walls, there stood a glowing, amber lava lamp. It seemed out of place in such an otherwise formal decor.

Across the table stood Kimber's associate with a few stacks of folders and papers on the table in front of her. She was a petite woman in a sharp, gray suit jacket over a matching pencil skirt and frilled white blouse. She had shoulder length, auburn hair and hazel eyes. A spray of freckles, almost invisible under her very conservatively applied makeup, wrapped over the apexes of both cheekbones and across the bridge of her nose.

"Good morning, Dr. Lopez," Kimber said as the pair walked into the room. "This is Dr. Dennis Foster."

She reached across the table and shook his hand, "I'm pleased to meet you, Doctor."

"Thanks. I'm not used to being called 'doctor'." He commented.

"With your degrees and your credentials, it seems appropriate," she replied.

"For the time being, Dennis," Kimber interrupted, "We'll use that title. It may seem a bit out of character for you but it's legitimate and, to impress General Sangster tomorrow, let's get used to it."

"I'll try to remember."

"Don't worry, we'll work on that."

For a moment, Foster looked across at Lopez, studying her face as she busied herself arranging some of the folders on the table in front of her. Suddenly aware of his stare, she looked up at him and asked, "Is there a problem, Doctor Foster?"

"Uh, no — no problem. It's just that you look kind of familiar to me. But, no, I'm sure I'm wrong."

"I'm sure you are, Doctor. I think I'd remember if we'd ever met before."

"As would I. I can't place it, but you must have a dopple-ganger out there that I'm recalling. Sorry."

"It's alright. Please, sit down. Let's get started."

Foster laid his briefcase down on the table just to his right and then pulled out a chair to sit. Kimber walked around the table and sat on the opposite side near where Lopez was standing but far enough removed to remain more of a spectator than participant. It would be her show, her expertise.

She picked up the first folder on the top of one of the stacks and set it in front of herself. She remained standing across from him. Being just a couple of inches over five feet tall, she had developed strategies to maintain the power position in such meetings, to be able to look down on a subject and cause them to look up to her as she'd question them.

She opened the folder and lifted out a few sheets of paper stapled together in the top corner and glanced at them quickly. Then she looked over at Foster, "You were born in Florida, grew up there. Is that right?"

"Yes. We lived in Winter Haven. Moved out when retirees began to overrun the town."

"You sound bitter about that. Does that make you angry? Do you feel that you were chased out of town?"

"Chased? In a way, yes, I suppose. But I wouldn't say that I'm angry about it. My life has been pretty good since then. I don't believe that, if I had stayed in Florida, I would have had the life that I've had."

"You met your wife, Olivia Lauper, when you were at California Polytechnic Institute?"

"Yes, I did."

"Was she a fellow student there?"

"No, she was going to a different school. She was working as a waitress at a restaurant that some of us frequented. One of my friends dared me to ask her out. I was kind of awkward around women, but she was beautiful with a great smile — still is, actually. With a little encouragement, I got up the nerve and, well, a few years later — after I graduated — we were married."

"Did you know that your father-in-law, George, is associated with a known communist organization in Oregon?"

"Communist? George? No."

"Are you a communist, Dr. Foster?"

"No!" Foster replied sharply, "I *love* my country! I helped put men on the moon for Heaven's sake!"

"Do you love your wife?"

Caught off guard with such a non-sequeteur question, he took a moment to collect his thoughts before replying, "Uh, yes, I do."

"Children?"

"No."

"You don't love your children?"

"I don't *have* any children."

"Why not?"

"Uh, we've talked about it and even tried a few times, but it just isn't happening for us."

"Shooting blanks, Dr. Foster?"

"Blanks?"

"Infertile — low sperm count?"

"Not that it's any of your business but, in point of fact..." He stood up from his seat and leaned in toward Lopez, "Are these sorts of questions really relevant? Why are you asking me this kind of stuff? How could this sort of thing possibly be at all important?!"

"It's all a matter of psychology, Dennis," Kimber injected. "When the general gets here with his interrogator, they're going to try and get you off of your stable footing. To get you to become agitated and maybe make mistakes and blurt out some kind of unguarded answers to the questions that actually *are* important. Mind games, Dennis, that's all it is."

"Well, I don't like it. Not at all."

"I know, nobody does. But it's all part of their process. Just keep your cool, tell the truth and since you now know what their game is, you can more easily keep a level head through it all. Whatever you do, don't try to evade their questions no matter how uncomfortable they might make you feel. And don't lie. They back-check everything."

"That is why we're doing this preparation today," Lopez added. "These questions are mild compared to what they're likely to ask you tomorrow."

"I hope you're right, Doctor Kimber. I hope this is all worth it."

"Trust me, Dennis, it is." ∎

CHAPTER TEN

Just Relax and Tell the Truth

Dr. Lopez's rather grueling interview prep that he had endured in St. Louis and the encouraging words of Doctor Kimber had, hopefully, prepared him for his first encounter with Pentagon officers. The subsequent meeting with General Sangster and his aide from the Pentagon the following day went well enough, or so he thought. As Lopez had warned, a lot of probing questions were asked, deeply personal things that didn't seem at all relevant, but he kept his composure, heeding her advice — she had prepared him well.

At home, he continued to address envelopes and cover letters to innumerable businesses and consulting firms in the aerospace industry to continue his quest on his own. Surely, someone out there would need a man of his extensive experience and impressive credentials.

As he sat at his desk, he could hear voices from out in the living room. He had an album of Mozart classical music on the turntable playing softly in his office as he worked but still could hear the voices talking — a man and a woman. He could hear them but from that distance couldn't make out any actual words. Did Livvy have the television on? It was her day off from working at the dress shop, but normally she wouldn't just sit in front of the screen. She'd be busy catching up with laundry, baking, running errands to the market and other such things.

Eventually his curiosity got the better of him and he had to go and see whose voices he was hearing. He set down his pen and got up from the desk. He grabbed his nearly empty coffee cup as he went, thinking that once his curiosity had been satisfied, he'd top it off before going back to his desk and the task at hand.

He walked out through the kitchen and, as he got closer, he recognized Livvy's voice and then that of their new neighbor, Ted. He set the cup down on the kitchen table as he passed and walked out into the living room.

"There he is!" Ted called out, looking past her and seeing Foster walking into the room.

"Oh, hi, dear," Livvy said looking back behind her. "Ted's here."

"Thanks, I can see that. Good morning, Ted."

"Morning, Denny."

"Something we can do for you — Ted?"

"I was just telling Livvy about a surprise visitor that I had yesterday."

"Oh?" Ted's unannounced, random visits to just talk with them were annoyingly frequent and tended mostly to be directed toward his wife, Livvy. She would smile a lot when he'd tell his Hollywood stories, dropping names of celebrities, and swoon just a little bit when he'd compliment her. He'd always comment to Foster, though (to his continual chagrin), what a lucky man he was to be married to such a beautiful, sexy and vital woman.

Any man would be gravely suspicious of Ted's ministrations and any ulterior motives — any *other* man, that is.

Perhaps it was the long-established trust between himself and his wife that he would never suspect anything inappropriate. It was something he'd always just presumed. Maybe it was his abysmally low regard for Ted in general that he didn't take him any too seriously. Or, perhaps it was his immense intellect that caused him to be so oblivious to things that other men would be quick to pick up on in the real world.

Or maybe he just took Livvy for granted.

"Yeah, these two serious lookin' guys dressed in suits came to my house and asked me a whole lot of questions," Ted explained.

"I don't know a whole lot about you, Ted, but I have to say that I'm not entirely surprised."

"They were asking me questions about you, Denny. Showed me their badges — they were FBI."

"FBI?" Foster paused for a moment and then smiled, "Oh, sure, the background check. Sorry about that, Ted. I'm up for a government job. They're doing a background check on me. They said the FBI would be contacting people I know like my former employer, co-workers, friends — that sort of thing. They didn't say anything about canvassing my neighborhood."

"It's okay. I guess it means that they're seriously considering you. If that's the case then this is a good thing, right? *Congratulations!*"

"Yes, dear, that's great news!" Livvy added.

"Thanks, but let's not put the cart before the horse — not just yet. Sorry for any intrusion, Ted. I didn't expect that they'd be doing this now after just the first interview. But then, maybe you're right, maybe it is a good thing."

"Well, I'd like to think so," Ted encouraged. "We need to celebrate. Let me take you two kids out for dinner tonight. Whaddya say? On me."

"Oh, I don't know," Foster generally felt uncomfortable in social situations anyway, but especially with people he didn't know very well and, considering that he didn't much like Ted, he was all the more reluctant to go along.

"We don't have anything planned, dear," Livvy commented to him, then turned back to Ted, "Will your girlfriend be joining us, too?"

"I'm sure she wouldn't miss it for the world."

"Come on, dear. Let's make a night of it. You need to get out of that office of yours for a bit. A double-date, it'll do you good — it'll do us both good."

"I suppose — alright. Thanks, Ted."

"Hey, again, congratulations, Denny. I've got a good feeling about this!"

"Well, nothing's etched in stone quite yet, but I definitely think I could use a night out."

"That's the spirit! Be seeing you!"

* * * * *

A little more than a week later, Foster got a call from Dr. Kimber telling him that the FBI's background investigation had concluded and that General Sangster would like for him to fly out to Washington DC for the next phase of the interview process. It would be conducted at the J. Edgar Hoover building downtown. He'd need to be in town for a few days. He packed a bag and put a few things in his briefcase that he thought might be of some interest to his interviewers including photocopies of his various diplomas and certificates, copies of the journals that he'd been published in and, of course, his pocket protector.

Again, Livvy dropped him off at the Burbank airport, kissed him goodbye and wished him luck. As he had done before, Kimber had arranged a round-trip boarding pass for him to pick up at the check-in counter. He'd fly from Burbank to Tempe and after a short layover, fly from there to Atlanta where he'd have to wait for a few hours to finally catch the flight to Washington DC. He'd be staying at the Watergate Hotel just across the Potomac in Virginia. Dr. Kimber got him a room with a view of the city.

A livery service picked him up in a black town car the next morning and drove him into the city. Wearing the nicest suit that he owned with the same conservative maroon tie (he only owned a couple of ties so his selection was pretty narrow — and simple), he carried his briefcase into the lobby of the J. Edgar Hoover building and was met in the lobby by Dr. Kimber and his associate Dr. Lopez.

"Good morning, Dennis."

"Good morning, Dr. Kimber," he shook his hand and then reached over and shook hers, "Dr. Lopez."

"Did you have a nice flight?" she asked.

"Pretty routine. I brought some reading materials for the layovers. Nice room at the hotel, by the way. Thank you."

"I wanted you to be well rested for this," Kimber explained. "This will be a pretty thorough interview. It will take several hours."

"Well, I think I'm ready."

"Good. Let's go then."

They stepped up to the desk in the lobby and were issued visitor badges, then rode the elevator up to the ninth floor. When the doors parted, an agent was waiting for them in the hallway. He escorted them to an empty conference room and let the three of them in, closing the door behind them. Foster was too nervous to sit. To break the ice, Kimber asked him what he had in his briefcase.

"Oh, just copies of my CV, some references, the journals that I was published in, a note pad and some pens — just some essentials if they ask."

"No slide-rule?"

"Slide-rule?"

"A joke, Dennis. Just trying to lighten things up a little." He stepped up to him and very soberly explained. "I guess people like us don't tell jokes very well."

"Or get them," Lopez quipped.

"Uh, yeah. Or get them." He put his hand on Foster's shoulder, "I wouldn't have offered you up for this if I didn't have every confidence that you were the perfect fit for the job. This security process can be tedious and intimidating, I know. But remember what I told you, they're going to try and get you off your base, unstable, maybe get you to accidently blurt out some hidden truth in an unguarded moment."

"Just relax and tell the truth, Dr. Foster," Lopez inserted. "Be honest with them, answer them as quickly as possible and keep your cool. Whatever you do, don't lose your temper with them."

"Right — stay cool — got it."

The door from the hallway opened and two agents dressed in black suits, white shirts and narrow black ties walked into the room followed by the uniformed General Sangster who had met with him at Kimber's office in St. Louis along with another man whom he introduced as Mr. Duwan Freeman. Freeman looked out of place in his brown jacket, red bow tie and wire-framed glasses. Still, the look on his face was just as grimly serious as the general's and the two agents in black who had posted themselves intimidatingly in two opposite corners of the room. Silent, but nevertheless impossible to ignore.

"Dr. Foster," the general began, shaking his hand, "we have some papers for you to sign before we get started. Have a seat."

Foster pulled one of the chairs out from the table and sat down. Freeman laid a folder down next to him and opened it up. He handed him a pen and then laid a form down on the table top and slid it in front of him.

"What's this?" Foster asked.

"It's your promise to keep all of what you experience from this moment on entirely confidential," Freeman explained, "under penalty of law."

"Can I read it first?"

"Of course. We wouldn't want you to sign anything without checking it over first. When you're ready, initial each page and then sign and date on the line at the bottom of the last page."

Foster began to read the small print, trying to read as quickly as he could. He felt all of the eyes in the room impatiently watching him as he flipped to the next page. He scanned it from top to bottom quickly and then, feeling pressured to hurry, he flipped to the last page and just signed where the line appeared at the end of the last paragraph.

"Don't forget to initial all of the other pages," Freeman reminded.

"Right," he quickly flipped back through each leaf and scribbled his initials in the bottom right corner.

Freeman took the form from him as Foster handed him up the pen. "No, keep that — you still need it."

He then put another multi-page document in front of him and told him to sign it. It was a general release for all of his collegiate transcripts and employment records. He signed it without reading it over.

The next form was a medical release allowing them to administer life-saving drugs and procedures should he become stricken in any way or an undiagnosed medical condition should cause some sort of trauma while he was there.

After having signed that form, General Sangster handed Freeman a Bible. He held it out to Foster and told him to put his left hand on it and raise his right hand, "Do you swear to tell us the truth, the whole truth and nothing but the truth, so help you God?"

He glanced up at Kimber, then nodded and replied, "I do."

Freeman handed the Bible back to the general and then slid another form in front of Foster, "This one confirms the oath you just took and your intent to hide nothing from us in our interviews."

Foster signed the form. It occurred to him that all of the forms were just part of the theater of intimidation. He began to think that much of it was just ersatz boilerplate text and otherwise unnecessary.

Finally, Freeman slid one more form in front of him and said, "This one gives us permission to administer the polygraph test."

"Polygraph?"

"Lie-detector," Lopez explained.

"I know what it is."

"It's routine, Dennis," Kimber added. "Don't let it rattle you."

Foster looked up at him for a moment with a leering expression and then, begrudgingly, turned back to the table and signed the form.

"That's it. That's the last form," Freeman said.

"Gee, already?" Foster grumbled sarcastically under his breath.

Freeman put all of the forms back into the folder and told Foster he could keep the pen. He then turned to the door and said to Sangster as he left, "I'll be ready for you in about ten minutes." The general nodded to him as he walked out of the room.

"Alright, Mr. Foster," Sangster said as he sat down at the table across from him. "I'm sure Dr. Kimber and Dr. Lopez have warned you about what will happen here today. There are various levels of security clearance within our government and the intelligence community itself. In order to take on the position that we need you for, you will need to qualify for one of the highest levels. Normally, when someone is first hired, they might qualify for a lesser level and be elevated as they gain experience and prove themselves with us over time. That process could take years and this is a rather urgent matter of national security — we don't have the luxury of time. If you get hired for this position, we need you to walk into that lab and hit the ground running. So we need to put you on the fast-track and go through this rather involved process to get you one of the highest levels right out of the gate."

"I understand."

"Am I right that you drive a racing car?"

"Uh, yeah. Sort of a hobby."

"Hobby? Most folks collect things like coins and stamps or build model airplanes. Driving a racing car seems to be a lot more involved than what other, uh, 'normal' hobbies might be."

"To the best of my knowledge, General, people don't collect stamps competitively."

"Competitive? So that's what it's all about — the competition?"

"There's a rush, I'll admit. But there's a team effort, too. Something one prepares for — not just the car — but mentally, emotionally. Practice, reflexes and instinct. A singular sensation of accomplishment in running the race and finishing well — especially if you walk away with a trophy."

"A competitive spirit, I like that."

"When I had first started working at Cyberdyne, we sat around the television on July twentieth back in sixty-nine and watched Neil Armstrong step off the ladder onto the surface of the moon, we were all really proud of the work we'd done to help make that happen — but the real celebration was that we had beaten the Russians. We got there first. We did the work, made the sacrifices, rallied the greatest minds and resources on the planet *and beat them*. That's what racing is all about to me, General."

"I think I can understand that, yes." He looked up at one of the men in black standing in the corner who took a quick look at his watch and then nodded. "Alright, looks like we can go join Mr. Freeman now. He should be ready for us."

The two men in black escorted Foster, Kimber, Sangster and Lopez down the hall to a blank, gray painted steel door. One of the men opened the door and held it open for Foster to go inside.

"We'll wait for you out here," Kimber said. "Remember, just relax, keep your cool, be honest and you'll do just fine."

"Alright."

"Here," he reached out for Foster's briefcase, "I'll keep that out here for you."

He looked down at the case in his hand for a moment and then reached it out for Kimber to take the handle. Then he turned and walked into the room, the two men in black followed in behind him and closed the door.

Freeman was sitting at a small metal table in the center of the room facing a large one-way mirror on the opposite wall. The rest of the walls were covered with sound-deadening tiles painted a dull gray. Freeman sat in a wooden chair facing the mirror from across the table with the polygraph machine in front of him. Another wooden chair was positioned at the end of the table, turned perpendicular to it and facing the mirror and away from where Freeman was sitting.

On tripods ahead of where Foster was to sit were two video cameras, one a few degrees to the left and the other a few degrees to the right. Hanging from the ceiling was a microphone that, when extended, would hang just a few feet in front of his face.

"I'll take your coat and your tie, Dr. Foster," one of the men in black offered.

He removed his coat and handed it to him and then pulled the knot loose on his tie and handed that to him as well. The man hung the coat on a hook beside the door and draped the tie over it to keep it as smooth and neat as possible. Then he instructed him to sit in the chair at the end of the table and roll up his right sleeve, the arm that would be closest to the machine, and to unbutton the top few buttons of his shirt.

The machine looked like something that Foster had seen in numerous movies and television shows. It was a metal box about as wide and long as a standard briefcase lying on its side, but about twice as thick. The top of it had a broad, flat deck with a narrow control panel along the left edge a couple of inches high and wide. A continuous paper graph exited from a roll inside the box, under the control panel and across the surface of the machine. As the test would proceed, the machine would continually feed itself from the blank roll inside, the paper would creep across the top surface and than off of the right edge and onto the table.

A row of delicate metal arms extended a few inches out from the side of the control panel over the paper, bent down at their tips to lightly touch it with their ink-filled styluses. Pivoting from the control panel, they would each move to register the responses of the various probes and sensors that would be attached to his body.

Freeman got up from his seat and began to pick up the various devices and cables that would be attached to him for the test, he asked, "Have you ever had a polygraph test administered before, Dr. Foster?"

"No, I haven't."

"Not even at Cyberdyne Technologies? Such a high-tech company, working on sensitive government projects?"

"I know that they gave the tests to some of the employees there, but I'd never had one. Maybe it was just random, or maybe I just have an honest face," he let out a nervous chuckle.

"Well, this is a pretty standard PDD examination that we'll be administering today. The machine measures your heart rate, blood pressure, galvanic responses on the surface of your skin, electrical impulses, breathing — all in response to certain questions that I'll be asking you. The machine will track those responses on a graph. The video will record your facial expressions and body language and the microphone will record any stresses in your voice."

"Oh, is *that* all?"

"Just try to relax and stay calm. It will just take a few minutes to get you hooked up here and we'll begin with some control questions. Alright?"

"Okay."

Freeman then connected Foster to the machine. It all seemed pretty complicated, but he sat patiently while the man attached and hooked up each sensor and cable. First, he wrapped an accordion-like band around his chest. Next, he wrapped a blood pressure cuff around his upper arm and then clipped sensors to the tips of three fingers on his right hand which he had him rest along the top edge of the table next to him. He then adhered electrical sensors to four places on his chest and to each of his temples and then, finally, plugged all the tubes and wires into the appropriate ports and sockets on the side of the polygraph machine.

It all seemed so very tedious to Foster, but the inquisitive scientist in him just couldn't help but be somewhat fascinated by all of it. He watched Freeman intently as the man went about his well-choreographed routine.

Finally, Freeman pulled the microphone down and adjusted it into position. He glanced over at the two video cameras. Red lights on each one showed that they were on and recording.

Freeman then sat down behind the machine and adjusted some of the knobs and dials along the control panel. He then opened up a loose-leaf notebook, removed a pen from his pocket and clicked the button down to extend the ball-point. He reached over the top of the machine and jotted a quick abbreviation on the slowly-passing paper chart and then looked up at Foster, "Are you ready, Doctor?"

"Ready." ■

CHAPTER ELEVEN

Meltdown

Behind the interrogation room's broad mirror, a gallery of observers watched the examination, Dr. Kimber and Dr. Lopez were joined by General Sangster, Dr. Damon Tryst, the CIA's Psy-Ops Director with his associate Dr. Brooke Hidleman who had already been designated to play the role of the director of Facility R-Four-Seven. Donald Pittman, from the White House's National Security Council, hovered in the background to observe and report back to the president.

Freeman finished connecting up Foster, made his preliminary adjustments to the polygraph machine and then told him, "Just relax, Dr. Foster, and please remember to respond to each of my questions with simple 'yes' or 'no' answers. Okay?"

"Alright."

"First, I'll ask you a series of control questions expected to elicit one obvious response or the other while I make any final adjustments. Are you ready?"

"I'm ready — go ahead."

"Is your name Barney Rubble?"

Foster smiled and replied, "No."

Freeman reached up to the machine's control panel and turned two of the knobs a fraction of a degree to fine-tune the response of the pens on the graph. He then looked down at the paper in his notebook and asked his next question.

"Do you live in California?"

"I do."

"Yes or no, please, Dr. Foster."

"I'm sorry. Yes."

"Is your wife's name Olivia?"

"Yes."

"Is your father still alive?"

"No."

Freeman made a few more minor adjustments and then looked up at the mirror and announced that he was ready to proceed. Foster noticed that he could see Freeman clearly in the mirror in front of them both without having to twist around and look back over his right shoulder at him. He settled in, squared up his shoulders and prepared to answer all of the man's questions.

"Alright Dr. Foster: Until recently, were you an employee at Cyberdyne Technologies?"

"Yes."

"And you worked as a particle physicist while you were there?"

"Yes."

He saw Freeman through the mirror reach up to the slowly traversing paper grid after each of his answers and quickly jot down a note as it crept by him.

"Did you work in any other capacity during your employ at Cyberdyne Technologies?"

"Yes."

"Did you work as an isotope analyst?"

"Yes."

"Did you hold a security clearance at Cyberdyne Technologies?"

"Yes."

"You worked on sensitive projects for the National Aeronautics and Space Administration?"

"Yes."

"You were involved in the effort to send astronauts to the moon?"

"Yes."

"Are you a communist?"

"What?"

"Just answer the question, Dr. Foster. Are you a communist?"

"No."

Again, Freeman made a quick note on the passing grid and then continued.

"Does your wife work at a job outside the home?"

"Uh, yes."

"At a dress shop?"

"Yes."

"Has anyone ever approached you to offer money for secrets from Cyberdyne Technologies?"

"No, never."

"Are you a member of the John Birch Society?"

"Never heard of it — no."

"Do you know a man named Luke Robbins?"

"Yes."

"A friend?"

"Yes."

"Co-worker at Cyberdyne Technologies?"

"Yes."

"You race cars together?"

"Yes. It's a hobby."

"Is Mr. Robbins a communist?"

"No!" Foster was starting to become visibly agitated, he could hear it in his own responses. He took a second to take a deep breath to calm himself before Freeman would ask the next question.

"Do you have any children?"

"No."

"Have you ever wanted children?"

"Yes."

"Infertile?"

"What the hell has this got to do with…"

"Just answer the question, Dr. Foster. Are you infertile?"

He grit his teeth and grunted, "Yes."

"Impotent?"

"Impotent?"

"Erectile dysfunction, Mr. Foster."

"Hmph — I know what it means — *no!*"

"Have you considered adoption?"

"Yes, we've talked about it."

"Have you considered adopting a minority child?"

"No. It never came up."

"Would you adopt a black baby?"

"I don't know — maybe."

"Yes or no, Dr. Foster."

"I said 'I don't know'!"

"Are you a racist?"

"What?! *No!*"

"Are you a member of the Ku Klux Klan?"

"For crying out loud! *No!*"

"Are you afraid of flying?"

The sudden shift in direction caught him off guard. Most likely, he thought, that was the intent. He took a breath and replied, "No." He settled back into the chair but his hackles were already raised. He listened intently to each question that followed and any implied nuances.

"Do you get air-sick?"

"No."

"Have you ever stolen anything?"

"No."

"Not even as a child? Never even a candy bar or pack of gum?"

"Hmph — yes."

"Did you get caught?"

"Yes."

"Did the storekeeper call the police?"

"No. He called my mother."

"He knew your mother?"

"It was a small town. Yes."

Freeman quickly made another note on the passing graph paper and then asked, "Did he sleep with your mother?"

"Are you freakin' *kidding* me?!"

"Please, Dr. Foster, just answer the question."

"No! *Of course not!*"

"Do you hold a PhD degree from the Massachusetts Institute of Technology?"

He leered at Kimber through the mirror in front of him, presuming he was standing behind it, and growled, "Yes."

"You also hold two doctorates?"

"Yes."

"One from California Polytechnic?"

"Yes."

"Did you protest the war while you were in college?"

"I was too busy — no."

"Did you have feelings about the war?"

"I don't like war — any war. Science is all about discovery, exploration, advancing civilization. War is only about death and destruction."

"So that's a 'yes'?"

"Yes."

"Pretty strong feelings, it would appear."

"Is that a question?"

"Are you now or ever been a member of the American Communist Party?"

Foster groaned and finally growled in response, "No."

"Did you vote for Richard Nixon?"

"The first time, yes."

"The second time? When he ran for reelection?"

"No. I was busy, forgot to vote that year."

"Would you have voted for him?"

"At the time — yes. He got us out of Vietnam. We didn't know about the other stuff until later."

"Other stuff?"

"Watergate and all that."

"Oh." Freeman flipped over a page in his notebook and then asked, "Do you know Bruno Keeler?"

"Yes. My wife's uncle."

"Do you know him well?"

"No. Met him at a few family functions."

"Are you aware that he's a communist?"

"*What the hell?!*" Foster twisted around in the chair to look back at Freeman.

Freeman looked up at him and repeated the question, "Are you aware that your wife's uncle is a communist? Yes or no, Dr. Foster?"

"We don't talk about politics or religion at family gatherings. Whatever his political leanings are, I haven't a clue!"

"Did your parents have a normal sex life — as best you recall?"

"Huh? I don't know — I guess so — yes."

"How often did you walk in on them while they were engaged in intercourse — more than ten?"

"What the hell! *You're sick!*"

"Less than ten?"

"Never, you pervert. *Never!*"

"Are you, Dr. Foster, a communist?"

He stared at Freeman in the mirror, his face flushed red and eyes bulging behind the lenses of his glasses. Then he reached over with his left hand and began yanking the clipped-on sensors from the fingertips of his right. "Alright, that's it, *I've had enough!*"

"Dr. Foster — please — what are you doing?!"

He pulled the adhesive sensors off of his forehead and snarled, "I thought this was a job interview! What the hell are all these questions about my mother and whether or not I'm a damned impotent commie!?" Foster yanked up the velcro and pulled the blood pressure cuff off of his arm and threw it down onto the table top. He stood up sharply from the chair, the backs of his knees sending it flying backward, tumbling onto the floor. "*That's it — I'm outta here!*"

Freeman stood up and began sternly instructing Foster to stop and sit back down in the chair. Foster, instead, turned and began storming off toward the door. Some of the cables and wires were still attached to him and the machine and began to pull it off of the table. Freeman reached out quickly and grabbed hold of it as Foster sharply twisted himself away, yanking some of the wires out from their sockets on the machine's side and snapping the rest off at their source.

"*Screw you, Freeman!* You perverted, sadistic punk!"

He pulled off the strap from around his chest and threw it on the floor as he neared the door. One of the men in black stepped out to block his path to the door but Foster, unaccustomed to physical violence, unexpectedly body-checked him and knocked him aside. He grabbed the door knob and pulled it open and paused, looked at the mirror on the opposite wall and snapped, "If you want to hire me for what I know and what I can do, that's what I came here for! I'm a scientist and a damned patriot, but if you want to play these sick-o games, you can take this government job and *shove it!* I'd rather wash cars in LA than trash what's left of my dignity in the name of national-*freakin'*-security!"

He stormed out into the hallway.

Immediately, a pair of FBI agents who happened to be in the hall when he burst out of the room. They drew their pistols and shouted to him to stop.

Instantly realizing that perhaps he'd gone a little too far, Foster put his hands up into the air and froze in his tracks as he stared down at the muzzles of the two guns.

Kimber and Lopez rushed out of the observation room and came up behind him. Kimber called out to the two agents, "Please! Please! It's alright, just blowing off a little steam here. It's alright, no need for all that!"

As General Sangster came out into the hallway and approached from behind Kimber, he nodded to the two agents to stand down. They relaxed their threatening postures and returned their sidearms to their holsters.

"You can lower your hands now, Dr. Foster," Lopez advised.

He slowly lowered his arms and turned. "Sorry, Dr. Kimber, I guess I blew it."

"I told you to keep calm, Dennis. Those questions were *meant* to rattle you, to get an unguarded response."

"Well, it appears to have worked." He subconsciously pushed his glasses up with his finger. "Again, sorry. Can we go back and pick up where we left off?"

"I don't think so," Lopez glibly injected, "I think you broke their machine."

"Oh, for the love of..."

"It's alright, Dennis. There will be other opportunities. Maybe this was just a case of us aiming a bit too high for a scientist of your temperament — just not meant to be. Don't worry."

"Thanks, Dr. Kimber. I guess I should go back and get my stuff."

"Mr. McCloud is bringing your jacket, I've got your briefcase right here. Why don't you go on back to the hotel, maybe have a drink to calm yourself and we'll catch up with you when we get done here."

"Alright," he took the briefcase from him and then draped his coat over his arm. "Again, sorry for all this. Sorry I wasted everyone's time."

"You just head on back now, Dennis. I'll see you in a little while."

Foster just nodded his head and then turned and walked dejectedly to the elevators while the others lingered in the hallway until the doors closed behind him and he was gone.

* * * * *

Gathered in a conference room down the hall, Drs. Kimber, Lopez,

Tryst and Hidleman gathered with General Sangster, Duwan Freeman and Donald Pittman around the end of a long table, standing and turned facing a pair of large television monitors on stands at its end. A camera was pointed at the group from a tripod between them. A piece of paper was taped beneath each screen displaying the words "New York" and "Hollywood" respectively.

A technician wearing a pair of headphones was seated at a small table off to one side behind a control box with three small monitor screens mounted to it so that he could control the feeds from the two remote locations and the signal going out from the camera in that room.

"Are we all set?" General Sangster asked him.

"Yes, sir, everyone is ready."

"Alright, let's get started."

The technician turned a few knobs and the images of their colleagues appeared on the two large screens at the head of the table. The screen from North Brother Island in New York showed CIA agents Felix DeSantis and Aaron Baer with M7 director George Weisz, Scott Desaultus of the NSA and facility director Elsa Kendrick seated around a conference table in a formal looking room. From the Fantasy Factory in Hollywood, Max Garner, Benny Taffin and their foreman, Ray Costello, sat on the edge of a large work table with Colonel Raymond Baker of the Army Corps of Engineers, Major Lucas Alberston, Director of the Groom Lake air base, and Peter Hunt, engineer from Northrop's Skunkworks special operations division.

"Good morning, everyone," Weisz said, getting the cross-country meeting started.

Responses of "Good morning" and other similar greetings were hailed back in response.

"Thank you all for taking the time today for this meeting. This is our 'go/no-go' moment. As NASA spends months and years planning, building and calculating for each mission, it all comes down to that moment when the astronauts are in the capsule, the fuel is pumped into the rockets and a hundred people make one last check of everything. Any one of them can throw up a red flag and stop the launch if they think that something is wrong — or likely to go wrong. This is our moment."

"Let's start with our subject, Mr. Foster," Dr. Kimber began. "You all saw the feed from the polygraph session?"

The others nodded or commented that indeed, they had seen it.

"Any thoughts?"

"Dude had a major *meltdown!*" Taffin commented.

"Wouldn't you?" DeSantis quipped.

"Lots of personal and apparently inappropriate questions," Garner said. "Sure, I'd get pissed off after a while. I'm surprised he didn't get up and slug you, Freeman, or start pitching furniture around the room."

"He did clobber one of your M7 security guys pretty good," Lopez pointed out with a wry smile. "Slammed him into the wall — and broke Freeman's little machine,"

"Pretty aggressive for a lab rat," Albertson added. "Can we afford to have someone so volatile in this program?"

"Yeah," Taffin continued, "What if he goes full-tilt berserk on us? What are you guys gonna do — shoot him?"

"No, of course not," Sangster replied.

"His response was exactly what we were looking for," Freeman explained. "The questions that I asked him were engineered to do precisely what they did, to elicit a violent, impassioned reaction."

"Why the hell would you try to get him to flip out like that?" Hunt asked.

"Don't forget the point of this whole operation, people," Weisz interrupted. "When this is over, we want our subject to be motivated to go public. We don't want him to just go off and lick his wounds and start looking for another job. He drives racing cars for a hobby because he likes the thrill of it and, more importantly, he likes to win. He has a strong moral base as Ted and Bambi have been testing and he's a man of integrity. He has all the credibility we need — and then some — to make this work. We want him to suspect having been given a raw deal, to have been minipulated — to ignore his morality just long enough to seek revenge, and we have to drive him to it. With all that in mind, his meltdown during that polygraph test was exactly what we were hoping for."

"Hmmm," Garner, mused, "I see where you're coming from. Makes sense. Do you have some way to keep him contained throughout the operation, though? We have a lot of secrets built into this facility and the people who are staffing it. Our scenario is pretty carefully planned. What if he goes off on us inside and charges into some space where he really shouldn't go?"

"Facility R-Four-Seven is, theoretically, a high security installation. There will be a very overt presence of armed security guards, locks, signs, scanners, all sorts of things to put the fear of God and the US government into him and, if he should somehow see behind the curtain, we have contingencies."

"Contingencies?"

"Trust me, Mr. Garner, we're pretty good at what we do. You have nothing to be concerned about."

"I hope not."

"You have to excuse him," Taffin injected. "Max is a congenital worrier."

"Tell me, not to change the subject," Weisz continued, "but how are things coming along out there?"

Garner looked over at Baker, seated next to him, "Well, the military guys have been really great. Everything that we needed on site, they got built for us in no time — they're obviously not union."

Taffin rolled his eyes and nodded in sympathetic agreement.

"We've got all of the rooms and systems in place. Ray and Colonel Baker and his crew have been working around the clock."

"Colonel?" Weisz addressed, "what's your assessment?"

"All of the infrastructure is completed, the electrical, plumbing and air are all in place and running," Baker replied. "The Fantasy boys came in with spray guns and barrels of synthetic dust to make the place look used. Major Albertson procured a few truckloads of used office furniture from the base's warehouses to fit the place out and we have a lot of technical gear on loan from Lockheed and complicated looking props from the Fantasy guys. We fitted out the labs with whatever equipment your Dr. Dillard told us to get — whatever Lockheed didn't have, we leased. We've got it all set up just the way our subject would expect to find it and it looks totally convincing. And certain machines and testing equipment in the labs have been rigged by our Hollywood special effects people to show our subject the test results we want him to see."

"It looks perfect," Albertson interrupted. "It looks like it's been up and operating for years. Even the vending machines and coffee makers in the break rooms are stocked and working."

"That's great. And what about the people?"

"I've been working with the boys from Hollywood to train our people in the various scenes that they have worked up," Dr. Hidleman explained. "We have people from the base, a few people from Skunkworks to give us a real tech-specific authenticity, even a few guys from the Army Corps of Engineers have signed on to help. All told, we have a crew of about one hundred and seventy-five and all of them have been training for the past few months. I believe we are ready."

"And Dr. Lopez? I mean, Dr. Teller?"

"I've been out there several times," Lopez replied. "I had to fly back to Burbank a few times, too, but Dr. Dillard has been working with me and I have my part down pretty well. He gave me a few books and journals to study so I can get the nomenclature down. I've had a lot of reading time on the planes and he'll be around to coach me if I need some help during the op."

"So I guess the only thing left is the base itself," Weisz said. "Major Albertson, are we all set to receive our guest?"

"He'll fly in on one of our regular flights from McCarran and be culled out from the group of legitimate workers along with a few other new employees — shills from our own crew here at the air base. We have quarters for him, fully wired, and he'll be accompanied at all times by security of one form or another. We'll keep close tabs on him but he'll never know it. I've got a couple of mini-buses assigned to be a shuttle service from the housing compound out to the the facility and back. He'll be given all of the normal access that any of our employees might have as far as the dining hall, post exchange, and that sort of thing, but kept out of certain hangars and other sensitive areas. We'll be scheduling any flight tests for when he is out at the facility and unable to see."

"And I guess the last part of this is surveillance off site. Mr. Desaultus, does the NSA have everything in place?"

"The Foster's home, both vehicles, their friends' homes and vehicles are wired for video and sound and the vehicles are tagged with trackers. We've also wired their favorite restaurants, the grocery store and pharmacy where they shop. The dress shop where the wife works is also wired for sound and video as is the neighbor, Ted's, place. The CIA has also placed undercover agents in each of these places, too. They won't be able to make a move without us hearing and seeing."

"What about communications?"

"Phones are tapped in all of these locations, we have access to area pay phones through the phone company. This also gives us access to their online connections through their computer whenever they dial up."

"Sounds pretty thorough. And you'd left them some bugs to find?"

"Yeah, we made them pretty easy for them to stumble on."

"Alright. It sounds like we're ready to go. Any last reservations? Concerns?"

Everyone on all of the monitors either quietly shook their heads or just remained silent.

"Then we're a go — good. Dr. Kimber..." Weisz addressed, "... you may inform our boy that he has the job and we'll be sending him information by courier, including an SF-86 to fill out just to be thorough. Start in two weeks? Everyone? Does that time frame work for everyone?"

"We're ready." "Yes." Every face nodded and agreed, they would be ready in two weeks to kick the operation into gear.

The subject had been prepared, the facility readied, the props set up and all of the people rehearsed and in place.

All that was left was for Dr. Kimber to go back to the hotel where Foster was kicking himself for thoroughly blowing the opportunity of a lifetime and give him the good news. ■

PHASE 4
THE SET-UP

CHAPTER TWELVE

Welcome to Area Fifty-One

Sunday afternoon and Livvy Foster pulled into the main driveway of the Hollywood-Burbank airport with her husband, Dennis, to bring him to the terminal to catch the flight out for his first week at his new job. They drove slowly past the long, glass-faced terminal building, watching the signs all along the covered sidewalk looking for the name of the airline that he was to board among the usual, commercial airlines whose signs were hung, evenly spaced all along its length. Watching the swirling traffic of taxis, livery cars, shuttle busses and other drivers like themselves who were just dropping someone off to catch a flight, she kept her eyes on the roadway and the crisscrossing vehicles. Foster kept watch of the passing signs from the passenger seat, looking for one that would show the name of an airline that was in the instructions that he'd received, an airline he had never heard of.

When they finally got to the end the long terminal building, nearly to the end of the driveway, and still hadn't found it, she asked, "Did we miss it? Should I go around and make another pass?"

"I don't know," he replied. "I guess so."

Just at that moment he noticed a small building off by itself about one hundred feet beyond the long, main building. It looked just like the larger, main building — the glass facade looking much the same. On the front of it was a small, lone, red sign with bold, white letters that read simply, JANET.

"That's it." He announced. "Over there."

She looked up at where he was pointing and began wending her way through the traffic toward the curb. "Who's Janet?"

"I don't know. The airline owner's wife, maybe? Daughter? I suppose I'll find that out during orientation."

She pulled up to the curb and stopped, pushing the button to activate their hazard flashers while they were unloading.

Dennis leaned across the front seat and gave his wife a kiss, "You just stay in the car, sweetie. I just have my briefcase and the one suitcase."

"Well, you have a safe flight, dear. Call me when you get there."

"I will, at my first opportunity, I promise." He pulled up the handle on the car door and pushed it open. He looked back at her over his shoulder, "I'll see you Friday — I love you!"

"I love you, too!"

He climbed out of the car and walked back to the trunk to retrieve his luggage and then, shoving the lid closed, he bent down so that she could see him through the rear-view mirror, smiled and waved to her.

She waved back though he couldn't see her smile through the mirror.

He walked up to the curb and across the sidewalk to the glass doors as she pulled away and out into the flow of traffic to head back home.

He pulled the door open and walked into a vestibule and then through a second glass door into the terminal building. As he entered, a man wearing a dark blue blazer stood behind a kiosk with a computer monitor and keyboard on it. A stern-looking man in a black suit and mirrored aviator-style sunglasses stood just behind him. The man in the blazer asked to see his identification badge.

"I don't have one, sorry. It's my first day."

"Oh? What's your name, sir?"

"Foster, Dennis Foster."

The man typed his name into the terminal and found him on a short, auxiliary list, "Ah, Mr. Foster. Welcome to Janet." He checked Foster's name off on the list and waved to another man in a gray uniform shirt and matching ball cap, "Peter will take your bag."

"Shouldn't I check that in? How do you know which plane it should go on? Which airport I'm going to?"

"There's only one plane, Mr. Foster, and it only flies to one destination."

"Hmmm, I suppose it's kind of hard to mess that up, then."

"Never thought of it that way, but I guess that's true. Here," the man handed him a card with his name written on it and a red rubber stamp that said JANET in bold letters over a block of small type that he'd probably not bother to read anyway. "Keep this with you and show it to whoever asks you for your ID badge until you get there. They'll take your mug shot during orientation and issue you an official badge — like the ones you see the other passengers wearing."

He took the card from the man and slipped it into his pocket, "Thanks."

"Find a seat and make yourself comfortable. There's coffee and tea. The plane will board in about fifteen minutes."

"Okay. Again, thanks."

He picked up his briefcase and walked out into the bright, wide open terminal building. It looked very much like any other that he'd ever been in, just a lot smaller. Large windows faced out to the runways and he could see planes taxiing past wearing the livery of numerous familiar airlines. Parked out on the tarmac just outside the glass were a trio of plain white airliners sporting just a single broad, red stripe that ran along their flanks from nose to tail and a small black registration number just below it at the rear. There were no other markings, no logos and no mention of the airline's name anywhere. One of the planes was pulled up close to the building, the door was open with a portable boarding ladder rolled up to it.

In the center of the room were rows of padded, chrome framed seats with about a half dozen people seated, scattered among them. As he walked out into the waiting area, he passed a counter island with a couple of polished stainless steel coffee urns and empty clear plastic pastry cases that he presumed would be filled for the passengers taking early morning flights during the week.

Along the wall to the right of the large windows beside a door with the word "gate" on a sign above it, was a counter looking much like the one adorned with coffee urns. On the counter was a computer monitor with a young woman in a blue polyester blazer and silk scarf standing behind it looking like a stewardess or airline hostess that one would find at the gate of any other commercial airline.

The biggest difference was the presence of a pair of military guards in camouflage standing at either side of the door to the plane holding MP5 machine guns. He noticed that neither of them had any sort of insignia on their uniforms and, for that matter, he realized neither did the woman behind the counter or even the man who met him at the door.

He then became aware that there were about half a dozen men in black suits and mirrored sunglasses that were hovering here and there around the periphery of the room. To him, they looked even more sinister than the men with the machine guns at the door but the other passengers didn't seem the least bit concerned and paid them no mind. He was well aware that the job he was about to take on required the highest level of security. It was probably all just a matter of routine and something that he would — as it appeared his fellow travelers already had — get used to.

Conspicuously absent in that waiting area was a schedule board listing the flights in and out of the terminal, their arrival and departure times and whether or not they were on time or delayed. The information that a courier had delivered to the house a week and a half before explained that the flights left on the hour every two hours from five o'clock in the morning until seven o'clock at night, seven days a week and returning flights arrived every alternate hour. Each flight left Burbank for McCarran International airport in Las Vegas. There they would pick up others who lived in and around the city, and continue on to the facility in the desert. Some employees flew out and back each day, others flew out on Sunday nights and returned again on Friday afternoons as he himself would be doing.

He glanced up at the clock on the wall behind the counter as he walked past and then found himself a seat.

Quiet music played and no one spoke to anyone else. It was all part of the secretive culture he had signed onto. He was kind of an introvert anyway so that would be something easy for him to adapt to.

He noticed a few of the people were reading newspapers and books to while away the time. He didn't see a newsstand or newspaper rack anywhere so he presumed that they'd brought them with them. He'd have to remember to pick something up when he was back home over the weekend. But for the time being, it was all brand new to him and his mind was just drinking in the experience. He wouldn't be able to concentrate on reading anything on that first trip anyway.

What he was not yet aware of was that many of the people in the waiting room, and those who would fly in and out of that terminal each weekday, worked at Lockheed's nearby Skunkworks facility. A large, unmarked building right there in Burbank on the other side of the runways.

He'd passed by it whenever he'd fly out or back. It had always been un-noticed and uninteresting to him. But then, that was the whole idea.

In a short time, one of the camouflaged security guards opened the door out to the tarmac and the awaiting 737 and chocked it to stay open. The woman in the blue blazer stepped out from behind the counter and stood with a carbonless form on a clipboard that she would fill out with names of each person who stepped up to her and showed their identification. The form would become the flight's manifest. The gold-enrod copy, the last page in the form, would stay with her in Burbank while the rest of the parts would fly to Las Vegas. The names of those who would board there would be added and the pink copy would be left with the ground crew there, and when the plane would reach its destination, the yellow copy would be given to the authorities there while the original, white copy, would be logged by the airline. It was so very routine and so like a typical government operation.

The plane itself was just like any other airliner but with far fewer passengers. They made daily commuter flights which were normally much fuller but the Sunday flights for the weekly dormitory employees were much less so. There was a single stewardess on board who offered cold drinks, coffee and tea in-flight as well as snacks like bagged peanuts or crackers. Though it was a government contracted private airline, it was still the intent to make civilian passengers feel comfortable and to never consider that unique and necessary requirement of their jobs to be a hassle for them.

The plane flew to McCarran International in Las Vegas where it remained on the tarmac for about fifteen minutes while a few additional passengers boarded and then made the short hop from there to so-called Homey Airport on the Nellis Air Force Base — the FAA code name for Groom Lake, the Area Fifty-One airfield.

As they descended into the valley to land, Foster watched out the windows to see whatever there was to see but all that was in view was desert surrounded by barren, rocky mountain ridges and, beyond those, more desert as far as the eye could see. A few small, scattered buildings were in view at a distance with narrow dirt roads that scratched across the dry ground — and everything seemed to be some shade or other of brown and beige.

In a word, the view was unremarkable and unexpectedly boring for an installation of such notoriety.

Eventually he could feel the plane leveling off in preparation to touch down. Still there was nothing but rocks and desert outside of the window but, as the plane neared the ground, he began to see a lot of low buildings and then, as the wheels touched the pavement with loud, screeching chirps, a long row of large hangars with their doors closed rushed past his window. When the plane neared the end of the runway, it slowed to a stop. The entire conclave of buildings had passed by as they'd landed and all that was left in view were some parallel taxiways, chainlink fencing and the same sort of barren mountains and desert all around in the near distance.

It all seemed so anti-climactic. He began to wonder what all the legendary hoopla was all about.

The plane turned around at the end of the runway and rolled slowly back on one of the taxiways until it finally stopped in front of a small, two story, white masonry building whose second floor was nearly all glass across its face toward the runways and partway around each side. He could see a few other plain white jets parked nearby through the plane's window with the same, simple red band painted down their flanks. It was the Homey Airport terminal for Janet Airlines.

A truck pulled slowly up to the side of the plane with a stairway mounted on the back of it that reached from the ground up to the door. The jet engines whined down to a quiet stop as the stewardess pushed open the door. Most everyone else on board had made the trip numerous times and knew the routine. They gathered their carry-ons and filed along the aisle to the front of the plane, out the door and down the stairs. They flashed their identification badges to a couple of men in black suits who waited on the tarmac at the foot of the stairs. They gathered up their suitcases from a row that the ground crew had unloaded from the plane and set out for them and then either walked or caught rides on golf carts that would bring them to their quarters somewhere behind all of the hangars.

Foster followed the throng and stepped off the plane, not sure yet where he was going. He showed his temporary identification to one of the men in the black suits at the foot of the stairs who told him to pick up his suitcase and step over by a waiting white mini-bus with four other "newbies" to be brought for a quick orientation before being taken to their own assigned quarters.

A couple of young men wearing light blue uniform shirts with Air Force insignia, dark blue slacks, sunglasses and shiny black, rubber-soled shoes collected up the suitcases for the five first timers and loaded them into the back of the mini-bus. Another man with another clipboard in his hands stepped down off the bus. He was wearing the same sort of light blue Air Force uniform shirt and dark sunglasses, Foster thought he looked awfully familiar. The man had a disturbing resemblance to his new neighbor, Ted White, but it was obviously just another coincidence.

The man stood on the pavement just outside the door to the mini-bus and introduced himself to the group as Lieutenant Bishop. Foster smiled to himself, thankful that he hadn't said anything embarrassing within the first few minutes of his arrival at his new job.

The man then looked down at his clipboard and called off each of the five names listed on it. As each of the newcomers acknowledged him, he waved them on board the bus. They'd all be taken to a place where they'd get an introduction to their new work environment.

Once everyone was on the bus, he followed them up the steps while the driver pulled back the lever to close the doors. He paused for a moment standing at the front of the aisle and announced, "Welcome, everyone, to Area Fifty-One." ∎

CHAPTER THIRTEEN

Orientation

The white mini-bus drove away from the Janet terminal building at the northernmost end of the airbase and past a long row of large hangars, all of which were closed, their contents hidden from view. The last hangar near the southern end of the airfield was partly open. The door was slid back just far enough for the bus to pull inside out of the hot desert sun to deliver its passengers. Foster would learn later that, during daylight hours, the hangar doors were rarely opened as prying eyes covertly — and illegally — poised on the mountain ridges to the east could get a glimpse of what might be parked inside, most of which was highly classified.

The mini-bus came to a stop and Lieutenant Bishop stood up to announce that they were to get off there and make their way to a row of tables and chairs set up inside, over to their right. They could help themselves to cool drinks waiting for them inside to mitigate the intense desert heat that none of them were yet acclimated to. They would quickly find the importance of keeping hydrated in the arid environment with frequent reminders and ready sources of cool water just about everywhere.

As he stepped into the cavernous building, it took Foster's eyes a moment to adjust to the much dimmer lighting after having stepped in from the brilliant desert sun. The space was enormous. To his amazement, to his left was parked a sinister looking, long, black spy plane — an SR71 Blackbird. He'd seen a few photos of them in magazines but never in person. It was sleek and, even just parked inside the hangar, intimidating. It seemed huge, so much larger than he had imagined from those photos.

He paused for a moment and just gawked.

There were also a few other planes parked in there as well including a pair of black T38 jets that were used as chase planes for the Blackbird. They were dwarfed by the spy plane parked beside them.

He lingered for a moment just absorbing the unexpected scene before him in all of its breathtaking detail. Suddenly aware that he was being left behind and would likely soon be urged to catch up, he turned and followed the rest of the small group into the open space at the other side of the hangar. A row of tables had been set up with folding chairs along their length facing across to a single table a few feet away with a free-standing, rolling blackboard near the wall a few feet behind it. On the table up front were a few papers, an unmarked cardboard box and a glowing green lava lamp undulating almost hypnotically at its center.

Looking around the vast space inside the hangar, he could see a few men in camouflage armed with M16s standing along the walls all around them as though posted a certain uniform distance apart from one another along the hangar's perimeter to protect the base's secrets from the uninitiated visitors. Two men in black suits and sunglasses stood at either side of the blackboard facing the group.

Foster and the group he was with were told to each find themselves a seat at the empty tables.

After a few minutes, a group of people walked out from a door behind the blackboard and around to the table in the front. A man in an Air Force uniform — obviously an officer with glittering metal insignia on epaulets on each shoulder — two men in business suits, one appearing somewhat older than the other and wearing a loud, colorful tie, and a woman in a conservative, gray skirt suit were all gathered in a group just off to one side.

Once they had arrayed various folders and papers that they'd carried out with them on the table, the officer in uniform casually stepped into the center in front of the table to address the group. "Good afternoon," he greeted. "I'm Major Lucas Albertson. I'm the director of operations here at the Groom Lake Air Base. You may have heard this place referred to as 'Area Fifty-One,' 'Homey International Airport,' or even 'Dreamland'. A lot of the engineers from Lockheed like that one.

"This is a top secret facility. You have all been vetted and cleared for the high level of security necessary to even be here. Some of you will have that clearance elevated for certain specialized work that you'll be doing here. I hope it goes without saying that you cannot tell anyone — including spouses and loved ones — that you work at this facility. You are not to refer to it by name, any name, and absolutely cannot divulge what sort of work you do here or anything that you might see or hear. Any questions?"

A hand rose from a young man seated to Foster's right, "Sir?"

"Yes, what's your question?"

"My wife and I don't keep any secrets from each other. Would it be okay if I told her?"

"This is one secret you absolutely cannot reveal — not to anyone. I don't care how transparent your relationship is. If you need help to develop a cover story, we have psychologists on staff who can advise you. This place and everything that happens here is a matter of national security. To violate that confidentiality is an act of treason and subject to arrest, imprisonment and, in certain cases, capital punishment. If you don't think you can handle that, then now is the time to say so."

The man who asked the question then shrank back into his seat and became gravely silent.

"Any other questions? No? Good." He turned to the younger of the two men in black suits who gave an understanding nod. On that cue, he gathered up a stack of folders as the major stepped back and walked up to the long row of tables. He looked at each folder, called out the name that was written on it and when that person acknowledged him, handed them their designated folder until all five folders had been distributed.

After the folders had been passed out, the woman in the gray suit stepped into the center to address them, "Good afternoon. My name is Doctor Brooke Hidleman. I'm the director of Facility-R-Four-Seven, the laboratory where a few of you will be working. All of you are weekly commuters — you'll fly in on Sunday afternoons and home again on Fridays. While you are here, you'll be living in our on-base housing. You've each been assigned an apartment in our Village behind the hangars and office buildings here on the air base. A commuter bus like the one you just rode in on from the plane will take those of you working at the labs to the Facility and back again each day."

She looked over at the group that was gathered to her right and at one man in a light blue airman's uniform who nodded to her. She turned back around to the group and added, "Airman Teasdale will take each of you, one by one, back into a room behind us to be photographed for your on-base identification badges. When your name is called, please get up quietly and follow him. The badges will be issued before you leave here. Please make sure you have it on you, visible, at all times."

The process began with Teasdale calling out the name of a woman who sat to Foster's left to come back to be photographed. When he'd return with her a few minutes later to again take her seat, he'd call out the next one in alphabetical order. The process didn't take very long and they were left to flip through the contents of their respective folders while they waited.

Finally, the last of them had been brought back from their photos and the group was again entirely present at the row of tables. While the photos were being taken and identification badges fabricated, the man in the black suit who had passed out the folders had brought out three small, bright yellow, aluminum cases and stacked them up on the table. Hidleman picked up one them and opened it, turning it for the group to get a look at its contents. "For those of you working in the laboratories, you will be issued one of these units. Inside, you'll find three of these pens." She lifted one out and held it up. "This is a radiation monitor. Some of you will be working with highly radioactive materials and the rest of you will be in an environment where you may be exposed if a leak or some other accident should take place inside the Facility. These devices will measure any sort of exposure that you might receive which you will log as you leave the Facility each day."

She replaced the pen into a fitted cavity in the foam lining and pointed to a metal box in the case next to it about eight inches wide and six inches tall with a switch, a single knob and a circular port in one corner covered with a screw-on metal cap that was tethered to the box with a short bead-chain. "The charger will be kept at your quarters. You will put one pen on the charger each day while you wear the other. Each morning, you will take a freshly-charged pen with you. Another pen will be on the charger while you are at work and overnight until you swap them again in the morning. The third pen in the kit is a spare. When you get to the Facility, you will be given more specific instructions during orientation."

Hidleman closed up the case and handed it back to the man in the suit to distribute with the others to each of the three in the group who would be working at the laboratory, including Foster. When he was finished, Major Albertson stepped up again and announced that the identification badges were ready. A group of airmen, who would conduct them to their respective quarters, were each waiting with golf carts to show them around the Village where they would be living for a week at a time for the duration of their contracts. Finally, they would be conducted to their respective apartments.

Foster noticed that, while Albertson and Hidleman did all of the talking and one of the men in a black suit handled all of the distribution of papers and other things, the older man in the loud tie stood off in the background with a stern expression as though he were supervising. He never addressed them, never said a word and he was never introduced to the group. It would appear that he was, in fact, the one in charge.

When Foster's name was called, he stood up, gathered up the folder that had been given to him, the metal case that he'd been issued with the radiation pens in it and his briefcase and followed a young airman who introduced himself as Peter Jordan. He handed him his identification badge, strung on a lanyard that he reached out and draped over Foster's neck as his hands were obviously full. He led him out past the array of parked, black aircraft to the open door and a waiting golf cart parked just outside in the building's shade. His suitcase was already stowed on the small cargo deck on the back of the cart. He piled his briefcase in beside it and then climbed into the passenger seat up front with the yellow case and folder of papers in his lap.

Airman Jordan explained a few basics to him as they drove between the hangars to a roadway behind them that would lead to the Village of apartments where he would be quartered. One of the things he stressed was the desert environment that they were in. He should invest in a few pairs of sunglasses — prescription if necessary since Foster normally wore glasses anyway — to wear a hat and long-sleeves to protect from the searing sun, and to hydrate continuously. The Air Force had stationed water coolers throughout the campus and made bottled water available at the commissary and the PX at no charge. Dehydration is an insidious thing that can sneak up on someone in such an arid environment, even indoors, and cause violent illness if one didn't vigilantly make all of that part of their daily routine.

"It's the one thing that the doc at our infirmary sees the most," Jordan intimated. "It can sneak right up on ya'."

The Village was comprised of four moderate-sized, four-story apartment buildings arrayed in an X-shaped cluster with one end of each building around a small central courtyard. They were somewhat separated from the phrenetics and noise of the airfield by the hangars a row of office and support buildings that were directly behind them, a buffer of sorts to give the inhabitants of the Village at least a modicum of peace and quiet.

Airman Jordan drove the golf cart around the complex and pointed out on the street level of the buildings the post exchange, the dining hall, commissary, laundromat, the civilians' club and a few offices, particularly the office of the buildings' management in case he should need anything. Finally, he parked his cart in front of one of the buildings' entrances and removed a slip of paper from a clip on the dashboard and announced that he was assigned room C-217. He hopped out of the cart and handed him his briefcase, then grabbed up Foster's suitcase and led him into the building's foyer. He pointed out the bank of mailboxes as they passed, noting that he wouldn't be getting any "real" mail there, but any internal mail or messages would be left in there for him and there was a shredder in each room to destroy them after they'd been read and acted upon.

They rode the elevator up to the second floor. A few of the residents of the building happened to pass them as they walked down the hallway and each greeted Airman Jordan with a smile as they went by. Apparently, Foster mused, Jordan was a pretty popular guy around there.

Finally, they arrived at room 217 and Jordan pulled a ring of keys from his pocket and opened up the door, then handed the ring to Foster, "Two keys for the apartment door and two for the mailbox downstairs. Keep one set with you and the spare set here in the apartment."

Foster looked down at the ring of keys in his hand, slipped them into his pocket and then followed Jordan inside. For a single bedroom apartment, it was a fairly large space and nicely appointed. Not as institutional or barracks-like as he had presumed, being a military base.

The short entranceway from the hall led past a kitchenette, open on their right, with the usual appliances but smaller versions of what might be found in the average home. A short dividing wall with a breakfast counter on top of it separated the kitchen area from the living area which was furnished with a small dining table with a couple of chairs, a comfortable looking sofa, coffee table, stuffed chair and a television on a stand. "The reception out here in the desert is pretty much non-existent. We're surrounded by mountains. The TV is the only snow this area ever sees." He paused for Foster's reaction to his attempt at levity. Genius scientist types — of which there were several inhabiting those apartments — never got his jokes. Any jokes.

He continued his explanation, "All the television programming here is closed circuit. Lots of reruns and occasional official announcements, but the really nice thing is: No commercials."

"What about the radio?"

"Same sort of thing, just base programming — we actually have a studio here with disc-jockeys who do a morning and afternoon show. They're not half bad. If you want to bring in a record player or tape deck or something, you're welcome to do that. Call down to the manager for a bookshelf and he'll bring one up for you. They have a lot of furniture and fixtures in storage here. You'll find that Groom Lake is pretty much self-sufficient and cut off from the rest of the world."

"Self-sufficient out of necessity, it would appear. Pretty isolated out here."

"Yes," Jordan turned down a short connecting hallway and pointed out the bathroom to the left as they passed it and then led Foster into the bedroom. "Queen size bed to stretch out on and get comfortable. Dresser, big closet and, again, if you think you need anything else, ask the manager and he probably has something stashed in storage."

He pulled out a folding suitcase stand from beside the dresser like the ones typically found in a hotel room and set Foster's suitcase down on it and then laid his briefcase on top.

"Is this where I tip you?"

"Tip? No, this isn't a hotel, Dr. Foster. But I do hope I've been of service."

"You have, thanks." Foster looked around the room as though he was trying to find something.

"Something you need, Doctor?"

"A phone. I promised my wife I'd call her once I got here."

"I'm sorry, I should have pointed it out when we were in the living room. It's on the wall at the end of the breakfast counter. It's one of those wireless phones so you can wander around the apartment with it. There's also a laminated card there with the phone numbers around the base that you might ever need to call. Just a friendly warning, phone calls are monitored here and are on a time-delay so that the censors can blank out anything sensitive that you might 'accidently' say. It's kind of awkward at first but you'll get used to it."

"Thanks again, Airman Jordan."

"My pleasure, sir. One last thing: The dining hall is open twenty-four hours and the shuttle bus to Facility R-Four-Seven leaves from there every hour, on the hour, from four until eighteen-hundred, seven days."

"Good to know. Again, my thanks."

"Yes, sir. Have a pleasant night, sir."

"Good night, Mr. Jordan."

"Good night, sir — be seeing you." ■

CHAPTER FOURTEEN

Day One

Dennis Foster rose from his bed on Monday morning in his new, temporary desert quarters. His first day at his new job, he was eager to get into whatever sort of research was waiting for him at the top secret lab. He showered, dressed, put on his identification badge and grabbed up his briefcase — a new morning routine not entirely unlike every other workday that he'd ever engaged in throughout his entire adult life. The biggest difference was the fact that he was going through the routine alone, without his wife, Livvy. He was already missing her but knew that the distraction of the work would keep him engaged.

As part of his new morning routine, however, he plucked one of the radiation sensing pens out of the charger where it had spent the night and clipped it into his shirt pocket, slipping it in behind the pocket protector as it was too fat to fit in with his usual array of writing implements and small slide rule. He then set a second pen onto the charger.

He left his apartment and made his way to the dining hall downstairs for a quick, light breakfast and then stepped outside to wait for the shuttle bus to come by and pick him up. The morning desert air was surprisingly cool, despite all of the warnings about the oppressive heat that he'd heard so far — and would continue to hear. Still, the air was dry. So dry that, despite how cool it may have been, there was no moisture in the air to condense, no morning dew on any outdoor surface. Everything was bone dry.

There was a park bench on the sidewalk at the bus stop out in front of the dining hall and a few other people were already sitting there and standing around behind it waiting for the shuttle-bus to arrive. He stood at the periphery of the group until a man in a light spring jacket turned to him and asked, "You're the new guy — right?"

Foster looked up at him and smiled, "Yeah, my first day."

"John, John Nolan," he reached out his hand in greeting.

"Hi. Dennis Foster," he shook the man's hand. "Nice to meet you."

"You'll love it here, trust me. Once you get the hang of the new routine."

"Well, so far, so good."

"I heard they just hired a new physicist for the particle lab — that you?"

"That's right."

"Ah, then you'll be working with Jennifer." He turned to the people seated on the bench and addressed the back of one of their heads. "Jennifer?"

She turned and looked impatiently over her shoulder at the man, "What is it, John?"

Foster was immediately struck with surprise when he saw her face. The shape and juxtaposition of her eyes, the shape of her chin — pale blue eyes and long blonde hair but the most alarming feature of all was an all-so-familiar scattering of freckles across the bridge of her nose.

The fact that his new neighbor's girlfriend, Bambi, might have had a doppelganger working for Dr. Kimber could easily have been written off as just random coincidence. But his new co-worker also being the spitting image of her was just creepy. Wearing glasses, different colored eyes, different hair, but unmistakably quite similar physical features and, despite any accents or syntax, the same timbre and tone of her voice. He was immediately suspicious but tried to dismiss his concerns. He'd been mistaken before and didn't want to embarrass himself on his first day.

"This is your new lab rat," the man announced to her, then turned to Foster, "This is Dr. Jennifer Teller. You'll be working in the same lab together."

"It's, uh, nice to meet you, Dr. Teller."

"You must be Dr. Foster. They told me about you."

"I am."

"So, you're the guy who's going to finally figure out what the hell it is we're dealing with out there."

"I am? They never really gave me any specifics about what I'd be doing here, just that my qualifications made me a good fit for whatever it is."

"Of course they didn't. Another unemployed rocket scientist? Accepted the first job offer that came along?"

"The first *viable* one, yes. Is there something wrong with that?"

"Hmph, join the club. There's a lot of you people around here. This job is unlike anything you've ever had before and, no doubt, anything you might ever take on in the future." She turned to watch as the shuttle bus turned the corner and rolled slowly up to where they were all waiting. "Buckle up, Dr. Foster, this is one wild ride."

Unsure what she meant by that, but certain that he'd likely find out quickly enough, Foster got on the bus with the rest of those who were waiting with him for the long, bumpy ride to the laboratories at Facility R-Four-Seven.

The airfield and its peripheral conclave of buildings, including the residential Village, is located in a long valley between so-called Freedom Ridge to the east and a low, parallel rocky mountain ridge to the west called Papoose Mountain. The entrance to the laboratories was on the southwestern face of that short mountain range. The entire facility is built inside, underground, carved out of the mountain itself. The road to get to it was not paved but a rather well-maintained gravel road that circled around the northern end of the mountains from the air base and then turned southward along the western side of the ridge. The road gradually climbed the lower slopes to the entrance of the laboratories. The ride could be uneven and, at times, jostling — particularly after a rare rain storm had washed out part of the road — and typically about an hour long.

Along the way, he watched out the tinted windows at the scenery that passed by. Most everything he saw was just more desert as far as the horizon. As they'd leave the base, he could see the dry Groom Lake lakebed with the long runway cut through the center of it and a row of low, rocky protuberances beyond, Freedom Ridge, until they rounded the north end of Papoose Mountain. On the western side of the ridge was just more of the same desert with no visible signs of landmarks or man-made construction of any kind.

The mountain itself was a remarkable, rugged and intimidating rock that jutted up from the blank, flat desert floor. Some low, scrubby foliage grew in amongst the boulders and large rocks gathered at the base of the mountain that offered a little bit of shade but there were no trees and no grass, no bit of green vegetation anywhere. It was just barren, colored in overall mottling shades of desert beige and brown.

When the bus neared the entrance to the facility, it slowed and turned left and climbed a gradual slope toward the mountain. A short driveway led to a level, fenced-in parking area controlled by a red-and-white striped gate. A row of massive steel teeth protruded up from a long steel plate that stretched across the width of the driveway just beyond the gate, their angled, pointed tips designed to rip apart the undercarriage of any vehicle that might try and pass without authorization. Armed, camouflage bedecked guards stayed out of the desert heat in an adjacent air-conditioned shack when they didn't have to walk out and talk with those in approaching vehicles.

Once the bus was cleared to enter, the striped gate rose and the massive metal teeth retracted into the ground. They rolled across the small, paved parking area to a broad concrete portal that extended about fifty feet from inside the mountain.

The portal was guarded at its mouth by a small contingent of men in camouflage uniforms and a group of military vehicles that included a pair of Humvees and an armored personnel carrier. Foster was fascinated by it all and not just a little intimidated but, at the same time, he noticed that his fellow travelers paid little attention. To them it was just part of the daily commute.

They drove slowly into the portal, through a wide, smoothly-paved tunnel that was large enough for two semi-trucks to pass by one another with plenty of room to spare and then through the massive open blast door. The tunnel had a gradual, even curve to it so that if one were standing at one end of it, they could not see the other end from that vantage point. Ultimately, they reached the massive blast door inside that was several feet thick and hung on hinges a few feet in diameter. The inner face of the open door exposed a complex array of mechanics that would lock and seal the door shut and protect from the shockwaves of any nearby nuclear blasts.

They pulled into another hangar-sized parking area inside the mountain where the bus turned around and came to a stop in a designated place and the driver swung the doors open. The people on board got up from their seats. Foster did the same, presuming that was the protocol, and followed them out with his briefcase in hand. When he stepped down off of the bus, he saw a huge, open space, easily as large as the hangar he'd been in the day before. Along the far wall was a long loading dock with a row of roll-up doors. Semi trailers were parked backed up to a couple of them. A small parking area to the right had about a dozen official vehicles parked in it including four unmarked, white Jeep Cherokees with red and blue police light bars on their roofs lined up side by side with a few gray Air Force sedans and desert-camouflage painted military trucks and Humvees.

The woman who had addressed the newcomers in the hangar the previous afternoon, Dr. Hidleman, was waiting for her three newcomers to disembark and then gathered them up in a group while the others walked past and into the facility through a large steel door that was opened up for them by an armed guard posted beside it.

"Good morning and welcome to Facility R-Four-Seven. In a moment, I'll bring you inside but first a few basics. To begin with, I want to be sure you each have your identification badges on and you're wearing your radiation pens," The three newbies each gestured to their own badges and the pens clipped onto their shirts. "Good. You'll notice on your identification badges a colored stripe. When you get inside, you'll see corresponding colored stripes painted along the walls." They lifted up their respective badges to take a look. Foster saw a red stripe across his.

"At first, you'll see all four colors along the walls. This is the area where you'll find common spaces like the cafeteria, administrative offices, infirmary, office supplies and janitorial storage spaces. As you go farther into the facility, the green stripe ends and the other three continue. You'll find a guard station that will not allow you to pass if you are only cleared for the green zone. Beyond that is the yellow zone, then the red and, finally, the black. The farther you go in, the higher the security level. If you don't see the color of the stripe on your badge painted along the wall, then you aren't cleared to be there. The guards will be checking your badges frequently while you are inside and will escort you out to an area where you are cleared if you should inadvertently wander somewhere you shouldn't. Be advised, they are also authorized to use deadly force to prevent any security breaches so it behooves you to cooperate. Does everyone understand that?"

The trio responded with affirmative words, nods and grunts.

"Good. There are restrooms located in each of the security zones so you won't have to go searching for one beyond where you are cleared to be. My office is in the green zone if you need to see me. Working hours are pretty flexible. If you're here late, can't get back to the Village for some reason at the end of your day, there are two dormitories in the green zone — one for the men, one for the ladies. I would recommend you pack a go-bag and keep it stashed here in your locker, just in case."

A hand rose from among the three new faces, "What's a 'go-bag'?"

Realizing that the group before her were civilian scientists and not military types, Hidleman explained, "It's a small duffle bag with a change of clothing for a day or two, toothbrush and basic essentials like that. We all have one here. Just talk with someone you'll be working with and they'll be able to suggest some specifics. Any other questions?"

The group just quietly stood shaking their heads.

"Good, then follow me."

A pair of men in black suits and sunglasses gravitated toward her as she walked to the door leading into the interior of the facility. They appeared to be the same two that were with her at the hangar the day before during orientation. They were never introduced and, frankly to Foster at that time, they all looked pretty much the same.

As she approached, she held up her identification badge for the guard to see and then looked back at her following brood and nodded to them to do the same. The guard pulled the door open and allowed them to enter with the two men in black following behind, shutting and sealing it behind them once all were inside.

Foster looked around at the inside of the hallway. It seemed to go on forever into the distance. The walls were painted blocks, glossy white from the high ceiling down to the longitudinal stripes that Hidleman had talked about at about chest height on both sides and then a neutral eggshell color down to the tan, asphalt-tiled floor below. About one hundred feet distant, he could see a desk positioned to face anyone who might approach with one of its ends butted up against the wall and partly blocking the hallway. Two armed guards in camouflage stood behind it.

Along both sides of the hall were several doors, all of which were closed. There were small, black plastic signs with engraved white lettering mounted on the wall just to the right of each door frame identifying what was inside by name and by room number. A few of the doors had small intercom boxes with keypads mounted beside them as well. He would find that some offices were accessible only by having identified one's self and being buzzed in or punching in the correct code number.

The ceiling was comprised of exposed, steel trusses that spanned across from one wall to the other and repeated every ten feet or so. Above the trusses was corrugated steel and innumerable pipes, conduits and cables were laced through the lattice of the trusses running the entire length of the hall, all of which painted black. Other pipes and conduits, painted to match the walls on which they were mounted on either side, some of which leading to or from gray, metal boxes of varying sizes mounted just above their heads. Some of the gray boxes were part of a network of of emergency lights spaced out along the entire length of the hall.

Waiting for them in the hallway were three people who would take charge of their new employees, bring them to their work areas and get them settled in. One man in a conservative suit and tie greeted a young woman in the group and then led her to one of the offices just a few doors down from where they stood. A middle-aged woman in a white lab coat introduced herself to the second member of the trio of rookies and began leading her down the hallway to a laboratory in the yellow zone just beyond the guards' desk.

Finally, an older man with short, partially-graying hair and matching mustache, wearing wire-rimmed glasses and a white lab coat introduced himself to Foster, "Good morning, Dr. Foster. I'm Brian Lebreau, I'm the director of the particle lab."

"My boss."

"Yes, I would be."

Foster shook his hand and smiled, "Pleased to meet you, Mr. Lebreau."

"It's 'doctor,' actually, but in the lab, we work so closely together we skip such formalities. We're all on a first-name basis. You can just call me 'Brian'."

"Alright — Brian. Again, pleased to meet you."

Lebreau looked down at the briefcase that Foster was carrying, "What's in there?"

"Oh, just some papers, calculator, slide rule, personal effects, lunch."

"The guards will have to search it when you get to the desk. Just for the record, everything you'll need is here — you'll see when we get to the lab — you won't be needing the briefcase."

"Good to know."

The particle lab was located two sections down the hallway in the red zone. Lebreau led him through first one and then a second guard station where he showed his identification badge and laid his briefcase down on each respective desk to be opened and inspected. Once the guards were satisfied, the pair continued down to a door in the red zone, a short distance beyond the desk on the left side of the hallway. The sign on the door said "Particle Laboratory" with an intercom box beside it. Lebreau paused before opening the door and turned to point out other doors in the hallway nearby, the rest rooms, an office supply closet, an employee lounge and other workspaces that he would show him later. He then took off his lanyard and, on the ring with his badge, was a key to unlock the door. He explained, "I don't like to use the buzzer when people are in here working. It's really annoying and distracts from the work. The put a keypad on the door to the lounge but for some reason, they didn't put one on this door so I've got a key for you, too, so whenever you need to go out for any reason, you can quietly come back in without disturbing everyone."

"That's a good idea."

Inside, Lebreau led him over to where four desks were set up in face-to-face pairings. Three of the desks had papers, file boxes and a few framed, personal photos displayed on them. One was essentially bare except for a desktop computer, monitor, blotter and lamp, "This is your desk. If there's anything you need, just let me know and I'll requisition it for you. I'll show you the basics on the computer a little later. Right now, though, I want to take you around and introduce you to your lab-mates."

Foster put down his briefcase and Lebreau beckoned him to follow to a counter along the back wall of the lab where one of his team was running tests using a large, white machine a little bigger around than a household refrigerator and standing about chest high. A computer monitor on the counter beside it was showing graphs and readouts of whatever the machine was measuring.

"Spectral analyzer," Foster mused as they approached, recognizing the particular piece of equipment as one that he'd made frequent use of at Cyberdyne Technologies.

"Yes, just one of our little toys. One of our tasks here is to break down and identify various materials and generate reports of our analyses." As they approached the counter, Lebreau called out to the man standing at the computer bent partly over, studying the images on the monitor with his fingers hovering over the keyboard, "Kyle?"

The man slowly stood upright and turned around. He was a young man, in his thirties, with a goatee and long dark hair tied back in a pony tail. He wore thick, black framed glasses and a white lab coat.

"Kyle, this is Dr. Dennis Foster."

"The new guy." he surmised with a welcoming smile as he removed his glasses.

"Yes. He'll be replacing Dr. McCaine." He turned to Foster, "Dennis, this is Dr. Kyle Bryant, our biochemical specialist."

"Dr. Bryant," Foster reached out to shake his hand.

"Just Kyle around here — Dennis, is it?"

"Yes. Pleased to meet you."

"And you."

"We'll let you get back to it, Kyle," Lebreau directed Foster, "Come on over here, I want to introduce you to our metallurgist."

They drifted to a large work table near the center of the lab where another white-coated technician had a number of small samples of material lined up in a row in front of himself, each of which was in an open-topped white plastic box. The samples were no larger than a few inches square. Each sample was a somewhat different metallic color, some subtilely different shades of silvery-steel, others resembling tones of copper, brass or bronze. A few of the samples had traces of paint or some other sort of finish on them. The boxes were numbered and he was engrossed in writing notes on a pad of paper as they approached while holding one of the samples in his other hand.

"Richard…" Lebreau quietly said as they stepped up behind him.

The man lurched as though he'd been poked in the back with a sharp stick. "It's okay," Lebreau explained, "Richard is a very focused sort of guy. He's easily startled when he's concentrating on something."

The man stood upright and turned around. He seemed a bit older than the chemist, appearing to be about the same age as Foster. He had a scarred, pockmarked face and wild eyes. He wore a blue jumpsuit underneath his white lab coat. A metal shop down the hallway — one of the doors that Lebreau had pointed out — was often his own personal workspace and when he would work there, he'd hang up his clean, white coat in the particle lab. The metal shop was a dusty, dirty sort of place.

"Dr. Richard Hart, this is Dr. Dennis Foster, our new particle physicist."

"Dr. Foster," Hart set down the metal sample that he'd been examining and reached out his calloused hand. "Welcome aboard."

"Thank you," Foster replied as they shook hands.

"So you're going to pick up where Dr. McCaine left off?"

"I'm not entirely sure just what I'll be doing here yet, but that's starting to look like the plan."

"Well, good luck with that."

"Uhhh, thanks — I guess," Foster curiously looked down at the metal piece that Hart had been studying so intently as they had approached and asked, "What's that?"

Hart turned and looked back at the work table behind him and then picked up the sample, "A most unusual sample. It apparently was broken off of something — we still haven't been able to match it up yet. It's absolutely fascinating, though. It's aluminum, but it's the purest, densest aluminum that I've ever seen. To my knowledge, there isn't a place on the planet that is able to produce an alloy this perfect."

"Oh? Where do you think it came from?"

"One more team member to meet," Lebreau interrupted, steering Foster away from what was, in Hart's and Foster's mutual exuberance, quickly becoming a suspiciously uncomfortable conversation to a corner behind them bristling with analytical machines and a large glassed-in compartment set into the block wall behind the counter. A young woman with her hair tied back in a long, blonde pony tail, wearing a pair of half-glasses perched on the freckled bridge of her nose clacked away at a computer keyboard. "Jennifer," Lebreau called to her.

Her shoulders heaved as though annoyed by the interruption. She reached up and slid the glasses off of her face, then swiveled around in her chair. When she stood up, she feigned a half-hearted smile, "Dr. Foster," she coldly stated.

"Dr. Teller." he replied.

"Oh, you two have already met?"

"At the bus stop," Foster replied.

"Well, good. The two of you will be working pretty closely together. Dr. Teller is a veteran of General Dynamics — worked on the design for nuclear reactors for submarines and other classified projects before we spirited her away."

Foster extended his hand to shake with her, she looked up at Lebreau who just proddingly nodded to her. She then hesitantly reached out and shook hands with Foster and then immediately yanked her hand back, snatched up a few facial tissues from a box nearby and vigorously wiped her hand off. She sat back down and turned around to get back to work.

"She takes some warming up to," Lebreau explained as he led Foster away. "I'm sure you two will develop a great working relationship pretty quickly."

Overhearing him as the two men walked away, Teller whispered under her breath, "Hmmm, I wouldn't count on it," just loudly enough for Foster to hear.

On the wall beside the door to the hallway was a row of coat hooks with four hooks, one for each of those working in the lab. Three hooks were empty and the last was hung with a white lab coat. Lebreau grabbed it and took it down, "Here," he said, handing it to Foster. "Now it's official. Welcome to the lab."

Foster took the white coat and smiled, "Thank you. I look forward to working here." ∎

CHAPTER FIFTEEN

Homesick

After having given Foster a fairly comprehensive tour of the particle laboratory, and after having met his three co-workers, Lebreau brought him to the employee lounge across the corridor of the red zone to sit with a cup of coffee and talk about just what was expected of him during his tenure at Facility R-Four-Seven.

The lounge was a comfortable place with chairs and a couple of tables and even an inviting leather sofa up against the back wall. Intended to be a bit more of an intimate oasis than a typical break room filled with vending machines and background music. It was a place for personal meetings away from the commotion of other areas where people could talk without interruption or spend some quiet time reading and studying materials that might need particular, uninterrupted concentration.

The two sat down at one of the small tables with their cups of coffee. Lebreau asked, "So, Dennis, what do you think of our lab?"

"For a secret lab built in a cave in the desert, yeah, it's pretty impressive."

"Thanks, but you haven't seen the half of it yet."

"Oh?"

"Well, you saw that Richard was working on metallurgical samples on that work table in there?"

"I did."

"That's the clean part of his job. He mostly works in that dirty, dusty metal shop down the hall. For obvious reasons, he can't light up acetylene torches or use grinders that blow sparks all around the lab so he has his own space for all of that. Likewise, so does our nuclear department."

"A clean room?"

"Yes, with *all* the latest tech — you'll love it. We'll suit up after lunch and I'll show you around."

"Now I'm *really* impressed."

"I thought you might be. We want to give you every tool you could possibly need to do what we hope you'll be able to do for us. It's that important."

"So what is it that you want me to actually do here? What is it that my predecessor had failed so badly at that I'm here to finish?"

"To be fair, Dr. McCaine didn't really 'fail' at anything. He just got frustrated when he reached a dead end. He got to a certain point in his research and our policies and security protocols at the time couldn't accommodate anything beyond that. Politics, in a word, Dennis. Since he'd left, we've taken a close look at those policies and tried to rectify the situation."

"Hence all the new 'toys'?"

"Well, that and a new approach to security protocols. We had a few meetings, took his complaints to heart and, knowing how critical it is for this particular facet of our work here, we made some adjustments. We tried to outfit the clean room with whatever we could possibly imagine that someone might need and instituted a policy whereby, if you think you might need something more, just ask. We have a pretty generous budget here and liberal procurement policies now. The work is important enough that we essentially have a blank check to hire and procure anyone and anything we need."

"That's great but, still, what is it that you want me to do here?"

Lebreau leaned back in his seat and took a sip of his coffee. He set the cup back down on the table and smiled, "We have a relic that we need you to identify for us. It's incredibly radioactive — much heavier than anything any of us has ever worked with before. All of our efforts have failed to come up with any sort of concrete analysis. We need you to break it down for us and tell us just what it's made of."

"Some kind of amalgamation? An alloy?"

"Maybe — we don't know. I can tell you that the consensus is that the relic is made out of something natural, previously uncategorized. But some believe, as you surmise, it might be some sort of alloy — we just don't know. McCaine got to a certain point in his research and hit a wall. He still couldn't say categorically one way or another."

"And that's where I come in?"

"Right. We need you to pick up where McCaine left off."

"Doesn't sound too daunting," Foster quipped with a sarcastic edge. "But tell me, if you had made all these changes to address his complaints, why didn't you just hire him back?"

"To be honest, we tried to. But he had already accepted another position elsewhere. Truthfully, this sort of secure, government environment isn't for everyone. I got the sense when I talked to him that the work wasn't the only issue he had with us."

"I think I understand."

"I've asked Jennifer to gather together all of his reports, notes and disks and set them out on your desk for you. To begin with, I want you to spend as much time as you need to study it all and come up with some kind of plan of action for me going forward. She'll assist you in your research. She's a nuclear physicist. Her function here ultimately is application — how to make this newfound energy source work for us in the real world."

"She seems to be a crusty, contrary sort."

"They call her the 'ice queen' around here — not to her face, of course. There's a hard shell with a cold heart in there somewhere but trust me, she's the consummate professional, imminently capable. She'll be a huge asset for you in your work."

"I hope so."

"Just don't try to get any too friendly with her. She can be pretty venomous, too."

"I'll keep that in mind."

When Foster returned to the lab with Lebreau, he found the stack of folders, notebooks and boxes of computer disks waiting for him on his desk as expected. He sat down and picked up the notebook with the earliest date written on its spine and began leafing through it as he stood behind his chair. McCaine's research was rudimentary to begin with, pretty much as one might expect — pretty much as Foster himself would have started with. The man had begun his approach to the problem with the basics. Foster wanted to spend some quality time with his predecessor's materials, studying and making his own notes.

He closed the notebook and took a quick look in the drawers of the desk but didn't find any sort of paper to work with. He asked Lebreau and was directed to the office supply closet where he was able to find a voluminous supply of spiral-bound notebooks, binders and writing tablets. He grabbed a couple of each and returned to his desk.

He spent the rest of the day reading the earliest of McCaine's notes, occasionally jotting down anything that he'd found that seemed to be pertinent. At that juncture, just beginning his review, he had no idea yet what would be germane and what wouldn't be, so he took copious notes as he went along.

Time flew by and, before he knew it, it was time to close up shop and catch the shuttle bus back to the Village. He'd only made it a short way through that first binder by then so he asked if it was alright to bring it with him back to his apartment.

"You can check out any of the documentation here in the lab with my signature," Lebreau explained. "You'll have a signed form to show to the security guards on your way out and if anyone were to ask on base anywhere. You can't, however, take anything home with you. Nothing leaves Area Fifty-One. Ever."

Pleased with the response he got, he had Lebreau sign out that first binder along with his own notebook to continue work at his apartment. He packed them into his briefcase which had suddenly found a purpose at the lab, and caught the bus back to his temporary home.

After stopping quickly at the commissary to pick up a sandwich and a bag of chips for dinner, he retired to his apartment to call home and tell his wife about his first day on the job — as much as he was allowed to anyway, which wasn't all that much — just that things went well and he had brought some homework back to his apartment to get himself up to speed on his new responsibilities.

She told him that she was proud of him and that she had had a good day working at the dress shop. The weather was nice and she missed him very much.

"I miss you, too, sweetie. This job is really awesome but I really wish that I could come home to you at the end of the day."

"I know. The house seems so empty without you here at night. I hate sleeping alone. But I guess we'll both get used to it — it's only for a couple of years until your contract runs out."

"Yeah, just for a couple of years — but I'll see you on Friday."

After saying good-night and "I love you" to one another, he hung the phone back onto the cradle mounted on the kitchen wall. He pulled his sandwich out of the bag from the commissary and unwrapped it, poured himself a glass of milk and sat down at the breakfast counter with the binder and his notebook to continue poring over his predecessor's notes.

It would be a long evening. Knowing how engrossed he could get in such study, he made a point to keep an eye on the clock lest he forget to turn in for a night's sleep until near morning.

He'd hate to wake up in the morning with his head lying on the open notebook still seated at the breakfast counter.

Although it wouldn't be the first time that sort of thing had ever happened. ■

CHAPTER SIXTEEN

Six Feet Apart

Tedious, intense and deeply complex but the work was exactly the sort of thing that Dennis Foster reveled in. It would bore any normal human being to tears, but his intellect and fascination with what he was doing just inspired him. He'd easily lose complete track of time if he didn't make frequent use of a small kitchen timer that he'd keep with him and set to make sure he got to bed, got off to work and left to get back to his apartment before the last shuttle bus would leave Facility R-Four-Seven for the evening.

At his apartment, he'd much rather pore over volumes of Dr. McCaine's notes and the numerous references that he'd brought with him from home than to watch black and white reruns on the base's closed circuit television system.

He filled a couple of spiral-wire-bound notebooks and innumerable scraps of paper and Post-It notes with his own observations. Dr. McCaine appeared to have done a most thorough job of analyzing the sample and came up with a number of cursory conclusions at the beginning of his study.

Friday morning had finally arrived — and that first week had flown by surprisingly quickly. He was excited to be doing what he was there to do and, moreover, to be doing it at a secret underground laboratory at Area Fifty-One.

But he couldn't tell a soul.

On Fridays, much of the staff in the lab began to drift out sometime around noon to catch the afternoon Janet flights back home to their families. The evening before, as he was studying Dr. McCaine's notes, Foster was beginning to get curious about the relic itself. Thus far, all he was able to do was read about it and see a few of McCaine's crude sketches intermingled within columns of his scrawled handwriting. He hadn't been able to see it in person. He wanted to at least get a look at it before he would leave for the weekend.

When he arrived at the particle lab that morning, he set his briefcase on the desk, pulled on his white lab coat, and unloaded all of the papers that he'd brought back to his apartment the evening before. The briefcase, though he was told wouldn't actually be needed while he was there, became a convenient way to transport papers and books back and forth between the lab and his apartment in the Village. For the weekend, however, it would stay there under his desk.

He looked across the row of desks and saw Dr. Lebreau sitting at his, his face hidden behind his computer monitor as he worked on some sort of report. Foster called out to him, "Good morning, Brian."

Lebreau leaned over to look around the screen and smiled, "Good morning, Dennis. Did you have a nice evening?"

"I did. And you?"

"Yes, brought back some homework. You know how that is."

"I do. I've read a lot of Dr. McCaine's earliest notes so far. I'd really like to get a look at the sample before I head off for the weekend. Would that be possible?"

Lebreau rose from his chair and began walking around his desk, "I don't see why not. I'm sure that seeing what it is you're supposed to be analyzing would be crucial. After all, a doctor can't diagnose his patient without seeing him in person — right?" He waved his fingers to invite Foster to follow him across the room.

They walked up to the counter where Dr. Teller was typing at a computer terminal. Still standing some distance behind her Lebreau called out as they approached, "Jennifer?"

She clacked a few more words and then straightened up, slowly slid off her reading glasses and turned around in her chair, "Dr. Lebreau. Good morning."

"Good morning, Jennifer. I'd like you to take Dennis in to see the relic that he's studying."

Visibly annoyed, she replied, "Now?"

"If you don't mind," Foster said as diplomatically as possible. "I've read through some of Dr. McCaine's reports and I'd have a much better understanding going forward if I could actually see just what it is I'm supposed to be working with instead of his rough sketches."

"It does make a lot of sense, Jennifer."

She looked up at Foster coldly and then turned to Lebreau, "I'm in the middle of something. Can't it wait?"

Lebreau looked across at Dennis, "Can it?"

"I was hoping to connect a few dots before leaving for the weekend. If it's not too much of an inconvenience."

"It is."

"We work for the government, Jennifer," Lebreau reasoned with a sly smile. "Wasting time has its own reward — inefficiency is always rewarded with bigger and bigger grants. I'd really appreciate it if you'd take a few minutes and bring Dennis over just to get a quick look at it — nothing more. Please."

"Alright, alright. Let me just save my document here and close things up. I'll be with you in a few minutes."

"Thank you," Lebreau added. "I appreciate it."

"Yeah, yeah…" She curtly replied as she turned back around and slipped her spectacles back onto her freckled face.

Lebreau walked back to his desk with a knowing smirk on his face and Foster just hovered around waiting for Teller to announce to him that she was ready to go.

When she finally got up from her chair, folded her glasses and slipped them into the pocket of her white coat, she waved to him and led him silently out through the door to the hallway. He followed her a short way until she paused in front of the door to the clean room. "It's in here," she explained. She punched a four-digit code into a keypad beside the door jamb and pushed the lever to unlatch it. The door opened with a whoosh of air entering the previously sealed space beyond.

They walked in and stopped in the air-tight vestibule just inside. Hanging in a row were six hazmat suits complete with helmets and disposable booties and gloves. Teller pulled the door to the hallway closed behind them and pulled down a lever in the center of it, latching it and activating a mechanism that compressed the door into the frame to create an air-tight seal.

They each took off their lab coats and hung them up, taking their respective radiation exposure pens from their pockets and setting them down on a counter while they suited up. The pens had to be visible

— especially while they were inside the clean room itself. The suits had a narrow pocket on the front designed to hold them. With the helmet on, it was very difficult to actually see one's own pen so protocol directed that nobody goes into the clean room alone and they were to watch each other's pens for indications of radioactive exposure.

When they were ready, she grabbed the handle on a large, stainless steel door that looked very much like that on a commercial, walk-in freezer. The seal gave off a momentary hissing sound as the air pressure equalized between the two rooms. Once inside the lab, she closed the door behind them, yanking on it to make sure it was secure and pulled down the handle just like the one on the door to the hallway, sealing them in.

Virtually everything inside was either gleaming, polished metal or painted bright white. The overhead lights illuminated everything in a pure, daylight spectrum of white light. The space just glowed with sterility.

The room was a jungle of complex machines, assorted cabinets and counters with cables, pipes and conduits ascending to a web across the white-painted ceiling above.

She led him up to a large Plexiglas panel built into a metal frame that protruded about a foot from the wall and was about five feet wide and five feet tall, the lower sill being at about waist high on him.

Hanging from the ceiling outside of the glass were two control arms, each coming down from a large, overhanging white box mounted on the wall just above the window. Each arm was comprised of a trio of polished stainless steel rods with a coiled cable that was contained between them. The arms were then connected to hand controllers on both the left and the right with space enough for a person to stand between them.

Inside the glass box in front of them were a pair of robotic arms that also extended down from the ceiling with pincers at the end of each one. She placed her gloved hand on one of the controls and asked, "Ever use one of these before?"

"When I was in college. It's been a while."

"These are state of the art. I imagine you'll get the hang of it pretty quickly."

He stepped closer and she ferociously snapped at him, "Back off,

Dr. Foster! You're too close!"

Confused, he froze in his tracks and then quickly took a step back, "What? What's the matter?"

"Personal space, Dr. Foster! You don't violate my personal space, especially when we're alone."

"I'm sorry, I didn't know," he awkwardly apologized. He wasn't sure what to do. Being a scientist who deals with specifics, he pointedly asked, "How far back should I stay?"

"Six feet. You don't come within six feet of me. Understand?"

"No, I don't, but I will if that's what makes you comfortable."

"It does." She cooly replied and then stepped away from the controls to allow him to step in.

Foster walked up to the glass and looked inside the large containment box in front of him. He could see the two robotic arms extending down from the ceiling and rows of what appeared to be clear Plexiglas drawers in a rack along the back wall. He slipped his hands into the two controllers hanging just to either side of his shoulders and then pulled down on them. The arms inside the box responded as he then twisted and manipulated them forward and back, side to side and worked his fingers to open and close the pincers at the end of each arm.

"I think I've got it," he announced after just a few minutes of practice. "Which drawer is it in?"

"Drawer thirteen," she replied, standing at a console behind him and watching what he was doing inside the containment box on video monitors arrayed in a row in front of her.

The rack on the back wall had two rows of smaller, numbered drawers only a few inches wide and tall and then, below those, was one row of larger drawers, one of which was numbered "thirteen." They each had large, kludgy handles on the exposed ends into which the pincers could fit and lock onto. He maneuvered the one on his right into the handle, slid out the drawer and set it down on a small, stainless steel table in the center of the containment chamber. While he used the right arm to hold the drawer in place, he reached in with the left, lifted the lid and then lifted out a small, metallic box with metal straps and a bright warning placard on its lid warning of extreme radiation danger.

He moved the drawer out of the way, set the box onto the table and opened it up. From where he stood, it was too far away from the glass to get a very good look at the contents so he lifted it up and brought it closer to the window to see better what was inside.

The interior of the box had a brown panel in it that filled it from edge to edge inside with a triangular cavity at its center. All around the perimeter of the cavity were rows of small, metal clips with braided wires extending from each one and disappearing into a row of shallow, black rectangles to the left and right and below just about an inch from each edge.

Held in place in the center of the box was a silvery metal triangle. It was about three inches along each of its three equal-length sides and the edges were beveled. Inside the box, it was impossible to tell just how thick it was. Engraved in two lines near the bottom edge was lettering that he could not make out, characters he didn't recognize. The metal was a sort of dull silver but still it seemed to emanate its own blueish light, a faint sort of glow.

"So that's it? That's your relic?" he quietly said as he studied it through the glass.

"Yes, it is. We have a few of them inventoried at the moment."

"And you have no idea what it is."

"That's why you're here, Dr. Foster."

"Well, it's obviously manufactured. Somebody out there made this so it would follow that they would know just what it's made of — no?"

"We've been trying to contact them for years. So far, no response."

"So you know who made this?"

"Not precisely, but we have a pretty good, general idea."

Foster placed the box back on the pedestal and closed it up. He removed his hands from the controls and turned to Teller, "I don't understand. If you know who made this, why all the subterfuge? Why all this cloak and dagger? Is it the Russians?"

"Well, one thing we know for certain, it was not the Russians."

"So where to you *think* it came from?"

"I'm afraid I can't divulge that information."

"Can't or won't?"

"You're not cleared for that, Dr. Foster — it's strictly 'need-to-know' and, for the time being, you don't."

"That doesn't make any sense."

"It's the government, it doesn't have to."

"How am I supposed to work with only bits and pieces of information?"

"For now, you'll just have to make do. It's a scientific problem to be solved. For the moment, the logistics are irrelevant."

"Irrelevant? Hmph," he chuffed as he put his hands back into the controllers and began putting the box back into the drawer to replace into the rack. "Alright, I suppose I can work with that — for now. I suppose it will just have to do."

"I imagine as your need to know might increase, they'll reveal more of the details to you. Just be patient."

"Not in my nature, but I'll do my best."

Once the sample was again secured in the drawer and sealed from any possible exposure, Foster raised the two control arms back up to their home positions and slid his fingers out. He and Teller then walked back out into the vestibule, closing and sealing the clean room door behind them to remove their hazmat suits. Before taking off any part of either suit, they made one last check of each other's radiation sensor pens to make sure that they hadn't been exposed while inside.

As they removed their protective suits, each part was set into a metal box resembling a small chest freezer. When everything had been removed and set inside, she closed the lid and sealed it. The contents would be taken out to be decontaminated and returned to the ready hooks behind them to be donned again in the future with the exception of the disposable booties and gloves.

When he returned to the particle lab, Dr. Lebreau asked him if he was satisfied with his visual inspection of the sample.

"I am, well, for now. I got a pretty good look at it through the glass with it still in its case."

"Was Dr. Teller helpful?"

"She was for the most part. It got a little weird at one point. She snapped at me and told me to keep back out of her personal space. Six feet. She wouldn't let me get any closer to her than six feet. It's going to be difficult to work with her if I have to keep so far away."

"Six feet?" Lebreau asked.

"Yeah."

"Used to be three. Couple weeks ago I heard that it grew to four."

"It would appear the woman has issues."

"Yeah. She, uh, has issues." ■

CHAPTER SEVENTEEN

Back in the World

The beginning of what would become their weekly routine, Foster's wife, Livvy, picked him up at the Burbank airport on Friday afternoon. When he walked out from the Janet terminal building, she was waiting for him at the curb. She rushed around and unlocked the trunk for him, gave him a quick peck on the cheek, and he loaded up his suitcase. He didn't have his briefcase with him, she noticed it missing but didn't ask about it. Since he wasn't allowed to bring any work home with him, there was no need to carry it back and forth from work to home. It would simply be set to the task of shuttling papers and books between his office and his apartment within Area Fifty-One for as long he'd be working there.

After they'd both gotten back into the car, Livvy pulled away from the curb and began the relatively short drive across town toward home.

"So, how was your week, sweetie?" He asked as they drove along.

"It was quiet. I missed having you around, though. With you home all this time since you lost your job, I sort of got used to you just being there. It's kinda strange now with you gone — especially at night."

"Ha, ha! Yeah, I kinda got into that 'stay-home' mindset, too. But it's good to get back out and back to work again. Not just for the money, but there's a — I'm not sure how to explain it — maybe just a sense of having a purpose again. Purpose aside from mailing out resumes, I mean."

"I get it," she replied with a smile. "I'm glad I kept the job at the dress shop when you got hired, though. I love being around people all day."

"I'm glad, too — glad that's working out for you."

"Ted came by this morning," she said matter-of-factly.

"Ted?"

"He wanted me to come and play tennis with him. He had on his white tennis shorts and one of those white sweaters with the red, white and blue collar."

"Does he know you don't play tennis?"

"Well, I don't anymore, but I did in college. I suppose I could get the hang of it again."

"What did you say?"

"Oh, I had to work today. Friday is one of our busiest days and I have to leave early to come and pick you up at the airport. There was no way I could go and play tennis today."

Foster felt uneasy about the situation. Leaving his wife home alone for a week at a time with a predator like Ted in the neighborhood sniffing around his front door was, at best, unsettling and, at worst, disturbingly suspicious. He trusted her implicitly, however, but still felt uncomfortable.

He wouldn't go so far as to admit to himself (or her) any sense of jealousy. Not yet, anyway.

"Don't worry, dear," Livvy continued with a knowing smile as he sat quietly in the passenger seat mulling over the situation, "I have no plans to go and play tennis with Ted — or anything else for that matter."

"Well, that's good. Not that I was worried or anything."

"No, of course not." She chuckled as she sarcastically answered.

Jealousy wasn't something that had historically been part of Foster's makeup. In his mind, everything in his life — including Livvy — was neatly ordered, everything aligned. It was an emotion that he was mostly uninitiated with and the feelings that he was then experiencing were confusing to him. He knew his relationship with his wife was solid. She'd never betray him.

Still, it was annoying how Ted was so persistent, finding all sorts of lame excuses to spend time around her. He was considering that, perhaps, he should have a talk with the man and tell him to stay away. Maybe threaten him a little bit.

But not that first weekend. He'd missed his wife while he was away and she had been missing him, too. He wanted to spend as much real quality time with her doing the sorts of things that they enjoyed doing. He didn't want to ruin the moment. He'd make the most of things together before she'd once again have to drive him to the airport on Sunday afternoon and say good-bye for another week.

Besides, maybe if Ted kept getting rebuffed by her, he would eventually lose interest and just give up on her. He couldn't understand why, with an oversexed porno queen as a girlfriend, Ted would have any interest in any other woman on the planet. But then, he was thinking logically and the situation was devoid of logic which only caused even greater elusion for him.

Before they got home, Livvy unexpectedly turned into the parking lot of a steakhouse they frequented not too far from the house. It was one of their favorites. She hadn't had time to actually make any sort of dinner at home and, besides, she wanted to treat him at a nice place to celebrate the first week at his new job. As they pulled in, he smiled.

They were shown to a booth near the back of the dining room. He didn't recognize the waitress who came to their table, although he wasn't paying very close attention. He hadn't yet become suspicious of his situation so wasn't at all vigilant. Being such regular customers, they knew many of the waitstaff and they knew the Fosters, but he didn't give it another thought as she asked if they would like to start with drinks while they were looking over the menus. Livvy ordered a glass of wine and he ordered a beer, the waitress took note on her pad and walked off to the bar to get their drinks.

"It's so nice to have you home, dear," Livvy commented.

"It's nice to be home, sweetie. I missed you all week. It's so weird living under all that security. Being away like that, I feel like I'm working twenty-four-seven, not the usual nine-to-five like a normal job. It's disorienting without the usual break of coming home at the end of a day."

"You don't have any sort of your own place there?"

"Oh, they have a few apartment buildings there and I have a nice one-bedroom in one of them. It's set up like a military base but I guess they understand that the nature of working there can be stressful for civilians like us so they try and make some of it more comfortable than barracks and chow halls. A little more like the real world we all come in from."

"So is it actually a military base you're working at?"

"I'm not sure how much I'm allowed to tell you but, well, part of it is. There are people around in uniform and all of that, but the rest of it is more like a corporation, like Cyberdyne was but with a lot more security."

"Sounds like something out of a movie."

Foster grinned, "I guess it does at that."

The waitress returned with their drinks and then asked if they'd had a chance to check over the menu yet. They hadn't but, because they had eaten there so often, they both knew what they wanted. She ordered the broiled haddock with rice pilaf and he ordered a New York strip, medium-well, and a baked potato with butter — no sour cream.

"Thanks," the waitress said as she jotted down their selections on her pad. "I'll get this into the kitchen right away."

"Thank you," Foster replied as he handed her the menus to take back with her.

Once they'd been left alone again, Livvy took a sip of her wine and then asked, "Do you like the job so far? The people?"

"In some ways it's very different from what I'd been doing but, in other ways, it's very much the same. There seem to be a lot of people working there at the lab, but I haven't actually met too many yet. I have an eclectic crew of co-workers in my own department, four of them. The one person that I'll be working most closely with is a young woman with a really bad attitude — not about the work, but about people. She's severely socially challenged. She announced to me that she had a rule about personal space, that everyone had to keep at least six feet away from her."

"Six feet? Really?"

"The supervisor in the department keeps talking to her from a distance. I'm not sure what he's afraid of — or what she's afraid of."

"Maybe he's just trying to be respectful."

"I suppose."

"You don't notice it so much being one of them, but genius types can often be, let's just say, a bit eccentric."

"Like me?"

"Well, to be honest, dear, you *do* have your idiosyncrasies."

"Which is why you love me — right?"

"Oh that, and, well, we'll get to the other reasons when we get home."

"*Other* reasons?"

"Do I have to spell it out for you?"

"Uh, I'm not sure."

She leaned over the table and whispered with a sly smile, "I'm not wearing any underwear."

His eyebrows raised — suddenly he understood what she was eluding to and a broad grin spread across his face.

* * * * *

Foster found himself wide awake at about five o'clock Saturday morning. He rolled his head over on the pillow and glanced at the clock and then groaned to himself. He closed his eyes hoping to fall back asleep but it was useless.

He slipped out from under the covers, trying not to disturb his sleeping wife as he did. He pulled on his bathrobe and pushed his feet into a pair of slippers and then walked out to the hall, quietly closing the bedroom door behind himself.

It was still pretty dim outside, but he hoped that the paperboy had been by with the morning paper by then so he went downstairs and opened the front door. There, about halfway up the walk from the street, lay his Saturday morning paper. He stepped out onto the porch and took a deep breath of cool, fresh, morning air, arching his back and stretching his arms up and out as he did.

He stepped down from the porch and walked out to pick up his rolled up newspaper. He unfolded it and took a moment to glance at the headlines on the front page. While he stood there panning his eyes across the page in the dim light, he heard a voice call out, "Mornin', Denny!"

He looked up over the top of his paper and saw Ted jogging past on the sidewalk across the suburban street from where he stood with his girlfriend, Bambi, alongside. Ted was wearing a pair of short gym shorts and a blue t-shirt while she was wearing a French-cut bikini bottom and a t-shirt cropped off and exposing her taught belly, her braless breasts bouncing freely beneath it with each step.

For the sake of being neighborly (as Livvy would encourage), Foster waved back to them as they jogged by, then just shook his head in annoyance and turned to go back inside.

As he walked into the house, Livvy was coming down the stairs in her bathrobe and greeted him with a kiss, "Morning, dear."

"Mornin', sweetie. I was just about to put the coffee on."

"Oh, that's good."

"I thought I might take a ride out to the hardware store and get a timer for it so you can get up in the mornings, go right into the shower upstairs, get dressed and the coffee would be ready when you came downstairs. Would you like that?"

"A timer?"

"Sure. I can take a ride up to the store after breakfast."

"The coffee machine has a timer on it, dear. I just don't know how it works. If you can show me how to set it up sometime, we could try it out."

"Ha, ha! Shows how much I pay attention to things like that — I had no idea. Sure, I'll take a look at it while I'm in there this morning."

Livvy smiled, "Thanks," she said and then turned back toward the stairs, "I'll go up and take my shower then."

As she climbed back up the stairs, her slippers gently slapping against her heels with each step, Foster walked into the kitchen and set the newspaper down on the table. He pulled out a box of filters, set one into the coffee machine's basket and then filled it with coffee grounds. He filled up the glass pitcher with water. Before starting up the machine to make a potful, he took a quick look at the face of it.

There was a small, analog clock on it, he'd noticed it before but never realized that it was also a timer. He studied the knobs next to it and began to fiddle with them and quickly figured out how the timer worked — or at least how it was *supposed* to work. Like the scientist/nerd that he was, he'd have to test his hypothesis.

He poured the water into the reservoir at the back of the machine and set the empty glass pot on the heating plate underneath. He then set the clock up so that the timer would turn everything on in just two minutes and pushed the start button.

He took a quick glance up at the clock on the kitchen wall and then stepped back to wait.

He watched the second hand go around and around twice and then heard a loud "click" from the coffee maker. An orange light then illuminated and it began to groan as it started to heat up the water and the dark brown drizzle of coffee ran out from the port at the bottom of the basket of coffee grounds and into the glass pot.

It worked — Livvy would be thrilled.

Despite being a certified genius, Foster wasn't a very handy sort of guy around the house. He could figure out electronic gadgets like the coffee machine pretty readily and he knew every nut and bolt of his race car — though that was more of a discipline learned by necessity and experience — but if he ever had to fix the dishwasher or the dryer, he'd be lost. He was, however, quite adept at dialing the phone and calling repairmen for help.

At breakfast, he asked Livvy if she had any plans for the weekend. She didn't.

After a week apart, the first of an unforeseeable number for them, he wanted to spend as much time with her as possible. Since there wasn't anything that had to be dealt with or fixed at home, or events that they wanted to (or needed to) attend, he suggested a leisurely drive up into the mountains to some of their favorite places and lunch at the little hot dog stand up there that overlooked the valley and the Pacific beyond. She agreed that would be a fabulous idea. They grabbed a couple of light jackets and tossed them into the back seat of her car in case it got chilly up in the hills and left for a relaxing day out in the fresh air.

When they returned home late that afternoon, Foster pulled the car into the driveway. As they were getting out, Ted came sauntering up from the sidewalk. Foster sighed to himself as the man approached, his hand extended with a broad grin, and greeted him.

"So how was your first week, Denny?"

"It was okay."

"Just 'okay'? Livvy told me that it was just the sort of work that you loved to do."

"It is, to be fair, once I get the hang of the new routine, I'll be able to focus on it better. It's all brand new right now."

"Oh, I get that." He looked over the hood of the car at Livvy. "Every new picture I work on is an all-new routine. Different directors, different producers, they all have their own ways of doing things. Gotta learn to adapt all over again each time."

"I'm sure Denny will get the hang of it pretty quickly," she replied with a friendly smile.

"Oh, I'm sure," he turned and looked back at Foster, "You folks had dinner yet? Looks like a nice night for puttin' some steaks on the grill."

"Not tonight, thanks. We'd really like to just have some personal time this weekend before I have to go back."

"Sure, I get it..." he leaned in and smiled slyly at Foster, lowering his voice, "...you dog, you!"

Foster felt like lashing back at the man just then but nerds like him aren't really good at snappy comebacks — although he'd probably think of something clever later. He envisioned himself, though, taking a swing at him while his face was in so close, but nerds are even less adept at physical violence. He just stared at Ted with gritted teeth.

Before he could say or do anything he might later regret, Livvy wrapped her arm around his and urged, "Come on, dear, let's go inside. I rented a video and bought a jar of Oriville Reddenbacher so we can have a movie night tonight."

He stared at Ted for a long moment while Ted just continued grinning glibly back at him, then turned to his wife and relaxed his posture a bit and said, "That sounds like a really good idea, sweetie. Let's go."

As they turned around to head for the front door of the house, she called back, "Good night, Ted!"

"Good night, kids — raincheck on the steaks! Be seeing you." ∎

CHAPTER EIGHTEEN

Hangar Two

Over the next couple of weeks, Foster incrementally acclimated to his new daily and weekly routines. He brought a few things from home — photos mostly, and some books — to make his little apartment at Area Fifty-One a bit more of a home-away-from-home. Photos of his wife, Livvy, of course, along with a few others like the one of himself and his friend, Luke, standing in front of their race car holding a trophy for having won a race a few summers before. It seemed such a long time ago, so much had happened since that day, and so quickly.

He wondered to himself if he shouldn't sell off his half of the racing operation to Luke or even just give it to him outright as it was unclear how long he'd be away from it. His new work/lifestyle didn't afford much for leisure time, certainly not nearly enough to engage in auto racing even at the amateur level that he and Luke had. Before too long, the car would become outdated and uncompetitive. It would be such a waste to let it just languish in his garage.

He set up a cluster of framed photos on the dresser in the bedroom where he'd see them regularly and, each night, vicariously wish his wife "good night" before clicking off the light and going to sleep.

For the time being, his time at work was mostly spent continuing the study of his predecessor's notes and reviewing records of the various test results that he'd gotten in his pursuit to identify the makeup of the strange, triangular sample. Foster, familiar with the processes and test equipment that McCaine had utilized, broke down each of the tests and considered how he, himself, might pursue each one with a somewhat fresh approach. Perhaps a different perspective would produce different results.

McCaine's procedures and the basic tests that he'd made were all very much within the accepted standards of the scientific community and, more specifically, that of the nuclear physics field. Foster considered that, if he were confronted with the same situation that McCaine had — starting from scratch — he'd likely have followed along much the same path himself.

Several blank notebooks became filled with his hand-written observations and hypotheses as he drilled down on each process and thoughts on additional tests that he'd add to the regimen. Hours at his desk, alone in the relatively quiet lounge down the hall from the lab and evenings at his apartment were devoted to his obsessive study.

Dr. Lebreau had asked him to work up his own plan to proceed, picking up where Dr. McCaine had left off when he had resigned. Foster was intensely fascinated by the challenge but one thing kept nagging at him. The sample that he'd seen was obviously manufactured by somebody, somewhere. It wasn't natural. It wasn't something that someone had found in a deep, dark hole in the desert or a cave in the mountains or at the bottom of the ocean. So, therefore, someone, somewhere, knew what it was and where it had come from. Without that information, he felt he couldn't come up with a viable plan.

He had to have some sort of context to work with, a starting point. He had to go in and insist that he be told what he needed to know.

That appeared to be the point in Dr. McCaine's research efforts where he'd finally quit in frustration. When he had insisted that he know that information to continue his work, he was stonewalled. Foster read in his notes how again and again he was told that he didn't have the proper clearance and would just have to proceed without that information. In some of his last notes he commented bitterly about his frustrations and Foster was beginning to get a fuller picture of the situation.

So, after months of unrequited contention, McCaine had given up and quit.

Sitting on his sofa in his apartment noshing a proper roast beef sandwich for dinner, Foster continued his deep study of his predecessor's work, reading each of his comments and making his own notes. And finally, he came to the last page of the last binder of McCaine's research.

LeBreau had told him that, after McCaine had walked out, they took a look at their policies and made some fundamental changes. He'd go in and talk with him and see just how fundamental those changes actually were and if they'd relaxed any the security roadblocks. He'd ask to find out what was kept from McCaine. After just a few months at his new job, he'd really hate to have found himself painted into the same corner that McCaine had found himself in and then also feel moved to quit in frustration.

After arriving at the particle lab that Thursday morning, Foster pulled on his white lab coat, carried his briefcase to his desk and unloaded the notebooks and binders, sliding the empty case under his desk where it had come to reside.

He returned many of McCaine's volumes to the bookcase from whence they had been taken and then logged onto his computer. He began to work on the massive project in front of him, opening up his notes and typing his findings and hypotheses into various documents that he'd set up on the computer, but his mind kept drifting to thoughts of McCaine and the circumstances of his final frustration. He sat back in his seat and dropped his hands away from the computer's keyboard, pausing for a brief reflective moment. Finally, he got up and walked over to Lebreau's desk, "Good morning, Brian."

Lebreau looked up from his computer screen, smiled and replied, "Good morning, Dennis. How 'ya doing this morning?"

"Doing well, thanks."

"Good. How's it going with your research so far?"

"Funny you should mention that."

"Oh?"

"I've studied all of Dr. McCaine's notes and dissected all of his various tests, examining the results that he'd gotten from them. I actually got to the end of them all last night. He never actually reached any sort of difinitive conclusions, all of his work seems to abruptly end at the same place."

"Unfortunate, I know."

"I'm at that same place now."

"Oh? Already?"

"I need to know — I need to know where that sample came from. Who made it? I need to know as much about it as I can before I'm able to go any farther."

"That's a complicated request — you have no idea. You can't come up with a plan to continue McCaine's work without that information?"

"From a thirty-thousand-foot perspective, I intend to re-do all of his tests and perform a few more of my own — that's the overview of my plan so far. But that's not much more than what McCaine did and I presume I'll get much the same results. I have to have some sort of a starting point. Right now, it's a moving target in the fog. The more I think about it, the more elusive it becomes and the more I understand how he got so frustrated with this that he finally quit."

"Are you saying that you're considering quitting?"

"No, I'm not thinking about quitting. I'll proceed as best I can if I have to, but you're effectively tying my hands."

Lebreau stood up from his chair and leaned up against his desk, "I'm afraid you just don't have the security clearance for that information — not yet."

"Do you?"

"I do, but I don't have clearance to share it with someone else who doesn't."

"Who does? Does Dr. Hidleman have that clearance?"

"She has clearance for everything around here."

"She does, eh?"

Lebreau was taken aback when he saw Foster's expression abruptly change. He asked suspiciously, "What are you planning to do, Dennis?"

Foster stood silent for a moment then, without saying another word, his face looking mischievously pensive. Then, suddenly, he turned on his heel and walked quickly toward the door.

"Wait!" Lebreau called after him, "Dennis!"

Teller looked up from where she was working as he rushed past her, making a bee line to the door, "Dr. Foster! Where are you going?!"

He didn't acknowledge her. He just grabbed the door handle and yanked it open.

She jumped up from her seat and ran after him, "Dr. Foster! *Hold up!*"

She chased after him down the hallway, past the security desk between the red zone into the yellow zone and finally caught up with him at the desk leading into the green zone. He stopped and and finally turned around, "Where the hell are you going?" she asked, "What's wrong?"

"I'm going to see Dr. Hidleman and demand that she tell me everything I need to know about that sample. I can't do my job without it — Dr. McCaine got this far and quit. I don't want history to repeat itself."

"She won't tell you. This is crazy!"

"Look who's talking about 'crazy'." He turned away and continued walking past the security desk just as Hidleman stepped out of her office with a stack of folders in her hands.

She glanced up and saw Foster storming down the hallway toward her with the diminutive Teller jogging along behind trying to keep up.

"Dr. Hidleman!" Foster called out. She stopped and stood in place as he came closer. "A word!"

Hidleman patiently asked, "Yes, Dr. Foster. What is it?"

He stepped up and insistently stated, "I need to know."

"Know? Know what?"

"He wants to know about the relic," Teller explained. "He wants to know where it came from."

"Oh, does he, now?"

"I do, yes. It's critical that I know to continue with my research."

Hidleman stood quietly considering the moment and then looked past him at Teller without responding.

Teller commented, "See? I told you. She won't tell you."

But then Hidleman calmly said to her, "Alright. Let's show him."

"Really? He's not cleared for this!"

"We can't keep hiring people and then hamstringing them when we think they're getting too close, Dr. Teller. Sooner or later we just have to trust someone," she looked up at Foster. "I can trust you, Dr. Foster? Trust you to keep this critical, national secret?"

"Uh, sure. I can keep your secret."

"But, Dr. Hidleman…" Teller protested. "…he's not cleared, he hasn't gone through the proper protocols."

Hidleman looked at Foster and cooly said, "*I'm* cleared for this, Dr. Teller and I call the shots around here. Come with me."

He couldn't believe that he'd actually convinced the facility's director so easily but, then, they had gotten that far in the research before. Perhaps they realized that if they wanted to get any real results, they had to be more forthcoming. Maybe whatever discussions that had to take place already had and the decision had already been made. He'd just gotten to the threshold of it being implemented a little sooner than expected.

But, perhaps, it wasn't quite as easy as it might appear. Maybe there was something else going on.

He didn't care. He was following Dr. Hidleman down the long corridor past the security desks for the yellow zone with Teller, then the red zone and finally, into the black zone, beyond which he was not cleared to enter but followed along as a guest of two who were.

The hallway ended at a "T" shaped intersection. A perpendicular corridor extended out to the left and the right. Along the opposite wall were a number of closed doors spaced far apart from one another. Large, gray doors unlike any of the others at the offices and laboratories behind them. They were set in wide, steel frames and each was about five feet across and eight feet tall with a row of bolts all around their perimeters. They appeared almost midievil. Hidleman led them to a door a few feet to their right as they emerged from the long hallway.

She punched a code onto a keypad in the center of the door which then released its lock with a loud, echoing, mechanical clanking sound. She pushed down a large lever that unlatched the door and, as it moved away from the frame, the air-tight seal was released and a hiss of air emanated from the room beyond.

Foster followed Hidleman and Teller inside. They emerged in the center of a long wall along one side of an expansive space. A hangar that measured easily a couple hundred feet wide and deep from where he stood to the distant back wall topped by a ceiling over twenty feet over their heads. The walls were painted shades of gray, the floor was a polished concrete surface with yellow and black striped lines delineating certain areas. Signs posted along the walls and hanging from yellow saw horses warned of radiation hazards and to keep back unless authorized to venture beyond them.

But the vast, cavernous room was not what took his breath away.

Parked inside that hangar were two very unusual aircraft — at least he thought they were aircraft. He had no other worldly context to categorize in his mind just what it was that he was seeing.

To the right was a disk-shaped craft about fifty feet in diameter. It was silver colored like brightly polished, bare metal. The center of the disk was thickly domed both on the upper and lower surfaces, tapering down to a narrow edge around its perimeter. A tinted clear dome capped the top made of a dark green, translucent material not unlike the dark green lenses of a pair of sunglasses. The smooth upper surface was broken up into recessed panels all around, each with a narrow, horizontal window made of the same dark green tinted material as the dome at the top.

The craft stood on its own retractible legs which, unlike any airplane he'd ever seen, were devoid of wheels. It stood on four broad, flat pads which suggested that it didn't need a runway to take off or land. Apparently, it rose and landed vertically under some sort of its own power.

Various panels were open around its surface, mostly small openings, their lids standing open with cables and wires leading out from them. A couple of much larger panels were open on the craft's underside, one of which appeared large enough for a man to climb in through.

Arrayed around the perimeter of the craft were an assortment of tables, trailers and test equipment to which the innumerable umbilical lines were attached and were themselves, in turn, cabled to several large, gray boxes on the walls nearby.

Workmen in blue jumpsuits wearing goggles and hearing protection against the persistent low hum of the machines attended to the equipment and the craft itself. They appeared, at that moment, to be running some sort of specific test on it, signaling to one another with hand signs from the podium of the test machines to those who were standing or crouched at various stations around the underside of the craft.

In silent amazement, Foster eventually turned his gaze to his left, to a second craft looking for the most part to be identical in design to the one on the right but its shiny metallic surface was dull and tarnished, stained in places with dirt and black carbon. It was smashed and had obviously experienced a fire. Part of it was torn away, severely charred around the jagged edges of a gaping hole exposing some of the mangled interior. Numerous twisted bits were lined up against the back wall, the larger ones on black-painted racks, the smaller ones stacked in metal cases.

Quietly, Foster asked, "Are these for real?"

"Yes, Dr. Foster," Hidleman replied, "They are very real."

He continued to stand there, dumbfounded and silent. His mouth was agape as he panned his eyes across the scene before him. Unidentified flying objects — UFOs, flying saucers — two of them parked side by side right in front of him.

He took a few tentative steps toward the intact craft to his right but once his foot stepped over an unnoticed yellow-striped line, a pair of armed military guards stepped quickly up to him and he stopped short.

"I just wanted to take a closer look," he explained.

"You're not even cleared to be in this room, Dr. Foster," Hidleman explained. "In time, I'm sure I can get you clearance to work more closely but for today, just stay behind that line."

He glanced down at the floor and spied the line painted across it below him and stepped back behind it. The two guards backed off and posted themselves a few feet beyond the line, hovering nearby just in case Foster should suddenly become more spontaneously ambitious.

"Flying saucers. *Really?* Is that what I'm seeing in here? *Flying saucers?*"

"Some call them that, yes," Hidleman replied. "We prefer the term 'extraterrestrial craft.' It's less conspiracy-theory-sounding."

"Lest we sound like the crackpots out there who keep reporting UAPs to the authorities," Teller added.

"UAPs?" He asked, still with his back to the two women, staring ahead in disbelief.

"Unidentified aerial phenomenon."

"Uh-huh."

"The one on the left, Dr. Foster," Hidleman explained, "crashed in the desert outside of Roswell, New Mexico in 1947. The debris was collected and brought to Wright-Patterson Air Force Base in Ohio where it was stored for several years. The space there wasn't conducive to any sort of in-depth study so later, when this facility was built, it was brought here."

"This is where your triangular sample came from," Teller added.

Foster turned around and pulled his glasses off to face her and Hidleman, "How did you find out how radioactive it is?"

"There was an accident at Wright-Patt," Teller explained. "A man was killed from exposure when he opened a containment capsule that was found inside. Others nearby were exposed when it happened. Some were crippled, a couple of them died years later of radiation poisoning and cancer. That's when it was decided to button it up and ship it here where we can keep anything like that contained."

"I now understand the need for all of the warnings and signs and these pens in our pockets," Foster commented, slipping his glasses back on and momentarily glancing down at his own. "And what about the other saucer? It doesn't appear damaged."

"No, that one was acquired through diplomacy, the State Department" Hidleman replied.

"Diplomacy?"

"A deal worked out by President Kennedy and a few eminent scientists of the day with envoys of the extraterrestrials who built it and flew it here."

"We worked a deal with the aliens for one of their space ships? You realize how crazy that sounds?"

"For a few of them, actually. Their technology is far beyond ours but the deal is that we have to figure it out for ourselves. The purpose of this facility, Dr. Foster, is to reverse-engineer these alien technologies and develop applications for scientific, commercial and military uses."

"Where are the other ships?"

"We have a couple of them here in hangars one and three. The rest are stored at Wright-Patt in a hanger there."

"That's unbelievable."

"Yes, but it's all true" Hidleman assured.

"What about the crews?"

"The crews?"

"This one crashed — right? Someone was at the controls when that happened, no doubt. What happened to them?"

"Uh, we're not privy to that intel, I'm afraid."

"After all these years, I can't imagine that this is the only space ship that ever crashed. I mean, we hear about airplanes crashing now and then all the time. Are there others? Other crashed alien craft?"

"Not here, no. Any other recovered wreckage is in Hangar Eighteen at Wright-Patt."

"With the corpses? What about the survivors of any of these crashes?"

"Again, I'm not read into that intel. Sorry."

"But you have your answer now," Teller injected. "Do you think you can work with the relic now?"

"Knowing that it came from somewhere other than this planet, yes. I kind of have to wrap my mind around that concept first but, knowing that, the whole thing becomes a blank slate. There is no earthly context to build any research on. I can see why Dr. McCaine was so frustrated. If he only knew about this, I think his work would have taken a much different tack."

"It appears you've already formulated a plan of action."

"Well, maybe not a 'plan' quite yet, but definitely a somewhat different direction. I think I'll be visiting the UCLA library when I get home. I need to look some stuff up."

"Not a word, Dr. Foster," Hidleman warned. "No to anyone."

"Oh, I know. The librarian doesn't need to know what I'm working on. She just needs to point me to the cosmology section in the reference room."

"You can't mention that you've seen these or heard any of what you've just been told to anybody. You're not cleared to even be in here yet. I bent the rules to show this to you to help further your research. Remember, there are serious consequences."

"Oh, don't worry about me. After years of working in aerospace, I've become quite good at keeping secrets."

"And your wife?"

"She's gotten used to it." ∎

CHAPTER NINETEEN

Suburbia Revisited

Foster didn't get much sleep that night in his small apartment in the Village at Area Fifty-One. He had seen behind the curtain and then knew without a doubt what the great secret that all the tight security was about. Why the secret base in the desert, the underground laboratory, the private jets and guns — all the guns. All around him. All the time.

The thoughts haunted him and kept him awake most of the night.

But people report seeing flying saucers constantly. Why keep it such a secret? Why spend the time, effort and expense on programs like Project Blue Book to dispel any such suspicions by explaining them away? Even with the most preposterous of rationales? It seemed that they would go to any length to keep the whole thing swept under the rug. But, again — why?

His mind just turned over and over as he laid in bed. He could hear jets taking off and landing on the long runway not far from his pillow. Some were remarkably loud and he could only imagine those might have been the powerful twin engines of the Blackbirds that were capable of propelling them to well over three times the speed of sound along with, too, the little black chase planes that would accompany them out from the airfield and then meet them again on their return to escort them back in.

After having been there for several weeks, he was usually nearly oblivious to the sound, it had become just background noise by then — well-muffled by the thick block walls filled with sound-deadening insulation all around him. Even the windows were double-paned, built with the inner and outer panes slightly angled away from one another to keep sound waves from transferring from the outside pane to the inside pane through a nitrogen-filled gap in between.

But that night he was unable to turn his brain off enough to fall asleep. The only solace was that, by noon the next day, he'd be on his way home and could peaceably nap on his own sofa in his own living room or just make an early night of it and climb into his own bed and let the exhaustion just overtake him until Saturday morning.

The six o'clock alarm finally sounded. He reached over and fumbled for the button on top of the wood-grained plastic box. He rolled his head over to glance at it to confirm to himself that it was, actually, in fact, time to get up for the day.

Groaning, he peeled the bedcovers back, swung himself around and got to his feet.

A hot shower, clean clothes and a gargle of mouthwash helped to perk him up enough to grab a cup of black coffee at the commissary before heading to the bus stop. He packed his bag for his flight home and left it near the door to grab later on his way to catch his flight back to Burbank.

In his briefcase were a number of Dr. McCaine's binders filled with his notes from the assorted tests that he'd conducted on the sample along with about half a dozen wire-bound notebooks filled with his own notes and observations that he'd compiled over the previous months. He came to the realization that both he and his predecessor had been coming at the whole research project from the wrong direction. Now that he knew just what it was that he was looking at — and, more poignantly, where it had come from — he needed to take all of the information that he had thus far absorbed and redirect it into an entirely new approach.

But it would take some time to formulate the details of that plan. He'd have to review everything, starting almost from scratch. He hoped that Dr. Lebreau would understand.

With his identification badge dangling from the lanyard around his neck, his radiation monitoring pen clipped behind the pocket protector in his shirt pocket, and his briefcase in his hand, he slid on his glasses with a pair of clip-on sun-shading lenses fixed to them and headed out the door. He grabbed a quick breakfast at the dining hall with his first cup of black coffee to start his day. He'd take a second large cup to go to sip on the bus on his way out to the lab. His morning would be primarily fueled by caffeine and the adrenaline of scientific curiosity that day.

When he got to the lab, he pulled on his white lab coat and parked his briefcase under his desk.

Dr. Lebreau walked over to him and asked, "So, Dennis, I hear you got quite an eyeful yesterday afternoon?"

"Uh, yeah, I sure did," He took off his glasses, unclipped the sun shading lenses and set them down on his desk.

"So tell me, what do you think?"

"I'm still processing it all — it was a long, sleepless night last night. One thing that I came to realize, however, is that I'm going to have to rethink the entire approach to this research."

"Oh?"

"I can see why Dr. McCaine came up empty after a few years' work at this. He was trying to identify something that he presumed was earthly, trying to fit it into a known square of the periodic table. Trying to put a round peg into that square hole, as it were — and he never realized that it would never fit no matter how hard he tried."

"Hmmm, I can see that now. We really tied his hands, didn't we?"

"I think instead of trying to identify what the sample is made of based on anything known, we need to identify its unique properties, break it down atom by atom, isotope by isotope. The one thing that's common throughout the universe is that everything everywhere is built with the same structure. We need to dismantle this structure particle by particle and then develop a strategy to synthesize it here on Earth."

"Synthesize it?" Lebreau was caught by surprise.

That scenario wasn't part of the plan. Garner and Taffin hadn't included that in their script, but they did assure that they had contingencies and backup plans for any eventuality. He'd have to trust that they'd anticipated something like that so he'd play along and see where it all might lead.

"That's, uh, pretty ambitious."

"I know, but I believe it's the best approach knowing now what I need to do."

"Well, you certainly know this stuff way better than I do, Dennis. Is this something we might actually be able to do?"

"Do we have a collider?"

"Uh, no. No we don't."

"Would it be possible to book time on one? Maybe the one in Tennessee or Cern in Switzerland?"

"I'd have to look into it. It's literally never come up before. How soon would you need to do this?"

"Oh, we're probably a year or more away I would guess, but we have to prepare a workable experiment and propose it to them to even be considered and get onto their calendar. I have a lot of work to get us there."

"And you're confident that you can do this?"

"Certainly. This is what I do. Once we know what we're trying to create in the lab, I can define the parameters and then devise a plan for the experiment." Foster smiled broadly, "This could be the missing element on the periodic table."

"The elusive ununpentium, element one-fifteen."

"Yes. We may very well be on the cusp of discovering an entirely new and unique element. It's terribly exciting!"

"Uh, I can see that," Lebreau was taken by Foster's childlike enthusiasm, hoping that those directing the whole production could quickly work up a plan "B" to take the new detour. "Let me make some phone calls."

Foster spent the rest of his morning reworking his research plan based on his new insight into the origins of the sample he was working with. The possibility of identifying and subsequently synthesizing a previously unknown element from another world was fantastic to him. He'd never dreamed that he'd ever have such an opportunity. A particle physicist's wildest dream.

But he also knew that he couldn't let his emotions and unfettered excitement cloud his thinking. As far as the research work was concerned, he needed to be as focused and sober as ever — for that particular project, perhaps even more so.

That afternoon Foster took the shuttle bus back to the Village, grabbed his bag at his apartment, and made his way to the Janet terminal per his new, weekly routine. The moment the 737 lifted off from Groom Lake, he dozed off and unexpectedly slept soundly through the stopover in Las Vegas right up until the plane landed in Burbank and the stewardess gently jostled his shoulder to rouse him.

His wife, Livvy, was waiting for him at the curb out in front of the Janet terminal building and greeted him with a kiss as he climbed into the car. She drove him home for a barbecue with their neighbor, Ted, and his girlfriend, Bambi. Foster wasn't really in the mood to endure Ted's bombastic personality or Bambi's unfiltered salacious rhetoric, but Livvy insisted that they were just trying to be good neighbors and that Ted had thought that, after a week away at work, the plane flight back home along with all of the associated logistics, he'd like to just kick back with a beer, a couple of burgers and some light conversation.

To be fair, the idea actually, fundamentally, appealed to him and, besides, she'd caught him in a really good mood just then. Livvy told him to just ignore the sketchy stuff and enjoy himself. He promised he'd do his very best — after a few beers, it would be easier to deal with the overtly inflated personalities of their new neighbors.

After unpacking the car and leaving his suitcase just inside the front door of the house, he and Livvy walked across the street to Ted's place. Bambi, in her customarily revealing, skin-tight wardrobe, greeted them cheerfully at the door in bare feet and led them through to the sliding patio doors at the back of the kitchen to the back yard where Ted was already getting the grill readied out on the patio.

"Denny!" he called out with a smile that showcased his glistening, white teeth as the three of them stepped down from the kitchen doors. He enthusiastically grabbed Foster's hand and gave a vigorous shake, "Did you have a nice flight?"

"Actually," Foster replied, recovering his hand and gently rubbing it to sooth the ache from such compressions. "I slept for most all of it. So I guess it was a nice flight."

"A rough week, eh? Well, grab yourself a beer out of the cooler and take a load off. I'll put the burgers on."

"Not rough, really. Just actually quite busy with a few late nights."

"Livvy, hon?" Bambi addressed, "You wanna glass o' wine?"

"Oh, that would be nice, thank you."

"Traffic in and out of the airport can have plenty of its own stresses," Ted commented to her. "Am I right?"

"Hmph," Foster grunted.

"Yeah, Ted," Livvy replied. "But I'm figuring out the ebb and flow of it all, where to go and how to thread through it. I'm getting pretty good at it, actually."

Bambi came back from the kitchen with a pair of wine glasses filled with red wine and handed one to Livvy. She took a sip and thanked her.

"So tonight's kind of a special occasion," Ted explained. "Won't be seeing Bambi around here too much for a little while."

"Oh no?" Foster quipped, not entirely disappointed by the news.

"She's been cast in a new movie. She'll be workin' up in Vancouver for a a month or so."

"It takes that long to film one of these, uh, 'movies'?"

"Well, actually, hon, they'll probably shoot enough footage for three or four flicks," Bambi explained. "This kinda film making is really economically efficient, don'cha know."

"I never knew," Livvy commented.

"I never cared," Foster grumbled.

"That must be a lot of lines to remember — for four whole movies!" Livvy diplomatically observed.

"Yeah, Ted and me are gonna practice some later. I got a copy of the script."

"There's a script?" Foster rhetorically asked.

"Gotta work on bein' able to talk with her mouth full," Ted chuckled. "If you know what I mean!"

"I'm afraid I do."

Livvy was becoming starkly aware that her husband, despite his previously good mood, was growing increasingly impatient with the base sort of subject matter already. She turned to Bambi and asked, "Can I help with anything in the kitchen?"

"Oh, sure, hon!" she replied. "Gotta get the salads outta the fridge."

"Great." The two women walked back into the house while Foster, slouched in a lawn chair with his feet up on a picnic table bench, and Ted at the grill were left to themselves out on the patio.

"So, Denny, I was thinkin', what are you gonna do with that race car of yours? Doesn't look like you've got much time to go racing these days."

"I'm not too sure. If this job works out like it looks like it will, I'll be too busy for any of that for at least a couple of years."

"You gonna pick it up again when this is all over — when the contract runs out?"

"The car probably won't be so competitive after all that time. Besides, it really shouldn't just be left parked in a garage unattended for that long. It needs to be taken care of."

"You gonna sell it?"

"Probably. I'm thinkin' of offering it to my friend, Luke, first."

"The guy you used to go racing with?" Ted quickly began scooping up each burger from the grill one by one and flipping them over.

"Yeah. It's not really something anyone can do alone — although I've seen some guys who do. If he can find another teammate or two to throw in with, he can just pick up in the season wherever they're at right now."

"Hope you give him a good deal."

"Oh, I will. But I'm sure gonna miss it."

"I can imagine. Tell me, what does Livvy think?"

"I guess she would miss it, too, but I think she'd be happy to get the other half of the garage back and me home weekends during the season."

"She's hot, Denny, a genuine babe. You're a lucky guy, you know."

"Oh, I know."

The women came back from the kitchen with the bowls of salads and set them out on the picnic table. The rest of the evening was pleasant enough. Ted and Bambi made an effort to reel back their usual, sordid subject matter and kept the conversation light.

Foster was obviously tired and after dinner he was beginning to have trouble keeping his eyes fully open and the alcohol in the beer was only making it worse. He was becoming even more of a social wet blanket than he normally was.

Livvy ultimately offered their wishes to their hosts for a good evening and excused themselves to return home and put her exhausted husband to bed. ∎

CHAPTER TWENTY

Contamination

Dennis Foster arrived at the particle laboratory early on Monday morning. He put on his white lab coat and got himself a few large pieces of blank paper and spread them out across an expanse of the counter near where Dr. Teller was typically found working among the various diagnostic machines and computers. He began to plot out the succession of tests that he would want to do based on the facilities available to him on site. Most of the tests, especially the first ones in his plan, were the same ones that Dr. McCaine had performed previously but with somewhat different parameters to search for somewhat different answers considering what he then knew about the origin of the sample.

He modified each test procedure to find the results he'd need to build a new hypothesis with all-new data, hoping to get them closer to an understanding of just what it was they were dealing with. Instead of trying to match results to any sort of known data, he would take the results at face value and work up a unique profile of the yet undefined ununpentium. He was working to develop a target to shoot at whenever he might get the opportunity to run an experiment at one of the world's largest and most respected super-collider facilities.

He was in the big league. There was no room for mistakes.

Long weeks of intensive work revisiting his predecessor's tests on the alien relic would be tedious and dull for most people, but Foster reveled in it all. He was truly in his element. A nerd in nerdville.

Dr. Teller was assigned to assist him throughout the process per their supervisor, Dr. Lebreau's, directive. As a nuclear physicist, she found the work at least interesting and, at times, particularly fascinating. The pair spent many long hours together over the succeeding weeks, alone, in the clean room. Sealed up in white, plastic hazmat suits with helmets, clear visors, gloves and booties on their shoes to prevent any sort of intrusion of stray radiation that might leak during their experiments.

The relic itself never left the glass isolation enclosure and was always handled remotely via the mechanical claws at the ends of the two robotic arms. Every precaution was taken in every session. Never did they become complacent knowing how lethally potent the sample they were studying could be if ever it were ever exposed to the air around them.

Foster and Teller had been preparing the next planned test for over two weeks, arranging everything inside the glass chamber in advance. The containment chamber was tightly sealed and secure and ready to begin work that morning.

They walked down the hallway together to the clean room and donned their protective suits, routinely checking to be certain that their respective radiation sensing pens were clearly visible to one another. Everything was checked and double-checked. Every seal was secured and nothing was overlooked.

When they were satisfied that all was ready, Teller punched in the code on the keypad and then pulled the lever on the vault-like door that would then open up into the clean room itself.

Carrying with them a couple of binders with their procedures laid out in detailed steps along with any other tools that they might have needed to bring with them from the lab, they walked inside, sealed the door behind themselves, and went about setting up to begin work.

Teller booted up the computer at the control panel behind where Foster would be standing at the large window as he manipulated the robotic arms inside the chamber. From her vantage point just a little off to his left, she would be able to see most of what he was doing outside and video cameras inside the enclosure showed live images on a pair of monitors in front of her.

Inside the enclosure, a broad, polished stainless steel pedestal had been set up with a few test probes to use in their experiment that Foster would pick up and manipulate with the claws. The probes would feed their readings back to Teller's computers.

He opened up the binder and laid it on the counter in front of himself, flipping it open to the page where the first steps of their first test were listed. Teller ran a last seal test on the chamber and, when all of the lights on her console had turned green, she initialized the program on the computer that they would be using to take the measurements in their test.

When she gave Foster a thumbs-up acknowledgement, he slipped his gloved hands into the controllers for the robotic claws to begin work.

Carefully, he reached one of the arms across to the airtight rack at the back of the enclosure and pulled open drawer number thirteen. He lifted out the small, metal containment box from the drawer and set it down at the center of the raised platform.

Holding the box in place with one of the claws, he used the other to unclip the latch on the front of it and then lift the cover up to reveal the glowing, triangular relic inside. For that particular test, the chip would not have to be removed from the box so he just hinged the lid all the way back to lie flat and out of the way.

"Alright, we're ready," he announced to Teller.

She tapped a few keys on the computer keyboard to set up the program to begin the test. After a minute or two, she was ready for him to start. "Okay, Dr. Foster, you can proceed."

With one of the claws, Foster lifted up a probe that was set out at the edge of the platform, its length sheathed in a long protective plastic tube clamped to the side of the table save for an awkwardly large, flat handle designed to be grasped by the mechanical claw. He clamped the pincers on it and pulled it up and out of its holster. He moved it directly over the sample, positioning it perpendicular to it and carefully aligning it using the images from the cameras that he could see on the monitors in front of him to be as precise as possible.

Slowly, he brought the tip of the probe straight down, closer to the metallic triangle. Teller read off the readings from her computer screen as it neared. The numbers increased gradually until he had brought the probe to within about a foot and then, from there on, they leapt upward quickly.

Foster was alarmed by the figures that were being called out to him from behind. He had expected a similar response but nothing of that scale, or that quickly. He slowed his approach, carefully bringing the tip of the probe ever closer until it was about an inch away from the sample's face.

"These results are not what I was expecting, Dr. Foster!" Teller called out from behind the computer terminal.

"I know," he replied. "This is far more potent than anyone had even guessed."

"Dr. McCaine never got this kind of response."

"I know. But he did this test differently, he was looking for something else entirely."

All of a sudden a loud buzzer began blaring in the room and red strobe lights began flashing, seemingly from every direction.

"What the hell is that?!" Foster called out. "A fire drill? Now?!"

"That's no fire drill, Dr. Foster!" Teller shouted back to be heard over the alarms, "We have a leak! We're exposed!"

He turned his head quickly and could see the radiation monitoring pen clipped to Teller's suit was flashing. With his helmet on, he couldn't see the one on his own suit, he reached down and slapped it against his chest with one hand, "Yes, Dr. Foster, you're exposed!"

"Yours is flashing, too!" He confirmed.

"We have to evacuate!"

"Not until I close this up. We can't risk any more exposure!"

Teller quickly began shutting down the computers, saving her results and closing everything in preparation to run for the door.

Foster slipped his hands back into the controllers and, as quickly as he was able, closed up the containment box with the sample inside, sealed the clasp, and then returned it to the airtight rack at the back of the enclosure. Once it was safely sealed shut, he pulled out his hands and waved to Teller to follow him to the door.

He grabbed the handle and pulled on it, but the door wouldn't move. He yanked on it a few more times but it was useless.

"Don't bother, Dr. Foster," Teller advised. "It's sealed up until the decon team gets here."

"You mean we're *trapped* in here?!"

"Not trapped, really, not permanently. There are protocols for this sort of thing. They're outside setting up in the hallway right now. Once they're ready, they'll open the door from the outside."

"How long is that gonna take?!"

"Not long…" Just at that moment, they could hear the clanking sound of the massive lock releasing and then watched as the door began to slowly swing open.

A man in a white hazmat suit wearing a rebreather pack on his back stood in the open doorway, "Dr. Foster? Dr. Teller?"

The pair waved and acknowledged him.

"Good, you're both still on your feet, that'll make this all easier. Please follow me."

They followed him through a tube made of clear plastic film that extended from a hard seal around the door frame from the clean room, through the outer room where they had suited up before entering, and out to an airtight plastic tent erected in the hallway up against the outer door. When they walked in, they found four plastic bins with hinged lids on them. A pair of attending technicians helped each of them remove their hazmat suits and drop each element into two of the bins. Then each was instructed to completely disrobe and place their clothing into the other two bins.

Teller just leered at Foster when they'd been given that direction.

"I won't look," he assured. "I promise."

He dragged the empty bin around to one side so that he could keep his back turned to her and then began unbuttoning his shirt. Item by item they each removed their clothing and dropped everything into the plastic bins. When they were both entirely naked save for their glasses, the technicians handed each of them a package in a clear plastic bag sealed with red and yellow striped tape that contained a sterile, white, terry cloth robe and a pair of plastic flip-flops.

They each tore open their respective bags and put on the robes as quickly as they could. They dropped the sandals onto the floor and slipped their bare feet into them. The technicians then handed each of them a plastic clamshell case for their eyeglasses.

"I can't see too well without these," Foster protested.

"I'm sorry, sir, but everything has to either be decontaminated or destroyed."

"Destroyed?"

"Hard items like your glasses, wallets, any money in your pockets — that sort of thing — will be decontaminated in a chamber kind of like an autoclave and returned to you. Soft items like clothing will be incinerated."

"But that's one of my favorite shirts!"

"I'm sorry, Dr. Foster. We've got to take radiation leaks like this very seriously."

"Hmph — I guess I understand."

A voice from outside the tent announced that they were ready for them. One of the technicians inside with them unzipped a panel on the side of the tent and a man on the outside directed both Foster and Teller to quickly exit the tent and climb into a plastic bubble on the back of a waiting golf cart and sit down. They both did as they were instructed, awkwardly trying to keep the fronts of their robes pulled closed and extended as far down their thighs as they could to maintain as much modesty in a compromising situation as possible.

The bubble was zipped closed and the cart began to roll away, down the hallway into the black-striped security zone. They rode past all of the hangar doors until the cart turned into a large room with a door wide enough to allow them to drive through and then seal them off from the hallway outside.

Inside the room were a few hazmat suited technicians waiting for them. Once the cart came to a stop, the plastic bubble was unzipped and the two scientists were helped out and onto their feet. One of the technicians told them to follow him to the showers.

They walked into another, separate room that was lined with glossy, light green tiles from floor to ceiling and corner to corner. Inside, there were six large shower stalls separated from one another by a tiled wall, open at the back with a tile-covered sill low enough to easily step over to enter. In the space where they were standing behind the showers was a row of hooks, benches and a few small tables. Behind and between the first two shower stalls stood a group of technicians at a table with a stainless steel tray on which were four syringes, two with a clear liquid in them, the other two with an amber colored fluid.

"You can hang your robes up there," one of the technicians pointed to the hooks on the back wall.

Standing in an open space, there was no opportunity for any sort of modesty except for the waist-high table between them. They each removed their robes and hung them up, trying their best to keep their backs turned to one another. Teller kept her arms crossed across her chest as they returned to the table with the syringes. Foster stood on one side of the table and Teller on the opposite side, each facing away from the other.

"Before we get you two into the showers," the technician explained as two others swabbed a small patch of skin on their respective left upper arms with an alcohol pad, "we need to give you a couple of preventive drugs. These will help to counteract any radiation exposure and hopefully prevent any organ damage."

"Hopefully?" Foster grumbled.

Each of them was stabbed in their left arms and injected with the clear drug first. Immediately afterwards, they were injected in their right arms with the amber colored drug. Then they were herded into each of the first two shower stalls.

For Teller, this was not new. She'd been working at the Facility for a few years by then and was familiar with the procedure. She'd had to go through the process once before — though that didn't make it any easier. But the fact that they could likely have been exposed to a deadly dose of the most powerful radiation ever known on earth made it begrudgingly tolerable knowing that it was a potentially life saving protocol.

Foster, on the other hand, had only read about it all in the hand-books he'd been given during orientation — dry, clinical descriptions that did little to prepare him for the real experience. He stood in the center of the tiled space directly over the metal drain in the floor, his feet spread wide apart, his arms outstretched and his chin lifted up. He closed his eyes tightly and then sucked in a deep breath and held it while he was sprayed down with almost scalding hot water from spray nozzles from every direction — above, below, in front, behind and at either side of him. When the hot water first hit his skin, he instinctively recoiled but then forced himself to keep his body as fully extended as possible.

After a few minutes of being wet down with water, the flow was shut off and two technicians with brushes on long poles stepped in and began scrubbing him vigorously from the top of his head to the soles of his feet with a foaming soap that strongly smelled like some kind of chemical solvent. They skipped over one small area in their otherwise intrusively thorough assault to spare him any undue discomfort. When they were done, one of them handed him a sponge that was dripping with the same foaming soap and nodded toward his previously unas-sailed crotch.

He stood for a moment and looked down.

"Radiation exposure can cause sterility and even testicular cancer,

Dr. Foster," the technician explained. "Be thorough, don't let a little embarrassment today cause bigger regrets later in life."

The man made sense. He and Livvy hadn't had much luck conceiving in the past but he didn't want to risk losing any chance at all for the future nor did he want to toy with the possibility of cancer so he took the sponge from the man and scrubbed himself in and around his crotch, being as thorough and forceful as he dared without hurting himself and then handed the sponge back to the technician.

"Alright, Dr. Foster, assume the same position — spread-eagle — time for the rinse cycle!"

He shrugged his shoulders and turned back around, faced the front wall and spread his feet and arms out to be blasted again with the hot water jets all around him. When he was completely rinsed off, one of the technicians handed him a large, thick, white towel to dry off with.

As he was burnishing himself dry, he looked up at the technician and asked, "Now what?"

"Debriefing and quarantine," the tech replied.

"Quarantine? For how long?"

"I don't know, sir. They'll fill you in on all that at the debriefing."

He was led back out to the open space behind the shower stalls. One of the technicians took the wet towel from him while another held up a clean, fresh robe for him to slip his arms into and then handed him a new pair of flip-flops — the ones they'd worn in from the clean room had been sealed up and taken away to be incinerated. As he was tying up the robe, Teller came out from the adjoining stall with her towel wrapped around her. He quickly turned around so that she would be able to don her own robe with some small shard of privacy.

They were each then told to take a seat in one of the two wheelchairs that were set there waiting for them. They were then rolled out through a door into a narrow hallway with several doors on either side. Everyone that he saw there were wearing a hazmat suit. He never saw any faces except through clear plastic visors.

Teller was rolled into a door on one side of the hallway, Foster was pushed just a little farther to a door on the other side. His wheelchair was rolled up to a door which was opened from the inside, then he was pushed inside and up to a small, metal table in the center of the room. There was a chair on the opposite side and a door in the center of the wall behind it. The technician who had rolled him in stood by to keep him company until another man, also in a white hazmat suit, walked in from the other door and set some papers and a small tape recorder down on the table.

"Dr. Foster," he addressed. "Good morning, I'm Jeffery Goss. I'll debrief you and then we'll get you a bed in the quarantine ward and make you as comfortable as we can."

"Uh, alright."

Goss pulled the chair out from the table and sat down across from him. He opened a folder and reached over to the tape recorder, stood it up in the center of the table between them and turned it on. "As you might imagine, it's difficult to write with these suits and clumsy gloves. I'll be recording this to transcribe later."

"Sure, that makes sense."

"So, Dr. Foster, for the safety of everyone who works in this Facility, we take every modern precaution. We know that we're dealing with things we don't yet understand, and so, try to be prepared for anything. When the unexpected happens, like this accident, we want to know everything we can about the details so we can improve our readiness and maybe prevent the same sort of thing from happening again."

"I understand."

"This is not about blame. I want to be upfront about that."

"Okay, I get it."

"Then let's start at the beginning. You and Dr. Teller had been preparing the tests that you planned to do today for some time, is that right?"

"It is. We'd been working at this project for the past few months."

"I'm no scientist, so please explain to me your procedure in laymen's terms."

"Hmmm, alright. Well, after planning things out on paper, we'd get together whatever equipment we'd need to perform the test and get it all set up inside the containment chamber which could take several days."

"So you're actually inside the chamber doing this?"

"Yes. Once the sample is exposed, the space inside there is toxic. We have to set it all up in advance, hook it all up to the computers, set up the parameters in all of the software that we'll be using and test everything to make sure it's all working properly. It's quite time-consuming, but if anything isn't right when we do the tests, we can't go in and fix it."

"And where is the radioactive sample while all of this is going on?"

"The sample is sealed inside of a small containment case that, in and of itself, shields its radiation from the outside. But that case is then stored inside a sealed compartment at the back of the chamber."

"Redundant protection."

"Yes."

"Okay, so you've got your tests all set up and the day that you'll actually do the experiments comes around — today — take me through that."

"We walked into the outer room, outside of the actual clean room, and put on our suits. We checked each other and made sure that our pens are visible to each other and all of the seals in the suit are closed and then punched in the pass code to open the door and go inside."

"This door is totally sealed."

"It is, like a bank vault with a thick, rubber gasket that seals it air-tight."

"And you made sure that it was latched behind you when you went inside."

"When you pull that door shut, the lock latches it closed and then some motors inside tighten it down all around the perimeter to make sure it has a tight, perfect seal."

"Really? I had no idea. So go on — you're inside the clean room."

"Well, we were both carrying whatever papers and notebooks that we'd need when we went inside. Dr. Teller walked over to the computer console with the video monitors and began to get things set up there. It's all planned.

"She booted up the computers, turned on the cameras, and opened up the programs that she'd need for the tests. Before we started anything, she ran a seal test — routine for this sort of environment. It showed all green lights for every seal.

"I walked up to the glass panel in front of the containment chamber and set down my binder, opened it up, and then powered up the robotic arms to begin working."

"So far, the sample is still sealed in the back of the chamber?" Goss asked.

"Right. The next thing that I needed to do was to get the sample out and set it up on a raised platform inside the chamber."

"You used those robotic arms to do that?"

"Yes. We never go inside, never even open the door. Once I had the case laid open, we were ready to begin the first test. When Dr. Teller told me that she was ready, I picked up the first probe with one of the claws and began to bring it in close to the sample. As I got it closer and closer, she was reading off the numbers that were being registered on the computer screen behind me and calling them out. That's when the alarms started going off."

"While you were doing that test?"

"Yes."

"Did you hit the sample with the probe?"

"No. The test didn't require any sort of actual contact, the probe only got to about an inch away from it. The plan was to get a little closer but when all hell broke lose, I put the probe back in its holder as quickly as I could and then closed up the sample and sealed it back in the rack so that no more radiation could leak from the chamber."

"It was already too late, though."

"For us, maybe, but I've never dealt with anything so powerful in my life and I knew that, if I'd left it out and we two were ushered away — as it turned out we were — it might continue to leak and contaminate the entire Facility. I didn't want to take any chances."

"But it was sealed inside that chamber."

"Which was already compromised, it would appear."

"Were you sure that, when you and Dr. Teller had been in there setting things up in the days before the test, you had closed and sealed the doors on your way out?"

"Yes, I'm sure."

"Well, obviously *something* failed."

"That's clear, but I can assure you that any doors or portals that we'd been using were secure when we were done."

"What about the robotic arms?"

"What about them?"

"Could radiation have somehow transmitted through the metal and leaked out into the room?"

"It doesn't work that way. Metal doesn't conduct radiation like it can electricity. But I suppose all the seals around the mechanism in the ceilings — around all the metal rods and wires and servos — could have worn over time. Maybe just enough to allow a small leak. Like I said, this is the heaviest element I've ever worked with, it probably wouldn't have taken much, just enough to set off the alarms."

"And you're absolutely sure that the doors you two had used to set up your tests were tightly sealed?"

"If you're trying to put the blame for this leak on the two of us — or just me — I can assure you that we are both professionals. We double and triple-check everything. We know full well the danger in dealing with radioactive materials, this one in particular. There's a reverent fear in our approach and meticulous attention to every detail, especially where it comes to safety precautions. If you're trying to write this off as 'human error,' you're barking up the wrong tree."

"If you're right, if the seals in that containment chamber have been compromised, we'll have to have them all replaced. Maybe even redesigned to be more effective. That will shut down the lab for weeks, maybe months."

"So you're trying to make it my fault to avoid having to spend the time and money to make those improvements? And what happens if you're wrong? What happens if you just brush this aside as being our fault and we continue with things the way they are in there today? You could be looking at a much more catastrophic event. *Lives are at stake, man!*"

"I understand, Dr. Foster, I do."

"Then take my word for it. Have someone go in there and inspect all of those seals. Make sure they're not worn or that they haven't compressed from use to no longer make tight contact or maybe dried out over time and formed small cracks — it doesn't take much. Dr. Teller and I have plenty to keep us busy in the meantime while you're making sure that your equipment doesn't kill us."

"That's a pretty stark way to put it."

"This is not the time to play politics, Mr. Goss." ∎

CHAPTER TWENTY-ONE

Exposure

Dennis Foster, still wrapped in a white terry cloth robe and sitting in a wheelchair, was rolled into what looked for all intents and purposes to be a civilian hospital emergency ward with several curtain-enclosed spaces sectioned off along one side of a long room. Each cordoned off space was set up with a hospital bed at its center, a counter along the back wall and innumerable panels of sockets, connections and cables arrayed across each wall within easy reach of a nurse or technician who might stand at either side of the bed.

As he was rolled down the center aisle, he noticed that all of the beds that he'd passed were empty.

All of the handful of people he saw in the room, including the technician that was pushing his wheelchair, were wearing white containment suits just like all of the others that he'd already encountered since the alarms had first sounded in the clean room.

As they reached the end of the room, the last bed was encircled by a curtain and he could hear voices talking from behind it. There was a nurse and another technician waiting for him in the adjacent space just before it, suited up like everyone else with the exception of wearing surgical gloves instead of the bulky ones that normally attached to the sleeves of those protective suits.

The technician stopped the wheelchair and set the brakes while one of the others pulled the curtain closed around them. The bed had been turned down for him and the nurse helped him up from the chair and then handed him a johnny coat.

He took the folded scrap of fabric from her and looked down at it, "Seriously?"

"I'm sorry, Dr. Foster, but it's protocol."

"Can I at least keep the robe?"

"Yes, there's a hook back here. You can put it on whenever you need to go to the lavatory or we need to take you out for any tests that might need to be done."

"Hmph...alright." Begrudgingly, he removed the robe and threw it across onto the bed and then slipped on the johnny coat, awkwardly trying to tie the cords in the back.

"Here," the nurse said from behind the plastic face shield of her suit, "let me help you."

He sighed as he surrendered any remaining bit of his dignity and turned his back to her so she could tie up the back of the garment for him.

Realizing that any attempt at modesty at that juncture was entirely futile, he hopped up onto the bed and swung his legs around to stuff his feet under the folded bedcovers at the base of the mattress. He sat upright and took a moment to straighten out the fabric of the johnny coat and then the nurse unfurled the covers up to his waist.

"Comfortable?" she asked as she raised the end of he bed behind his head and then grabbed one of the pillows behind him and lifted it up for him to settle in.

"Under the circumstances, I suppose so," he answered with a deflated tone as he lowered himself down.

The technician then told him to lift up his arms and then untied one of the cords under his armpit that connected the sleeve and opened up a panel down the side of the johnny coat. Without a word of explanation, he reached in under the fabric and stuck adhesive sensors to a few places on his chest. He then removed a bundle of cables out from a drawer under one of the monitoring machines behind him and connected each of the leads to the sensors. The nurse then retied the cord of the johnny coat for him.

He was then instructed by the technician to extend his left arm and make a fist.

"What's this for?" Foster asked.

"Intravenous line, sir. To keep you hydrated and allow us to introduce any sort of drugs in an emergency."

Defeatedly and without any more questions, he did as he was told. He reached out his left arm and laid it out flat alongside himself on the bed. He clenched his fist and the man then inserted the needle into the crook of his elbow, taping it over to keep it in place. "That should do it, Dr. Foster."

He breathed a sigh of relief as the tubing from his arm was then connected to a bag of clear fluid hung from a pole behind his left shoulder. The wires from his chest were then plugged into color-coded sockets on the front panel of a machine on a rolling stand and then, when the machine was turned on, it began to make quiet, regular beeping sounds. The screen illuminated with a glowing, bright green graph of fine vertical lines on a black background with four thicker horizontal lines that extended out from the left, punctuated by a small, bright dot at their ends near the center. The graph moved slowly across the screen from right to left while the lines tracked various wavy paths across it. One of the lines moved in vigorous up and down spikes that appeared to be showing his heartbeat.

Once the technician was satisfied that everything was connected and working as it should be, he and the first technician who had wheeled him into the ward left with the wheelchair. The nurse then explained to him that he couldn't get out of bed for any reason without help. She showed him the button for the nurses' station and told him to push it to get someone to come out. She then showed him the controls to raise and lower the sections of the bed to make himself comfortable.

As she began to walk away, he asked, "So there are only two of us in here?"

"This ward is for emergencies like this, radiation exposure in particular. We're prepared for a much bigger group and much worse circumstances. We'd much rather have the place altogether empty but just a couple at a time is way better than what we drill for."

"Who's the other guy in the next bed? Was there another accident?"

"No, just the one. That's your colleague, Dr. Teller."

"This isn't the men's ward?"

"We don't have multiple wards, Dr. Foster — this is it. We like to think that we're all grown-ups in here and the crises that anyone may be dealing with are distraction enough. Besides, there are cameras everywhere. We watch everything."

He glanced up over the foot of his bed and saw a video camera mounted to the ceiling, its lens pointed down directly at him.

"These machines are also connected to monitors in the nurses' station which is manned twenty-four-seven. We keep very close tabs on our patients. We haven't lost one yet."

"Hopefully we won't break your streak."

"Hopefully." She smiled, although he couldn't see her expression through the plastic visor, then turned to leave and grabbed the edge of the curtain, "Would you like this open or closed?"

"Uuuh, open, I suppose. Probably won't be so claustrophobic and boring as staring at the same patterns in the curtain for hours."

She smiled and then pulled the curtain back, opening the front of the space to the busyness of the rest of the room. Before leaving, she asked if he'd like something to help relax him, to maybe get some sleep.

"I don't think so, thanks. I have a lot to think about. Don't want to waste this time."

"Alright then. You just relax, buzz us if you need anything. We'll check in on you from time to time — be seeing you."

"Thanks."

The nurse walked away. From his vantage point, propped up in the hospital bed, he could see the empty room beyond with all sorts of carts of electronic equipment parked in their designated places along the opposite wall, a couple of folded up wheelchairs kept at the ready and the occasional person walking past in their protective white suits.

Unlike any hospital that he'd ever visited, there was an overriding silence. No soft music, no blaring public address announcements, no one being paged, no loud beeps, buzzes or bells. Just quiet with the barely audible, rhythmic sounds of the monitors next to his bed.

He could hear rustling from the bed behind the curtain to his right, "Dr. Teller?" he quietly asked.

No response.

"Dr. Teller? Is that you?"

Still no response.

"Doctor?"

Finally a reply, "In case you haven't figured it out with your stratospheric IQ, I'm not interested in any sort of conversation — certainly not with you."

"You're not talking to me? I'm sorry, I didn't mean for all of this to happen. You know this isn't because of anything either of us did wrong."

"You don't get it, do you?"

"Get it? I guess not. What's this about?"

"I've never felt so violated in all my life."

"Violated?"

"Having to take off all my clothes in front of strangers."

"And that's my fault?"

"No, but you didn't have to gawk at me — *damned pervert!*"

"What?! I wasn't gawking at you!"

"I could feel your eyes all over me. It was disgusting."

"You're imagining things. I was too busy being roughed up and pushed around — as I assume you were as well — to even think about that sort of thing. Besides, I tried my best to keep my back to you so I wouldn't have to look at you at all."

"You don't want to look at me? Why? You think I'm ugly?"

"Oh, for cryin' out loud! No, I don't think you're ugly!"

"How would you know if I'm ugly or not if you hadn't taken a good look?"

"I got a glimpse, to be truthful — okay? But just an *accidental glimpse* — for a split second — before I could turn away. I was caught by surprise, but my attentions were thoroughly monopolized by everything else that was happening at that moment."

"So you *did* look. You saw me naked."

"For a nanosecond, to be completely honest — yes."

"Pervert!"

* * * * *

That was the first weekend that Foster had to spend away from his wife. The quarantine would last for five days. Having to spend those days in the same room quarantined next to the frosty, accusatory Teller with just a thin panel of fabric between them, they were ponderously long days indeed. He pined for the day that he'd be released and allowed to fly home.

It was also the first time he'd ever intentionally lied to his wife. He had been evading certain topics thus far but never came out and told her an out-and-out lie. He couldn't tell her why he was having to stay "at work" so he made something up. Something simple. She had a vague idea of the nature of his work so he just told her that he was working on an experiment and couldn't walk away from it just yet. He had to stay and see it through. In a way, it was sort of true. She'd heard that explanation before but, when he was at Cyberdyne Technologies, it typically meant that he'd just be late for dinner. With his profound apologies, she said she understood, told him again that she loved him, and would miss him until he could come home the following Friday. He didn't say anything but sincerely hoped that he'd be released before then.

He had gotten a message out to Lebreau who brought him a stack of his notebooks and other references that he had asked for so that he could at least continue some of his work from the hospital bed and not have to endure the sensation of ice cold, seething anger radiating from the other side of the curtain without, at least, the distraction of work. Perhaps he might even get something accomplished during his unfortunate period of incarceration. Maybe the the time wouldn't be entirely wasted.

On the following Tuesday evening, he and Teller were finally released from quarantine and allowed to go back to their respective apartments at the Village. They were each given some basic underwear, surgical scrubs and slip-on canvas shoes to be able to walk away dressed well enough to be seen in public. They were also handed zip-sealed plastic bags with their decontaminated personal effects.

Teller made a bee-line to the bus stop to catch the next shuttle out to the Village but Foster had an armful of books and papers that he wanted to leave on his desk before he left. He'd take care of that task first and then catch the next shuttle in an hour.

No homework for that evening. He knew that once he got to his apartment, all he'd be interested in doing would be taking a hot shower and putting his feet up with a beer for a while. But before any of that, he'd call Livvy just to hear her voice and catch up with her. To let her know that he was okay because he knew that she'd worry. Finally, he'd turn in early for a decent night's sleep in a familiar bed. ■

PHASE 5
THE HOOK

CHAPTER TWENTY—TWO

Apologies

The rest of the week after having been released from quarantine was, in a word, a drag. Foster had a really hard time getting and staying focused on his work. The twice-a-day visits of a nurse from the infirmary to draw a blood sample to monitor his recovery from being exposed in the accident were glaringly distracting — and a little painful. He really didn't like needles. It was all so intrusive into his normal thought processes.

Teller was distant and curt to him and he made sure to give her as much space as possible but didn't feign from telling her what he needed her to do as his assistant although he couched it all as congenial, professional requests rather than taking on any tone that might be in any way perceived as orders. He tried to soften the atmosphere a little bit and show her some overt respect, even if it might have sounded a bit over-the-top.

She seemed to respond well to that approach and the two were able to work together again with certain understood boundaries and no more words between them than absolutely necessary.

He didn't bring any work back to his apartment in the evenings, either. He was mentally and emotionally exhausted each day and only wanted to get a bite of take-out dinner at the commissary to eat alone in his apartment and ultimately turn in early each night.

Thursday evening, his wife Livvy called to tell him that the next day she wouldn't be able to pick him up at the airport. She would have to work the whole day at the dress shop as the woman who normally would take the afternoon shift hadn't shown up for work for a few days without calling. Alma, the shop's owner, presumed that she had quit. She asked if there was any way that Livvy could stay on Friday, typically one their busiest of the week. She called to ask if it would be alright for him to get a cab home from the airport that day.

He knew that it was always a possibility that she'd need to do that and one day he'd likely have to get his own ride home. Though he was anxious to see her after the singularly difficult couple of weeks he'd just been through, he agreed. She promised him that they'd do something fun on Saturday to make up for it. The thought made him smile for the first time in several days. He'd look forward to spending time with her as soon as he could.

Working Friday morning in the lab was stressful with Teller's overtly dark countenance. She cast an oppressive, icy pall over the entire department. All of his co-workers kept their distance from her and none of them spoke to her. He avoided her as much as possible — as he'd been doing ever since they'd been released from quarantine. He was just going through the motions on autopilot, watching the clock and ready to bolt out the door at noon for the terminal and that much-anticipated flight out of Area Fifty-One to get home.

In Burbank, it was raining lightly when the plane landed. He hailed a bright yellow cab at the curb out in front of the Janet terminal building. The cabbie, a friendly young man with a thick middle-eastern accent, carried on a light and energetic conversation with him as he brought him to his driveway. He pulled the cab up as far as he could to keep Foster from having to walk in the rain any farther than necessary. He paid the driver before getting out of the dry car, quickly grabbed his suitcase out of the trunk, and dashed through the drizzle to the front door to let himself in.

In the quiet, empty house, he set his suitcase down at the foot of the stairs. He was alone with his thoughts. That wasn't a good thing, and he knew it. He didn't want to dwell on the negative and without Livvy there, that's just where his mind kept drifting off to. He wanted to enjoy his time at home compartmentalized away from the concerns of the job, especially once she got back from work in a few hours so they could enjoy a quiet, pleasant evening together.

His first thought was his stomach — he hadn't had a thing to eat since a quick English-muffin breakfast sandwich that morning. It was just after two o'clock and he was feeling the pangs so he carried his suitcase to the basement door and set it down there while he continued into the kitchen to make himself a sandwich. Livvy had made a pitcher of iced tea that he'd found in the refrigerator so he poured himself a glass, put a couple of ice cubes into it, and then sat at the breakfast counter to eat.

He turned on the radio so the house wouldn't seem so empty and quiet while he ate. He got to thinking of whatever he might do with himself until his wife got home later. He had a few hours to kill and didn't want to just sit like a lump on the sofa watching Judge Wapner or something equally as intellectually void. As he finished up his sandwich, he got the bright idea that it would be a good time to finally go out to the garage and work on cleaning up the race car and putting away all of the tools and equipment that he and Luke had unloaded after their last race together and just left in there.

He wistfully thought that that day was almost a lifetime ago. Maybe, when he was done, he'd call Luke and tell him to just come and get the car and get back out there with it. If his friend was waiting for him to go racing again, it might never happen.

He finished his lunch, rinsed out the glass in the sink, and then brought his suitcase down to the basement to toss all of his clothes into the washing machine not taking any care for whites, coloreds, or things that should be washed in either hot or cold water. He realized that he'd be putting on his race day grubbies to go work out in the garage so he stripped off his shirt and pants, emptied all of the pockets, and tossed them in as well. Once the washer started its first cycle, he grabbed up his empty suitcase and climbed the stairs in his underwear to put on his "Quantum Racing" denim shirt and a pair of well-worn blue jeans to get to work.

He walked out into the garage through the door from the kitchen. The first bay was empty, normally occupied by Livvy's car when she was home. He flipped on the overhead fluorescent lights and then pushed the button for the second garage door to open up and let in even more light from outside to work by. With the sounds of the whirring electric motor and the clanks of the metal wheels riding along in the tracks, the door slowly rose up to reveal his own pickup truck, glistening wet in the rain, parked just outside that second bay where the race car resided.

He turned on the radio that sat on a shelf above his workbench and then walked slowly around the car. It was a bittersweet moment for him. So much excitement and joy that he'd experienced campaigning that car in race after race with his friend. They were best friends, a real team the two of them — three of them, if one were to consider the car as well. Whether it was his turn to drive or to do the timing and scoring from the pits, it was always such a thrill contending for the win. Every once in a while they would take one of the top three places as all of the trophies on the shelves in their respective living rooms would attest. It would be hard to let go, but Luke could continue to enjoy those moments while he worked in a secret laboratory in the desert with extraterrestrial spacecraft.

The first thing he did was to jack up the car and remove all four wheels and stack them up at the back of the garage out of the way. It was all part of an oft-practiced, post-race ritual.

Likewise, he removed the engine cover, the nose and a few other body panels that were designed to be routinely taken off to expose the inner workings of the car for maintenance and repairs. Stripped of much of its blue and green skin, he stood there and looked at the polished aluminum underneath and exposed engine behind the cockpit. It brought a lump to his throat.

"Hey, neighbor!" a familiar voice called out from the driveway. It was Ted.

His thoughts interrupted, Foster turned his head to see him walking around the pickup truck and stop just inside the open garage door. He was carrying an umbrella and paused to fold it down as he walked inside.

"Hey, Ted." Foster replied with a mix of annoyance at his appearance at his door and that of welcome for the man's company.

"So this is it, huh? This is your race car?" He set the umbrella down out of the way to drip-dry.

"Yeah, this is it."

"Looks like it's broken or something. Did you crash it your last time out?"

"No, I just took some of the body panels and the wheels off of it to do some maintenance and cleaning — routine stuff. We just parked it here after that last race. It's been sitting here since then."

"Oh. I've never seen the inside of a race car before. Looks a lot different than under the hood of my Caddy."

"I'm sure it does."

"I saw the cab come by and drop you off earlier. Livvy didn't pick you up this week?"

"No, she has to work at the dress shop this afternoon."

"I thought you'd like some company." Looking over the race car as Foster began some basic maintenance, he asked, "Can I help?"

"I can't believe I'm saying this but I'd just appreciate you hanging around to talk with. I've had a pretty tough week."

"I don't suppose you can talk about it much — being secret and all that."

"No, you're right. But it's not so much the work, just some personality issues. Why don't you tell me about what you're up to these days. You working on a picture somewhere?"

"Oh, yeah. We've been shooting up in the canyons for the past few weeks. Nice to be working closer to home — able to come home nights, sleep in my own bed."

"That's nice. Hey, in that refrigerator over there, grab us a couple of beers — would you?"

Ted looked around and saw an old, round-topped refrigerator against the back wall of the garage painted in international racing orange and peppered with race sponsor stickers, he smiled and replied, "Sure!"

* * * * *

Over the next week, Foster worked late into the evenings at his apartment in the Village at Groom Lake. He'd sit with some of Dr. McCaine's notes and a few sheets of blank paper spread across his coffee table playing some of his favorite jazz records on the stereo with the volume turned down so that the apartment wouldn't seem to be so starkly quiet.

Before the contamination and quarantine and the weight of Teller's attitude afterwards, he found that his usual love of absolute silence as he worked caused him to feel uneasy, fidgety. He needed some sort of background sound. Nothing loud or raucous, just the radio or a record on the turntable playing softly was enough. Just so that his brain wasn't so apt to wander off into dark places as he found it had a penchant of doing those days.

Sitting at the edge of the cushion of his sofa and leaning over the table, he made some sketches on the papers and quickly jotted down some notes in a spiral-bound notebook that he had in his lap as he leaned over the table. Alternately, he would sketch out something and then make a note in the pages on his lap. The sketches helped him visualize what he needed to do for the tests that he would need to pursue.

Finally one morning, he approached Dr. Lebreau, "Good morning, Brian."

"Good morning, Dennis," Lebreau responded as he looked up from his computer screen.

"I was hoping I could talk with you about some tests that I need to do."

"Oh? Certainly," he looked back down at his computer and quickly hit a few keys to save what he had been working on. When he stood up, he grabbed his coffee mug and suggested, "Tell you what, let me refill my mug and we can head over to the lounge — Kyle is making a lot of racket over there this morning, it's a little difficult to concentrate."

Foster smiled, he had been thinking the same thing but, being the "new guy," didn't want to complain. As they walked past his own desk on the way to the coffee machine, he snatched up his mug along with one of his notebooks with a number of his sketches stuffed between the pages. The two each poured themselves fresh cups before heading off to the lounge across the hall.

Once inside, Lebreau set his mug down on one of the tables and pulled out a chair to sit down. Foster set all of his papers down on the table across from him and sat.

"So, Dennis, what have you got in mind? You know, you don't need my permission to do any of your experiments. I appreciate you keeping me in the loop, though."

"Oh, I know. But some of what I need to do is going to need some specialized equipment that I'm not finding in either lab. I'm hoping we either have them in storage somewhere or parked in some remote corner around here or, if not, you can get for me."

"We have a pretty comprehensively equipped lab. What more is it that you need?"

"For one, a slicer."

"A slicer? What do you need to slice?"

"I want to bisect the sample to analyze it molecularly."

"You'll have to forgive me, Dennis. I'm the manager of this department, I'm just here as the cat-herder and paper-pusher. I don't necessarily understand what any of you geniuses do in there."

"Ha, ha! Well, what I need to do is slice off a narrow chunk of the sample and then shave it down into molecule-thin slices to then examine through an electron microscope and do other tests like spectral analyses. I'll need to get it into a cloud chamber, too."

"Don't we have that equipment already? Kyle and Richard use that stuff in their work."

"Well, some of it, but it's not remotely controlled."

"Remotely...? Oh, so that you can operate it inside the containment chamber."

"Right. We need to be able to isolate them inside and operate them with the computers — or bring in other computers if the ones we have in the clean room aren't compatible."

"Sounds expensive."

"Yeah, I suppose it will be. But if we're going to be able to synthesize this element, we need to know everything about it, every characteristic, every chemical response and isotope. Dealing with earthly elements, there are certain known quantities and things that we can relate our results to. With this sample, it's a complete unknown. We have no benchmarks to align with."

"I suppose that makes sense. What do you need?"

Foster flipped open his notebook and tore out a page with a list that he had compiled the night before. He reached across the table and handed it to Lebreau. He looked over the list and, while his eyes were still reading across each line, he commented, "I was right. This is going to be expensive."

"You told me when I started here that we had a pretty limitless budget."

"We do," He looked up at Foster with a grin. "I'll make some calls. We may have some of this at Wright-Patt in storage. I'm not sure where one could go to purchase some of this stuff but we have procurement experts who can ferret that out for us."

"That's great. How long do you think that will take?"

"Honestly, I have no idea. I know you're anxious but, remember, we're dealing with the government here. They essentially have only two speeds: slow and slower."

"Oh, I know."

"But I promise I'll get right on it and once I know who's going to procure what, I'll keep on them."

"That's all I can ask, I guess. You'll keep me apprised?"

"Sure. I'll let you know as soon as I do."

* * * * *

Crews from Lockheed's Skunkworks came into Facility R-Four-Seven and, with help from technicians and tradesmen of the Army Corps of Engineers, stripped away all of the soft rubber seals in every orifice inside and leading into the clean room, putting on a weeks-long show of making sure that another so-called accident would not be possible. In a meeting with Lebreau, Foster, Teller, Facility director Hidleman and Major Albertson, they were told that the rubber seals had worn down over time and were no longer making solid contact with one another. It was just a matter of time before an accident would happen. Fortunately, it wasn't any worse than it was thanks to the quick actions of Foster sealing up the sample before he and Teller evacuated.

They would replace all of the seals with slightly fatter ones that would compress down tighter and were made of a more durable synthetic rubber that had been developed for NASA to use in the Shuttle program.

Work in the clean room could safely continue with Foster's tests on the highly radioactive alien relic as he had planned.

Those weeks were otherwise fairly routine — routine for working on studying an alien technology for which almost nothing was really routine. Flying in from home on Sunday afternoons, five days of working in the labs, and then flying back to his wife on Fridays. He had quickly adapted to the lifestyle and Livvy did her best to adapt as well. She faithfully picked him up at the airport each week and dropped him off again to catch his flight to somewhere unknown with a loving kiss good-bye.

Her curiosity would never be satisfied but, knowing the secretive nature of his work, she refrained from asking too many questions and understood when he would apologize for being unable to give her any sort of answers. After the years of marriage they'd shared, a certain unqualified trust existed. As a couple, they were uniquely prepared to cope with the unusual circumstances that many other marriages and relationships might be strained under.

Foster showed up for work on a Friday morning, typically a short work day to accommodate weekly commuters like himself to catch flights out later in the afternoon to go home for the weekend. As he walked into the lab, he took his white lab coat down from the hook just inside the door and pulled it on. He transferred his radiation sensing pen from the pocket of his shirt to the pocket of the lab coat where it would be visible at a glance.

He said good morning to his co-workers and made his way to his desk where he set down and opened his briefcase, unloaded all of the papers and books that he'd brought home to work on the previous evening, and then slipped it underneath the desk to its customary place for the day, out of the way.

Teller walked over to meet up with him at the coffee machine, something she'd never done before.

"Good morning, Dr. Teller," he tenuously greeted as she neared. Holding up an empty coffee cup, he asked, "Can I get one for you?"

"Oh, no, thank you. I'm still working on the cup I got at the dining hall this morning."

"Okay," He turned and set his mug down to pour himself a cup of black coffee. Since taking on the intense position at the lab, he found he much preferred the strong taste and no longer added cream or sugar.

"Can we talk?"

"Isn't that what we're doing right now?"

"I mean in private. I need to talk with you about something."

Knowing her abrasive attitude toward him since he'd begun working there and especially since the accident in the clean room and her accusations that followed — and convinced that she was at least a little less than entirely sane — he reluctantly agreed.

"Can we go to the lounge for a minute? Just for a minute."

"May I bring my coffee?"

She smiled, "Sure."

Smiling was something that he hadn't seen her do very often. He suspected that there was some ulterior motive in her invitation but, nevertheless, with his unspoken reservations he followed her down the hall to the lounge. She had a somewhat different tone to her voice and her face seemed a bit more relaxed than it had for the previous few weeks. He was hoping that whatever they would be discussing would help to ease the tension between them but still couldn't help but be suspicious.

Once inside, he noticed that there was no one else in the room — they were alone. He was immediately uncomfortable with the situation, there were so many reasons that the situation could go so terribly wrong.

He expected that he'd been lured into a trap, that she was about to unload both barrels at him, calling him a pervert (among other things) and maybe even take a swing at him. Any fragile professional relationship that may have still existed between them could be thoroughly shattered. He wasn't prepared to deal with any of that and so made sure that he remained between her and the door to facilitate a quick exit if necessary.

"Look, Dr. Teller," he defensively began. "I came here to work in the discipline that I've been trained in, as a particle physicist with years of experience, to analyze that radioactive chip in there. I'm not here to chase women or make your life miserable. I'm married — *very happily* married. And though you might be a very attractive..."

She cut him off, "Dr. Foster — Dennis — I wanted to get you alone in here to *apologize* — that's all."

"Apologize? For what?"

"For accusing you and being a perfect bitch these past few weeks. I read too much into what happened and spent all this time just being angry at you for no reason. I finally realized that it was really all me, nothing about you. I realize, too, that you tried your best to be professional about it all, a gentleman. I just wanted to take a little time, in private, to say that...and to say that I'm sorry for all of it. I clearly overreacted."

Stunned and caught somewhat off guard, he fumbled and replied, "Uh, I appreciate that — it's alright."

"No, it's *not* alright, and I intend to be a bit less standoffish. I'll try anyway. That six foot rule of mine? Let's make that three from now on — that okay?"

"It's a good start."

"Just be patient with me. The work we're doing here is far too important to let these sorts of personal issues get in the way. Am I right?"

She reached out her hand to him. He looked down at it for a quick moment and then reached out and grasped it, careful not to grip it too tightly, and shook it.

"Oh, I totally agree." ■

CHAPTER TWENTY–THREE

Shock and Awe

Foster got off of the shuttle bus from his apartment in the Village on Thursday morning — just another work day at a most unique sort of job. The ride along that gravel, desert road for an hour or so was the one thing that he never really got used to but, per his daily routine once he'd arrived, he walked down the long hallway, stopping at each of the security desks along the way, to get to the red zone where the lab was located. The guards in the camouflage fatigues knew him well by then, smiled and wished him good morning by name, but still had to inspect the contents of his briefcase and pass a metal-sensing wand over him before allowing him to pass deeper into the mountain Facility.

He used his key to unlock the door to the lab to avoid disturbing anyone who might already be working inside and walked in, set down his briefcase and put on his white lab coat. He clipped the radiation sensing pen into the coat's outer pocket — being all the more cognizant of it since the accident weeks earlier — and went to his desk saying "good morning" to each of his co-workers that he'd passed along the way.

Teller, as was her habit, was already there. She was already at the counter in the corner with her cup of take-out coffee deeply engaged in a project on the computer in preparation for a series of tests that she and Foster were planning to do in the clean room later that morning.

"Good morning, Jennifer," he said as he walked up from behind her with his own coffee in hand.

She stopped her work at the keyboard, took a deep breath and then sat straight up. After a moment's pause, she reached up to her reading glasses and slid them off of her face and then turned in her chair with a forced smile and greeted him, "Good morning, Dr., uh, *Dennis*. How are you this morning?"

He could tell that she was making an effort to be congenial and appreciated her doing so. It was already making for a much more relaxed working environment and he realized that it was not natural for her. "Doing really well this morning. Looking forward to getting back into the clean room this morning. I'm anxious to see what results we get from this next round of tests. I think these will tell us a lot."

"I'm getting all of the parameters programmed right now. I should be ready in about an hour."

"That's perfect. I have some numbers to run from last night and I should be done at just about the same time."

"Oh, good," Dr. Lebreau's voice said as he walked up to them from behind, "you're both still here. I got the word that the team in Hangar Three is inviting us all in to see a demonstration this morning. You gonna be free at around ten?"

"Uhh," Foster began to reply, about to beg off, not wanting to interrupt his much-anticipated next tests.

"I'm sure we can be here," Teller interrupted. She turned to Foster and explained, "I've been working with the Hangar Three team on applications, to try and get some of this alien technology to work again within our own earthly understanding. I've done a lot on the circuitry and shielding design for this."

"They're going to use one of those chips for something?"

"They've been trying to get one of them to fly," Lebreau excitedly added.

"Fly? That's *huge*."

"It is," Teller continued. "Worth postponing our test for a few hours or, maybe even, a couple of days. What d'you say?"

"If they can make one of these things fly, I want to be there to see it. Besides, considering what we're doing on this end, it might even be helpful in our own research to see how they do it."

"Inspiring, if nothing else," Lebreau quipped. "Ten o'clock, then. We'll all meet here at about quarter-to and walk back there together. You don't all have black security stripes so you'll have to come with me."

Foster grinned like a little kid and confirmed, "We'll be here. Wouldn't miss it for the world."

The next hour and a half seemed to be an eternity as Foster and Teller continued their work with one eye on the clock the whole time.

Finally, he saw the others in the lab gathering by the door so the pair got up from their respective keyboards to join them.

Like a mother hen leading her chicks, Lebreau walked down the hallway past the last checkpoint with his team and then turned right when they got to the perpendicular hallway at the end. Six massive, steel doors were spaced along the length of the hall on their left. The first two led into Hangar One, the second pair led into Hangar Two where Foster and Teller had seen two of the spacecraft weeks before, and farther down the hall the last two doors led into Hangar Three. By the time Lebreau and his team had arrived, there were already about a dozen others loitering in the hall waiting to be let inside.

Among those waiting was Director Hidleman who, when she saw them approaching, turned and greeted Lebreau and those that had come along with him. She looked at Teller and said, "You must be pretty excited about this."

"I can't tell you, ma'am. Years of work and finally a breakthrough."

"This one's a giant leap, to coin a phrase. If they succeed today, your research, Dr. Foster, becomes all the more important."

"I can see that. Working backwards, as it were. Application first, then the power source."

"'Reverse engineering' we call it. The more we dissect their technology and understand it, the better we can understand all that we're dealing with here — including that chip of yours."

With a clanking sound that echoed off of the solid block walls of the hallway, the door to the hangar opened and a man in a blue jumpsuit stepped outside holding it open and announcing that it was alright to enter then — and to stay behind the barriers for their own safety once they got inside.

Stepping into the expansive hangar, there was a relatively small area just inside the door cordoned off with a rectangle of yellow saw horses strung together with yellow caution tape. It was pretty clear that they were not allowed to venture beyond that line.

In the farthest corner of the hangar sat the alien saucer. It looked almost identical to the one that he'd previously seen in Hangar Two. The most notable difference was that it had no landing gear under it. Instead, it rested in a circular, steel stand a few feet high like a soft-boiled egg nested into an egg cup. Around it were four large yellow supports with broad pads on the ends of them that braced against the underside of the ship.

Several cables and tubes extended from various open ports scattered around the ship's surface, a few draping down from the upper surfaces, the rest from its underside, and led to a control console and a row of small trailers and large, gray boxes on the walls behind it. A group of technicians in blue coveralls were busy making last minute adjustments, checking all the cables and the controls on the various machines on each of the trailers and connected machines.

Standing closest to the saucer were four men in white containment suits with headgear, visors and air tanks on their backs. They were checking all of the connections on the ship itself, squatting down underneath and climbing up onto step ladders to check the connections on the upper side.

"In a few minutes we'll power up the ship. Once we do that, you will not be able to leave. The doors to the hallway will lock and seal in case of a radiation leak," the man in the overalls standing with the group by the door explained. "As you all know, we are dealing with technologies that we know very little about and, if this experiment goes wrong, this room may be flooded with radiation. If anyone wants to leave, now is the time. Those who stay, please be sure you're wearing your pens and keep an eye on them — just in case."

Sobering warnings, but taken to heart. Everyone in the Facility had heard about the accident in the clean room. Two or three people took the man's warning to heart and left before the experiment began but the rest remained. He then handed out goggles to everyone remaining with admonition to put them on as the test was about to begin.

The area that they were corralled into was small but there was still enough space for everyone there to spread apart and get a good, clear view of the saucer. As they watched, they heard someone call out for the ropes to be manned. Attached to four points around the disk were heavy ropes attached to the outer rim of the ship. The men in hazmat suits grabbed them up and stepped back to take up any slack. They would hold the craft centered over its stand like the people who hold the ropes under the giant balloons in the Thanksgiving Day parade in New York City. Low-tech, but effective.

Clearly that flight test would not be one for distance, just proof of concept of the technology. Inside the hangar there wasn't much room for it to fly around much anyway.

Next, a voice called out for everyone around the ship to stand clear as the four yellow clamps that held it in place were released and retracted out and away, hinged at the floor, they opened up like a gigantic yellow flower.

Technicians standing at the control panel podium began turning knobs and then pushed one of a pair of large levers forward. Foster watched them carefully as a quiet hum began to be heard echoing around the interior of the hangar. It started out soft and low. A deep-throated hum that grew gradually louder and louder as that first lever was moved.

Then another hum at a slightly different but harmonizing pitch as the technician pushed the second lever forward. It grew in volume along with the first. A deeper sounding tone.

The small gallery of spectators watched with rapt anticipation, almost breathlessly.

After a few minutes of these tones gradually growing together in volume, someone in the group of spectators pointed and shouted, "Look! I think I saw it move!"

Sure enough, very slowly, almost imperceptibly at first, the craft very slowly rose just a few inches up from the rim of the support stand, its bulbous belly still hovering inside the metal ring.

Floating in the air, the men holding the ropes seemed to be taking a moment to make sure they had a good grasp on it and were still keeping the craft centered over its stand.

The onlookers watched in silent amazement. Foster's mind reeled through innumerable thoughts as he instinctively and involuntarily worked in his head to analyze just what it was he was seeing. Something that he'd never given any credence to, conspiracy theories and urban legends. But there it was, a flying saucer — and it was *flying!*

After a brief pause, the technicians at the control panel slowly moved the two levers together and the alien craft rose upward — a little at a time — until it completely cleared the support stand below it and hovered a few feet above with nothing but air beneath it.

The gallery burst out in applause, cheering the monumental accomplishment of the team who had made it possible. Foster couldn't believe his eyes and clapped wildly along with the others around him — he couldn't help but smile broadly at the sight like a little kid at the circus.

The significance of the event was not lost on him in all the excitement of the moment, though. An alien craft, a flying saucer from some other part of the galaxy, defying Earth's gravity and flying — tethered and contained as it was in that hangar — before his own eyes.

The saucer hovered for about five minutes while the men on the ropes made sure of their grips. The descent would be tricky, to guide it back down into the stand and then reattach the clamps to support it.

The gallery got quiet again as the technicians at the control console began to back the levers down again that controlled the power of the heavy-metal ununpentium chips contained inside the craft and it very slowly sank back down. Once the lowest part of its bowl-shaped underside had dropped into the open ring around the top of the stand, the four men on the ropes began pulling and adjusting it until it gently settled back into place.

The hum stopped. Teams rushed in to grab the four locking arms and swing them up into position and then clamped them onto the sides of the saucer just below its outermost rim.

After a moment of quiet, the gallery once again erupted into applause, congratulating the team who had just put on such an amazing demonstration. A milestone in their collective research had been achieved. It had been a long and hard-earned journey to get to that moment. They couldn't help but show their enthusiasm and excitement — even Dr. Hidleman, whose face beamed in a proud, effervescent smile.

As the technicians around the spacecraft began the work of detaching the cables, coiling up the tethering ropes and shutting down the various systems that had been powered up to make the test possible, the man in the blue coveralls asked them all to check their radiation pens. Once they all did and no one reported any undue exposure, he thanked them for coming to witness such a triumph and then held the door open to allow them all to leave again.

Foster was amazed. So much to have taken in in such a short time. The whole UFO/flying saucer thing had always been nothing more than a dubious legend to him — the stuff of questionable theories and sensationalistic television specials. Being a scientist, he had intuitively just dismissed it all.

There seemed to be no rational explanation for any of it. Just a lot of unsubstantiated sightings of lights in the night sky and self-credentialed talking heads who kept arguing that the government was fully aware of the situation, that they were actually working shady deals with extraterrestrial visitors, and lying to the public all the while.

How could a government that had put men on the moon possibly be guilty of all of that? It didn't make any sense to him but then, before his very eyes, he watched an actual flying saucer lift off under its own power. He was doing experiments on a metallic chip made of a material previously unknown on planet Earth. How could he deny the reality of it all any longer? Maybe his government wasn't so vested with inscrutable integrity as he had previously, naively thought.

As he walked back down the hallway with rest of the gallery of observers returning to their respective offices and laboratories, he noticed a row of windows along the wall to his left across from the hangar doors. He hadn't noticed them on the trek from the lab to the hangar. He'd been too engaged in conversations with his co-workers along the way anticipating what they were hoping to see. At the time, the windows were dark, but as they were leaving, the lights behind the glass were on and the glow caught his attention as he neared.

The window sills were at about waist level and the glass was a little taller than he stood. Each pane was about a yard wide and there were six of them in a line separated from one another by a metal sash a few inches wide. Inside, curtains were drawn across all of them to hide whatever was in the room beyond from view and what was happening inside. He noticed a gap where one of the curtains wasn't quite pulled all the way across leaving a space several inches wide where his curiosity drew him like a magnet.

Peering in, he saw a large, brightly lit room. Along the back wall were rows of polished, stainless steel doors. Each door a few feet square with a pair of oversized hinges along the left edge and a large, polished metal handle at the right. In the center of each door was a small metal bracket that held a paper card, some of which with some bold handwriting on them that he couldn't make out from where he stood on the other side of the glass.

Midway in the room, between there and the windows, were three stainless steel tables. They looked like operating tables with a large, movable light array hanging over each one of them. In a sobering moment, he realized that the tables were not for doing life-saving operations. In consideration of the rows of polished metal doors along the back wall, the revelation that the room was in reality a morgue and those tables were used to perform autopsies sent a chill up his spine.

Gathered around the table in the center of the room were four people in light green surgical gowns wearing matching hair coverings, surgical masks, goggles and gloves. Two stood on one side of the table and one on the other while the fourth stood with her back to him at the foot of the table, blocking his view of whatever it was that they were doing between them.

One of the faces at the side of the table looked up and noticed the gap in the curtains and a face peering in. He pointed it out and shouted out loudly enough to be vaguely audible through the glass. The woman at the foot of the table turned to look and then quickly marched toward the windows to pull the curtain closed. When she moved away from the table, she suddenly revealed what it was that the four of them were so engaged with.

Foster gasped in complete revulsion. The shock caused him to stand bolt upright and instantly step back from the glass as he felt a cold chill envelop him.

The woman grabbed the edge of the curtain and yanked it closed. He stood there staring at the blue and beige pattern of the curtain's fabric through the glass for a long moment in numb disbelief.

"Dr. Foster!" He heard his name as though it were being called out from a distance in the echoing canyon of block walls. "Dennis?!"

Snapping out of a fog of incredulence — enough, anyway, for a fleeting moment of lucidity — he turned his head to see the last of the group he'd been walking with disappear around the corner. Teller lingered behind, calling out to him to catch up.

He took a breath, turned from the window and waved to her, "I'm coming! I'm coming." ∎

CHAPTER TWENTY–FOUR

The Ramos Project

Foster worked through the rest of that Thursday in a fog. His mind was completely captivated by all that he'd seen that morning — both the amazing and the deeply disturbing. He told Teller to postpone the tests that they were planning to do until the following week. He just couldn't focus on much of anything for the time being.

"Are you alright, Dennis?" She asked.

"I just witnessed one of the most amazing things I'd ever seen. I need time to process it all — I'm sure I'll be fine."

"I understand," she consoled. "I'll finish up the numbers and then we can pick it up again on Monday."

"Sure, that sounds good. Monday, then."

He went back to his apartment that evening still feeling dazed. He bought a sandwich at the commissary for dinner but then ended up putting it, still wrapped, into his refrigerator as his appetite was entirely absent.

He grabbed himself a beer and then sat down on his sofa and just stared at the opposite wall for a while in silence. He so wanted to talk with someone about all of what he'd seen. He picked up the phone intending to call his wife but then recalled that the line was tapped. If he were to inadvertently blurt out something about what he'd just experienced, he might get himself — and her — in all sorts of trouble.

In all of what he'd seen and experienced thus far, he was becoming more aware of the need to shelter her from all of it, to protect her.

He set the phone back down again.

He put on some music to perhaps ease the infesting quiet. He put a Miles Davis record onto the turntable and set the stylus down on the grooves. Still, he found himself wandering aimlessly around his apartment — pacing. He had to shake the bedazzlement out of his head. He finally decided to just take a hot shower, have another beer and then get to bed, hoping that he would be able to actually sleep.

He went through the morning on Friday in a daze, his mind totally distracted by what he had experienced the previous day. Everyone else in the lab left him alone at his desk as he tried to make some sluggish progress on his computer. Teller only spoke with him a couple of times that morning, once to say "good morning" to him when he had first arrived and once to ask a question to which she'd received a halting, meandering response. After that she just left him alone for the rest of the morning.

Finally the clock on the wall was creeping ever so close to noon and Foster couldn't wait to be up and on his way home. He rode the shuttle back to the Village, grabbed his already packed suitcase at his apartment and made his way to the Janet terminal to catch the next flight back home to his wife to whom he knew he couldn't confide any of what was bothering him. But, still, he just couldn't wait to get home. Just to be with her would be solace enough.

When Livvy met him at the airport, he seemed distant to her, distracted. He loaded his suitcase in the trunk and got into the passenger seat. He leaned over to kiss her and she noticed the look on his face. She asked if everything was alright.

"Yeah," he dejectedly responded through a fake smile. "Everything's fine."

She didn't believe him. She knew him far too well. His demeanor told a very different tale. Nevertheless — presuming that he wasn't allowed to share what was bothering him — she pulled away from the terminal and drove them home.

He spent the rest of the afternoon in silence. He wanted so badly to tell her everything. He'd never kept secrets from her before except for Christmas gifts and birthday surprises and that sort of thing. He felt guilty that the job had caused him to have to lie to her so often — and the lies were getting bigger all the time. He'd have to tough out the funk that he was in without being able to confide in his singlular best friend and confidant. It was eating him up from the inside.

He spent the afternoon in his office alone. She kept away, respecting his need for solitude even though she didn't understand the reasons.

She brought him coffee and made him a sandwich as dinner time approached. He worked on his curriculum vitae, picking up where he had left off when he'd sent the unfinished draft to Dr. Kimber nearly a year before. He was so conflicted about the position that he was in and the compromises that it was demanding of him that he was sincerely considering going in on Monday morning and giving his notice. With such a high-security government job, he wasn't sure how that would work, but if he didn't change his mind in the meantime, he wanted to be prepared to begin his job search anew.

Still, he vacillated. The discoveries that he'd made so far and the possibility of breaking through with the definition of the elusive unknown element ununpentium and the subsequent renown for being the scientist who had figured out how to synthesize a previously unknown alien element would be monumental. It's the sort of thing that scientists like him live for. Could he really walk away from that? An opportunity like that would likely never come along again.

But, just in case, he worked to update his resume. He knew that at that moment he wasn't thinking clearly. Best, however, to be prepared for any possible scenario.

On Saturday morning he decided to go and take his truck down to the car wash and give it a thorough going over, a good hand-washing, vacuum out the interior and clean out the trash that may have accumulated from the last road trip. It had been parked unused in the driveway for so long, it really needed to be driven at least a little bit.

He thought he'd fill the tank when he was done and then maybe take Livvy for a ride to look for antiques. It was one of her favorite things to do — he didn't understand the attraction himself. Why would anyone want to buy worn out old things off of a dusty shelf in some dark, junk-congested shop somewhere? But she loved it and he thought it would be a good way to get his mind in a better place. Maybe get some lunch at some roadside stand somewhere and get out in the fresh air with his wife.

He felt so guilty about her and that he couldn't tell her about any of what was going on in his head so maybe it would make up for his dark mood. And who knows? Maybe he might even find it in himself to smile a little bit before they'd get back.

It was a perfect day, sunny with a light breeze from the west. The couple spent the day meandering north through the back roads to stop at several shops along the way that he knew she'd loved to explore. By the time they got back home to Burbank, he felt refreshed. The weight he'd carried home with him was somewhat relieved. They rented a movie on the way home and settled in with a big bowl of popcorn and a bottle of wine for a quiet evening together.

Early Sunday morning, Foster went out to pick up his newspaper that had been tossed out onto his driveway by the neighborhood paperboy. He ventured out a little later than he customarily did, trying to time it so that he'd miss the spectacle of Ted and bouncing Bambi out on their morning jog but, as he bent down to pick up the rolled up newspaper, he heard Ted's voice call out from across the street, "Morning, Denny!"

As he stood back up with newspaper in hand, his eye was arrested by the passing movement of Bambi's pointed, unrestrained breasts vigorously rising and falling, jostled sharply with each foot-fall under a tight-fitting cropped t-shirt as she and Ted ambled by on the opposite sidewalk, smiling and waving to him as they went past.

It was almost like they'd waited for him to come out of his front door before trotting by. Each week he tried to go out and fetch the paper at a strategically different time — earlier, later — that morning was the latest that he'd ever ventured out and, still, he got an unwelcomed eyeful.

Maybe, he thought, he'd wait until lunchtime the next week. Maybe that would be late enough. He could take the paper with him on the plane. Maybe that would work.

That afternoon Livvy drove him to the airport and the Janet terminal building to catch his plane back to the secret facility in the desert where he worked. Before he got out of the car, he said to her, "I'm so sorry I've been such a downer all weekend. I've just got so much on my mind right now."

"I wish you could tell me about it, but I understand."

"I hope you had fun yesterday hunting for antiques."

"I did, but mostly I was glad to be with you all day and maybe help perk up your mood — a little bit, at least."

"Well, you certainly did. I may not look it, but I feel a lot better now than I did when I got home on Friday. Thanks."

"I *love you*, Denny."

"I love you, too, sweetie. Thanks for being there for me."

She leaned over and kissed him, "You have a good week this week and call me if you want. I don't care how late or if you can't tell me about what you do there, I just like to hear your voice."

He smiled, "I will. You have a good week, too. Say 'hi' to Alma for me."

"I will."

He got out of the car and gathered up his suitcase from the trunk and then waved goodbye to his wife. As she drove away, he walked into the terminal with the Sunday paper folded over and clutched under one arm as he walked in.

As he worked through his Monday, he seemed to be in better spirits but, still, wasn't quite his usual self. Lebreau noticed and remembered the way he was the previous Friday morning and approached him to quietly ask if everything was alright at home.

"Home? Everything is fine. Why?"

"Well, I can't help but notice the way you've been acting these past couple of days. It seems pretty obvious that your mind is elsewhere."

"Don't worry, I'm here in my entirety. After seeing that saucer actually fly last week, I have a somewhat different perspective, that's all."

"Look, it's okay if you're having issues, it's not all that unusual. This job can be really demanding in so many ways and put a lot of stress on marriages and families. We have a psychologist here if you need someone to talk with. You can't talk with friends or family and I know that can be really frustrating. Take advantage of that. His name is Dr. Tryst. Go down to the secretary's office in the green zone and ask for him."

"Thanks, I'll keep that in mind. But, really, I'm fine."

"Don't let the job consume you, Dennis. It can do that if you're not careful."

"I can see that. Thanks."

Foster finished out his day at work and took the shuttle bus back to the Village for the evening. He stopped to have dinner at the dining hall. They had a meatloaf special that night. He'd had it before and thought they made a pretty good meatloaf, so he decided to indulge. Although the meal was as good as he had expected, he just didn't have much of an appetite so just picked at it and ended up tossing out half of it and left for his apartment.

When he walked in, he put his keys on a small table just inside the living room and removed his identification lanyard and laid it down next to them. Just as he laid his briefcase down on the coffee table, there was a knock at the door.

"I'm coming!" he called out and then turned to walk back.

He peered through the security lens in the door and saw a familiar forehead and pulled-back scalp of hair, "Who is it?" he asked, fairly sure who it actually was standing outside in the hallway, barely tall enough to be seen through the viewer, but unclear as to why she might be there at his door.

"It's Jennifer," came the presumed response.

He had no idea why she was at his apartment but he wasn't going to make her stand out in the hallway while he grilled her through the door. He pulled it open and greeted her, "Hi — uh, Jennifer — what are you doing here?"

"May I come in?" She asked.

"Uh, yeah, sure," he stepped back out of the way to let her walk past. "I don't mean to be rude, just kinda surprised to see you here."

As she walked in, she looked around and smiled, "These places are all pretty much the same, aren't they?"

"I wouldn't know," he replied as he closed the door. "This is the only one I've been in."

"You haven't been here very long, but when you get to know some people, you'll get around."

"I guess. So, again, I'm surprised to have you show up at my door — why are you here?"

She stopped in the center of his living room and turned back to look at him with a concerned look on her face, "I'm worried about you, frankly. I know you might find that hard to believe, but when you work closely with someone for a while, you naturally become invested in their well-being. I just wanted to come by to check on you — away from work, away from ears that might overhear so maybe you'll feel freer to get something off your chest in private that you wouldn't at work."

"I appreciate that, but..."

"But, what? You're 'fine'? You're obviously *not* fine. Look, I have a pretty good idea what it is that you're so upset about and I also know that you can't go back home and tell anyone about it. Your traditional network of confidants is no longer available so you've got to keep it all bottled up inside. I know, I've been there. I live alone because, working here, I destroyed any relationships I've ever had back in the world. This lifestyle can do that after a while if you let it."

"So you've come to try and convince me to go talk with Dr. Tryst?"

"Shrinks? Ha! Quacks! Voodoo science, if you ask me — and Tryst is one of the worst. No, I came to be a friendly face to talk to. I'm not a professional psychologist. I'm not going to tell you it's all okay or what to do to absolve yourself of the nightmares — I've got plenty of my own. I'm just a sympathetic ear who has seen it all before and can relate. I'm here and I'm willing to listen, that's all."

Foster stood there for a moment and pondered all that she had just said to him. After what she'd put him through over the previous weeks — despite her more recent apologies and overt efforts to be more congenial to him — he still couldn't bring himself to accept her as being at all sincere. He tried to graciously sidestep her offer by explaining, "I was just going to call my wife."

"Your wife? And tell her *what?*"

"Well, that the meatloaf was really good tonight — I guess."

She just looked at him with a sly smirk on her face as if to silently punctuate her words.

"Hmph, I see what you mean." Maybe, he thought, he could actually trust her. Maybe a little bit, anyway. Besides, it would be nice to unload to someone, to get it off of his chest. "Look, I was about to get myself a beer — you want one?"

"You know, that sounds good. Sure."

"Okay, have a seat," He turned back to the kitchen and grabbed out a pair of brown bottles from the refrigerator, twisted off the metal caps, and returned.

She took the bottle from him, nodded her thanks, and then looked to put it down on the coffee table but hesitated. "No coasters?" she asked. And then answered herself with a grin, "Of course not. It's a guy's apartment. I should know better."

"A guy with a touch of OCD," he elaborated with a smirk and then handed her one from a neat stack of coasters that he kept at the end of the breakfast bar behind him.

She chuckled quietly as she set it down on the coffee table and put the bottle on top of it. She sat down at the end of the sofa and then waved to the stuffed chair across from her and invited him to sit, too.

"When I looked back to find you after we'd left the hangar, I saw you standing at that window. I had a pretty good idea what you were looking at — that's our morgue."

"Yeah, I could see that," he sat down with his beer. "I guess I didn't notice the windows when we were walking out to the hangar. The lights must have been off. But when I saw that one of the curtains was partly open, I couldn't help but look inside. There were people standing around in surgical gowns and a child on the table. His skin had turned a strange color and they had him cut open like a trout. One of the people was lifting out what looked like one of the kid's internal organs and set it into a metal dish that one of the others was holding out to him."

"That was no child, Dennis."

"It sure *looked* like a child — small, except for his head. It was as large as any of the adults' that were standing around him."

"Do you recall asking me about the crew members of the alien crafts in the hangars?"

"I do — wait — you mean, that was one of *them?* That was an alien from another world?"

"It was. You were watching an autopsy in there."

"Oh, my word," he whispered.

"You didn't at least suspect?"

"Well, I'll admit that the idea had crossed my mind but it seems too fantastic to be credible."

"We not only study the aliens' advanced technology, but we study the aliens themselves. That one was lucky. He was dead before they started the autopsy."

"What are you saying?"

"Did you notice that the autopsy tables have tie-down straps on them? You don't have to strap down dead aliens before you cut them open."

"You can't be serious — that's *murder!*"

"Is it? They're not human, after all."

"They're sentient beings — they have the intellect to build flying disks that we, in all our wisdom and technology, can't yet figure out. We think it's such a big deal that we were able to get one of them to lift a few feet up off the ground. They fly them all over the place at speeds that leave our fastest jets in the dust. We pat ourselves on the back for figuring that much out and these, these *people*, are so much farther advanced but we still think they're no more than animals to be studied and dissected like frogs in a high school biology class? I have a real problem with that!"

"I know it's hard to accept and it took me a while to get even a little comfortable with it all — being a part of this whole thing."

"It's sick. It's Nazi-concentration-camp sick. Have we so thoroughly abandoned our humanity in all of this?"

"It's a tit-for-tat deal that we have with them. I'm sure you've heard of people who have been abducted by aliens. People who disappear never to be seen again and a few escapees who tell horrific stories of their experiences being experimented on."

"On the front page of *The Enquirer* at the supermarket checkout line, sure."

"They're allowed a quota of humans to study and we're allowed to keep any of their crewmen who happen to crash or just land here and get themselves captured. It's a deal worked out between the Truman administration and the aliens after World War II."

"I had no idea."

"And then there's the Ramos Project. Genetic experiments trying to develop an alien-human hybrid. A super-soldier, so they hope."

"That's disgusting. Aliens impregnating human women? Inter-species sex? I can't begin to tell you how offended I am by that thought."

"Well, there's no actual sex involved. It's all done in a lab with a human egg and alien sperm and then implanted in a surrogate to carry to term."

"Where are these freakish hybrids now?"

"Mercifully, none has lived very long, most have miscarried over the years and a few of the surrogate woman didn't survive to term."

"How do they get women to volunteer for such a macabre experiment?"

"Volunteer? No, Dennis, they're just grabbed off the street. Young, healthy runaways, prostitutes, women who have nobody to miss them if they just disappear. They're taken to Wright Patterson's genetics lab, cleaned up, given physicals, vitamins and then impregnated and confined for the duration. If they survive, they're either kept to be used again or released into some city far distant from where they'd disappeared from, addicted to heroin or some other illicit drug. Nobody is the wiser and, more importantly, nobody would ever believe their dubious, drug-scrambled stories."

Horrified, Foster sat back in his chair and just stared at Teller for a few long minutes. He finally took a sip of his beer and then a long breath, "And now I'm a part of all of this. An accomplice of sorts."

"As are we all."

"I'm not sure I can be associated with this anymore, knowing what I know now."

"I thought that myself at one time. It's a real blow when you first find out the scope of it all. But I considered the technological gains that are possible in the work that we do in our own little corner. I've seen the reactors that are in these alien spacecraft. I've studied the gravity repulsion projectors and worked out how they function. That's how they got that one ship to fly. If we can figure out how to synthesize the chip that powers those reactors — just imagine, Dennis — the ramifications of such powerful clean energy! The gas crisis that we just went through, coal-fired power plants belching black smoke and soot into the atmosphere, poisoned water and oil spills — all a thing of the past. Think of the ecology, what your breakthrough could mean to the planet, to all of mankind. Don't quit, Dennis, please. It's way too important."

Foster was dumbfounded. He stood up from the chair and put his bottle down on the table. He turned away from Teller and then wrapped his two hands around his forehead and slid them back over his scalp as he heaved a long, heavy sigh.

"Dennis?"

He turned to her, "I know, I know. I've thought about all of that, too."

"Look," she stood up and walked over to stand in front of him, "Promise me you won't do anything rash — okay? Promise me you'll give this a lot of thought before you make any decisions."

He dropped his hands to his sides, "I promise."

"At least now you know the truth."

"I appreciate that — I do."

"And you can't let on to anyone that I told you. Not even anyone here."

"I won't. I promise."

She quickly glanced back over her shoulder at the door, "I guess I've done enough damage for one night," she said with a slight smile, "I should go."

"I guess. I have a lot to think about. Thanks anyway for being honest with me," They drifted down the short hallway past the kitchen to the door.

"I know we didn't get off on the right foot when you first got here — I'm really sorry about that — but I hope you know that now you can talk to me about just about anything."

"Thanks, Jennifer. I appreciate that," He pulled the door open and stood back to let her past and out into the hallway.

She walked by and then stood just outside the door and paused. She turned with a sullen expression and said quietly, "Just one more thing." He stepped out to stand closer to hear better. She threw her arms around him and laid her head on his chest. Instinctively, his arms just fell around her and he held her to himself. "I hope I can count on you to confide in, too. I don't have many friends. I'd like to call you my friend."

He released his embrace and planted his hands on her two shoulders as she stepped back from him, "Jennifer, there's nothing I'd like better than to be your friend. You can count on me."

"I'm so glad to hear that." She stepped away and began to turn toward the stairwell. She looked back over her shoulder, "See you in the morning?"

"In the morning, yes. Have a good evening."

"You, too, Dennis." ■

CHAPTER TWENTY-FIVE

Financial Anomaly

When he was at home with his wife, Livvy, or on the phone with her during the week, Foster could nearly bust for having to keep so many secrets. So often he would open his mouth to say something and then suddenly check himself and change the subject. Livvy tried to be patient with him, knowing that he wanted so much to tell her about what he was doing at work, but that he wasn't allowed to and could get into a lot of trouble if he did.

He called home one Tuesday evening to find her crying. She was almost inconsolable. "What's the matter, sweetie? What's happened?"

"Alma had to let me go from the dress shop," she explained. "She said that business was slow and she had to cut back," she quickly yanked the phone away from her face to sniffle into a Kleenex and then continued, "I was the last one hired, I had the least seniority — so I was the first to go."

"I'm so sorry, dear. I know how much you enjoyed working there."

"I'll really miss it, I will. But at least I won't see that creepy stalker anymore."

"Stalker? What are you talking about?"

"Oh, I didn't want to bother you about it. You have so much on your mind."

Suddenly gravely concerned, he encouraged her, "No, no, please — what's going on? Are you alright?"

"Yeah, I'm fine," she reluctantly began. "I first noticed him a few weeks ago, just standing outside on the sidewalk across the street from the store. All dressed in black like one of the Blues Brothers — without the hat — wearing a pair of those mirrored sunglasses so you can't see his eyes. Even had a black umbrella when it was raining."

"Just standing there?"

"Yeah — creepy. He wasn't *always* out there but, every once in a while I'd look out the front window of the store and there he was, just staring across the street at us through those sunglasses."

"And you think he was stalking you? I mean, you and not Alma or one of the other girls who work there?"

"Once we noticed him out there for a while, we started keeping track. He would only be out there when I was at work. And sometimes I'd see him in the grocery store, outside the pharmacy and at the bank, too."

"Why didn't you call the police?"

"We did — a few times — but by the time they'd get there, he was gone. It was like he knew they were coming. Alma brought her camera to work one day and we snapped a photo of him but the man at the drug store said that that particular negative was exposed — completely blank. Somehow right out of the middle of the roll of film. Weird, huh?"

"Yeah," Foster suspiciously replied, "weird."

"Well, I've never seen him around home so it looks like he doesn't know where I live."

"Don't be afraid to call the cops if he ever does show up."

"And keep all the doors and windows locked — I know. I make sure I'm not followed home, too. I take a different route once in a while just to throw anyone off."

"Smart — that's my girl."

When their conversation ended with strained but loving words of goodbye, Foster hung up the phone and felt that his wife's description of her stalker was disturbingly familiar. It sounded suspiciously like the men in black that he'd seen silently hovering around from the time he had first interviewed for the job to the day he'd first arrived at the Groom Lake airbase. They were always around somewhere throughout the campus at the Village and throughout Facility R-Four-Seven. The man she had seen seemed too much like them — too much to be just a coincidence.

They always seemed to be watching. With their ever present sunglasses on, one never saw their eyes.

Like soulless insects, they were just there. Just always there.

When he arrived at the Facility for work the next day, he stopped in at Dr. Hidleman's office in the green zone before continuing down the long hallway to the particle lab. Her young secretary, dressed in an Air Force uniform, greeted him in a small outer office lined with file cabinets and office machines. Hidleman was always in her office, as though she lived there. He knew he'd find her at that early hour.

"Just a moment, Dr. Foster," the secretary said, "Let me buzz her and let her know you're here."

He patiently waited while the woman pushed the button on her phone and then spoke quietly into the receiver informing Dr. Hidleman that he was there to see her. After a very brief, hushed conversation, she said "Yes, ma'am," and hung up.

She looked up from her desk at Foster and announced that he could go right in.

As he entered her office, Hidleman was just finishing up a conversation on the phone. He kept away, respecting her privacy and standing back near the door. He overheard her mention the relic that he was analyzing saying that it had the potential to be the most powerful nuclear fuel ever discovered. Some of what she said made him think that the work he was doing would ultimately be used to create horrific new weapons with unspeakable power. He felt a chill as she finished up the conversation and hung up the receiver.

He stood and waited and, in a few moments, Hidleman looked up at him and greeted, "Good morning, Dr. Foster. What is this early morning visit about?"

Foster approached the director's desk, "I just had a rather disturbing phone call with my wife last night."

"Marital problems?" She knew better. The call was, as with all of his phone calls, monitored and recorded. "Not uncommon for people who work here, but not the sort of thing that I usually get involved with."

"No, nothing like that — she's being followed by your men in black suits. One of them has been stalking her and hanging around where she worked. She was let go from her job and I know it was because this guy's presence was creeping out the store's owner and the other women who work there."

"I'm sorry that your wife lost her job. You may recall that you signed a document giving us permission to surveil you and keep tabs of your home life as part of our monitoring you for national security purposes."

"I know. I expected that you'd be watching me, but I didn't realize that it would include stalking my wife."

"The so-called 'men in black,' as you call them, are part of our security team. They are charged with watching everyone and everything and, when necessary, intervening in the interest of national security. It's all part of the deal, Dr. Foster."

"Can I explain all of this to her?"

"No, of course not."

"So I have to just let her be afraid? That's wrong, *just wrong!*"

"It's part of this security-driven life we lead, Dr. Foster. I'm sorry."

"I am, too."

"Is there anything else, Dr. Foster?"

He paused for a moment and then replied through clenched teeth, "Apparently not."

"Look, if you need some help with your marital situation, I recommend you make an appointment with our staff psychologist. He can help."

"Dr. Tryst?"

"Right. Have you met him yet?"

"No, I haven't — but I've heard about him."

She quickly walked around behind her desk and pulled out the top drawer, "Here," she reached in and took out a business card, "Here's his card. Hang on to it and give him a call. He understands the stress of working in this environment, he can help. Really, he can."

He took the card from her and quickly glanced at it before slipping it into his shirt pocket, "Thanks."

"So, if there isn't anything else, Dr. Foster, I'm sure we both have a lot of work to do today."

"Yes — yes I do," Foster replied curtly.

He stood and glared at her for a moment then turned and left the office without another word.

As he walked past the secretary in the director's outer office, she cheerfully wished him a nice day and added, "Be seeing you."

When he arrived at the particle lab, he set down his briefcase on his desk before rearranging the lanyard with his identification badge, the pocket protector and radiation monitoring pen, transferring them from his shirt pocket to that of the white lab coat before buttoning it up. As he was doing this, Dr. Teller came across the room carrying a cup of coffee for him and just set it down on the corner of his desk. He glanced down at it and then at her, "Thanks, Jennifer."

"You're late. I presumed that something might still be wrong."

"You presume right. I think some caffeine might get me back on track, though."

"Are we still planning to get into the clean room today for that next test?"

"Yes, that's my plan. I'm hoping this will give us all the data I need to finally put the proposal together for the super-collider experiments. I want to meet with Dr. Lebreau by the end of the week and have something substantial to present to him so we can at least get onto someone's calendar."

"That's exciting," she commented. "For a scientist in this field, that's the Holy Grail, to get an experiment accepted at someplace like Cern and to discover an unknown element. For people like us, it just doesn't get any better than that."

"That's why I'm still here, frankly — the only reason. Besides, the sooner we get this done, the sooner I can get home to my wife and return to some sort of a normal life."

"Well, I for one am glad you're sticking around for all of this."

"So," he picked up the cup of coffee and took a sip, then unlatched the briefcase with his free hand and lifted it open, "I've got some figures that I'd worked up last night. Got a minute to go over them?"

"Sure," she grabbed the chair from the next desk — Hart never used it anyway — and pulled it up to have a ringside seat to start work with Foster on the day's details.

* * * * *

Friday morning, Foster was at his desk working at his computer to compile some of the data from the last tests that he and Teller had done that week. Lebreau walked up to him from behind, "Dennis?" he interrupted.

Foster stopped his typing and looked around to see him standing there with a rather serious expression on his face, "Brian. Yes, what is it?"

"I just got a call from Dr. Hidleman. She'd like you to come down to her office."

"Oh? What's this about? I'm pretty busy here, trying to get this proposal finished up."

"She says it's important. I don't know what it's about but she said that she needs to see you down there right away."

The tone of Lebreau's voice added enormous weight to the request. He quickly turned back to his computer, saved his work, and closed out the files that he had open.

"Alright," he said as he stood up from his desk, "I'm on my way."

Without any clue as to what Dr. Hidleman could possibly want — and so urgently — he left the particle lab in the red zone and began walking out to the green section to meet with the Facility's director. Perhaps it had something to do with his request — demand, really — that the men in black would leave his wife alone. Maybe she had been able to call them off and wanted to let him know in private.

Otherwise, he couldn't imagine what she could possibly have wanted to see him about that it couldn't wait.

He walked into the outer office and the secretary looked up from her desk at him, "You can go right in, Dr. Foster. They're waiting for you."

"They?"

The secretary didn't respond. She just looked at him for a long moment and then looked down and returned her attentions to the papers on her desk.

Anxious to get done with whatever the matter might be about and get back to his own work, Foster knocked on the door and then walked into Hidleman's office.

"Ah, good morning, Dr. Foster," she greeted. "Won't you have a seat?"

He looked down at the chair that faced the front of her desk and then up at one of the seemingly innumerable men in black suits and sunglasses that stood behind the desk to her right. The man's expression was grim as he looked down on him — at least he presumed that the man was looking down on him, it was difficult to be sure through the mirrored lenses.

"I think I'll stand, thanks. What's this about?"

"As you wish — this is Mr. Steele, he's the head of our security team. He's discovered some financial anomalies with your banking accounts and needs to ask you a few questions."

"My bank accounts? You've been reading my mail? Reading my bank statements?"

"We don't need to read your mail to monitor your banking activities," Steele replied. "Banks are required to report any large transactions above a certain threshold."

"Son of a..."

"Specifically, we noticed a sizable, cash deposit and need to ask you to explain it. When we see this sort of thing in the accounts of someone who works in such a high security position as yours, we naturally become curious. Were you paid for secrets? Did a representative of another government pay you to divulge information about what you're working on here? About this Facility? About Area Fifty-One?"

Foster was furious. Still, he took a moment to collect himself before responding. "Don't be ridiculous. You follow me around like a herd of lost puppies, you see who I see, who I spend time with. And, besides, when the hell would I have time to meet with anyone like that? I'm here five days a week, with my wife for two and in the air the rest of the time! You can't be serious!"

"You could meet with someone who appears perfectly innocent on the outside and is, in fact, an agent of a foreign government."

"Aside from my wife, the only people I see are people that I've known for years. My friend Luke, my barber, people like that. I think if they were agents, I'd know about it."

"What about that new neighbor of yours, Ted White, and his pornography actress girlfriend? They'd just moved across the street shortly before you were hired for this job."

"Ted? He's imminently annoying, but he's harmless. He's no agent for anyone. He's just some Hollywood phony working in the movie industry and she's as air-headed as they come and talks about sex all the time."

"You and Mr. White spent a long time together talking in your garage a few weeks ago. What was that all about?"

"What the hell are you talking about?"

Steele opened up a folder that he was holding and handed a large black and white photograph to Hidleman who, in turn, passed it to Foster. It was a photo of him and Ted standing with bottles of beer in their hands on either side of Foster's partially dismantled race car in his garage. It was grainy, shot with a long telephoto lens. His pickup truck parked in the driveway in front blocked some of the view, but his and Ted's faces were unmistakable. A strip of laminated paper was attached to the bottom of the photo with typed information as to the date and location that the photo was taken.

"This was actually a few *months* ago," Foster explained. "I had had a rough week here at work and missed my wife. When I got home, she had to work late and couldn't come pick me up at the airport. I went out to the garage to work on the car when Ted wandered over from across the street. He was just keeping me company, actually offered to help."

"Just kept you company? What did you two talk about?"

"Talk about? I don't know — nothing really. He asked a lot of questions about the car, said he'd never been up close to a race car before. His conversations always seem to deteriorate into the boring business of movie-making finances or his sexual exploits and bragging about his girlfriend, Bambi's, unique talents. I always try and get him off the subject. Don't want to hear that kind of stuff. But that's all. Oh, and I made him my gopher."

"Gopher?"

"Yeah, *gopher.* Go for this, go for that. I had him fetch beers from the fridge, wrenches from the work bench, that sort of thing."

"Hmph, alright."

"So, getting back to the reason I've been summoned here, what is this banking anomaly that you claim to have found?"

"A ten thousand dollar deposit, in cash, to be specific. An oddly round number. It smacks of a drug deal, maybe some sort of payola or bribe."

"And when did this deposit supposedly take place? Let me guess, just about six weeks ago — am I right?"

"As a matter of fact, yes."

"I sold the race car."

"You sold your race car? I thought that was your hobby, your passion. Why would you sell it?"

"Since I started working here — and since I had begun my job search before that — I have had no time to pursue auto racing. The car had been sitting in my garage since the day that we'd come back home from our last race. It broke my heart but I sold my half of it to my partner and friend, Luke, with the trailer, tools, spare parts — everything. He paid me in cash, hundred dollar bills if you need to know. Satisfied?"

"We'll have to verify that information, of course, but it tracks. We've noticed that the car and the trailer are now gone."

"Tracks? Damned right it 'tracks.' And while we're in the same room together," he peered into the mirrored lenses of Steele's glasses, "leave my wife alone."

"Your wife?"

"You guys in the black suits and sunglasses, following her all around, hanging around where she worked. You got her fired! This has to stop!"

"Surveillance isn't my department, Dr. Foster. But I can tell you that everyone who works at this Facility and other high security installations like it are routinely monitored. They and their families and the people they regularly interact with."

"Dr. Hidleman tells me that I can't explain that to her, to relieve my wife's fears that she's being stalked by creepy, sinister looking men in black. She's afraid of being attacked! She's called the cops on them more than once."

"I'm sorry for that but Dr. Hidleman is correct. You can't tell her about us or about anything related to this Facility or what it is you do here. I'm sorry but I hope you understand."

"I've never lied to my wife before in my life, but since I took this job I seem to be lying to her all the time now. I *hate* it."

"National security, Dr. Foster. It's all very necessary to maintain national security."

"Thank you, Dr. Foster," Hidleman interrupted, handing him a form and a pen.

"What's this?"

"It documents our meeting here. Sign it to acknowledge that you've met with Mr. Steele and myself this morning and that we talked about this banking issue with you."

He took the form from her and scanned it over quickly, "What if I don't sign it?"

"It will be noted in your HR file that you were uncooperative and the unsigned form will be included."

With his teeth gritted, he silently leered at her eye-to-eye for a long moment and then laid the form down on the corner of the desk closest to him and signed the bottom. He handed the paper back to Hidleman and tossed the pen onto the blotter.

"We'll check on your explanation, of course, and add an addendum to your file with our findings. In the meantime, is there anything else?"

Foster seethed for a moment in silence and then grumbled, "No, I guess not."

"Alright then, you're dismissed."

"Yeah, so it would appear." He turned and grudgingly walked out the door. ■

CHAPTER TWENTY-SIX

A Whiff of Infidelity

Friday evening, Livvy Foster picked her husband up at the airport once again and drove home via a favorite, local restaurant for dinner. Once they'd been seated and placed their drink orders, he looked up at his wife and said, "I'm so sorry you got let go from Alma's dress shop, sweetie. I know how much you enjoyed working there."

"I did, but I suppose I might be able to find some other part-time job. We don't really need the money. You've got a really good job right now. With you gone so much, it's just nice to get out of the house and be around other people — to have some kind of purpose — you know?"

"I do. Have those men in black been around anymore?"

"Well, I wasn't going to tell you but, yes. I saw one standing on the sidewalk across the street from the house yesterday."

"So they know where we live?" In a whisper, he then reasoned, "Of course they do."

"Ted happened to be out in his yard at the time and saw him. He confronted him and chased him off."

"Good ol' Ted to the rescue," Foster said sarcastically.

"Don't be like that, now."

"Why didn't you just call the police?"

"I was about to when I saw Ted walk up to him. I watched from the window to see what would happen but when the man walked away, I just went out and thanked Ted for chasing him off."

"Did he invite you in for drinks or something?"

"He said he would have, but he was working on some financial stuff for an upcoming movie project and had to get back to it. He asked me if I'd take a raincheck."

"And what did you say?"

"I don't know — I think I just said 'thanks' or something and went back inside."

"Hmph," Foster snorted.

"You know, dear, if I didn't know any better, I'd think you were jealous of Ted."

"Me? Jealous?"

"Yes, you — Dennis Foster — I believe you're *jealous*."

"I'm sure you're wrong."

"I think it's cute."

"Cute?"

"After all these years of marriage, to think that my husband might be jealous if another man gets too friendly with me is really nice. It says a lot."

"Well, okay, I'll admit it. But I know you'd never cross the line, sweetie, so if I'm jealous at all, it's that he's able to spend more time with you than I can these days. That's all."

She smiled and then, changing the subject, asked, "So how is work going?"

"Oh, it's going alright, I guess. I'm finding all of this high security stuff a little hard to deal with sometimes, but I'm managing."

"The red tape getting in the way of your work?"

"It's very distracting."

"I could hear that in your voice sometimes when you call me."

"I wish I could tell you about it all. I really can't talk with anyone about any of it." The waitress returned to take their orders. Having been so engaged in conversation, neither had had a chance to look at the menu. But they frequented the place enough that they had their favorites. Foster still asked the waitress what the specials were for that evening in case something different might sound enticing.

Ultimately, however, they both ordered what they usually ordered anyway.

When the waitress had walked away back to the kitchen, Foster just slouched a little bit in his seat and lamented, "I used to be able to tell you everything — *and did*. Now I'm forbidden to tell you anything at all. They tap the phones, watch me all the time, watch you..."

"Watch *me*?"

"Uhhh, well, you know..."

She leaned over the table and lowered her voice, "Is that who these men in the black outfits are? They're government agents of some kind — watching me?"

"Well, uhh, do they *look* like government agents?"

"Honestly, I'm not sure what a government agent is *supposed* to look like, but they sure don't look like James Bond or Napoleon Solo."

"Yeah," he surrendered. "I think that's actually the idea."

* * * * *

Foster got off of the shuttle bus first thing in the morning at the R-Four-Seven facility and walked toward the large, metal entrance door. The guard standing there checking identification badges stopped him and told him that Dr. Hidleman wanted him to report to her office before proceeding down to the particle laboratory for the day.

He rolled his eyes, "What now?" he thought to himself.

He walked into Hidleman's outer office and was again greeted by her secretary who, in turn, announced him via the intercom on her phone to her boss. She looked up from the speaker box and said, "You can go right in, Dr. Foster."

"Yeah, I heard," he snarked, having overheard their conversation from where he stood.

When he walked into the office, Hidleman was again standing behind her desk with the imposing Dwayne Steele, the man in the black suit who had confronted him about supposed banking irregularities a couple of weeks previous.

Foster took one look over at Steele, sighed, and asked, "What is this about?"

"You remember Mr. Steele?" Hidleman asked.

"Try as I might, how could I forget? Did my explanation of the so-called banking anomaly not satisfy you? Did you check me out?"

"Yes, Dr. Foster," Steele replied. "That matter is resolved, thank you for your cooperation. But this is another matter entirely."

"Now what?"

"When we hire people for such high security positions as yours, we are very concerned with their stability — at every level, in every part of their lives."

"You think I'm unstable?"

"Let me finish, Dr. Foster."

Impatient with the personal intrusion, he dismissively retorted, "Yeah, yeah — go ahead."

"Finances are often times a sign of outside influences of various kinds but also personal relationships can be destabilizing as well and could lead to subjects doing irrational things."

"Irrational? What are you talking about?"

"Well, for example, if a man's wife were having an affair with another man and that other man were to offer to him that he'd leave her alone in exchange for something, maybe some secrets from a top secret facility like this one or money for which such secrets might be sold to a foreign entity."

"Affair? What are you suggesting? My wife? Having an affair?"

"We see that sort of thing here a lot," Hidleman explained. "Employees spending days, weeks away from loved ones. There's a certain element of loneliness inherent in this sort of lifestyle that sometimes needs to be satisfied. It's not all that unusual."

"Not my Livvy!"

"We have pretty reliable eyewitness accounts of her spending an extraordinary amount of time with a neighbor of yours," Steele elaborated.

"Who? Ted? You asked me about him last time. He's a jerk, to be certain. But like I told you, he's harmless."

"What do you know about Mr. White's politics?"

"Politics? The man talks about sex more than anything else — that and the intensely boring business end of making movies. He's never mentioned anything about politics and he's never asked me how I might have voted in any elections or any of that sort of thing. Again, he's completely benign."

"Were you aware that he's a member of the American Communist Party?"

"Obviously, I am not. Nor do I care."

"You *should* care, Dr. Foster." Steele opened up a folder on the corner of Hidleman's desk and lifted out a few 8-by-10 glossy photos and handed them to Foster, "Eyewitness photos, Dr. Foster," he explained, "...of your wife with Mr. Ted White."

The photos were a shock for him to see. In each black and white image was Ted and his wife, Livvy, shot from over her right shoulder. They showed the pair embracing and, in one of them, kissing with seemingly great passion that initially made his blood boil.

"What have you got to say now, Dr. Foster?"

"I don't believe it — I *can't* believe it!" Then something caught his eye, partly revealed under the woman's hair in one of the photos was a tattoo on her neck and behind her ear. He couldn't make out just what the image was, but he knew that Livvy didn't have any tattoos anywhere on her body. He then began to study the photos more closely and saw numerous other inconsistencies. He instantly knew they'd been faked.

For some reason, they (whomever "they" might be, he wasn't yet sure) had found a model, actress, volunteer of some sort who was the right height, the right build and had the right sort of hair, though she could have been wearing a wig in the photos. They were taken outdoors in bright sunlight and both the woman and Ted were wearing sunglasses and none of the images showed the woman's face fully enough so they could have gotten away with a model who looked just similar enough from an oblique angle for grainy, black and white surveillance photos.

Something was up but he thought he'd play it cagy. He continued to express his outrage without letting on that he knew the photos were faked.

"You told her that the security agents that she'd seen were ours." Steele accused.

"You tap my phones, you bugged my house and my apartment here and have cameras everywhere I go — I'm imminently aware of that — when would I have been able to tell her anything like that?"

"Over dinner."

"You bugged the restaurant?"

"We know it's a favorite of yours. We have some of our people on the inside, too, keeping an eye on you."

"The waitress — she's one of yours?"

"I can't confirm that, of course."

"No, of course not — *that's obscene.*"

"Careful, Dr. Foster," Hidleman chided. "You signed up for this, you gave us permission to monitor you in every way — in the name of national security."

"Hmph, 'national security.' Dr. Kimber warned me about that

'Catch 22' of yours. The universal excuse, the universal rationalization for just about anything that you people can think up to intrude and screw with people's lives. You think you can do *anything* to *anybody* while you chant 'national security' like some kind of justifying mantra!"

"I think you need some time to cool off, Dr. Foster," Hidleman sternly said. "Take the day — I'll let Dr. Lebreau know that I sent you back to your apartment. Get some rest, unwind and clear your head. I'll see you back here tomorrow morning."

"I don't have to 'unwind,' I can see what's going on here clearly enough. I'm okay to get back to work."

"I will see you in the morning, Dr. Foster." She repeated with a more forceful tone.

Foster stood quietly for a moment. He knew that he had no answer or any control over the situation just then. His only reasonable response was to do just as he had been told, to get back on the shuttle bus and go back to the Village and his apartment there. He threw the photos onto the desk and then picked up his briefcase and silently turned and walked out of Hidleman's office. He stormed back out to the parking area at the mouth of the cavernous Facility R-Four-Seven and got onto a waiting shuttle bus. At that hour of the morning most everyone was riding the busses in from the Village to the Facility, he had it all to himself for the long, solitary ride back again.

* * * * *

After Foster had left on the bus, George Weisz walked into Hidleman's office to join her and Steele for a conference call with General Sangster and the CIA's Felix DeSantis. When the two men were dialed up and heard on the speaker phone on Hidleman's desk, Weisz began by asking, "So, what does everyone think? Do we think that Dr. Foster is ready for the next phase?"

"I think he's getting ready to explode," DeSantis replied. "He's starting to unravel. I think he's ready to break."

"Dr. Hidleman? You see him here every day — what do you think?"

"He's seen the saucers, saw one of them fly which, by the way, I honestly didn't think those Hollywood characters would be able to pull off. I almost believed it myself, it was so well done. He got a glimpse of the morgue and an alien autopsy. Jennifer has filled his head with all sorts of macabre ideas and now has him all primed and ready to pull the trigger on him. And Ted, or whatever the guy's name really is, has Foster all but convinced that he's sleeping with his wife. Yeah, I think he's ready to snap."

"Steele — I guess my question to you isn't whether you think Foster's ready, but whether or not you and your people are."

"Everything's in place, Mr. Weisz. Just say the word and I'll be on the phone with Washington."

"Very good. And General Sangster, I guess then the last piece of this is the Air Force. You folks have a lot of involvement from here on out. Are you all ready?"

"We're ready, Mr. Weisz. Everything is in place."

"Alright then, we're a 'go' for the next phase. Mr. Steele, call the IRS and Dr. Hidleman, tell Jennifer to make her move."

"Yes, sir. I'll have a meeting with her right away."

* * * * *

Fuming and angry in his apartment that afternoon, Foster paced around, sipped on a cold beer or two and just talked to himself, sometimes forgetting that the apartment was bugged and that his words were probably being listened in on.

He didn't care.

In his rage, he picked up the ever-present glowing lava lamp intent on hurling it across the room but, once he'd wrapped his fingers around it, the hot surface caused him to yank his hand back. Just as well, he thought. He'd be the one who'd have to clean it up anyway.

Talking out loud to Livvy — lamenting, ranting, arguing with himself — he paced around the apartment. "I can't believe they're doing this to me — *to us!* If I had only known that they'd intrude into our lives like this, I never would have taken the job. Really, sweetie, I would *never* have!"

After a few hours, he had walked and talked himself out and calmed himself enough to sit on the sofa and think to call his wife. Talking with her, even if he couldn't talk about anything that was actually happening to him, would at least give him some sense of not being so alone at that moment. He picked up the receiver and dialed his home phone number.

The phone rang once, twice, a few more times until, finally on the sixth ring, a man's voice answered.

"Hello?" the man sounded like he was out of breath.

"Hello? Who the hell is this? Ted? *Is that you?*"

"Denny?" the voice answered. The sound of the man's baritone voice confirmed to him that it was, in fact, his dubious neighbor.

"Ted!? *What the hell are you doing in my...*"

The line went dead. Ted had hung up the phone leaving Foster's imagination to fly into the darkest places that it ever had.

He threw the phone down onto the sofa and let loose a primal scream at the top of his lungs.

His handlers were right. If ever he might be ready to step off of the precipice, it was then. ■

PHASE 6
THE BURN

CHAPTER TWENTY–SEVEN

The Honey Trap

Mid morning on Friday, Foster was working at his computer when Teller walked up to him from behind speaking softly so as not to startle him as he worked, "Dennis?"

He turned, slipping off his glasses as he did, "Jennifer — yes, what is it?"

"You know how I offered to you that if you should ever need a friend here at the Facility to talk to — someone whom you could tell things to that you can't tell anyone on the outside — that you could always come and talk to me?"

"Sure I do. Do I look like I need to have one of those conversations right now?" He rubbed his hand over his face quickly as if to smooth out any fretful wrinkles that might be showing.

"Well, you have had a look of concern on your face these days, but I figured that you'd come talk to me if you felt you needed to. No," she looked him in the eye, "it's my turn. I was hoping that I could lure you away to the lounge for just a few minutes."

"Me? After all the time that you've been working here, I'm the one that you'd trust to talk with? I haven't even been here a year."

"These other people have me pegged as some kind of a bitch. They don't know me any deeper than just the surface. But then, none of them had to spend a week with me in quarantine and, frankly, none of them have seen me, you know, naked. After what we'd been through together, I feel a certain level of trust with you that I don't with anyone else here."

"I'm flattered, I am. Sorry that that trust had to come about by such uncomfortable circumstances."

"But you conducted yourself like a gentleman, as much as any man could have in such an urgent situation and I appreciate that. Your wife must really appreciate that in you, too."

"Maybe not so much these days as I would have thought."

"Oh? Trouble at home?"

"Actually, no, I don't think so — no, not really — I'm not sure. It's this job, being away for a week at a time, not being able to be there. It's probably just the stress getting to me. Sometimes it's hard to keep it hidden."

"Well, if you like, we can talk about that, too."

He slipped his glasses back on and began to get up from his chair, "It would be nice to get it off my chest. Maybe I won't be so preoccupied and actually get some work done today."

Teller smiled. He got up from his desk and followed her to the door and down the hallway to the lounge, away from the phrenetics of the lab and the busyness and noise of the rest of the Facility. She paused to punch the access code into the keypad next to the door and, when they heard the lock mechanism click, she pushed it open and walked inside.

He followed her in and around the tables expecting that they'd take seats at one of them to talk but she stopped and turned to him, "You know, Dennis, you're right. I've been working here for a long time. In most work environments, people would get to be friendly with some of their coworkers, go out for drinks and maybe even develop relationships. Here, we might accidently find ourselves having dinner in the dining hall at the same table and then go back to our apartments afterwards — alone. That's about as good as it ever gets around here."

"I know, not much of a social life here. Most of us will be getting on planes for home in a few hours and then it's back to work again on Monday morning."

"Our lives are all somewhere else."

"I guess that's true."

"It gets pretty lonely when you don't really have much of a life somewhere else to go to."

"I imagine that would be true. I sympathize, I really do."

She stepped up closer to Foster.

She reached her hand out and gently grabbed his wrist for just a moment, "I like that I can talk with you like this."

"I do, too. Getting to know the real Jennifer Teller has been nice. I don't feel so isolated out here as I used to."

She leaned in just a little closer to him, "Me either."

As she inched closer, Foster was beginning to feel uncomfortable.

"You know, Dennis," she said looking down and taking his hand in hers. "I haven't really had any sort of, you know, *physical* contact with anyone in a long, long time. Scrubbing me down with push-brooms full of chemical-smelling soap doesn't count. What I mean is," she looked up at his face again, "by someone who actually cared about touching me — for the *pleasure* of it — you know? I miss that. I miss that a lot."

"I, uh, can relate," he was suddenly feeling very uneasy about the turn that the conversation seemed to be taking. "I find my time at home with my wife to be quite a recharging for my well-being," He felt it necessary to mention his wife at that particular moment, awkwardly as he did, as things seemed to be going in an increasingly dangerous direction.

She smiled, "Not to mention recharging your libido, I imagine."

"Uhh, yeah," he said nervously. "That too — I suppose."

She let go of his hand and then reached up and unbuttoned the top button of her lab coat, "You know, Dennis, I could use some recharging about now myself."

"You, uh — you could?" He replied with a wavering voice, suddenly noticing that she didn't appear to be wearing any sort of blouse underneath the white coat. "What, what are you talking about?"

"We could be friends, Dennis — really *good* friends — with certain 'special' benefits while we're both so isolated out here in the desert." She stepped up and pressed herself against him, wrapping her arms around him. He stood, frozen, his arms fearfully extended out to either side of himself. With her head resting against his chest, she rubbed her leg up against his and softly asked, "We could fill those pent-up needs for each another — no strings. What would you say if I told you that I wasn't wearing anything under my lab coat?"

"You, uh, you *aren't?*" He replied, sounding terrified.

She moved her hands down to the small of his back and pulled him in to herself, pressing her pelvis tightly against him, "Does that excite you?"

"Uhhh..."

"You've seen it all before," She stepped back from him and then reached up and pulled off the clip that held her hair gathered up behind her head and let her tresses fall free. "Haven't you just been thinking about me? Dreaming about me? Wanting to *touch* me?" She slipped her fingers through her hair, tipping her face downward and looked up alluringly into his eyes and added, "To *have* me?"

Dumbfounded, he stood there silently frozen. She reached out and took his hand and led him to the sofa at the back of the room. She turned to embrace him again and then sat down, perched on the edge of the cushion, and unfastened the next button on her coat.

"I, uh, have something I have to do," he fumbled. "Maybe we can talk — *actually talk* — some other time. Okay?"

"But I want you, Dennis! I *need* you — I need you *now!*"

He stood like a deer in the headlights of an oncoming semi-truck for several excruciatingly long moments as she slowly finished releasing that button and then moved her fingers down to the next one below it, nimbly gripping it with her fingertips as she seductively looked up at him standing in front of her.

He became aware that his hands were trembling.

He felt trapped.

With everything else that was going on in his life at that moment, he couldn't believe what he was experiencing. One more complication out of his control that potentially threatened everything.

An overwhelming sense of fight-or-flight suddenly overwhelmed him.

He chose flight.

Like retreating from an unexpectedly encountered venomous snake coiled and threatening to strike, he took a couple of slow, silent, tentative, backward steps. Then he suddenly just turned and quickly walked out the door, trotting down the hallway and back to the lab.

He rushed to his desk and sat down to catch his breath and then tried to bury himself again in the work that he had interrupted to follow Teller to the lounge.

His head was spinning with all sorts of thoughts that he just couldn't justify with one another. Staring almost catatonically at his computer monitor, he realized that he could not even hope to concentrate. With his hands poised over the keys he realized that they were still shaking.

He decided to shut it all down and leave. Obsessively, almost in some sort of robotic mode, he methodically arranged all of his papers and books into neat stacks at the center of his desk so that he could pick up where he'd left off on Monday morning.

He looked around the lab. He saw everyone else engaged in whatever projects they were each working on at various stations paying no attention to him, but he didn't see Teller anywhere. Hoping to escape before she might return from the lounge, he told Lebreau that he was going to catch an early flight home to take care of some personal issues and then slipped out the door and out to the next shuttle bus as quickly as he could without bothering to wait for his supervisor's approval. ■

CHAPTER TWENTY-EIGHT

The Breakdown

After having spent a weekend at home brooding about all that had suddenly happened to him, Foster flew back to Area Fifty-One on Sunday evening. For the entire time he'd spent with his wife that weekend, he barely said more than a few words to her. She respected the mounting stress and frustration that he must have been feeling but had no idea of the accusations that had been leveled at her by his employers or what had transpired in the lounge with a coworker whom he had been by that time convinced was certifiably insane.

Even though he was entirely innocent of anything inappropriate, he still felt guilty. Having to keep the whole situation hidden from Livvy only helped to intensify his feelings of guilt. To have an attractive woman try and seduce him was territory that he was entirely unfamiliar with. He felt like he was standing on paper-thin, shifting, ice.

When he got back to the lab on Monday morning, Teller was not there. Dr. Lebreau informed him that she hadn't flown out on Sunday like everyone else. She was still home and feeling ill. "I expect she'll be in on Wednesday, Thursday at the latest."

"Thursday? That won't give us time to get much of anything done this week," Foster commented.

"Well," Lebreau lamented, "I suppose when you're sick, you're sick. I don't know what's ailing her. All she said was that she needed a day or two and then she expected she'd be feeling well enough to come back in."

"Alright, I guess it is what it is. I'll just have to work around that. By the way, have you had any luck contacting anyone at Cern?"

"Oh, yes, I meant to tell you last week. I did. I talked to the director over there who said that he's very interested in running your experiment. He's anxious to see your proposal."

"Wow, that's great! Are we on the calendar?"

"No, not until he sees your actual proposal and knows what they're getting into. So, how's that coming?"

"I have just one more test to do to confirm a few things. With Dr. Teller out, I suppose it may have to wait until next week. But, in the meantime, I can work on the portions that I have the data for. I've already begun on it. Most of my evenings in my apartment here have been spent making notes and doing some last-minute calculations."

"Not a television-watching sort of guy?"

"There's only so much 'I Love Lucy' that a man can absorb in one lifetime. The base's closed circuit service is sorely lacking in fresh material. It's all good, though. I'm excited about this project and, besides, working on this stuff in the evenings keeps my mind from dwelling on *other* stuff."

"Other stuff?"

"Just a few personal things — nothing really — just a distraction that I'd rather not waste any mental energy on."

"I understand. Well, keep me posted on your progress. As we get closer with this, I'm getting excited about it, too."

Encouraged by Lebreau's progress report on arrangements being made with the Cern laboratories in Switzerland, Foster got back to work on his computer on his proposal for an experiment that, if successful, would synthesize an element never before identified on Earth. Since he discovered it, he would get to name it. After himself? After his wife? No time for such mental meanderings just yet, there was still a lot of work to do to get ready.

On Tuesday, he arrived at the lab to once again find that Teller was absent and would likely be for the next day as well. That clinched it for him. There was no way that they'd be able to prepare for and execute the last tests that he needed to do that week, even if she came in on Thursday. It would have to wait until the following week. Perhaps the extended absence would help him — help both of them — put the events of the previous week in the lounge behind them and hopefully forget them altogether. As things stood, it would be very difficult to work with her until they'd cleared the air and gotten things back to normal.

He sat at his desk, logged onto his computer and spread out his notes to begin work. Using the calculations that he had done the evening before in his apartment, he worked on the narrative to present to the people at the Cern laboratories to convince them to put his experiment onto their calendar to run on their super-collider. It was a physicist's dream and he was on the fast track to having it realized.

He took a short break for lunch at mid-day, anxious to just keep working, and returned to the lab to find Dr. Lebreau standing at his desk waiting for him.

"Dennis," his demeanor was grim as he greeted him on his return.

"What's the matter? Did the people at Cern call? Is there something wrong?"

"No, nothing like that."

"What is it, then?"

"Dr. Hidleman want you to report to her office immediately."

"She does?" Taking into account the look on Lebreau's face, he grumbled again to himself, "Now what?"

Reluctantly, Foster saved the work that he had been doing on his computer and walked out of the lab. He walked down the corridor from the red security zone through the yellow and into the green zone to Hidleman's office door. He paused for a moment, heaved a quick sigh, and then walked into her outer office where her secretary curtly greeted him and instructed him to take a seat and wait.

The room was silent aside from the noises made by the secretary as she shuffled papers and alternately tapped on the keys of her computer terminal and the calculator that sat at the corner of her desk blotter. Over those subtle sounds was the continuous, echoing sound of a ticking clock. Loud and regular. Having to listen to it only made the time seem to drag on and on as he waited the few minutes to be admitted into Hidleman's inner office.

As he sat there facing the secretary's desk across the narrow room, his eyes were involuntarily captivated by the undulations of a brightly glowing lava lamp on a shelf behind her chair. There was one in his apartment when he first moved into it. Fully-furnished as it was, it just came with the place. He had unplugged it and put it up on a high shelf in the bedroom closet on the first day presuming that it had been left behind by the previous occupant.

Periodically, he'd come back on a Sunday afternoon to find it had been taken down from the closet by the cleaning crew over the weekend and set up again on a small table in the living room. Again, he would pack it up and store it in the closet. Eventually, he just threw it in the trash hoping that it would finally just go away.

The next Sunday he found a replacement that glowed with a different colored light set up on the same table. He opened the window and tossed it out.

Finally, the intercom on the secretary's desk sounded with Dr. Hidleman's voice saying to send him in. The secretary rose to her feet, walked to the office door and opened it for him, "You may go in now, Dr. Foster."

He stood up, "Thanks." He walked by her and into the office. She closed the door behind him.

He took a couple of steps into the office and stopped cold in his tracks. Standing around Hidleman's desk with her was the man in the black suit, Dwayne Steele, along with General Sangster who had first interviewed him for the job and CIA psychologist Dr. Damon Tryst whom he hadn't previously met. No introductions were made.

"Have a seat, Dr. Foster." Steele offered.

"No thank you, I think I'll just stand."

"Sit down, Dr. Foster," General Sangster sternly ordered.

Hesitantly, Foster complied. A chair set in the center of the space in front of the desk and facing toward it was the only one in the room. He sat down and looked across the desk at Hidleman standing behind it, "What is this all about? What is it this time?"

She turned and looked over at the man in black, "Mr. Steele?"

Steele was holding a few folders in his hands and set them down on the corner of the desk. "Dr. Foster, as I'd explained to you before, for the sake of national security we have to be sure that the people who work in such a facility as this are immovably stable. To be sure that they can be trusted with the highly sensitive information that they deal with every day. Certain red flags tell us when their stability may be eroding and action might need to be taken."

"I thought I explained about that bank deposit. And those photos you showed me of my wife with my neighbor, Ted, were obviously faked. They were so badly done a kid in grammar school could see it. So what is it now?"

"First of all, I assure you that those photos were not faked and they would most certainly stand up in a court of law."

"Only if the judge is one of you people — my wife doesn't have a tattoo," Foster snarled.

"A lot has happened over the time since our last meeting, Dr. Foster. Are you aware that the Internal Revenue Service has launched an investigation into your finances?"

"No, I hadn't heard."

"I wouldn't be surprised if a certified letter was waiting for you at home."

"Of course."

"You seem to be pretty resigned to this. Did you know that this was a possibility?"

"With you people, I find that just about *anything* is a possibility — anything *bad*, that is. You seem to have your tentacles into everything in my life. Not much surprises me anymore."

"Do you think that this is all some kind of conspiracy, Dr. Foster?" Tryst dismissively asked.

"I'm not sure that I'd use that word, but it sure seems too much of a coincidence to be random. Somebody, somewhere, is pulling the strings."

"And you think that's us?" Sangster injected. "You think your government is manipulating you somehow?"

"*You* said it, General, *not me*."

"I can assure you that is most certainly not the case, sir," Sangster insisted.

"Typical case of paranoia," Tryst offhandedly explained. "Possibly the result of some sort of recreational drug abuse or some form of psychosis. Perhaps some combination. Could take years of psychoanalysis to sort that all out. The man is obviously unstable."

"Dr. Hidleman," Sangster looked across the desk at her, "you have something else you wanted to add?"

"Regretfully, I do." She looked down at Foster, "I — we — can overlook a lot of things. We know that this job is stressful, it's unlike any other in the world and puts unique demands on those who work here. An occasional financial anomaly, like the money you got for selling a car, can be easily explained away and set aside. But one thing that we cannot abide, is harassment among co-workers."

"Harassment?! What...?"

"This is a small, tight working community here. We work very closely with one another, we eat together and live together in a very small Village of apartments filled with people who have lives elsewhere that they have to keep entirely compartmentalized from what they do here. It puts a strain on everyone," She picked up one of the folders that Steele had set down on her desk. She opened it up and then continued, "When a predator among us makes someone else feel uncomfortable — threatened — it effects all of us and it effects the important work that we do here as well."

Sensing that she might have been eluding to the events in the lounge with Teller the previous Friday, he thought to defuse the issue and be magnanimous, "I understand that, I do. But I don't feel at all threatened — maybe a bit annoyed, but not threatened. I don't think it's necessary to throw anyone under the bus."

"Dr. Teller came into my office on Friday afternoon, Dr. Foster. She was destroyed. She sat in that chair and cried her eyes out and told me the whole story."

"Story? What story?"

"That you threatened her career if she didn't perform certain sexual favors for you. Alone and lonely here and having marital problems at home, you forced her to follow you to the red zone's lounge wearing only her lab coat. That you've been obsessed after having lusted at her while you two had gone through decontamination procedures several weeks ago."

"That's a lie! More than that, it's *insane!* None of that happened — *absolutely none of it!*"

"We have pictures, Dr. Foster. You should have known better, there are cameras everywhere in this Facility." She took out one of the photos in the folder and handed it to him. It showed Foster and Teller standing together in front of the door to the lounge, Teller's fingers were on the buttons of the keypad, apparently punching in her security code to unlock it.

"Okay, we went into the lounge together. She said that she had some sort of personal problem that she wanted to talk with me about. We'd done that on a few occasions. This time, when we got in there, she told me that she wasn't wearing anything under her lab coat — I never saw anything, she only ever got a couple of the top buttons undone before I walked out and left her there. I'm not sure what she wanted from me but I had a pretty good idea and I wasn't going to stick around for things to get any more weird."

"Oh? I'm not sure I can believe that, Dr. Foster," Hidleman removed the next photo and reached across her desk and handed it to him.

The photo showed Teller sitting on the sofa from a high angle, the camera mounted on the wall above and just behind his shoulder. She was sitting at the edge of the cushion where he had left her. Her white coat had been unbuttoned down to the last button in her lap and she was unmistakably naked underneath. The collar was draped down and off of one of her shoulders and the sleeve slid down to her elbow nearly exposing one breast entirely. Foster stood directly in front her.

"That's you in the photo, is it not?"

"It is, but..."

"And that is Dr. Teller sitting on the sofa?"

"Obviously."

"You're standing only a foot or so away from her, her eyes are fixed directly ahead of her, not looking up at your face. It doesn't take a rocket scientist to figure out just what it is she's looking at and why."

"*That never happened!* When she sat down on the sofa, she wasn't all exposed like that, *I swear.* I never got closer to her sitting there than six or eight feet and then I walked away. I just left. *This never happened!*"

"Photos don't lie, Dr. Foster."

"Well, *this* one sure as hell does!"

"Do you mean to tell me that, after having seen her petite, naked, young body in that decontamination tent, you didn't fantasize about her? Obsess over her? Lust after her?"

"No! *Absolutely not!* I tried my best to keep my back turned to her, to be professional about it the whole time. It was definitely not a fun experience for either of us — I did my best to show the utmost of respect for a co-worker in an intimidating and compromising situation!"

"So, you're saying that Dr. Teller is lying?"

"I don't know why she would, but if you say that she told you these things, then yes! *She's lying!* And those pictures are faked somehow. *None of that happened!*"

"There are more photos, Dr. Foster. Even more damning than that one and, I assure you that they are not faked, there is no way that they could be," She closed the folder and set it down on the desk and then picked up another one. Inside she retrieved another photo, "This photo was taken by the surveillance camera in the hallway outside your apartment door," she handed the photo to him. It was a picture of him and Teller embracing just outside his door after she had shown up unannounced at his apartment to apologize and talk about the two of them being friends to make their close working relationship more comfortable.

Hidleman then handed him a second photo that showed Teller by herself standing at his door, her right hand balled into a fist as though she were knocking on it, "Notice the time stamp at the bottom of each photo," she directed, "Three hours and forty-seven minutes difference. What did the two of you do in there for three hours and forty-seven minutes, Dr. Foster?"

He studied the two photos for a moment and replayed the events of that evening in his mind but couldn't imagine that they'd been together in his apartment anywhere near that long. He set all of the photos down on Hidleman's desk and stood up, "She couldn't have been in my apartment for more than half an hour — probably not even that long. The hug happened, she was thanking me for letting her off the hook for being such a bitch before that. The other picture could have been posed hours before just to frame me for something — or you could have added the time stamps later!"

Steele picked up an accordion folder, pulled off the elastic strap and folded over the flap lid. He reached inside and removed a clear plastic bag, sealed with red evidence tape and handed it to Hidleman. She, in turn, handed it to Foster, "This was found by the cleaners that weekend. It was wedged in between the sofa cushions in your apartment. Care to explain this one away?"

In the plastic bag was an obviously worn, lacy red French panty. It was bunched up and stuffed into the bag, but still unmistakable. It was a relatively small size, apparently a size that could fit someone as petite as Teller.

Foster was momentarily speechless. He just looked up at Hidleman and then at all of the grave faces focused on him from all around and then just defeatedly asked her, "Why are you doing this to me?"

She snatched the plastic bag away from him. "Dr. Foster, your personal effects from your apartment have been packed into your suitcase. It's waiting for you at the terminal. The photos and other personal effects at your desk have been packed up into your briefcase. It's waiting for you in my outer office, my secretary will give it to you as you go out. Leave your lab coat, radiation pen and identification badge with her," she handed him a large white envelope. "There's a temporary identification in here that will get you home."

She never offered any sort of explanation and he knew that pressing the issue was pointless. They'd somehow arrayed all of these things against him, it seemed the culmination of a specifically planned process. "You're done here, Dr. Foster."

They were discarding him like yesterday's trash.

He took the envelope from her and stood stoically until General Sangster interrupted by placing a form on the desk in front of him and handing him a pen, "Sign this," he sternly directed.

Foster took the pen and looked down at the form — several pages of text with his name at the top of each one and a blank line for him to sign on the last page at the end of all the text with the date next to it, "What's this?"

"Nondisclosure agreement," the general explained. "You agree not to divulge anything about this Facility, the people or the work that is being done here, anything that you've seen or heard here or any of the work that you've done under penalty of law. If you say anything to anyone, it's a felony and you will be subject to prison for a long, long time. Is that clear?"

"You people are nothing if not thorough, I'll give you that." He had already signed a few such documents but begrudgingly leaned over and signed the bottom of the last page and dropped the pen on the desk.

"If it's any consolation, Dr. Foster," Hidleman offered, "the work you've done here has helped us make great strides. I can't tell you how disappointed I am that things worked out this way."

"You're kidding with that — right?"

"No, Dr. Foster, I truly am disappointed in you, disgusted." She pushed the button on the intercom on her desk and told the secretary that he was ready to leave. "You're dismissed."

The door to the outer office opened and two armed men in camouflage stood just outside. Foster walked out between them with the white envelope in his hands. The door closed behind him and he stopped to remove his lab coat, taking the radiation sensing pen from the pocket as well as his own pocket protector filled with writing instruments and his slide rule. He lifted the lanyard with his identification badge at the end of it up and over his head and reached it out to the secretary. Once he had handed everything over to her she just nodded to the two in camo to proceed with escorting him out. One of the guards was holding his briefcase and handed it to him as they walked out of the office. He followed them to an unmarked white Jeep Cherokee that was waiting for him at the shuttle bus stop.

When they got out to the large parking area, he took one last look around — the loading docks, the parking area with other white Cherokees and Humvees and several people in both civilian and military garb milling about attending to their respective tasks. He was instructed to sit in the back seat with one of the soldiers who'd escorted him from Hidleman's office, the other sat up front in the passenger seat beside the driver. They drove the long, bumpy route back around Papoose Mountain to the airfield and the Janet terminal.

His packed suitcase was waiting for him at the gate and one of the intimidating men in camouflage would escort him out to the plane and ride along with him to Las Vegas and then on to Burbank, California where he'd finally put him into a cab to take him home.

As the plane lifted off, it was the last time he would see the Groom Lake airbase and Area Fifty-One as it just disappeared into a brown, blur of endless desert stretching off into the distance. ∎

CHAPTER TWENTY-NINE

Fist to the Face

"Hello? Livvy?!" Foster called out as he walked in through his front door. He wasn't able to call her when he was abruptly ejected from Facility R-Four-Seven and quickly ushered off to a plane to take him back to California.

"Who is..." she walked out from the kitchen with a dish towel in her hands and into the living room to see him with his suitcase and briefcase just then closing the front door behind himself. "Denny — I wasn't expecting you home. It's only Tuesday — why are you here?" She tossed the towel back onto the kitchen table and then began walking toward him. When he turned back around, she could see the look on his face — an all-too familiar look. "What's wrong? What's happened?"

"They let me go," he hesitantly replied. "Called me into the director's office this morning and, before I knew it, I was on a plane for home."

"Why? I know you can't tell me much of anything, but I thought you really loved what you did there."

"I'm not sure I should tell you. It'll probably only upset you."

"Honestly, I don't think that I could get any more upset than I already am."

"What, what is it?" Rattled by her comment, he immediately suspected that their neighbor, Ted, had done something to upset her or maybe one of those insidious men in black had been lurking around. He wasn't prepared for her next question.

"Do you know a woman named Jennifer Teller?"

An icy spike drove through him at the sound of the woman's name. He had never mentioned her to his wife before, not by name. He stepped up to her and reached out to hold her but she pulled away from him.

He stood frozen for a long moment with a mixture of shock and disbelief. She had never recoiled from him like that before.

Haltingly, he quietly admitted that he knew Teller, that she was a co-worker at the Facility.

"She called me last evening."

"She called *you?* How the hell did she get the number?" He thought for a moment, "She's one of them," he continued in almost a whisper. "Of course she had the number."

"She said that you raped her."

"What?! *Raped her?!*" He couldn't believe what he was hearing. "So now it's escalated to *this?!*"

"Escalated? What are you talking about, Denny? Did you attack this woman?"

"Of course not! Geez, Livvy, I would hope you'd know me better than that."

"Ever since you got this job, you've been keeping so many secrets from me. I know you had to — a lot of them anyway. But you seem to be someone else lately, what *other* secrets are you keeping from me?"

"I didn't rape her! I never *touched* her and never *tried* to. *You have to believe me!*"

"She said she has photos."

"I know. They showed some of them to me this morning. Last week they also showed me photos of you and Ted hugging and kissing out there on the sidewalk."

"Me?! Ted?! *Never!*"

"I know."

"You do?"

"Of course I do. First of all, I know you. I know that you would never do that but I also know that the photos are faked. As soon as I saw them I could tell that they were."

"And the photos she has with you?"

"Also faked. They did a better job with them, I'll have to admit, but still not good enough. If you should ever see them — which I hope you never do — you know me well enough to see the flaws right away."

She sat down on the sofa and reached for the box of tissues on the side table. Foster sat down on the edge of the coffee table right in front of her. He placed his hand on her thigh while she wiped the tears from her eyes.

"This is why they fired you? Because this woman said you raped her?"

"Well, they just used the term 'sexual harassment.' Apparently the story got grossly embellished by the time she called you."

"You're saying that this is all a conspiracy?"

"It's really starting to look like one — yes."

"Why? Why you?"

"I've been thinking about that all the way home on the plane. Why? Why would they go through all the official gyrations of hiring me, security checks, surveillance, access to such sophisticated equipment to do the study that I was doing there — only to toss me out a year later? I don't know, but I did get the research advanced to the next level, far beyond what my predecessor had before he quit and left. A genuine breakthrough. I got them to the point where they could move forward with a series of experiments at the super-collider in Switzerland. Maybe that's all they wanted out of me.

"Maybe they set all of this up in advance so that they would have a mechanism to be rid of me when they were ready to. Ejected with a nondisclosure document and a wheelbarrow full of threats to ensure my silence. Maybe that's it. Maybe that's all there was to it."

"They used you."

"They *screwed* me — both of us. A lot of the fallout comes down on you, too. That's just *wrong*."

"What are you going to do?"

"I don't know. It all happened so fast. I have to think about this."

As he said that, the doorbell rang. He looked back over his shoulder at the door and glanced at his watch. Livvy suggested, "Could be the mailman with a package. He usually comes around at about this time."

"Alright," he said, getting up on his feet, "I'll get it."

While his wife wiped her eyes with a tissue, he opened the door and found standing on the porch, in fact, the mailman. "Certified letter, Mr. Foster." He was holding an envelope in his hand with a green card attached to the front of it. He handed Foster a pen and then pointed to the box at the bottom of the card where he needed to sign.

Foster braced the envelope up against the open door and signed inside the box, then handed it and the pen back to the mailman who tore off the green card at the perforations and handed the envelope back to him, "Thanks, Mr. Foster. You have a nice day."

"You, too, Mr. Beazly."

He closed the door and looked down at the envelope, the return address in the corner had an icon of an eagle's head beside the words "Internal Revenue Service." He groaned.

"What is it, Denny?"

He walked back into the living room, tearing the envelope open as he did, "It's from the IRS. They said something about this at the meeting this morning. Adding more injury to insult," he quickly scanned the content of the letter. "The government is seizing our assets for nonpayment of our income taxes for the past eight years."

"What?! We paid our taxes, we *always* pay our taxes! We hire an accountant to do our taxes just to be sure we get it right and send them enough every year."

"I know, I know. It's just another stab in the back to remind us of how much of a reach these people have — that they can reach out and hurt us any time they like. I'll call our attorney in the morning and sit down with him about this. I'm sure he'll be able to clear it up."

"I sure hope so. I'm scared. If they can do this, what else can they do to us?"

He sat down again on the coffee table and then reached out and wrapped his arms around his wife. She held him tightly and he whispered to her, "It'll be alright, it'll be alright. I promise. I'd never do anything to hurt you or our marriage. Believe me, it will be alright."

"I'm sorry, Denny — I know. I love you, I do."

"I love you, too, sweetie…"

A knock on the front door interrupted their consolances. Foster sat back upright, his hands still holding onto his wife's shoulders, and looked back around at the door. "Who in the world could it be now?"

"I honestly don't know. The mailman's already been here."

"Probably some salesman or something. Just ignore him, maybe he'll just go away."

The knocking repeated. Foster continued to ignore it.

The person knocked again, even louder, as though trying to be heard should the first couple of attempts hadn't been.

"I don't think they're going away," Livvy sighed.

Foster stood up, "Hmph — I'll get rid of them, whoever it is."

He walked to the front door calling out, "I'm coming, I'm coming!" as he walked across the living room floor. When he pulled the door open, there stood his neighbor, Ted, on the porch with a broad smile on his face.

"Hey, Denny, I saw the cab drop you off, thought I'd come by and…"

Before he could finish his sentence, Foster swung the screen door open and awkwardly swung his right arm, slamming his fist into Ted's face. The blow catching him entirely by surprise and sending him reeling backward, tripping and tumbling down the porch steps and landing sprawled on his back on the front lawn.

"Denny!" Livvy shouted, seeing what happened from where she was sitting in the living room. She jumped to her feet and ran to the door as Foster, shaking his hand from the pain of the impact, ran down the steps to pursue Ted out onto the grass.

"You're one of them! Aren't you?! *Aren't you?!!*"

Ted, splayed out on the lawn with blood oozing from the nostrils of his broken nose and his hands raised, frantically trying to defend himself from the rampaging Foster, groveled, "One of *who?!* What are you talking about, Denny?! *Please!*"

Livvy caught up with her husband and just grabbed his arm from behind, "Denny, please stop! You said yourself the pictures were all fake. I promise you, Ted has been a perfect gentleman all the time you've been gone! A pest sometimes, but he never tried anything."

"Yeah, yeah — a pest! I guess that's fair!" Ted, still on his back on the grass, was trying to squirm away from Foster lest he get any more of a pommeling, "But I never touched her, Denny! Never! *Honest!*" He begged, "*Please don't hit me again!*"

"Denny, please, I think he's had enough!" Livvy pleaded, trying to hold him back.

Foster stopped chasing Ted, pathetically trying to wriggle away across the lawn. Besides, he was a physicist, not a pugilist. His hand hurt and he feared that he may have even broken a bone or two — but it felt so good to have made contact with his nemesis' face, so satisfying that he badly wanted to do it again, even if he ended up in a cast for a few weeks.

"Get up, Ted," he growled.

"You're just gonna to punch me again!"

"No, as much as I want to — and I *really do* — I'm not going to punch you again. Get up and get the hell off my lawn!" He turned away from the groveling Ted and wrapped his arm around Livvy to walk back into the house. As they walked away from him, he added over his shoulder, "I never want to see you again, Ted. Never." ∎

CHAPTER THIRTY

The Breaking Point

A few weeks later, early on a Sunday morning, Foster was up early because he couldn't sleep and was beginning to develop a headache lying in bed after hours of staring at the ceiling in the dark and obsessing over all that had happened to him and his new circumstances suddenly thrust upon him. He wrapped his robe around himself and slipped his feet into slippers, then began walking down the stairs to start the coffee maker in the kitchen.

With the Mr. Coffee machine gurgling, making the first pot of the day, he shuffled through the living room to the front door to go out and gather up his newspaper from where the neighborhood paperboy typically would toss it in the middle of his driveway. As he opened the door, he looked out and saw a tow truck in the dim morning light at that moment rolling out of his driveway with his pickup truck hung on the back of it and then quickly drive up the street and around the corner before he had a chance to even step off the porch.

All he could do was stand there and watch in stunned silence as his repossessed truck was towed away and disappear out of the neighborhood.

Out of the corner of his eye, he noticed a shadowy figure standing on the sidewalk across the way. A man dressed in black wearing mirrored sunglasses was looking directly across at him.

Foster's face flushed with rage. Without a moment's thought he dashed down the steps and across the lawn. He ran out into the street in his slippers, but before he could get to him, the man in black had calmly slipped into a dark sedan idling at the curb and driven off leaving Foster standing in the middle of the street in disbelief and steeping with inconsolable anger.

The IRS had frozen his bank accounts. The checks that he'd written for the previous four months had all retroactively bounced and had arrived at his home from the bank by courier stamped "NSF" — insufficient funds. Not just the checks for the payments on his truck, but all of the payments they'd made for everything.

Though he actually had enough money in the bank to support himself and Livvy fairly well for a short time while he looked for another job, it was inaccessible. He was, for all practical purposes, suddenly and thoroughly broke.

He dejectedly turned and walked back across the street and up his driveway, scooping up the newspaper along the way, and stepped up onto his porch. Before going into the house, he glanced across to the empty space where his pickup truck had been parked in the driveway and happened to notice Ted standing alone on the sidewalk across the street in front of his own house. The man didn't say anything, didn't wave or make any sort of gesture. He just stood there.

Convinced that Ted was one of "them" and probably had something to do with all of their suspect financial difficulties and his truck being towed away that morning, Foster didn't respond. He just turned and walked back into the house and shut the door.

* * * * *

With their bank accounts frozen, collection agencies were continually hounding them on the phone (until their phone service was ultimately disconnected) and knocking at their front door. The IRS case was going nowhere fast. Foster needed to get a job, and quickly. He continued to send out resumes and check the help-wanted listings in the local newspapers but wasn't able to get much of even a nibble.

He was desperate to sign on for anything that would help them pay the bills until something permanent came along. It was as if he had somehow been flagged as some sort of pariah by someone — and he had a fair idea by whom.

Livvy was able to get a job as a waitress at a local restaurant. She had been a waitress in her college days which, ironically, was the way she and Foster had met. She hated it, but considered that something was far better than nothing. The paycheck wasn't much but tips were pretty good — and in cash. Foster thought he'd try his hand as a car salesman at a local dealership that was looking for help and willing to hire any warm body still drawing breath. He soon discovered that he just wasn't cut out for it. Besides, he would occasionally walk out onto the car lot and see one of the men in black suits loitering about. Even there, they wouldn't leave him alone.

He finally found a second shift job at a warehouse picking orders of office supplies and packing them up for delivery or shipping out during the following day shift. It was back-breaking work that he wasn't accustomed to and he'd often come home and make his first priority the bottle of aspirins kept on the kitchen counter just for him to cope with the hard, manual work that he had come to pursue. But the evening hours allowed him the day to look for a permanent position in his field of aerospace expertise. With his degrees and very specialized experience, there were any number of jobs that he could do — he just had to find the right opportunity and make that all-so-critical connection.

For the next few months, he and Livvy worked hard together to try and make ends meet. He was working the second shift at the warehouse and she, the day shift at the restaurant. They rarely saw one another when one or the other of them weren't sleeping.

They sold whatever they could to bring in a little more money and even held a garage sale one weekend. Still, with the two jobs that they had and the median income that they were able to bring in, it wasn't enough. Tensions incrementally rose between them as the weeks and months passed.

At first, realizing that money had become a wedge and intent throughout their marriage, they would never allow that to happen. They'd always had more than enough and had never been in such a situation before. They both tried hard to set their concerns aside and recommit themselves to their marriage and to one another. But, like an exposed nerve, things only got more and more difficult and tensions gradually intensified.

Depression, despondent frustrations and some lingering suspicions grew in their relationship like invasive weeds, sucking away any remnants of a happy life together. Eventually it just became a daily routine of just going through the motions of going to work, eating, sleeping and repeating day after trackless day until the pair were simply existing like some sort of emotionless robots trapped in an endless loop.

Both wondered just how much longer they could go on. ■

CHAPTER THIRTY-ONE

Separate Ways

More and more frequently, when the Fosters might happen to both be home at the same time, disagreements would quickly flare into arguments. Arguments escalated to shouting matches which would eventually lead to days of bitter silence. Neither of them had ever heard the other raise their voices at them more than a few times in all they years they'd been together but, by then, it was an all too regular occurrence.

Each blamed the other but mostly, at its root, Foster shouldered most of it. The dubious specter of infidelity haunted them both. It was the ever-present nine-hundred-pound-gorilla in the room. Unspoken suspicions continually laid just under the surface and would more and more frequently rise to fuel heated arguments laced with more and more pointed accusations.

Neither wanted to believe the worst of the other, especially knowing that whatever allegations had been leveled at either of them had been fabricated by powerful people for reasons that they could only surmise. But the nagging thought — especially as their relationship continued to disintegrate — that where there was smoke, there was probably fire, continually haunted them. Such thoughts populated their sleep and nagged at them throughout each day.

When they weren't at one another's throats, the silence between them was almost deafening.

Foster woke up one day at around midday and made his way down the stairs to the living room. When he lighted onto the first floor, he found Livvy standing there with the stack of mail that she'd just brought in from the mailbox in her hand, leafing through it. Red-faced, she was obviously on the ragged emotional edge of tears, she looked up at him, "We're not going to make it, Denny — are we?"

"What are you talking about? It's been a little rough but we're okay so far."

"What about the IRS? Have you heard anything from the lawyer?"

"I'm going to call him today before I head out for work."

"So you haven't?"

"No, not yet." He walked past her, heading for the kitchen and a much-needed cup of coffee.

"So, when are we going to hear something?!"

"I told you, I'm gonna call him *today*."

"This is really hard, Denny! I don't know how much longer I can take this!"

"What are you saying?"

"You've got to find a good job like *now* or we're going to lose *everything!*"

"I'm trying — you *know* I am!"

"Maybe you need to try *harder!*" The dam of her tears finally burst and she began to break down.

"Can't you see? They've got it all rigged! I'm doing the best that I can!"

Livvy reached for the roll of paper towels on the counter to wipe her face, "It's not good enough! I'm sorry — it's just *not!*"

"It damned well better be! It *has to be!*" He stormed out of the kitchen into the living room, she chased after him in her anger.

"I know you're thinking about her!"

"What? Huh?" Foster stopped in his tracks and turned back toward his wife. "Thinking about *her?* About *who?*"

"That *Jennifer* woman!"

"You think I'm fantasizing about her?! You can't be any more wrong! The woman is certifiably *insane,* lied *through her teeth!* Destroyed my career!"

"I can't believe *anything* that you say anymore!" Her voice rose even louder. "You saw her naked — *another woman!* A sexy, younger woman!"

"And what about Ted?!" he shot back.

"Ted!?"

"Yeah! Why did he answer the phone all out of breath when I called home?!"

"I have no idea what you're talking about!"

"And you say you can't believe what *I* say!?" In his rage, he reached out to grab something off of the shelf behind him to throw against the wall. He blindly picked up the first thing his hand fell onto and reeled back to hurl it.

Livvy shrieked in shock when she saw what he was holding.

He saw her reaction and froze for a moment.

He looked down at his hand. He was holding the plastic figurines that had topped their wedding cake, preserved and long displayed on the shelf as a memento and symbol of their vows. Realizing how fragile it was, he quickly opened his fingers and just stood there with it resting on his open palm.

Livvy could no longer contain herself, she burst out into uncontrolled tears. Bawling, she just turned and ran up the stairs. A moment later he could hear the bedroom door slam shut.

Foster carefully replaced the cake topper onto the shelf and looked at it for a long moment realizing that he had nearly destroyed the last symbol of their union and how poignant that thought was. How the two of them were progressively doing the very same thing in real life.

Maybe her question to him was right. Maybe they weren't going to make it.

The following morning, Livvy got up early and left the house. Foster had spent the night in the guest bedroom which would, from that day forward, become his own.

She drove into town and parked in front of a three-story office building on Main Street. Sniffling and clutching a handkerchief, she sat in the car for a little while to get a grip on her emotions. Finally, she wiped her eyes one last time, grabbed her purse and pushed the door open. She climbed out of the driver's seat and walked up to the front doors of the building.

In the small vestibule inside was a directory sign on the wall. She quickly studied and saw that the office she was looking for was on the third floor. She rode the elevator up and, when she stepped out into the hallway, another sign pointed her in the right direction.

She found the door she was looking for and paused for a moment in the hallway just outside. She took a deep breath. She hesitated but finally planted her hand on the knob, turned it, and walked into the reception area.

"Good morning," a woman dressed in classic office attire sitting behind a desk in a small lobby greeted her. "May I help you?"

Livvy took a breath and replied, "I think so."

"You need to see Attorney Jenkins about something? Do you have an appointment?"

"No, I don't have an appointment — I need to talk with someone about getting a divorce."

* * * * *

On the fateful day that the IRS finally seized the Fosters' house and its contents, a county sheriff pulled up and parked along the curb out front with one of his deputies who also pulled up and parked right behind. They walked up to the front porch and rang the bell. Foster answered the door and saw the two men in uniform standing there looking grimly at him.

"Dennis Foster?" the sheriff asked.

"Yes," he knew that was the day that they were to vacate the house, but wasn't expecting law enforcement officers at his door.

The sheriff handed him some papers which essentially told the Fosters that they were each allowed only to take one suitcase with them. He'd gotten that same notification from the IRS a couple of weeks before with the final payment demand. He glanced over it and Livvy walked up behind him and looked over his shoulder at it.

"We're all packed," she told the sheriff.

"Good. I'm hoping we can do this with as little grief as possible."

"I don't envy your job," Foster quipped as he folded the paper and laid it on the top of his suitcase already waiting by the door next to his wife's. "I know this isn't your fault. We know who's to blame for all of this — we'll cooperate."

"I'm glad to hear that. The guy from the IRS should be along shortly with some papers and then we can wrap this up."

Just as he said that, a gray sedan pulled up and parked along the curb across the street from the two sheriff's patrol cars and two men in dark suits got out, one of them carrying a briefcase. They crossed the street and walked up the driveway to join the officers on the porch.

"Mr. Foster," one of them addressed.

"Yes. You two are from the IRS, I presume?"

"We are." The man reached out with an envelope, "I'll need you to sign this, please."

Foster pulled the envelope open and pulled out a document of a few sheets stapled together in the top corner. He glanced over it quickly and then reached out to hand it to Livvy, "It doesn't matter, Denny, we've got to sign it anyway — right?"

"I suppose so."

The sheriff plucked a Cross pen from his pocket and handed it to Foster. "Thanks."

Leaning the papers up against the open door, they each signed the last page where their names appeared and effectively surrendered the house and all of their other remaining worldly assets to the Internal Revenue Service to be auctioned off.

He handed the papers back to the IRS agent and the pen to the sheriff. As they stood there, a pair of yellow taxi cabs pulled up into the end of the driveway and parked side by side.

"Well, I guess this is it," The sheriff said, noticing the two cabs and, too, that the Fosters were not leaving together.

"Yeah, I guess it is," Foster whispered.

He and Livvy then picked up their respective suitcases and walked past the officers and agents on their porch and out toward the driveway. When they got to the two cabs, they looked back at their house that had been for so many years their happy home as the two IRS agents were stretching yellow tape across the door, stapling a notice to the center of it and screwing on a hasp at its edge to padlock it shut.

Both of the Fosters couldn't help but feel a painful lump in their throats, their eyes welling up. How, they thought, did it all come to that? How did such a life of love and devotion come crashing down so thoroughly?

The two of them stood in their driveway looking across the tops of the two taxi cabs at one another silently for many long minutes as the two cab drivers put their suitcases into the trunks.

There was so much they each wanted to say to one another but just couldn't find the words.

Perhaps they'd already said more than enough by then — maybe too much. If either of them had uttered a syllable just then they might just make things worse or break down altogether, or both.

The sadness in both their shattered hearts was overwhelming.

Then, finally, the expected inevitable happened.

Dennis and Livvy Foster turned away from one another, got into the back seats of the two respective yellow cabs, and went their separate ways. ■

CHAPTER THIRTY-TWO

Shabby But Clean

With the small paycheck he'd gotten from working at the warehouse, Foster was able to save up a small nest egg and buy himself a used car — a very used car. It wasn't much, a twelve year old Dodge Dart with a lot of miles on it. It burned a little bit of oil but it had been well cared-for by its one owner and was in pretty good condition for its age. The car dealer that he had briefly worked for gave him a good deal on it knowing that, because of its age and mileage, no bank would finance a sale for it, so when he offered a few hundred dollars cash for it, they were willing to help him out and sell it to him.

Late one night, he drove to his house that still had the IRS's yellow warning tape across the front door and a hasp and padlock securing it closed. He parked in the space alongside the garage where he used to park the race car trailer. It would be, for the most part, out of sight from the street in the dark. He then snuck around to the back of the garage and found a window that he'd always forgotten to lock when he lived there, hoping the feds hadn't stumbled on it.

They hadn't. It wasn't locked.

He pushed it open and climbed inside, landing on top of the washing machine in the dark and clumsily tumbling onto the concrete floor. He groaned to himself, reached up to grab the corner of the machine for support and pulled himself up onto his feet. A few bruises would probably show themselves in the morning but, otherwise, he was fine. He brushed himself off and walked over to his work bench.

The power was shut off but he'd brought a flashlight with him. He found some of his tools and jimmied open the door from the garage into the house. Once inside, he went into his office and took all of his printed resumes and packed them into a cardboard box along with his computer, printer, disks and other peripherals. He took a quick look at his bookshelves and grabbed a few books that he thought he might need if he were ever able to get another job as a physicist. So many other things that he wanted to take, but he knew he just didn't have room in the car and nowhere to store them — at that moment he was homeless. There were other more important things to be gathered.

He grabbed up another box on the floor, the one still packed from when he'd left Cyberdyne Technologies that held his framed diplomas, certificates and his treasured photo with astronaut Michael Collins and whatever else he had stuffed in the box at the time. There was room in there for a few more items and then he took that, too.

He set the boxes and the computer monitor in the kitchen by the door to the garage along with a short stack of books as he walked out through the living room. Upstairs, he pulled an empty suitcase out of the closet and threw it open on the bed. He stuffed in some of his clothes — shirts, pants and a pair of dress shoes from the closet, underwear and socks from the dresser. He grabbed a couple of ties to be prepared for job interviews and pulled down a couple of his sport coats on their wooden hangers and covered them with large, plastic garbage bags that he'd brought up with him from the kitchen as makeshift garment bags. In the bathroom, he grabbed his electric razor and any bottles of over-the-counter preparations that he thought would be useful to take like aspirin, antacids and cold pills, a spray can of deodorant and a tube of Ben-Gay along with a tube of hemorrhoid cream — just in case.

He stuffed everything into the suitcase and a large, canvas shopping bag that he'd found in the closet with long, looping handles and brought them all downstairs to add to the pile by the garage door. In the dark living room, the streetlight shining through the front window glinted off of one of his racing trophies on the shelf. It gave him a moment's pause.

He wanted so much to take them all with him but there was no room for them and, besides, that was a lifetime ago. Still, some of the fondest memories of his adult life were contained in them as he studied them, slowly panning the flashlight's beam across the row of shining brass and gleaming silver. He decided to take three of them, the first place trophy for the first race that he'd won some years before, the one for winning the regional championship and the second place trophy that he had scored in the very last race that he and his friend, Luke, had contested together before he got the government job that had since flushed his entire life into the sewer. He had no idea what he'd do with them, but he took them anyway.

As he was taking the trophies down from the shelf and laying them down in a box, he noticed that, on the same shelf, stood the plastic cake-topper from his wedding to Livvy. The very same icon that he nearly smashed in a fit of rage just few weeks before. A lump rose in his throat. In the darkened room, he just stood and stared at it for a long moment, the guilt of what was happening to the two of them hung heavily on his heart.

Finally, with his throat choking up and his eyes beginning to well up, he reached up and took the small statue down and placed it into the box. Hope springs eternal, he thought. Maybe one day he would make things right again with Livvy and she'd come back to him.

He could only hope. Going forward from that moment, she would be his quest, his purpose, his obsession. As he saw things, there really was no other reason to go on.

Before leaving his garage, he filled an old backpack with a collection of essential hand tools that he thought he might need to fix his old car or, maybe, just hang a picture one day.

With the power having been shut off, he raised the overhead garage door by hand just enough to slide everything outside onto the driveway. He then closed the door, climbed back out through the back window and loaded everything into the trunk and the back seat of his car.

He pulled out of his driveway for the last time and began driving east to Las Vegas hoping that, if he could just get out of California, maybe he could make a fresh start in another state, another city. The areas around Las Vegas were rife with high-technology industries, he might have a much better chance of finding a good position out there and, maybe after he got himself established, he might be able to patch things up with Livvy and get their lives together back on track.

Maybe.

He drove all night and into the early morning. With a few dollars in his pocket, he could get enough gas to make it and maybe get a bite to eat when he got there. After that, if he didn't find work quickly, he'd have to live in his car for a while.

It wasn't much of a plan but then maybe that was the price to pay for trusting the wrong people.

* * * * *

Feeling very alone in his car stuffed full of his remaining worldly belongings, he rolled into the outskirts of Las Vegas and saw the iconic, triangular yellow sign welcoming him as he approached the famed downtown strip of casinos, towering hotels and miniature reproductions of the Statue of Liberty and the Eiffel Tower. Roller coasters swirled around many of the buildings, their windows glittering with reflections of the bright, golden early morning sun rising in the east.

It didn't look at all as he had expected it to. Bright, flashing lights give the illusion of fun and excitement by night, but then daylight has a way of illuminating the darkest of places with the stark light of reality. The homeless shuffling along the dirty sidewalks beginning their day long quest for whatever they might find to get by for just one more day. The grifters who were still plying their nocturnal trade as the morning sun rose, preying on tourists as they packed themselves up and left their hotel rooms to drive or fly home. The busses that had driven through the previous day, bringing excitedly anticipatory tourists into the city from miles around for a night of revelry, stage shows and gambling, lined up at the curbs to bring the disappointed, exhausted and financially drained back home again.

Traffic through the strip was slow and a little busier than he had expected it would be at that early hour. He drove through its length and found that, on the other end of town away from downtown and the flow of tourists from the west, the glittering oasis dwindled quickly. A few small hotels with storefront casinos were intermingled with two- and three-story retail shops with apartment flats on their upper floors. Eventually, he came upon Chick's Diner.

It was a shabby looking place, but not notably dirty. It just seemed like it had been out there exposed in the desert for a long, long time. The sign was sun-faded and somewhat sandblasted by the desert winds. The building's famously American looking stainless steel facades were dulled by the same gritty winds. But the windows were clean as though they were routinely washed and the parking lot was devoid of weeds growing up from its many cracks (save for those along its outermost perimeters).

Shabby, yes, but clean and well cared for by its owners for many years.

He pulled in and parked his equally shabby looking Dodge in an empty space near the front door. He made sure to lock the doors before walking away from the car as everything he owned was inside. As he walked in, he saw taped to the inside of the glass in the door, a sign saying "help wanted." The faded sign with yellowed, dried-out and peeling Scotch tape barely holding it in place looked like it had been there for quite a while.

When he walked into the dining room he noticed that, just inside the door next to a rack of tourist literature and maps, were a pair of slot machines. He was at once surprised to see them there in a diner of all places but then realized that in that town, that sort of thing was pervasive. They were literally everywhere. He didn't give them a second glance and took a seat at the counter. A rotund, middle-aged waitress with dark brown skin, her curly, black hair gathered up behind her neck and cascading down over her collar, smiled at him and welcomed him as she set a menu down on the counter in front of him. She hovered for a moment and then cheerfully asked, "Coffee, hon?"

He couldn't help but smile to himself in response, "Sure, coffee — please."

She turned to the counter along the shiny, stainless steel wall behind her and fetched a white porcelain coffee mug off of a tray half filled with them, flipped it right-side-up and poured him a cup of freshly-made coffee. She set the mug down in front of him with a spoon on a folded, paper napkin. She then set a small, metal creamer and fluted glass sugar dispenser next to the napkin holder in front of him. "Y'all know what you want, hon?"

"Yeah, I think I'll have the two-egg breakfast."

"Excellent choice," she complimented with a smile (she said that to almost everyone in response to whatever selection they might make). "How would you like your eggs?"

"Over easy, thanks."

"Toast?"

"Yes."

She grinned, "I mean, *what kind* of toast would y'all like, hon? White? Wheat? Raisin?"

"Oh, sorry. White, please."

"Okay — I'll get this right in for ya'."

"Thanks."

The waitress turned and walked to the large pass-through opening to the kitchen in the back wall and clipped the slip from her order pad up onto a revolving metal rack, spun it around so that the paper showed to the cook on the other side, and then slapped her hand onto a bell next to it to alert that there was an order in to be filled.

Foster reached for the creamer and the sugar dispenser and began to render his coffee when the waitress returned with a wire rack filled with small, rectangular plastic packs of jams, jellies and marmalades. She set it down in front of him and he nodded his thanks and then, rather spontaneously, he asked, "The sign in your door. You're looking for help?"

She stopped and turned back to him and smiled, "Yeah, we are. Short order cook, nights. Why — y'all interested, hon?"

"I think so. I literally just got into town, all my stuff is packed in my car out there. I was hoping to find a job to get me started here in Vegas."

"Well, it don't pay much but y'all get a cut of the waitress' tips and ya' can take food home if ya' like. But I gotta warn ya', the night shift is when all the freaks come out."

"Freaks?"

"Ha, ha, ha! Yeah, *freaks* — this is *Vegas,* hon! I don't care where ya' from, y'all ain't seen *nothin'* yet, I promise."

It appeared to him that the owners of the diner were probably as desperate to find someone to fill that position as he was to find a job — any job. Maybe in their mutual desperation, they'd overlook the fact that his only experience as a cook was burgers and chicken on his back-yard barbecue grill. Besides, he was literally a rocket scientist, a Mensa member — how hard could it be?

"I've seen some pretty strange stuff in my lifetime, I assure you. I doubt that I'd see much else that would shock me."

"Suit yerself," she chuckled. "If y'all still game for it, come on back around at six. Chick'll be here for the night shift and he can show ya' the ropes."

"I'll definitely think about it. Thanks."

With no other options presenting themselves in such quick order,

Foster went back that evening and took the job. He found that he actually had an aptitude for being a short-order cook. It required its own sort of expertise, but it really *wasn't* rocket science, after all.

Chick, the diner's owner, showed him where a couple of baseball bats were strategically kept for emergencies — one under the counter, the other back in the kitchen — and checked him out on the sawed-off twelve-gauge shotgun kept under the cash register. He explained that all of his employees who worked the night shift were checked out on these things, including the waitresses. On that late shift, he might have to deal with some undesirable and even potentially dangerous characters and it could get dicey at times.

Who knew that working in a diner could be so treacherous, he thought. But after what he'd just been through at Area Fifty-One and all that the government had put him through, he figured that he was ready for just about anything.

Chick gave him an advance so that he could get himself checked into a local motor inn, he'd at least have somewhere to sleep besides the front seat of his car. After a few weeks, once he had saved up some money and with Chick's endorsement, he would get an inexpensive apartment above a pizza shop in one of the buildings in that part of town not too far from the diner.

For the time being, however, he was thankful that things were working out as they were and so quickly. Maybe he really had been able to leave all of his trials behind in California. Maybe it really was a fresh start.

His only lament was that he was going it alone without Livvy. She was, after all, his goal once he got back on his feet. The diner gig seemed to be a good first step and he was grateful for it.

After a few weeks, Chick left him to solo on the overnight shift with one waitress and one other who floated between waiting on tables, bussing them and helping out in the kitchen. A few of the women rotated every few days on the night shift. Chick worked the late shift for Foster in the kitchen on a couple of nights each week so that he could have a break now and again. He got to know the crew that he was working with fairly quickly and they all got along reasonably well and functioned together like a well-oiled machine night after night.

Like his second shift warehouse job back in California, having the days free was opportunity to look for a permanent job in his field. Once he had found an apartment to settle into, he set up his computer and began his job search again in earnest. The area around Las Vegas was a hub for high-technology firms and parts of what was still a vibrant core of the aerospace industry. He watched the newspaper want ads and answered every ad that he thought he might qualify for. He also cold-called on every company that he could find, in person when he could, by mail when he couldn't.

He got a number of "thanks-but-no-thanks" and "we'll-keep-your-resume-on-file" responses along the way, but he tried not to get discouraged and persevered. Finally, he got a phone call asking him to come by for an interview. It was with a turbine engine manufacturer in an industrial park near the airport.

At last, maybe things were beginning to look up for him. Maybe he would finally be getting that second chance that he was hoping for. ■

CHAPTER THIRTY-THREE

Break In

Foster got up on Wednesday morning, shaved, showered, put on a freshly-ironed dress shirt, slacks, and a tie. He wiped his not-so-shiny dress shoes with used cooking oil that he'd brought home from the diner the night before in an empty soda bottle and buffed them up to make them as glossy as possible. Then he grabbed up his briefcase and suit jacket to head off for his interview at Consolidated Turbine Industries.

He felt good. The job sounded like just the sort of thing that he could apply himself to with some real potential. He was encouraged that perhaps he might get a taste of those heady days of Apollo and the Shuttle program again.

The roads around McCarran airport were a maze, especially in and around the industrial park where he was slowly meandering, looking for the address he'd written on a note taped to his dashboard. Most all of the corrugated metal buildings looked much the same as one another, some were beige, most of the others were blue. The signs were small and easy to miss as he drove around but, thankfully, he didn't get too lost. He had left early, anticipating difficulty in locating the place as he was still pretty unfamiliar with his chosen new city and didn't want to be late.

He finally found the driveway leading back to his destination and pulled into the parking lot. He took a glance at his watch — still fifteen minutes to spare. He breathed a quick sigh of relief and got out of the car. He slipped on his suit jacket and grabbed the handle of his briefcase then made sure that he'd locked the doors before slipping the keys into his pocket and walking up to the front door.

Feeling reasonably confident and imminently hopeful, he walked through the glass doors into the vestibule and through to the lobby. A guard at a desk directed him to the office of Mr. George Parsons, the man with whom he was to interview.

He found Parsons' office down the hall and walked in through the glass door to an outer reception space attended by a secretary who checked her appointment book and then directed him to have a seat in one of the chairs along the opposite wall to wait for his appointed time. She noted that Mr. Parsons was running just a little late but Foster, still enthusiastic about his prospects, was more than willing to wait.

Eventually, the door to Parsons' office opened and a young man in a suit and carrying a briefcase stepped out and paused just outside. Parsons, a stout, older, balding man with graying hair and glasses, shook the man's hand and thanked him for having come to meet with him.

"I look forward to hearing from you, Mr. Parsons." The man replied with a salesman's smile.

"I'll be making a decision by the end of the week. We'll be in touch."

"Thanks again." The man turned, glanced quickly at Foster as he walked past as though sizing up the somewhat older competition, and then walked out the door to the hallway.

Expecting to be called into the office immediately upon the previous appointment having left, Foster was just beginning to lift himself up off of the seat but then surprised to see Parsons quickly disappear back inside, closing the door behind himself.

Trying to remain positive, he reasoned to himself that Parsons probably had to return a phone call or use his personal rest room or something before welcoming in his next interviewee.

After a few minutes that seemed to pass like hours, the secretary's intercom buzzed and she got the word to send Foster in. He got up, brushed his suit jacket smooth, picked up his briefcase and walked up to the door. He gently knocked and then let himself in.

"Ah, Mr. Foster," Parsons said, rising from his chair behind the desk. "Please, have a seat."

"Thank you." He saw a few chairs arranged in front of the desk facing it and sat in the center, setting his briefcase on the floor beside him.

Parsons had a folder on his desk blotter that he opened up and glanced at the contents quickly before beginning. "Thank you for sending us your resume, Mr. Foster. At first blush it appears that you could be a perfect fit for one of the positions that we're currently looking to fill."

"Thanks."

"You worked for Cyberdyne Technologies out in Burbank for a number of years."

"I did."

"What did you do there?"

"Mostly I studied particle dynamics. We designed and built components for the space program. The systems and the astronauts needed to be protected from radiations of varying types while out in open space. I studied the isotopes and particles that we needed to protect them from and helped develop the shielding that we'd build into our own components and to help shield the spacecraft and its crew."

"Sounds like pretty intensive work."

"Sometimes it really was. We were always aware of our predecessors' race to beat the Russians to the moon. Those were pretty exciting times."

"I'll bet. Why did you leave there?"

"Well, the space program is winding down. A lot of people in technical positions like mine were being laid off. In fact, the entire department where I was working was being eliminated, a dozen people would ultimately be let go."

"I've gotten a lot of response to my job postings from people just like you, alumni of the space race."

"I can imagine."

"I need to tell you that much of the work we do here is on government contracts and many of them require a fairly high level of security clearance so we have to be very careful of whom we hire — not just their technical capabilities but their backgrounds to be sure they would be able to secure those government clearances. So we check out everyone pretty thoroughly."

"I understand."

"Your resume says that you have doctorates from California Polytechnic as well as one from the Massachusetts Institute of Technology along with a PhD from there. That's pretty impressive."

"Thank you. It's been a huge investment of my life but those degrees have served me well over the years."

"Were you aware, Mr. Foster, that falsely claiming to have such degrees when applying for a job is illegal? For a government position or one that would require a government security clearance, it's actually a felony."

Unsure of just why Parsons was telling him that, he replied, "No, I wasn't aware of that but, considering the gravity of that sort of work, it would make sense."

"We contacted both of these institutions to verify your credentials. Neither could find any record of you ever having attended either of them."

Foster sat frozen in his chair for a moment. He couldn't believe what he was hearing.

"I, I'm sure it's just a mistake."

"One school, maybe, could be some sort of clerical error, I'll give you that. But two schools on opposite sides of the country? Two schools of such esteem? That's too much to be a simple coincidence."

"But I have diplomas, transcripts."

"Diplomas can be forged — I've actually seen some pretty good fakes in my day."

"I'm sure it's a mistake, some kind of mix-up, computer glitch. I'll call them, I'll get this straightened out."

Parsons leered across his desk at the crestfallen Foster for an interminably long moment. "I'll tell you what I'll do, Mr. Foster, I'll give you the benefit of the doubt. I won't call the FBI on you. If you have any success with MIT or CalTech, call me. But if this is a scam, I expect you to give it up and stop trying to pass yourself off as being so qualified. You're wasting a lot of people's valuable time and, eventually, someone won't give you such a break and will call the authorities. As I said though, on paper you look like a good fit here and I know that you'd be a real asset so I'm really hoping you're right. But, for now, I just can't take the chance. Sorry."

Foster knew exactly what — or rather *who* — had happened. It wasn't the schools. Dwayne Steele, M7, the CIA — or whomever it was who was pulling the strings — was still dogging after him. They wanted to keep him down, keep him under the radar so that he could never be taken seriously anywhere ever again. So that he'd keep his mouth shut about what he'd seen at Facility R-Four-Seven. So that he would just disappear.

He left Parsons' office and dejectedly drove home to his second floor flat above the pizza shop and took off his dress slacks and suit jacket, brushing them down first, and then hanging them up in the closet, covering them up with a large plastic trash bag with a hole cut out of the bottom for the coat hanger's hook to protrude. He wiped down his shiny dress shoes and slipped them into a paper bag to keep them clean of dust — the desert air was pervasive and seemed to penetrate through every crack and crevice. He was constantly dusting the interior of his apartment and he wanted to preserve his one remaining pair of dress shoes for as long as possible.

He pulled on his freshly laundered but hopelessly stained white work pants and a white denim shirt. He looked at his watch and realized that he wouldn't have to report to the diner for work for a few hours. He didn't have anywhere to go, nothing to do to kill the time. Besides, he was far too distracted to be able to engage his mind on anything at that point so he just took a beer from his refrigerator, flipped on the television and sat himself down on the sofa to mindlessly watch whatever might be on the screen just then — a pass-time he'd abhorred and thus far avoided but, at that moment, resolved himself to. He feared that he was becoming just the man he'd hoped he never would.

* * * * *

The following evening, he arrived at work at the diner, pulled on his cook's apron, donned a ball cap to contain his hair while working in the kitchen per local health regulations and to try and keep the ever-present airborne grease from coating it as it tended to penetrate everything.

For the first couple of hours, Chick would work with him in the kitchen to have a couple of extra hands on deck during the dinner rush but then, by around six-thirty or so, he'd hang up his apron and leave Foster with a dwindling troupe of waitresses, bussers and kitchen help until it was just him with the usual pair to get through to two o'clock and closing time.

For most of the night, it was typically pretty slow until just about midnight when the second shift at the local factories would let out and they'd get a quick flush of customers, mostly looking for a late-night breakfast before heading for home.

At around eleven-thirty, before that midnight rush would ensue for that night, Foster was making up a large batch of homefried potatoes on the grill in preparation for the expected influx of breakfast orders when he heard the bell at the window. He glanced up and saw an order slip hanging from the revolving rack and Grace, the waitress who had first greeted him there when he'd just arrived in town, smiling at him from behind it.

"I got it!" he called out to her.

He yanked the slip of paper down and began to prepare the various items that were listed on it. Two cheeseburgers, medium-rare, one with bacon, both with fries. He could hear the milk shake blender whirring on the counter outside the order window and voices talking and laughing out in the dining room.

He finished grilling the two burgers and set them into a pair of toasted buns then put them at one end of a pair of oval plates, leaving room for a pile of french fries beside each of them. He gathered up the order slip and the two plates, set them on the shelf in the order window and slapped the bell, "Order up!" he called out.

Looking out at the sparsely populated dining room for Grace to make sure that she'd heard him, he saw a young couple sitting in a booth across from one another by the window talking, laughing and sipping their milkshakes. Grace cruised by, gathered up the two plates, and brought their burgers and fries out to them. As he watched all of the routine goings-on in the dining room, out of the corner of his eye he noticed a lone figure seated a couple of booths to the right near the door. He froze at the sight.

In the seat facing him with just a cup of coffee on the table in front of him was a man in a black suit and mirrored sunglasses, his face in a nearly expressionless, stone-like countenance. He looked up from his cup, turning toward the order window, and looked directly at Foster standing on the other side looking back.

Foster instantly recognized him, staring across the dining room at him with his eyes hidden by the sunglasses. It was unmistakably Dwayne Steele, the man who had crossed his path time and again during his experience at Facility R-Four-Seven. The man who accused him of tax fraud, financial improprieties, cheating on his wife and accused him of raping a co-worker. The man who had threatened him with prison and ultimately had him fired. The man who was probably instrumental in making his academic records evaporate, the IRS to destroy what was left of his life and shredded his marriage.

His sense of shock at seeing the man almost instantly evolved to outright blind rage. His face flushed red as it morphed into a scowl behind gritted teeth. The man continued to just coldly look up at him from the booth.

Foster turned sharply and stepped back from the window. He grabbed the baseball bat that was kept within easy reach leaning up in the corner nearby and raced around to the door to the dining room in a frantic, storming gait.

He shoved the door open and marched out and around the counter to the dining room, his face radiantly red with seething anger. By then, however, the man was gone. He could see the red tail lights of a dark sedan through the big plate glass windows slowly pulling out of the parking lot and turning down the street.

Grace stood behind the counter with a coffee pot in her hand and her mouth open, frozen in disbelief, and just watched as Foster stopped in his tracks in the middle of the dining room, balled up his fists, shaking the bat and groaned out loud, "Aaaauugh!"

"Dennis?" She hesitantly called out. "You okay, hon?"

He stood there for a moment just staring out the window at the parking lot — Steele's car long gone — and then heaved a long breath, turned to her and just grumbled with slouched shoulders, "Yeah, yeah — I'm okay."

"Y'all don't *look* okay. You know that guy?"

"Sort of." He walked back around the counter with the bat in his hand, the flushed redness in his face gradually draining out to a more normal pall. "Have you seen him in here before?" he asked her.

"Dressed like that, all black with sunglasses in the middle of the night? I think I'd notice. But we get all kinds of weirdos in here at all hours — this is Vegas, afterall — I can't really say for sure, hon. Sorry."

"Ahhh, it's okay," he pressed his palm against the swinging door to the kitchen and took a quick glance down at the bat clutched in his other hand. "Do me a favor, would you? Give that couple there with the burgers a free slice of pie for dessert — I think I might have scared them."

The couple were in fact, cowering in the booth, each of them slid as far back in their seats and up against the wall as they could get with a look of terror as though they'd both just seen a rampaging ghost.

"Sure thing — y'all get yerself a cold lemonade or somethin'. Calm down before ya' blow a gasket or somethin'. Yer hands are shakin'."

"Yeah, good advice, Grace. I will," he pushed the door open and walked back into the kitchen.

They had found him. He didn't know how, but they did.

Maybe when he'd taken the job there at the diner and filled out all that paperwork for Social Security and income tax and such, somebody in Washington noticed and passed the word. Maybe there was some kind of red flag on him — somehow, someone was keeping track of him and they had started to haunt him again.

He couldn't help but wonder to what lengths those people might go to destroy him? How far would they take it? What were they afraid of?

He just wanted to be left alone.

The diner closed as it normally did at two o'clock and by two-thirty he and the small crew of two had cleaned up, cashed out the register and locked the doors. Although he could walk to his apartment from there, at that hour of night in that part of town, he preferred to drive the short distance just for safety's sake. The three of them said "good night" to one another in the parking lot as they routinely did each night and drove home through sparsely travelled roads distant from the glittering downtown strip, nearly devoid of nocturnal tourists leaving only the most dangerous, depraved and desperate who inhabited the dark of the night.

Foster pulled into the parking lot behind the pizza shop which was, at that hour, dark inside and had been closed for several hours. He unlocked the back door to the stairwell leading up to the second floor. Exhausted from a night of work and emotionally drained, he trudged up step by step. When he got to the top, there were four apartment doors in the short hallway, two on the left, and two on the right. He walked up to his own door, the last one on the right at the front of the building. A couple of bare light bulbs in fixtures hanging from the ceiling illuminated the hall just enough for him to find his way and steer his key toward the deadbolt lock. As he inserted it, he glanced up along the door jamb and stopped abruptly.

The matchbook cover that he had folded over and closed into the doorframe whenever he'd leave his apartment was gone.

Someone had been inside.

Maybe they were still in there.

If it was Steele or one of his black-attired minions, he knew that calling the police would be futile. He and Livvy had learned that. They'd called them on the men in black who had been following them around back in California on numerous occasions and nothing had ever come of it. Obviously the government spooks had the local police wired.

He was in no mood for any of that. He was tired and was sick of running from those people. He refused to flee his own apartment. He was done being afraid.

Slowly and as quietly as he was able, he turned the key in the lock and then gently pushed the door open. The light from the hallway showed his folded matchbook cover lying on the floor just inside. His hope that perhaps it had just fallen out and gotten swept up in the hallway or that some prankster had simply plucked it out of his door were dashed. Someone had definitely been inside.

In the corner, within reach behind the door, he kept a baseball bat that he'd picked up at a pawn shop in town (taking a cue from the simplistic but effective security measures at the diner). For the second time that night, he grabbed it up and gripped the friction tape wrapped handle tightly in his right hand, choking up on it for quicker and more decisive leverage — and impact.

He flipped on the light switch in the short entryway just inside the door. The light spilled out into the living room and adjacent kitchen area with just enough that, if there had been someone there out in the open, he would have seen them.

Stealthily, Foster crept up the hallway to the end of the short wall that enclosed the kitchen to his right, reached around the end of it and felt for the light switch. Bathed in light, he could see that there was, in fact, nobody there.

He quickly stepped past the intersection with the short hall at his left that led back to the bedroom and bathroom and flicked the switch for the living room light to fully illuminate the room. He didn't see anyone in there but knew that someone could easily be hiding behind some of the few bits of furniture that he had — a sofa and a stuffed chair in the corner. He quietly stepped up to the sofa first, stood back with the bat firmly in his grip, and then reached out, grabbed the corner of it and sharply yanked it back from the wall.

No one behind the sofa.

He repeated the potentially revealing move with the chair and, again, found no one hiding behind it.

He realized that, whomever it was who had broken into his apartment — though he fully expected that it was some one of Steele's men in black — could equally be likely some sort of local drug gang member or just junkies looking to steal something to fence to buy drugs. He'd dealt with Steele's people before and knew them to be far more dangerous than the local street thugs, they didn't scare him. Besides, those people didn't leave the places that they'd break into so neat nor would they bother to re-lock the front door.

Turning toward the hallway again, he ventured down to the bathroom, again turning on every light along the way. He didn't see anyone in the bathroom but then used the end of the bat to quickly slide back the shower curtain to reveal the tub enclosure behind it. No one.

Finally, he came to his bedroom. He noticed a strange green glow coming from inside, something that he'd not seen before. He reached around the wall and felt for the light switch. When he had flicked it on, he quickly stepped into the room with the bat poised to swing. There, on his nightstand, he saw a glowing green lava lamp had been set up, the molten wax inside the globe bubbling up in perpetual undulations.

It was clear that Steele was sending a message. A continual reminder that he and his people could reach out and slap him around anywhere, anytime they'd care to. He could run, but he couldn't hide.

He noticed that the closet door was ajar as he walked in so, grabbing the knob in his left hand and holding the bat at the ready with his right, he yanked the door open. At first, he didn't see anyone inside. He stuck the tip of the bat between some of his clothes hanging on the bar and slid them to one side. Still, no one.

After seeing the insidious lava lamp, he knew both who had broken into his place and just why. He didn't really expect to find anyone still there.

Nevertheless, considering that a person may not have completed his task before Foster had come home, he could still be hiding behind some of the furniture — under the bed, behind the dresser or the chair by the window. He methodically worked his way around the room in an effort to be as thorough as possible and satisfy his own concerns. Part of him was really hoping to find Dwayne Steele cowering under the bed so that, in the privacy of his own apartment, he could beat the very life out of him — slowly, methodically, savagely, mercilessly.

He poked the bat under the bed sharply to stab at anyone who might be hiding under there but found he was only stabbing at the air. Just to be sure, he pulled up the skirts of the bedcovers and looked underneath. There was no one there, either.

Satisfied that he was alone in his apartment, he walked back out to the hallway door and made sure that it was locked, the deadbolt thrown closed and the security chain was fastened and then began to look around to see if anything had been taken — not that he had much of anything worth taking anymore.

Looking across to the living room, he could see that his television set was still there, the coffee maker and the toaster oven, also pawn shop purchases, were still on his kitchen counter.

In the bedroom, he kept a small cigar box on the dresser in which he had a couple of tie-tacks and tie-bars and a pair of cuff links for which he had no shirts anymore with French cuffs to use them. None of it was really of any value but they were shiny and a thief looking for something that at least appeared to have value could have just grabbed them and stuffed them into a pocket but, no, they were still in the box.

As he looked around it became pretty obvious to him that someone had done a pretty thorough search of his apartment. The drawers of the dresser and the nightstand had been removed and replaced after their contents had been rifled through. It was just confirmation to him that it hadn't been a common burglar. It was them.

The men in black or some of their henchmen with their own dark agenda.

In the closet, a cardboard banker's box that he'd kept important papers in had been searched through. He quickly leafed through its contents to be sure that his birth certificate, the papers related to his ongoing IRS case, and a few letters from his wife from when they had been dating so many years before were still there. He had always cherished those letters, he never realized just how much until he thought they'd been lost.

But, no, everything was still in the box. Shuffled out of order as though they'd been dumped out, examined and hurriedly replaced — maybe even photographed while they were at it — but still there.

What in the world could they have been looking for? He couldn't imagine. Perhaps it was just a scare tactic, another poke to remind him that they could reach out and hurt him at any time in any place as evidenced by the glowing lava lamp added to his bedroom decor. If that's what it was about, it was working.

But then, knowing full well whom he was dealing with, he realized that their greater purpose may have been to install listening devices and cameras — bugging the apartment as they had his home. They were professionals. He knew from that experience that he might find one or two of the devices if he looked really hard but probably wouldn't find them all. It was a frustrating turn of events but from that moment forward he would watch what he said in there just like he did when he was living in the Village at Area Fifty-One.

Part of him breathed easy finding no one still in his apartment but another part so wanted to find Steele in there, hiding, cowering in some dark corner. But then, maybe it was for the best. That wasn't who he was.

He walked over to the nightstand and unplugged the lava lamp. He gathered up the cord and carried it out to the breakfast counter to take down to the dumpster the next morning and be rid of it.

He flopped himself down onto one of the stools and sighed, "Livvy," he lamented, "I miss you so much — I miss us so much. I don't even know where you are tonight but I so wish I were with you. Anywhere — *anywhere else* — anywhere at all. To hold you, to hear your voice telling me it's all gonna be alright. I hope that someday you'll be able to for forgive me for all of this. Someday."

That night he slept uneasily and kept the baseball bat across the headboard beneath his pillows — just in case.

He felt choked up lying there in the dark. He so missed his wife and thoroughly racked with guilt. He hoped she was sleeping peacefully that night, that she was happy wherever she was and that those people would just leave her alone.

But for his part, he'd never felt so vulnerable and isolated in all of his life. ∎

CHAPTER THIRTY-FOUR

Sniper

A little early for his shift that day, Dennis Foster showed up for work while the diner's owner, Chick, was still manning the grill in the kitchen. He was more than happy to get an early respite from the hot, greasy work and pass the spatula off to him. When it got hot in Las Vegas, which it did most days, hovering over a grill for eight or nine hours can nearly drain a man of all of his strength. The air conditioning, while it made the dining room comfortable, was practically unnoticed in the hot kitchen. The key to surviving a day back there was to stay hydrated and they all drank glass after glass of ice water, iced tea and electrolyte drinks like Gatorade. As much as they'd take in, though, they'd sweat out again through the day from every pore of their bodies.

While Foster donned his apron, Chick gave him the lowdown on the day, who was scheduled to be in with him for the night shift, the specials for the day and which items they were getting low on.

"I understand you had an unwelcome visitor last night," he commented.

"Oh, you heard about that, huh?"

"What happened? You knew this guy?"

"From a lifetime ago, yeah. He's bad news. When I saw him in here, dressed all in black and just nursing a cup of coffee in the middle of the night, I knew he was up to no good."

"Grace tells me that you went after him with a bat. She said you looked pretty pissed."

"Well, we have a history."

"Maybe you can tell me the tale someday. If he's that kind of trouble — the kind of trouble that would hurt the business or the people who work and eat here — well, that's what the bat's for."

"Thanks. He ran out of here pretty fast. I doubt he'll be back."

"I hope not, but I'll alert the folks on the other shifts to keep an eye out and be ready to call the cops if he shows up again."

Foster smiled to himself knowing that Steele and his minions had no fear of the police. When Chick had first brought up the matter, he was convinced that he'd be fired for his explosive reaction to the man's presence in the diner. Another job that the man in black would have gotten him ejected from. But he was relieved — although the job wasn't much, it was secure and Chick actually commended him for his actions to protect the diner and its patrons.

Feeling pretty good about that and with the expectation of a fairly easy night, he took the helm in the kitchen but still kept an eye out for Steele's potential return. As he'd said to Chick, he really didn't expect the man would be back, but then, he knew how devious and unpredictable he and his people could be. Every time he took an order slip down from the window or set out a plate to be brought out to the dining room, he would take a quick scan of the patrons at the booths and all along the front counter.

Until closing time, he never saw a glimpse of Steele. Maybe he really did scare him off for good.

Though, he expected, not likely.

When it came time to lock up and head for home, Foster, Grace and Loretta, the other waitress whose turn it was to be on with them that night, walked out the front door to the parking lot. Since sundown, the air outside had cooled considerably. It was refreshing after a long, hot shift at the grill. There was still a warm breeze wafting in from the desert, but the night was still much cooler than the triple-digit heat the city had been enveloped in at midday.

He waved good night to the two women who got into Grace's car. She would give Loretta a ride home on her way. Foster got into his trusty, rusty old Dodge Dart and rolled the windows down. Because of the ever-present dust in the air, leaving the windows open for the day, even just an inch or so, could coat the interior of a car with a fine, powdery grit blown in from the surrounding deserts. The car was hot inside even so long after sunset. He opened the driver's side door, rolled the window down, and walked around to the passenger side to do the same, leaving the driver's door open as he did to allow the cool night air to flow in and the hot air to flow out as much as possible.

He got in behind the wheel, pulled the door shut and turned the key in the ignition. He backed out of the parking space alongside the diner and then pulled out of the lot onto the street, turning left to head the short distance up the street and around the corner to his apartment above the pizza shop.

Walking along the sidewalk and loitering here and there along the way were the sketchy night people. He'd see them on his way home every night. Some just down on their luck, homeless, with nowhere else to go. Others were predators waiting in dark corners for a likely victim to stumble into their presence to be descended upon, pimps with their sad-looking, painted and scantily-clad clutches of addict prostitutes and the ever-present gatherings of drug dealers and wannabe gangsters here and there along the way. Seeing some of the inhabitants of the underbelly of the city each night reminded him time and again just why he drove the eight blocks from home and back each day rather than walking. He'd always keep a close watch on them out of the corner of his eye.

A few blocks from the diner was a fairly substantial cross street with a stop sign at the corner. He could see some swarthy characters gathered on the sidewalk there as he approached. With the windows of his car wide open, he was concerned that they might rush out to him when he'd stop so he rolled slowly up to the intersection and quickly looked both ways on the cross street. At that time of night, the streets in that part of town were almost devoid of traffic.

With nothing in sight approaching from either direction, he quickly pressed the accelerator again before coming to a full stop to get through the intersection before any of the local predators could make a move toward him.

Bang!

All of a sudden his right rear tire went down flat. A blow-out, he instantly presumed, feeling the car quickly drop down on that side. On a short-order cook's paycheck, he couldn't afford to put new tires on that old Dodge. Typically it was shod with mismatched used tires and retreads. It wasn't the first blowout he'd experienced and probably would not be the last.

He knew the routine all too well. He just hated that it had happened in that place at that time of night. He coasted the car through the intersection and up to the curb, leaving enough room to work changing the tire. He was a bit nervous about stopping right there but he really didn't have any choice. Perhaps seeing a guy in greasy, dirty clothes reeking of the diner's kitchen and driving a pathetic old car would make the predators think that he wasn't worth their time.

He was right, to his relief. But, too, neither did any of them offer to help. Just as well, so he thought.

With the keys in his hand, he shoved the driver's side door open and climbed out to walk around and get the jack out of the trunk and swap on his nearly treadless spare. As he stood up from the driver's seat he heard another loud report.

Bang!

Immediately he heard something slam into the sheet metal on the lid of his trunk. The predators and night people all around him suddenly scattered. They knew just what it was they'd heard — and it wasn't another blowout or the backfire of some passing car.

A sniper on a nearby rooftop had shot out his tire and seemed to be looking to finish the job.

Terrified beyond anything he'd ever experienced before in his life, Foster quickly crouched down behind the car for cover. When he did, the street light shone across the rear fender to his left and he could see an exit hole just above the wheel well. Whatever the shooter was using was powerful enough to pass through the sheet metal of the car's trunk lid and then out through the fender. He wondered how much protection his hiding behind the old car was actually affording.

Should he make a run for it?

Should he throw his hands up and surrender?

No, that would be stupid. If they wanted to kill him, they wouldn't care. He'd just be making himself an easier target.

Pressed up against the side of the car, he tenuously reached his arm out and closed the car door hoping it would offer just a little more protection and then kept himself squatted down as close to the asphalt as he could get. Looking around, he saw the sidewalks had been completely deserted. A few curious faces peeked around from behind corners to watch what might happen next.

Steele and his people had destroyed his life, his marriage, taken everything from him and were finally looking to take the only thing he had left — his life. After everything they had already done to him, they were finally trying to kill him.

He kept crouched down behind the car, wondering how long he could stay there.

A couple of cars rolled by, seeing his disabled car at the curb and its driver crouched down beside it. They just presumed that he was working to fix the car so steered wide around him and continued past.

He was alone, abandoned to his fate.

It seemed just a matter of time.

Foster wasn't a religious sort of man but, as they say, there are no atheists in fox holes. He prayed. Shaking like a leaf, expecting a third shot at any moment that could tear through the metal of his shielding car and lay him out on the street mortally wounded. He was just waiting to die.

He cried, he prayed.

When he thought about Livvy, the guilt just overwhelmed him.

It was too late to fix anything. There was no going back.

Long minutes crept by as he cowered behind the car in the street. Eventually he heard approaching sirens. Someone unseen had heard the shots and called the police. At least a few cruisers were racing toward him from various directions. It was encouraging to hear them, the distant sound of their sirens growing quickly louder, but at the same time he knew that the men in black didn't concern themselves with local law enforcement.

But then, they jealously shunned exposure. Perhaps when the police arrived in force, possibly with a SWAT team and the media not far behind, the shooter would just evaporate — for the time being, anyway — to finish the job on another day.

Sirens and flashing red and blue lights quickly descended on him from everywhere and surrounded the perforated Dodge with Foster pressed up against it in mortal fear for his life. With guns drawn, the police swarmed out and took cover behind their own cars. Foster looked back over his shoulder at a couple of them right behind him and pointed up at the rooftop. One of the cops who could see him passed the word and they all began to train their pistols, rifles and shotguns upwards. A few ran in through the front door of the building and sprinted up the stairs inside to the roof. In a few minutes, one of them appeared at the parapet and waved down at the others. The sniper was gone.

They found a single shell casing up on the roof standing upright on the parapet as though staged for them. It was proof that there had been a shooter and he had fired down from that position. Proof to Foster, too, just who it was. There was no other evidence to be found.

After the "all-clear" had been called out, a couple of the officers helped Foster change his tire and he thanked them profusely. He was still shaking inside, almost unable to hold the lug wrench and stood like a deflated balloon as they questioned him about what had happened. They believed part of his story — the part about someone shooting at him (as the holes in his car attested) — the parts about men in black, Area Fifty-One and government conspiracies they just quickly made note of while they shook their heads. In that neighborhood, at that time of night, it was difficult for them to take seriously a scruffy looking man in greasy diner togs driving a rusty old car with nearly bald tires on it spinning such a fantastical yarn.

They wrote down what he said because they had to but would likely joke about him when they got back to the police station. It was Las Vegas, they'd heard that sort of thing plenty of times before.

He didn't care. It was what it was — that's what happened.

A few of the police stayed on the scene to await the detectives and a forensics team and then allowed Foster to go on his way as the rest of them got into their cars and drove away.

Foster, fitfully aware that Steele or one of his cohorts could be waiting for him at home, convinced one of the cops to escort him to his apartment door. Apprehensively, he drove the last couple of blocks to the building and parked in the lot behind the pizza shop. The patrol car rolled in behind him and one of the two officers got out and followed him to the back door. He unlocked the door and the two of them climbed the stairs and walked up to Foster's apartment door. He stopped in front of his door with his key in his hand and looked up at the corner of the doorframe. He saw the matchbook cover still wedged in where he had left it earlier that afternoon when he'd left for work. He reached up and plucked it out and then turned to the officer and said, "Thank you. I really appreciate you doing this. I think I'll be okay now."

"Are you sure, sir? You want me to go in with you and look around?"

Foster looked down at the matchbook cover in his hand and replied, "No, I'm sure. Thanks again."

"Alright, you stay safe, sir. Call us again if you need us."

"I will — believe me — I will."

As he pushed his door open, the cop turned and walked back down the stairs to rejoin his partner in the waiting patrol car. Foster walked into his apartment, grabbing up the bat that he kept in the corner just inside the door. He made sure the door was locked, the deadbolt thrown closed and the security chain in place. Then, just for a bit of added peace of mind, he wedged a chair under the door knob and pressed its feet into the carpet as forcefully as he could to brace it as tightly as possible.

He kept away from the windows and slipped down the dark hallway to the bathroom, groping his way along the familiar walls to avoid turning on any lights. Gripping the bat in both hands, he sat down on the floor between the toilet and the bathtub, leaning up against the wall. Fearing for his very life, he didn't know what else to do, where else to go. He couldn't think of anywhere that would be safe.

Whatever moral strength he might have had left was exhausted by then. He felt empty and so thoroughly alone.

How low they had brought him. How they'd thoroughly pulverized him. He pined for Livvy to just hold him at that moment and assure him that everything was going to be alright.

But Livvy was gone. He sobbed bitterly as he talked to himself — an angry argument at times.

It was all his own fault. He beat himself up as he sat with his back up against the wall.

As he sat there in the dark, his verbal meanderings drifted to addressing his painfully absent wife as his mind shifted seemingly at random forgetting that someone might be listening in.

"Livvy," he mused, quietly at first. "This is all my fault — I know. I wish that I could tell you that right now, to tell you how I feel. I wish things could just go back to the way they were before. I'm empty without you, so empty. I realize that more and more each day. I could face all of this with you but without you, I'm lost." His voice gradually rose in volume. "They've taken everything — *everything* — including you. Now they want to take my life, too. I'm thinking, maybe, I should just — you know — do that for them. There's nothing left but fear and pain.

I don't want to live like this anymore — *I can't!* I just can't."

He had reached his end, he clearly had nothing left to lose.

Exhaustion, however, eventually overtook him. His eyes gradually dropped closed, falling asleep propped up against the wall, sitting on the cold, hard bathroom floor. ∎

CHAPTER THIRTY-FIVE

KVGS

It was a long and physically painful night sitting on that hard floor trying to sleep. Although he only caught a few brief snatches of sleep, waking from time to time in nightmarish fits, the seemingly endless night gave him ample opportunity to think.

It's an interesting paradigm. When a man has nothing left to lose, he's at his most desperate moment — and his most dangerous.

He knew that Steele and his people would not give up. He also knew that he had gotten lucky the night before. Somehow the sniper on the rooftop had missed him. Surprising in light of the apparent professionalism of those people but, perhaps too, they were just trying to send him another message punctuated with a bullet.

Or perhaps, God was giving him a chance to fight back. If that were the case, he wasn't going to waste it.

Most of the sleepless night was spent pondering various scenarios for revenge but he realized that vengeance would only inspire more attacks on him. Eventually, they'd just end it, they wouldn't miss.

Besides, those weren't people that he had any sort of access to. Any plan for revenge would need some kind of resource, authority or intrusion into their lives that he just didn't have. The cold truth was that he was entirely powerless.

But if he did nothing, he reasoned, they would most likely hunt him down like a rabid dog and ultimately kill him anyway, silencing him forever. And nobody would ever know — or care.

What were they afraid of?

There was only one thing they were afraid of, he reasoned: exposure. They shunned the bright light of day, the spotlight of recognition for who and what they were.

From his very first contact with them in Dr. Kimber's office in St. Louis, he was handed one nondisclosure form after another to sign and swear that, under penalty of law, he would not divulge anything that he'd seen, heard or experienced. All those forms were clearly intended to instill a fear in him but it was the only power he had over them.

They might still kill him in the end but, once he'd publicly blown the whistle on them and told his story, it would seem that there would no longer be a reason.

It was a chance he'd have to take — a very narrow chance — but better than no chance at all.

His body ached and complained to him sharply as he got up from the bathroom floor that morning, gripping the rim of the bathtub for support as he got up on his feet. Before doing anything else, he grabbed the bottle of aspirin and downed a few of them.

He shuffled out to the kitchen and got an empty garbage bag from the roll he'd kept under the sink and brought it into the bedroom with him. He glanced at the door to the hallway as he walked past to make sure that it was still secure and that the chair he'd braced under the knob was still in place.

They were.

He stripped off his greasy diner clothes and stuffed them into the plastic bag. There would be no time to wash them. He gathered up his other changes of white chef's pants and grease-stained t-shirts — laundered and neatly folded in his dresser drawer — and stuffed them into the bag, too.

He went back into the bathroom, showered and shaved and very carefully and neatly combed his hair. He put on a crisply ironed dress shirt, creased slacks and a tie. Dressing, as it were, for another interview but what he was planning could turn out to be the most important interview of his life.

There was still a tiny amount of cologne left in a bottle that he'd taken from his dresser at home so he daubed on a few drops to make sure that any lingering air of the diner's kitchen was masked. Finally, he slipped his pocket protector into his shirt pocket replete with pens, mechanical pencils and his slide-rule.

He threw his empty suitcase on the bed, flipped it open, and packed up every bit of clothing and anything else that might have fit into it.

Then he loaded it and a few cardboard boxes containing all of the rest of his computer and other personal belongings from the apartment into his old Dodge Dart. Without looking back or saying a word to anyone, he just got in and drove away.

He rolled slowly down through the center of town, through the Las Vegas strip, starkly illuminated by the early morning sunlight. He paid no attention to the sad array of lost souls and predators that drifted along the sidewalks. The dust and the dirt and the darkness of "Sin City" would soon be just a brief and distant memory. But first, there was one last thing that he had to do before finally leaving Las Vegas for good.

Just beyond the strip, on the other side of downtown, was a modern, glass-faced office building a few stories tall. In keeping with the Las Vegas aesthetic, its facade displayed a large, neon sign that simply read "KVGS TV" in glowing magenta and purple letters over a background of small, racing white lights.

He pulled his car into the parking lot and parked behind a van so that it would be hidden from anyone who might drive by on the street. He knew they were out there somewhere. They obviously knew what he drove and he didn't want them to find him before he could complete his mission.

He got out of the car, brushed his shirt smooth with the heel of his hand, looked at his reflection in the car's window and took a quick moment to adjust his tie, then walked into the air-conditioned lobby. A receptionist greeted him with an effervescent smile and asked what it might be that she could do to help him.

"I need to speak with someone in your news department," he announced, mustering up all of the faux confidence that he was able to.

"Do you have a news story that you want to report?"

"Of sorts, yes."

"I can see if anyone is back there right now. Maybe one of the interns can come and take down your information."

"No, I need to talk with someone in charge. A reporter, or the supervisor of the news department — whoever's available. This can't be relegated to just an intern."

"That sounds pretty serious, sir. May I say what this is about?"

He thought for a moment. Should he tell a receptionist what his purpose was that morning? Could she be trusted? But then, he had nothing left to lose, he had to trust someone, so he told her, "I'm here to throw the curtain back on Area Fifty-One. I used to work there — now they're trying to kill me."

She just looked at him for a moment, her cheerful smile faded. So many people had come in or called to report sightings in the skies, alien visitors, abductions and other strange phenomena that they at the television station were almost numb from the nearly constant flow of crackpots, conspiracy theorists and folks who just honestly believed they'd seen something out there in the desert.

She reached for the phone, "Just a moment," and punched in an extension number.

Foster stood patiently and waited as he heard her tell someone on the other end of the line that there was a man in the lobby who claimed that he was there to blow the lid off of Area Fifty-One. He understood their dubious attitude, that was a bold claim and, really, what did they think he might tell them that they hadn't already heard before? Of course, they had no idea.

As he stood there listening to her side of the phone call, he heard her tell whomever was on the other end of the line that he was dressed in a nice shirt, tie and slacks. A moment later she responded that he was wearing shiny dress shoes. Her response to what was apparently the person's last question was that he was also wearing glasses and a pocket protector with a slide-rule in it.

The receptionist hung up the phone, looked up at him and smiled and then said, "Someone will be right out to speak with you." Then she motioned to a row of padded chairs and said, "Won't you have a seat?"

"No thank you," he replied. "I'll just wait right here."

She looked at him rather uncomfortably and silently stood while waiting for someone — anyone — to emerge from the offices behind her. After a brief few minutes, the door opened and a man in a white shirt wearing a solid blue tie loosely hanging from around his collar walked out into the lobby and briskly up to where Foster was standing with his hand out to shake his, "Good morning, sir. I'm Bradley Smith. I'm the news director here at KVGS. What can I do for you?"

"I have a story to tell you. A story about what's going on behind the facade at Area Fifty-One."

"Do you, now? Well, I have to tell you, truthfully, we get an awful lot of people in here who want to tell us stories about Area Fifty-One — aliens, flying sauces — all of that sort of thing. This is Las Vegas. It's practically in the neighborhood, part of the local culture here. You'll have to excuse my reluctance. Tell me, why is your story so unique?"

Foster leaned into the man, pushed his glasses up with one finger, and lowered his voice, "I'm a nuclear physicist. I used to work on the Apollo and Shuttle programs. Recently, I worked at a secret laboratory there studying alien technologies, Facility R-Four-Seven. I've seen things, touched things, heard things and got caught up in the whole government secret national security world. They got out of me all that they wanted to and then tossed me out. They've destroyed my life, taken everything from me and now they're trying to kill me. Is that credible enough for you, Mr. Smith?"

"I'll have to admit, I've not heard anyone make those sorts of claims before. You've piqued my interest." Smith thought for a few seconds and then offered, "Why don't you come back with me and meet our senior anchor — maybe you've seen him on the evening news — Wesley Brooks? He does an investigative magazine show every weekend and I think your story might be just the sort of thing that he'd want to sink his teeth into. You game?"

"I literally have nothing left to lose. Sure, I'm game."

Smith led him out from the lobby and down a paneled hallway lined with office doors on either side interspersed with framed photos of their on-air personalities including syndicated stars like John Tesh, Delilah and Rush Limbaugh. He stopped in front of one open door and knocked on it to get the attention of the occupant inside, "Wes?"

The man sitting at his desk was typing on a computer keyboard. He looked up from his work and replied, "Brad, yes, what's up?"

"I've got someone I want you to meet. He just walked in off the street and says that he's here to expose what's going on at Area Fifty-One. He says he worked at Facility R-Four-Seven and I immediately thought of you."

"R-Four-Seven, eh? I'm touched, really. Is he here?"

Smith stepped to one side and waved Foster into the room. As he entered, Brooks rose to his feet and offered his hand. "Good morning, sir. I'm genuinely anxious to hear your story."

As the two shook hands, he asked Foster for his name. His plan was to tell his story and then just disappear so he was hoping to do it all as quietly and anonymously as possible so he quickly, awkwardly blurted out, "Smith, John Smith."

"Smith, eh?" He looked over at his boss still loitering in the doorway, "No relation, I trust?"

Smith smiled and shook his head, "No. No relation."

"So, did *our* Mr. Smith tell you about my news magazine show?"

"Not much, just that it exists."

"If you check out, I'll have you on as a guest and we'll talk about your story."

"I have to do this today — now."

"Uh, *now?*"

"I expect that you can record it and use it later? My car is packed and as soon as I leave this building, I'm leaving Las Vegas for good. They're trying to kill me. They took a couple of shots at me last night, shot out a tire and put a couple of bullet holes in my car. I'm outta here as fast as I can."

"I think I read about that on the police blotter this morning," Smith commented from behind him.

"Hmph — okay, I think that could work," he looked up at Smith. "What d'you think? I've got time — worth taking a chance?"

"It's your call, Wes."

The newsman just grinned. He loved juicy stories about Area Fifty-One. He turned to Foster and asked, "So, 'John Smith,' that's obviously not your real name. You want to remain anonymous, I presume?"

"As I said, they're trying to kill me so, yeah. I've seen TV shows where the person is just a dark silhouette and their voice is distorted — can you do that?"

"Sure, we can do that," he looked up at Smith and added, "right?"

"It will take a little time to get it set up but, yeah, we can do that." He looked at his watch and then asked Brooks, "You got time right now, Wes?"

"For this? Sure. If Mr. Smith here turns out to be the real deal then I've got all the time in the world."

"Great. I'll go round up Jerry and Cal and find a couple of camera operators and we'll get set up. I don't think Brant has gone home yet. Give me about a half hour?"

"Yeah, that's good, I can spend some time with John here and get a little background to get things going. Just let me know when you're ready."

"Okay," Smith jogged down the hall to the break room to start gathering the crew of technicians that he'd need to ready everything on the set for Wes Brooks' magazine show and to keep his mysterious guest shrouded and his voice distorted to help maintain his anonymity.

Brooks had Foster sit down at his desk with him and took notes while he gathered some basic information from him so that he wouldn't be going into the rather impromptu interview entirely cold. Brooks had apparently heard rumors of Facility R-Four-Seven and was eager to hear whatever Foster had to say about it. As he related the events of the past couple of years in quick and broad generalities, Brooks became more and more intrigued by the story.

Las Vegas is not geographically very far from Area Fifty-One and the culture of flying saucers and visiting aliens was a popular theme among the locals. Any time that KVGS could do a fresh story about any aspect of that subject, they jumped at the chance. Whether anyone at the station lent any credence to the whole thing or not, it made for good television and, therefore, good local ratings and subsequent advertising sales.

As Foster spoke, Brooks asked a lot of pertinent questions. A bit of a UFO hobbyist himself, he was pretty familiar with some of the nuancical details beyond the pop culture of little green men and silver space ships so his query was well informed and garnered some deeper information than most would have thought to ask about. What had begun as a planned one hour magazine show (minus time for commercials, of course) became in his mind a multi-part exposé. He would sit with Foster in the studio for as long as it took to record as much useful material as he could and then edit it all down to at least a two-part show — maybe three. He was excited by the prospect. Rarely did such an opportunity come along and he wanted to take full advantage while he could.

When news director Smith returned to Brooks' office to inform him that they were just about ready for them, the anchor asked one last quick question before ushering Foster out of his office and down the hallway to the studio, "Are you married, Mr. Smith?"

Foster thought for a few seconds and finally replied, "At the moment, I'm not entirely sure. But she has been as much a victim in this as I have. I don't want to mention anything about her in the interview — for her protection."

"When did you see her last?"

"It's been a while."

"Do you miss her?"

"Of course I do. It kills me to be separated from her for so long but, wherever she is, she's safer out there than she could be with me. I want to keep it that way."

"I understand. We won't mention anything about that. I promise."

Before taking seats on the magazine program's set, Brooks led him over to a couple of chairs that looked much like those in a barber shop with a counter in front of each of them and a large mirror rimmed with rows of bare bulbs mounted so that they could each see themselves being made up and readied for the bright studio lights.

A pair of makeup artists began by stuffing tissues into their collars to protect their clothing and then mopped each of their faces down with a dry towel.

"I understand that you have your protocols," Foster mused to Brooks as the young woman began applying various creams and powders to his face, "but if I'm going to be hidden in shadows, why would I need makeup?"

"That's a good question," Brooks replied. "I really hadn't thought about that."

"Shine," the woman who was working on Foster replied.

"Shine? What do you mean?"

"We've done this before and found that, even though you're in the shadows, the bright lights around you can still reflect off of your skin in places and give away some of the shape of your face. This way, your face won't reflect the lights."

"You know," Brooks chuckled, "I've been in this business for a long time and that had never occurred to me."

"That's why you're the anchor behind the desk and I'm the makeup professional."

"You *do* make me look good out there."

She smiled and turned to Foster as she began padding his face with powder and quietly said, "It's nice to be appreciated."

"It is," Foster agreed. "And he's not trying to kill you, either. That counts for something, too."

Not knowing what he was referring to, she just shrugged and agreed. During the course of hearing the ensuing interview, she'd ultimately understand.

As they got into place on the set, a sound technician clipped a small microphone to each man's shirt and then took off his ball cap and handed it to Foster, "It'll help hide the shape of your face in the silhouette," he explained.

Foster thanked him and set the hat onto his head.

Finally, all was ready.

Brooks was the consummate professional. He made Foster feel comfortable and gave him time to formulate the responses to his various questions. But Foster gave him far more than he was expecting.

He told him about the secret airline that shuttled people into the Groom Lake airbase on a daily basis, about the Village where the weekly commuters and some of the Air Force personnel lived while they were there. But mostly, he talked about the secret lab, Facility R-Four-Seven. He told him about alien spacecraft and the technology that made them fly and maneuver the way they did. About gravity-amplifiers, quantum mechanics and about element 115, so-called ununpentium. He told about the morgue and the alien autopsy that he'd witnessed and about the macabre Ramos Project, alien-human hybrid experiments and live dissections.

He talked about government deals with alien visitors at the highest levels leading all the way up to the White House. About abductions and human experiments. About politicians, military and intelligence agencies who have maintained the depraved treaties since World War II.

And he talked a lot about the intense security measures that he had to observe while he worked there and that those in power were at that time still trying to intimidate him, going so far as to take sniper shots at him the night before, hoping to silence him forever.

The interview went on for a few hours. Brooks was thrilled that so much of it was fresh, things he'd not heard before, and would make for an exciting multi-part exposé. When it was finally done, Foster was asked to sign a release which he willingly did as John Smith (witnessed by Bradley Smith, just to be legal), shook hands with everyone, and left.

He got into his old Dodge and drove out of Las Vegas — never to return. ■

PHASE 7
THE TWIST

CHAPTER THIRTY-SIX

The Mike Casey Radio Show

The television interview on KVGS in Las Vegas did in fact end up as a three-part exposé. John Smith, as he was introduced, instantly became a celebrity among the UFO conspiracy theory community and the target of intense controversy from virtually every direction. Popular accusations of being a liar, mentally ill or some kind of con-artist, became fodder for radio talk shows and call-in armchair commentators rendering their own concerted opinions. Some thought that, clearly, someone who would make the outrageous and highly detailed claims that he did, must have had some sort of ulterior motive. He must be in it for the money or maybe for the notoriety — or both.

While self-appointed experts debated and argued, John Smith vanished along with Dennis Foster. Fame and fortune would have had a hard time catching up with him.

Nearly a year later, dressed in dusty, worn clothing and sporting a full beard, long hair tied back in a pony tail under a faded Boston Red Sox ball cap and thick, black-rimmed glasses, a recently familiar but ostensibly anonymous man sat at the counter at the Little A'Le'Inn Diner with a tuna melt sandwich and iced tea at lunchtime.

When he had first shown up in Rachel, Nevada, he was totally unknown and nameless to the people who lived there. The few who populated that tiny speck of a town knew every other face and mostly left them to themselves. To those who did bother to ask the stranger's name, they came to know him as Harrison Blake, or just Harry to those slightly more familiar like Barb, the waitress at the diner.

He sat quietly by himself at the end of the counter where he could best see and hear the small portable television on the shelf during the noon hour news and weather. From that vantage point, too, he could see the door from the parking lot and the entirety of the rest of the dining room and part of the gift shop beyond. He'd be able to dart out through the kitchen and the rear exit if the need should arise — if the boogyman in black, Dwayne Steele, should show up. Thus far, it hadn't, but he still couldn't let his guard down.

A profoundly elderly man came in that day. He was a regular though no one had seen him for a little while. The waitress greeted him by his first name and asked if he'd like coffee.

"Thanks, Barb," he replied and then shuffled his way along the row of stools at the counter with labored, almost painful looking steps. For a moment, he stood behind the stool next to Foster and asked, "Harry Blake?"

Foster slowly turned to look at him, half expecting to see Steele or one of his black-clothed minions standing there. Instead, he saw a tired looking old man standing slightly bent and resting his hand on the top of the stool for support. The skin on his face was a yellowish-pale with a few very noticible magenta and purple splotches here and there. His beard was short and spiny and mostly white as was the hair that skirted around the brim of his dust- and sweat-stained straw cowboy hat.

"Yes," Foster replied, "and you are —?"

"My name is Alan Black — most folks 'round here just call me Al. I own the trailer park where y'all live up on Canyon Road."

"Oh? Is there something wrong?"

"Wrong? Naah, just wanted to meet you, inner'duce myself. I know you're subletting that trailer from ol' Ben Jordan — I ain't had a chance to catch up with 'ya 'fore now."

"Oh, well then," Foster reached out his hand and shook with Black, "I'm pleased to make your acquaintance. Don't think I've ever seen you around the park."

"I don't get out much — got cancer. Some days are better than others though, today's one of the better ones."

"Sorry to hear that."

"Mind if I sit here?" The old man nodded to the stool next to Foster.

He smiled and said, "Not at all. You need help?"

"Nah, I'm okay — thanks."

With apparently great effort, Black swung one leg over the empty stool and pulled himself up onto the seat, gripping the edge of the counter for support. As he did, the waitress brought his coffee and set it down in front of him. "Thanks, Barb."

He began to add cream and sugar to his cup and began to explain a little about himself as he did, "Was one of them soldiers that was assigned to them nuclear tests in the desert back in the fifties. Got pretty bad exposed. We didn't know too much back then about what radiation can do to a body after a while."

"Well, I hope the government helped out once everyone finally realized."

"Nope. VA been officially denyin' benefits for this all along. Findin' all kinds of excuses and lame reasons. The folks at the VA in Vegas been good, though," he grinned a sly smile. "They keep lyin' to Washington and sneakin' in treatments. Had chemo a few years ago."

"Did it help?"

"For a while."

"So what're you going to do?"

"Just die, I suppose."

"Well, that sucks."

"Oh, it's not so bad. You live like this for a few decades while it gets worse and worse, dyin' looks better and better all the time. When my time comes, I'm gonna go see Jesus. We all gotta die, son, but it's all good."

"Hmph — Well, I'm glad you've made peace with it."

"I guess." The waitress, wanting not to interrupt the old man's story, came back and asked if he'd like his usual lunch, a roast beef and swiss on rye with mayo. "Yeah, thanks, dear."

"I'll get that right in for you, Al."

He leaned his forearms on the edge of the counter and intimated, "Docs say I shouldn't eat red meat or fatty stuff like cheese and mayo." He grinned like a Cheshire cat.

"So why do you?"

"I wanna die while I'm still livin', son. Ya' know what I mean? I don't wanna die after years of wastin' away eatin' baby food in my trailer and tryin' to watch 'The Price is Right' through my cataracts."

"I think I get it. Life is brief enough. Don't give up on it any sooner than you absolutely have to."

"Exactly — you *get* it, boy!"

"Easier said than done, so I've discovered."

"Ha, ha! I suppose it can be for some folks." He took a sip of of his coffee and turned to look at Foster. "Look, I didn't just stumble on y'all here today. I been lookin' for you."

"Town's pretty small, Al. Not too easy for someone to hide around here."

"Didn't say I was lookin' for very long," he chuckled. "Look, I came to tell y'all that Ben sold me his trailer. He was gonna come back to Rachel some day, that's why he sublet it out 'til then. But he's livin' in a home now down in Florida now. Looks like that's gonna be his last stop."

"Sorry to hear that. So now you're my landlord?"

"I am."

"Rent goin' up?"

"Ha, ha! Maybe. But actually, I have a proposition for you."

"A proposition? No offense, Al, but I've heard that sort of line before — typically hasn't ended well."

"I got a feelin' you're runnin' from somethin' — or maybe someone — that's why you're here in Rachel in the first place. That's why a lot of folks are here."

"Uh, something like that."

"Ain't no nevermind," he waved his hand as if to dismiss the whole subject. "Look, I'm havin' a hard time gettin' around the park these days and doin' maintenance on the place, waterin' plants and fixin' folks' plumbin' an' stuff. I was wonderin' if you'd like to be the super?"

"The super? Hmmm, sounds interesting. What's involved?"

"Well, gotta water them plants around the flagpole at the front gate, collect rents, fix stuff, pick up trash, keep the place lookin' nice. Pretty much on call all the time but it comes with a small paycheck and free rent."

"Free rent, eh? I like the sound of that."

"So, it's a deal?"

Foster thought for a moment and then reached out to shake Black's boney, discolored and trembling hand, "One thing, though."

"What's that?"

"I've gotta be paid in cash, off the books. I don't have a bank account."

"We ain't got a bank in Rachel anyways. Most folks just pay cash 'round here. That ain't a problem at all."

"Then you've got a deal, Al."

It was an arrangement far better than anything Foster could have dreamed of. If he had to live alone, it seemed to be a pretty good way to do it. The simple life, under the radar and off the grid. It appeared that providence was finally smiling on him, it was perfect.

For the next several months, he lived a fairly peaceful life, rustic and lacking in anything that might qualify as being at all luxurious. But oddly, he didn't miss any of that. He had food on his table, a roof over his head, gas in the car and, most of all, a purpose. Life was good.

The only part of his life that he really did miss was Livvy.

Black gave him a tattered old canvas tool box filled with well-worn tools to fix plumbing and wiring along with a collection of basics like screwdrivers and wrenches and, of course, the ever ubiquitous Vice-Grips and a roll of duct tape. Along with his own tool kit that he'd quickly gathered in his garage in Burbank before heading east, he was prepared to fix just about anything. Out there in the middle of the desert where plumbers and electricians were few and far between (for all practical purposes, nonexistent), one was essentially on their own. Surely, a rocket scientist who could operate a mass-spectrometer and help design a space station would be able to fix a leaky faucet when called upon.

Being a friend of Al Black in that town had its perks, too. Meals at the diner were often sharply discounted or on the house altogether. Harry Blake got to be pretty well-known in the little crossroads of Rachel, Nevada, particularly among the residents of the trailer park. He found the natives to be uniquely friendly and welcoming — even to the constant trickle of tourists passing through town on the Extraterrestrial Highway in search of aliens and the back door to Area Fifty-One, just down the road, to take pictures of themselves in front of all of the warning signs saying that photography was not allowed and to keep out or else deadly force is authorized. If they were lucky, they might even snap a photo of one of the unmarked white Jeeps lurking about with men in camouflage keeping an eye on them from a distance.

Normal people spend their vacations at the beach, camping in the great outdoors, visiting national parks or museums. Some folks, however, find that sort of thing boring and look for strange adventures instead like taunting the so-called camo-guys at Area Fifty-One.

To each their own.

Late one morning, there was a knock on Foster's trailer door. He took a quick look at his watch and then went to open the door. It was Jimmy Estobar, a teenaged boy he recognized who lived in the trailer park standing on the wooden platform just outside the screen door, "Mr. Blake?" he asked respectfully.

"Yeah, Jimmy. What's up?"

"It's Mrs. Jennings. She asked me to come get you to fix her sink."

"Her sink? Did she say what's wrong with it?"

"No, just said it was her sink."

"Okay, tell her I'll be there in just a minute — gotta change my shirt and grab my tools."

"Sure thing, Mr. Blake!" The boy turned and trotted away, back to Mrs. Jennings' trailer.

Foster took off his Hawaiian shirt and laid it neatly across the bed and pulled on a denim work shirt, laced up a pair of sneakers onto his feet and then pulled the old tool box out from a cabinet by the door. He walked up the dusty street to Jennings' trailer and knocked. She opened the door and the smell of freshly-baked cookies wafted out from inside.

"Oh, Mr. Blake! Thank you so much for coming so quickly. It's my sink."

"Yeah, Jimmy told me. Can I come in and take a look?"

"Of course," she retreated into the trailer to let him walk past her, shutting the door behind himself.

After twisting and fiddling with the faucet knobs he announced that the rubber gaskets inside them were badly worn and that's why it was leaking so much. He good-naturedly scolded her for not having called him when it was just dripping a little bit instead of waiting until it was a constant stream.

"But no worries, Mrs. Jennings. I can swap out the gaskets for you. I have spares back at my trailer — I'll be right back."

In less than an hour he had retrieved the gaskets from his place and repaired both her hot and cold faucets and stopped the leak. She was elated and gave him a plate of cookies to take back with him with her thanks.

He walked back to his own trailer with the plate of cookies in his hand. When he got there, he returned the tool box back to the cabinet where it lived and set the empty packages for the rubber gaskets that he'd just used on his dining table to remind him to add them to his list for his next trip to the hardware store in nearby Crystal Springs.

He took off the work shirt and kicked off his sneakers and washed his hands. He then put the Hawaiian shirt back on. It was just about lunchtime and he was planning to go to the diner for a sandwich. Before heading for the door to leave, he put the plate of cookies into the refrigerator so that all of the chocolate chips didn't melt into goo in the desert heat.

Just as he had slipped into a pair of sandals and approached the door to go out, someone knocked on it from outside. He rolled his eyes, "Now what?" he groaned to himself.

He opened the door and saw a man standing there on the platform just outside. He wasn't anyone he'd seen there in Rachel before. Perhaps a new resident in the trailer park whom he hadn't yet met but, as far as he knew, every space was filled with occupied trailers and he knew all of their inhabitants. The man was fairly well dressed in a short-sleeved dress shirt tucked into a pair of newish-looking, creased blue jeans. He had a short-cropped, full beard and wore tortoise-framed sun glasses and a straw fedora.

"Yes?" Foster said to the stranger through the still-closed screen, "Can I help you?

"You Harry Blake?"

Suspicious of a stranger unexpectedly appearing on his doorstep, Foster replied, "Who wants to know?"

"Hmmm, I can't blame you for being standoffish. My name is Mike Casey. I'm the director of the Extraterrestrial Resource and Research Center here in Rachel."

"The Extraterrestrial Research and — what? Never heard of it."

"It's a little ways out of town, on the Highway near the Area Fifty-One back gate."

"Can't say that I've ever noticed it, but then, I don't get out that way very often. What is it that you want?"

"May I come in?"

"Not a chance."

"Uh, okay. Look," he looked around to the left and the right and then lowered his voice. "I know who you are."

"Whoever you might think I am, I'm sure you're mistaken."

"C'mon, I saw your interview on TV, everyone has. I've seen you around town for the past few months and finally put two and two together. You're 'John Smith,' am I right?"

"I haven't seen that interview. I'm sure I'm not the guy you think I am."

"It's gone national — did you know that? The networks picked it up from the local station in Vegas. You talked about things that nobody has ever talked about before. I want to interview you on my radio show. I want to get your story out to the believers out there who know there's a cover-up going on. My audience is deeply invested in finding the truth about this vast government conspiracy. You could blow the lid off of it, motivate these people to put pressure on the right people to finally come clean."

"I've got nothing to do with any of that, I'm just the super here. I don't want to be on your radio program. Leave me alone!"

Foster pushed the screen door open as Casey stepped back and closed the inner door behind himself as he stepped out of his trailer and pushed Casey out of the way. He made sure the door was latched and then, ignoring his unwelcomed visitor, turned and walked away.

"Where you going?!" Casey called out as Foster got into his old Dodge Dart and backed out into the narrow dirt road.

He didn't say a word to him. He just drove away.

Annoyed, Foster drove up the street and then rolled into the parking lot at the Little A'Le'Inn. He walked inside and plopped himself down at the diner's counter in his usual place at the far end so that he could see everything going on inside.

"Mornin' Harry," the waitress said, looking up at the clock on the wall, "or rather, 'good *afternoon*.' Didn't know how late it's gotten to be. Ice tea?"

"Yeah, thanks, Barb."

"Lunch?"

"Turkey and swiss, small fries, please."

"You got it, dear."

As he sat there at the counter, sipping on his iced tea, the bell on the front door jingled behind him and in just a minute or so, Casey stepped up to the counter, standing behind him just off of his left shoulder.

Foster saw him walk in and just rolled his eyes, "What the hell do you want? Did you follow me here?"

"Sort of. It's lunchtime and, well, the options are pretty scarce here in town. Besides, I saw your car out there."

"A regular freakin' Sherlock Holmes, aren't you?"

"Look, I understand your reluctance — and hostility— I really do. I saw those interviews, I got a pretty good idea of what they did to you."

"And, hypothetically speaking, if they should find me?"

"They might just kill you — I get it."

"So why are you chasing me like this? You trying to get me killed? Just leave me alone!"

"This guy bothering you, Harry?" the waitress asked as she returned with his sandwich.

"Yeah, but I got it covered."

"You sure? I don't want things to get out of hand here in the diner. Don't make me have to call the paramedics again."

"I won't hurt him, I promise." It was all a put-on for the benefit of the stranger hovering around Foster, hoping to inspire him to just walk away. "Besides," he added, "there aren't any paramedics around here anyway, they wouldn't get here for an hour and he's probably bleed out by then."

"True. Would you just drag him outside to bleed, then?"

"Hell of a mess. Sure."

"Seriously, if you want me to have the boys in the back come out and bounce this guy, you just let me know, dear."

"I will, but I think it's all under control. Thanks."

"Uh-huh." The waitress looked up at Casey and just leered at him through squinted eyes for a few seconds. After having inspired a proper chill up the man's spine, she turned and walked off to the other end of the counter to serve another patron.

Foster took a bite of his sandwich and tried to ignore Casey as though he were just a pesky fly buzzing about. He wiped his lips with a napkin and looked back over his shoulder, "You still here?"

"Yeah, I'm still here."

"Hmph." He turned back around and sipped on his iced tea.

"You're gonna pester me until I admit to being whoever the hell you think I am? Talk on your radio show?"

"Pretty much."

"Wrong answer."

"Look, just come on out to the Center. We can talk there more freely. I know you don't want these people in town to know who you really are. I get that. I really don't want to complicate your life any more."

"I'll think about it — which *doesn't* admit to anything, you understand. What are the hours out there?"

"I live there. I'm usually around. If you see the Jeep parked out front, I'm in. Just come knock on the door."

"Alright. Like I said, I'll think about it." ∎

CHAPTER THIRTY-SEVEN

Not So Alone

Loneliness can be debilitating. Long periods of empty time when one's mind — and heart — have a penchant to wander. Often wandering into places where one vehemently does not want to go. Sad places. Dark places.

Livvy Foster found herself sitting alone in her apartment all too often pondering the circumstances that had brought her to such a lonely situation. Anger, guilt, depression — but mostly it was the guilt.

She'd moved from Burbank when she and Dennis had split up on that fateful, awful day. She moved to Santa Clara and rented a small apartment there for several months but it was still too close to familiar haunts that just kept reminding her of what she had lost. So again she moved, and again, until she found herself in the small town of Lockhart, off of any major route to or from any major city and distant enough from Burbank, Los Angeles and anywhere or anything familiar.

She found a small coffee shop there where she reprised her roll as waitress from her college years. It was enough to pay her meager expenses but only part-time which meant that she still had too many solitary hours in her days so she took on a second part-time job as a checkout clerk at the lone grocery store in town. Between the two jobs she barely had enough time to eat and sleep which suited her just fine. She kept telling herself that it was just temporary. One day she'd be over it all and maybe, just maybe, she could finally sign the divorce papers that she'd been carrying around with her from place to place for the previous couple of years, still undecided as to what direction she wanted her life to go.

She thought that maybe she would go back to college to refresh herself, to update her skills. She had a bachelor's degree but then, when she married Dennis, she never did much of anything with it. She could take some courses at a community college perhaps, to get up to speed and then get a job good enough to better support herself.

Occasionally, as she'd ready herself for bed, she'd look down at the wedding band on her finger and try and decide if she should just pull it off once and for all and leave it on the dresser. Maybe with its absence, she could muster up the courage to follow through with the divorce and finally be free of the dark cloud that hung over her.

On a couple of occasions she'd actually grabbed hold of the ring and, with some effort to twist it out of the fleshy trench that it had nestled itself into, pulled it off of her finger. She'd hold it in the fingertips of her right hand and just look at it for a moment or two, thinking about her husband and the years they'd had together. The good times that it represented, the bright moments, the things that had gone missing in the midst of the storm they'd both just endured. For richer or poorer, for better or for worse, till death they should part — she wondered, did she really mean those words when she married him so many years before? The thoughts just fanned the flames of her guilty feelings.

Finally, with a groan of surrender, she'd slip the ring back onto her finger. For the time being, anyway.

Perhaps remembering like that only helped to remind her of the gaping hole in her life and just how alone in the world she actually was.

The coffee shop was open early in the mornings, seven days a week. She typically worked the first morning shift five of those days (rotating with other waitresses on the weekends) and be there to greet her customers with a broad smile at five o'clock each day. Engaging with people was therapeutic for her and she enjoyed the busyness of working there.

She'd be on her way home at just after eleven o'clock. On the Sundays that she was scheduled to work, she'd drive down the street toward home through an intersection where the Evangelical Free Church was located at the corner. On a warm day when she'd have her windows open, she could hear the singing coming through the open doors from inside. It reminded her of her childhood when her parents were members of a Methodist church in the midwest where she grew up.

As a child, she would be in church virtually every Sunday with them. As a younger child, attending Sunday School and, when she was older, sitting through the service with the adults to hear the sermons delivered with vigor by the minister at the pulpit.

The thought would bring a smile to her face as she'd drive past on her way. She'd think to call home whenever she'd have a chance to talk with her mom and dad but she'd convince herself all over again that they'd just remind her again of being such a failure — on the cusp of her fortieth birthday with her marriage shattered, her college years wasted and working part time as a waitress and a grocery store checkout girl. She couldn't bring herself to face the chiding and embarrassment that she was convinced she'd have to listen to. It would only make things worse. She'd much prefer to dwell on the happy memories of her childhood.

But one Sunday morning, as sunlight streamed in through her bedroom window, she laid in bed alone and sleepily pondering her situation. Those thoughts of her childhood attending that church with her parents again filled her mind along with the recollections of her feelings when she'd drive past that little church and hear the inspired voices that wafted out from inside all just sort of merged together.

Realizing that that particular Sunday was one that she was not scheduled to work, she got up and began to get herself ready for a day off. She showered and walked back out into the bedroom in a bathrobe with her wet hair wrapped in a towel. She slid open her closet door to pull out a pair of jeans and a comfortable shirt to lounge around the apartment in to blissfully waste the day away with a few glasses of wine and maybe an old movie or two.

At one end of the bar in her closet hung some of her nicer clothes. The dresses, skirts and tops that she'd worn when she'd worked at her friend's dress shop back in Burbank or that she might wear to a nice restaurant when she and Dennis were still together. She paused for a moment and looked at them carefully and a thought suddenly captured her heart.

Where does inspiration come from? Ideas, motivations and such motivating thoughts? In her case, she just chalked it up to a combination of guilt and a desperation for human interaction — something less superficial than asking a customer what they'd like in their coffee and then wishing them a pleasant day as they'd leave.

But sometimes such inspirations come from somewhere else. Somewhere inside, deep inside. Some call it the soul, the spirit. Whatever that might be, somehow God had taken a hand in redirecting her trajectory. Why just then? Maybe she just hadn't felt the movement in her own spirit to do anything before then. Maybe she just didn't hear Him. Or maybe He was just waiting until she was ready.

Whatever the reason, the time seemed to be upon her that such inspiration should finally gain traction. She reached for a gray skirt and laid it on the bed followed by a white, ruffled blouse with a long white ribbon around the collar that would tie into a draping bow once the garment had been buttoned up.

She gathered up the other things that she would need, a slip, shoes, stockings, etc., laid them all out on the bed and then went into the bathroom to finish primping her hair, brushing her teeth and gargling before getting dressed.

She recalled from the sign out in front of the church (having driven past it innumerable times) that the Sunday service started at ten-thirty, Sunday school beginning an hour prior to that. She wanted to make it in time for the service. That Sunday may have been the beginning of something new in her life or, perhaps, just a passing fancy — a momentary shot in the arm — so she didn't want to get too immersed just yet. Just start with the basics and see how things went.

When she arrived at the church, there was still about fifteen minutes before the service would begin. Hoping to be as anonymous and unseen as possible, she avoided eye-contact as she walked in the front door. There were a few people loitering around in the entranceway who were cheerfully conversing and didn't appear to notice the stranger in the white blouse who wandered in but a man in a jacket and tie stepped up to her and smiled and handed her a copy of the week's bulletin. She took it from him, smiled back and nodded her thanks without saying anything. A woman in a paisley dress who stood beside him (presumably his wife) then reached out to shake her hand, "Welcome to our church," she began, "is this your first time with us?"

"Uh," Livvy's attempt at remaining invisible was apparently failing. "Yes, my first time."

"Well, sit anywhere you like. There are hymnals and Bibles in the racks in each row," she smiled broadly at her, "I hope you enjoy your time with us."

"Thank you." Livvy turned and drifted into the sanctuary and spied a number of empty seats near the back. She made her way to an unoccupied pew and sat at one end by the aisle.

The smell of the old church building brought back memories for her. Do all old church sanctuaries smell the same? The wood, the varnish, the dust settled into the crevasses of the wood-planked floor, the carved wooden pews. It was instantly a feeling of familiarity and comfort.

She opened up the bulletin and scanned its contents. Information about the church, its various ministries and meeting times and an outline of that day's service. It listed titles of the songs that they'd be singing, they were mostly familiar hymns and some not so familiar, all of them were numbered so she'd be able to find them in the hymnal — perhaps they'd come back to her from her childhood.

The organ and the piano up front began to play and the congregation began to gravitate into the pews and stood to worship together, singing the first of the hymns listed in the bulletin. She quickly yanked the hymnal out of the rack in front of her and flipped it open to the right page and found her place as everyone else was already well through the first verse. She joined in at the start of the second verse.

It felt good. She felt an inexplicable warmth and realized as they'd continued into the last verse that her face had begun to relax. The tension that she felt pulling at her forehead and her jaw was noticeably easing as she sang.

She stood and sang along with the next two hymns and then everyone sat down to hear one of the church leaders get up and make a series of announcements before they would pass the baskets for the morning's offering. She grabbed up her purse and pulled out a few bills, not wishing to be thought ill of for having passed up the basket without contributing but working two part time jobs, she was barely able to meet her expenses each month. She'd hoped that putting something in, however meager, would be looked upon more favorably than nothing.

The deacon that passed the basket through the rows skipped hers (she was the only one seated in it). She'd find out later that they didn't expect guests to contribute to supporting their church and he'd just assumed — since she was unfamiliar to him — that she was, in fact, a guest and passed her by.

The minister's message was poignant, as though he knew that she was coming that day. He spoke of things that touched on her feelings of guilt and loneliness, about commitments and most of all, love. It all made her think and reminded her of the things she'd heard in church as girl — things that somehow had been forgotten, or at least, pushed back in her mind over the years. Life has a way of doing that and one usually doesn't realize it until things start to crash all around some years later. Hearing the man's words would occasionally bring a tear to her eye but, too, encouraged her heart, making her feel just a little bit stronger, a little more confident and a bit less alone.

The singing, the message, even the wooden pews and the creaking floor held a familiarity that she found a certain comfort in. She felt like she belonged there somehow.

When the service was over, she felt refreshed and recharged. As she walked out of the sanctuary, the minister and his wife were standing in the doorway to the lobby and shook everyone's hands as they passed by. Some had comments of thanks for him as they walked by. When Livvy stepped up, the man smiled broadly and welcomed her, "Thank you so much for coming today. I hope you've been blessed."

She just smiled back, not sure how to respond.

He added, "I hope, too, that you'll come back and be with us again."

She looked down at the ring on her left hand and smiled again, "Yes," she replied, "I believe I will." ■

CHAPTER THIRTY-EIGHT

A Crazy, Terrible Idea

Curiosity finally got the better of him and about a week after his first encounter with Mike Casey, the director of the Extraterrestrial Resource and Research Center, Foster decided to drive out and see just what it was all about. Besides, if the man had somehow actually figured out who he was, he could ruin everything if he started to blab on his conspiracy theory radio show that he'd found John Smith — or worse yet, Dennis Foster — in Rachel, Nevada.

He drove out on highway 375, the legendary Extraterrestrial Highway that ran through the tiny town, south out of the village. Around him were endless acres of empty desert on all sides with a low mountain range in the distance to the west. The mountains stood within the confines of the Nellis Air Force Base, beyond which was situated Area Fifty-One and the Groom Lake airfield. Living so close to the base was a constant reminder for him to keep on his guard.

When he had left Las Vegas after doing the television interview, he just took the next turn off of that main road and drove on toward the desert with no thought as to where he was going. He was running for his life, he wasn't headed for any place specific. He'd never even heard of Rachel, Nevada, but that's where his gas tank started flirting with "empty" and he had to stop to tank up.

When he drove out of the television station's driveway, he turned left and kept making random turns until he found himself on a long, empty stretch of highway. So he just kept driving.

When he went into the building at the gas station to pay, he saw a file card tacked to a bulletin board near the cash register that advertised a place for rent at the Shady Acres Mobile Home Park. He asked the attendant where that was and, with the man's directions, drove out to find it on a side road off of the main highway.

When he pulled up to the front entrance, there was a flag pole with an American flag fluttering in the breeze surrounded at its base by a circle of whitewashed stones forming a border around greenery that included some hearty flowers and a couple of stout looking cacti and a wooden sign facing the road with the name of the mobile home park lettered across it. Everything else beyond that circle was dirt, rocks and desert dust. The name of the park was obviously either a joke or any sort of shade that might have once been there had long since shriveled up in the unrelenting desert sun and blown away.

He located the trailer from the advertisement and found a note on its door directing him to knock on the door of the next trailer where the neighbor, who had the keys, would let him in and show him around. If he wanted to rent it, he'd take his rent money and pass it on to the trailer's absentee owner. There was no lease. It was all quite informal, cheap and all in cash.

For a man who wanted to essentially disappear off the face of the earth, Rachel and the Shady Acres Mobile Home Park, seemed the perfect place for him to do it.

As he continued driving south looking for the Extraterrestrial Resource and Research Center, he ultimately saw a faded, weathered sign out by itself near the edge of the road with a smaller sign hung just below it displaying the call letters of the transmitter that Casey broadcasted his weekly radio show from. A dusty, old surplus Willys Jeep that had been crudely painted with hardware store spray cans in a makeshift pattern of brown and beige camouflage was parked out in front of a large camping trailer with similar, smaller signs on either side of it.

The trailer was on blocks with a weathered gray plywood skirt all around it that extended from its frame down to the dusty ground below. The trailer's walls apparently began life painted in an overall white with dark blue stripes which had been faded and sandblasted in the winds to a pale off-white, the stripes barely visible as a light blue cast over with desert dust that covered everything.

The door and the windows to either side of it were shaded by corrugated fiberglas awnings. Various gray wooden crates were piled up near the rear of the trailer and a large propane tank sat on a concrete pad beside the trailer's towing tongue.

Behind the trailer was a steel shipping container, the top of it slightly taller than the trailer's roof. Across the top of it was an array of radio antennae and small satellite dishes aimed in various directions. Standing on the ground off to one side was a large satellite dish nearly thirty feet in diameter pointed upward at about a forty-five degree angle.

Foster surveyed the scene and thought to himself, "What a dump! No wonder I'd never noticed the place before."

Well, Casey had said that if he were to see the Jeep parked out in front, then he was in. So he pulled the old Dodge up behind the Jeep and parked. He knocked on the door and, in just a quick moment, Casey opened it up and smiled, "Harry Blake, I'll be damned! I was hoping you'd come around some day. Come in! Come in!"

Foster stepped up into the trailer and pulled the door closed behind him. To the left of where he had walked in was a small kitchen with a two-burner gas stove and a small refrigerator below it along the back wall, a small sink in a short counter was along the front wall beside the door with cabinets above and below. A curtain closed off the back portion of the trailer where a bedroom and personal living space was. To his right, the entire front portion of the trailer was Casey's radio studio. A table with a mixing board, a computer and a rack filled with a few radio transmitting components and a mixing board faced away toward the trailer's front wall where Casey would sit at the microphone to do his shows. Across the table from the host's seat was a row of three chairs for guests with three microphones on retractible booms for them to speak into.

The walls were covered with bookcases, posters and maps. Casey pulled out one of the chairs from the studio's table and turned it around, "Have a seat, Harry. Beer?"

"Uh, sure." He sat down while Casey bent down and pulled a pair of cold bottles out from the refrigerator and twisted off the caps. He handed one to Foster and then leaned up against the counter and took a sip of his own.

"You don't recognize me, do you?" he asked with a knowing smile.

"Should I? I'm sure we've never met before that day you just showed up on my doorstep in the trailer park."

"I didn't think so. It's the beard I guess."

Foster looked more intently at him, studying his face. Then, considering the man's mannerisms and speech, his eyes suddenly widened with revelation and he blurted out, "Ted?"

"Yeah, Denny!" The man cheerfully admitted, "*It's me!*"

Foster leaped to his feet, "*You son of a bitch!*" He lunged toward his nemesis.

Suddenly realizing that the reunion wasn't going quite the way he'd expected, Ted quickly ducked and retreated back behind the curtain, clutching it for cover, "Denny! Please! Please! *Stop!*"

"Why can't you people just *leave me alone?!* Haven't you done enough freakin' damage?!"

"They screwed me, too, Denny! Please! *Let me explain!*"

Foster stopped trying to grab at him through the curtain and stepped back. The last time he'd seen Ted, he punched him in the nose and hurt his hand — and was ready to do it again if Livvy hadn't called him off. He hadn't been cut out for physical violence but he'd readily make an exception in Ted's case. But after working as the superintendent of the Shady Acres Mobile Home Park for a while, he so relished the idea of impressing the knuckles of his then calloused hand into the man's face.

Ted sheepishly peeked around from behind the curtain, "Denny? Come on, now. They burned me, too. That's why I'm here."

Foster, still furious, slowly stepped back toward the chair and turned around to take a sip of his beer, "What the hell are you talking about?" He stood there facing the radio studio, his back turned toward Ted. "What's this all about?"

"Well, first of all, the name's Tom, not Ted. Tom Finley."

"And you're — what — CIA? M7? Some other sort of national spook agency?"

"No, not exactly. I really did work in the movie industry. I was a bean-counter that managed the finances for various pictures — just like I told you. Accounts payable, sort of. I got recruited to play the part by the CIA. I was going through a dry spell, hadn't worked on a picture for a few months and they were offering a bucket of money so I bit for it. I had no idea what they would have me do to you. Honest!"

"Tell me one thing, Tom or Ted or whatever the hell your name really is: Did you sleep with my wife?"

"Never. I *never* even touched her, Denny. *As God is my witness!* A lot of talk, but I never touched her — ever."

"But they *wanted* you to."

"Oh, yeah, they sure did. They got really nasty about it, too — applied a lot of pressure, made a lot of threats — so I quit."

"And then they squashed you like a grape."

"Uh, something like that, yeah."

"So all this..." he waved his hand around toward the radio studio at the end of the trailer, "...is about revenge?"

"They rigged it so that I could never get a job in Hollywood ever again. My degrees in accounting somehow evaporated, the schools say they never even heard of me. My resume isn't worth the paper it's printed on. This is all I've got left — to expose them and make things as complicated for them as I can."

"A sad story, Ted. Annoyingly familiar, though."

"Tom."

"Whatever — I've heard it all before — lived a lot of it myself. How do I know you're not lying to me? Again. I've heard a lot of lies over the past couple of years."

"I know and, for my part in it, I'm sorry."

"What about your sketchy girlfriend, Bambi?"

"Hmph, yeah. There's a piece of work, gotta tell you. A real pro. She's one of those M7 spooks. She was your handler of sorts."

"My handler?"

"She was M7's eyes and ears the whole time you worked for them."

"Lopez," Foster mused.

"And that co-worker who threw you under the bus at the end."

"Teller? Are you serious? They were all the same person? I knew they all looked kind of similar but figured it was just a coincidence. Couldn't *possibly* be true."

"But it was."

"What about all that porno talk?"

"Hmph, she knew all the lingo, that's for sure. Acted the part around you two and wasn't shy about using her body as a tool. But she was all business. When you two would leave, she'd turn it off like a switch."

"That explains a lot."

"Like I said, she's a real piece of work."

Foster sat down and took a quick sip of his beer. After a moment, he sighed, "I can't believe it. They really played me."

"And they're still playing you, Denny — playing both of us."

"So what do you want me to do on your radio show. I don't want to give my real name."

"No, we'll stick with 'John Smith,' that's fine. Besides, that's what people out there know you as anyway. But I want you to blow the lid off the place. You've been inside, you worked there, met people, saw things that nobody had ever talked about before. I want you to tell it all."

"So how many people actually hear your show? I can't imagine you can broadcast too far from this trailer out here in the desert."

"Far enough. But I'm also syndicated. Some stations that can pick me up air it live, some record it to air later and I have a lot of stations that I send cassettes out to. Thousands and thousands of people hear the show all over the country. There's a lot of interest in conspiracies like this — you'd be surprised."

"I had no idea. This place sure doesn't look like much."

"That's kinda the idea."

"I'm impressed. But I'm not looking for revenge. I told my story to that TV station in Vegas and walked away. I'm happy here. Reasonably happy anyway."

"I get it, really I do. But I'm not there yet."

"I'm sorry for you."

"Look, if they could do it to a guy like me and to a bona fide rocket scientist with a much bigger IQ like you, they can do it to anyone. If we tell your story and pull back the curtain, maybe we can save some other poor schmuck from the same grief."

Part of him really wanted his pound of flesh but Foster knew that there was no way he'd ever even put a dent into that government machine. He'd done the interview in Las Vegas to hurt them, but it was all about them, not himself. Maybe Finley was right, maybe he could send up a red flag to warn anyone else who might get that knock on their door from a smiling government spook bearing dubious gifts. Perhaps open some eyes so they wouldn't get burned like he did. "There's something else."

"Something else? What's that?"

"You heard me talking about how they had me studying an alien element, the chip that powered the saucers?"

"Yeah, sure."

"It's the heaviest, most powerfully radioactive material ever known. They kept filling me with the idea that, if we could find a way to synthesize it, we could use it to generate almost unlimited amounts of power — clean, no emissions, an ecological miracle."

"And that was a lie?"

"I don't know if that part was — maybe. But I once overheard the director of the lab on the phone talking with someone about how it could be developed into the most powerful nuclear weapon ever. I've been thinking about it since then. From what I remember of the readings I got from it, a bomb that used ununpentium could destroy entire cities and the whole metropolitan areas around them, untold tracts, kill millions of people and render vast areas a radioactive wasteland for centuries in the blink of an eye."

"Wow — really? You think that's what they actually wanted you there for?"

"Yeah, I do."

"You need to talk about that, too. The whole UFO thing is huge, we have a big audience for that, but the world needs to hear about this, too."

"You might be painting a target on your back."

"Ha, ha! Look around, Denny. I've got nothing left to lose. My greatest revenge would be to shine a light on that plan and shut it down. People need to know about this. What d'ya say? You in?"

Foster thought for a moment and then responded, "Alright, I'm in. When do we start?"

"Great! Tomorrow night is my next live broadcast. On the air at seven. Can you be here by six so we can go over some stuff first?"

"Tomorrow? Anxious to get at this, huh?"

"You bet I am. Talking with you has me jazzed to get started right away."

"Yeah, sure. I can do that. Not that I've got anything on my social calendar, I'll be here."

For the next few weeks, Foster showed up at Ted's dusty trailer studio on Thursday nights at six o'clock to do a two hour long live talk show about his experiences at Area Fifty-One and the Facility R-Four-Seven labs. Letters and emails from listeners and phone calls from radio station program directors who subsequently aired the episodes told them that the public was excited by what they were hearing and were hungry to hear more.

When they had finished and signed off of the fourth show, Foster thought that they were done. The recorded episodes would likely get re-aired in the future all over the country, but he'd be able to just go on and live his anonymous life in the tiny town of Rachel where nobody knew who he really was. And that was just the way he liked it.

But Finley had an idea. A crazy, terrible idea for one more episode. Before Foster left the trailer that evening, he stopped him, "I want to show you something before you go."

Foster pulled on his jacket but waited by the door for Finley to fetch something out of a cabinet in the studio. He pulled out a backpack and set it down standing upright in the chair that Foster had been sitting in at the console. When he did, he unzipped it and reached in to pull out a gray and silver box with a number of knobs and a small, dark, rectangular screen on the top face of it.

"Digital recorder," he explained. "I can carry it in the backpack with a wire out to a headset mic and go totally mobile."

"That's pretty cool, Ted," Foster commented, somewhat impressed at the new technology but unsure why it was being shown to him.

"I have a great idea — if you're up for it. But you're literally the only guy on the planet who can do this."

"Do what?"

"Sneak onto the base and go check out that secret laboratory."

"You can't possibly be serious."

"Think of it! I can bring a camera, too, and we can post some pictures on my website to go along with the episode. Talk about credibility, man!"

"And what if we get caught? You have no idea what the security is like in there."

"I've been in there before — a few times — and got caught a couple of times. Essentially, the camo guys will pack you into one of their trucks and drive you out to the gate and kick you out with a lot of threats and scoldings. No big deal."

"I don't know, Ted. That lab is all the way around the other side of the base, the other side of a mountain. How far did you ever get?"

"To the top of Freedom Ridge. Got some really great pictures from up there, too."

"You didn't even scratch the surface. To get to the lab you'd have to go through the air base and then drive around the mountain to the other side. The ride I took from the apartments on the base to the lab each morning took about an hour. That's a long time to be out there and a big chance to get caught. Penetrating that deep could come with a lot more consequence than just getting kicked out the back gate."

"I know, but wouldn't it be worth it if we got away with it?"

"But if we didn't, they'd take your recorder and it would all be for nothing."

"Not for nothing. The recorder has a transmitter in it. It'll send whatever is recorded back here to the trailer in real time, so even if the recorder is confiscated, we've got the story right here on the computers."

"That's great — presuming they let us go."

"Ah, don't sweat it. What else you got to do? Water the flowers and fix people's plumbing?"

"I like my job. It's safe."

"But what about the adventure of it all? Where's that race car driver? That spirit? Can't you just feel the adrenaline already flowing?"

"I'll have to admit that, yeah, it does sound pretty exciting — daring. There is that potential rush, I suppose, but..."

"C'mon, what d'ya say, Denny?"

"Oh, alright. When do you plan to do this?"

"Saturday night. Most all of the Skunkworks people will be back home for the weekend. A lot of the security guys will have the night off, too. It's the best time."

"This Saturday — day after tomorrow?"

"This Saturday."

Foster thought for a moment and, figuring there being no point in putting it off, it won't be any more or less dangerous any other Saturday night, he agreed, "Okay, Ted, before I change my mind. I'll take you to Facility R-Four-Seven."

"Even if we get caught?"

"Even if we get caught." ∎

CHAPTER THIRTY-NINE

The Lucky Ones

An idyllic, moonlit Saturday night when some folks would be out for a romantic date night, going to the theater or gathering with friends in their back yards, Foster pulled up in front of the Extraterrestrial Resource & Research Center and parked next to Finley's camouflage-painted Willy's Jeep. Dressed in all-over black, he knocked on the door to the trailer and found Finley inside, packed and ready to go. It was about eleven o'clock. There was a nearly full moon high overhead which, in the clear desert sky, illuminated things just enough to see fairly well once one's eyes got acclimated. Still, Finley had packed a pair of powerful battery-powered lanterns. He'd put fresh batteries in them that afternoon to be ready.

Finley was excited about the anticipated excursion. Foster, to be fair, was feeling the adrenaline but was still pretty apprehensive. Frankly, he was having second thoughts. He really wanted to just walk away from all of it altogether and just live a simple solitary life but, at the same time, he thought about the fact that the same people who destroyed his life did the same to Finley — and could easily do it to anyone else. He thought that this one last incursion would help Finley to find closure and maybe he could walk away like Foster was trying to do.

There was still, however, that nagging thought that maybe it was all a put-on, just like so much of what he'd already been through over the previous couple of years. Maybe Finley, or Ted — or whatever his real name might actually be — was still one of them. Maybe this was just going to be one more stab in the back.

He'd go along, but he still didn't trust him. He'd keep his eyes wide open.

They got into the Jeep and Finley drove them a little farther south from the trailer on the Extraterrestrial Highway and then turned down a narrow dirt road that would lead out to the north gate of Area Fifty-One, the so-called "back gate" so famous in tourists' and conspiracy buffs' photos. It was nearly ten miles of rough, uneven road to get to the gate, but when they were about halfway, Finley turned off to the left and began driving across the open desert on a barely discernible trail.

"Where we going?!" Foster asked as he held on tightly to whatever he could reach.

"Short cut!" Finley replied.

They drove a short distance farther and he slowed to a stop.

"What's wrong?" Foster asked.

"Nothing. Gotta get something outta' the back."

Finley climbed out of the idling Jeep and went around to the back where he folded back a tarp and pulled out a small canvas case, then carried it around again to the driver's seat. He pulled it open and removed a set of night-vision goggles and strapped them onto his head.

"Night vision?"

"Yeah, got 'em in an Army-Navy surplus store a few years ago. State of the art." Finley leaned forward and switched off the headlights, then flipped the goggles down in front of his face and turned them on.

"You can *see* with those?"

"It's kinda tunnel-vision but, yeah, I can see everything."

"You got another one?"

"No, sorry Denny, I've just got the one."

Foster turned back around and looked out through the windshield. The moon was pretty bright and his eyes were getting adjusted to it so he didn't feel like he was missing much of anything. There wasn't much to see, anyway.

Finley put the Jeep into gear and started driving again.

"What about infra-red? Won't they be able to see us with that?"

"I packed a bunch of insulation under the hood and all inside the engine compartment. If they see us at all, it'll be a small, weak image. It'll look like a coyote or some other small animal — anything but a vehicle."

"What about us?"

"Okay — a *pack* of small animals."

They drove out to the fence line about a mile south of the Area

Fifty-One gate. He followed along the fencing, off-road across the desert for about half a mile farther south, and then pulled the car into a thicket of brush.

They climbed out and he unloaded his backpack with the recording and transmitting equipment in it from under the tarp in the back of the Jeep. He pulled off the night-vision goggles and packed them back into the car and then removed the two lanterns, a couple of canteens and a backpack for Foster. He then pulled out a folded up, tan camouflage net and Foster helped him to spread it out over the Jeep. Nosed into the brush and covered in the net, the Jeep would be practically invisible from any sort of distance, even overhead.

"Okay, there's a cut in the fence up here," Finley directed.

Along the chain-link fencing, one of the fence posts had a splotch of reddish-brown paint at its tip. The moonlight was just enough for Finley to locate it and just beyond there was an opening in the fence. The chain-link had been cut from the ground up to about five feet high and then held closed with a few bits of wire twisted together to hide the gap from the camo-guys' patrols. Foster helped untwist the wires and then pull the fence open to slip inside. Before venturing any farther, they tied the gap closed again lest anyone discover it while they were inside.

Finley took off his pack and opened the flap at the top. With a penlight that he held in his teeth, he looked inside and turned on a few switches to begin recording their adventure. When everything was all set up, he pulled out the headset and draped it out of the left side as he closed the flap back over. He had Foster hold onto the headset as he pulled the pack on again and then hand it to him over his shoulder so he could set it in place over his head and begin his narrative.

"We're through the fence," he explatined. "I'm with John Smith, the moon is bright and so far we haven't seen any camo-guys or headlights from any patrols. We're about to climb up Freedom Ridge."

He turned to Foster and explained, "There's a path from here that follows the fence for a little bit. We don't want to give away the location of the opening so it doesn't go directly up the mountain from right here."

"Lead on, Ted."

Finley put his hand over the microphone and corrected, "Mike. While we're on the air remember, you're John and I'm Mike."

"Right — sorry."

"No worries. Come on."

The trail paralleled the fence line for about one hundred feet and then took a ninety degree turn and headed straight up the slopes of Freedom Ridge to a vantage point at the top.

Freedom Ridge isn't much of a mountain, really. It's rocky and arid but not very tall and not very steep. A person in fairly good physical condition can make the climb pretty easily.

About halfway up the hill, they saw a glow from above them and off to their right. A narrow dirt road that ran along the apex of the ridge from north to south was used by the roving patrols in their white Jeep Cherokees giving them a good vantage point to see down the slopes on both sides of the ridge. The trail went through the most popular viewing locations for intruders and conspiracy-theorists who'd risk climbing up there to see the airbase at Groom Lake in the distance.

"Camo-guys," Finley whispered into his microphone. "We see a glow at the top of the ridge. Probably headlights. They're stationary right now. We'll keep climbing and try to avoid them."

"It would really suck to get just this far and get busted," Foster mused.

"It really would."

They picked their way along the rocky trail, trying to stay low and out of sight in the revealing moonlight.

As they neared the summit, they were surprised by one of the two camouflage clad patrol officers standing off by himself urinating into the weeds with his back to them. Finley quickly told Foster to drop down, waving his hands to him to get low. He crawled around behind him and took something out of his backpack and then crept up toward the camo-guy, "Mike!" Foster whispered out as loudly as he dared, "Where the hell are you going?!"

Finley didn't respond. He just waved back at him to stay down and stay quiet. As the man stood there peeing on a scrubby bush, Finley pressed the muzzle of a bright pink, plastic water pistol into the man's back. He instantly raised his hands in surrender. "No, no..." Finley said as he yanked the man's Glock from its holster and grabbed the radio from his belt, "...go on, finish up. We're not barbarians here."

The man quickly returned his hands to the task as Foster crept up in the dark. Finley handed him a roll of duct tape and directed in a loud whisper, "Zip him up and tape his mouth and his wrists."

"Zip him up?" He stood for a moment looking at the man frozen with his hands still at his crotch. "No way! I'll let him do that for himself." He turned to the man who was just then shaking out the last few drops, "You good with that?"

He just silently nodded and then put himself back together and zipped up his fly. Foster tore off a piece of silvery duct tape and pressed it across the man's face to seal his mouth shut and then had him put his hands behind his back to tape his wrists together.

"Okay," Finley directed. "Sit down and stay quiet."

"Where you going?" Foster asked.

"We need wheels, and we don't need these guys blowing the whistle on us."

"You're not gonna shoot anyone, are you?"

"Isn't the truth worth wasting one of these guys? But, No. Not if I don't have to."

Finley climbed up a little higher on the hill and hid behind a large rock anticipating the man's partner coming to look for him once he thought that he'd been gone too long. A few minutes later, as expected, the second camo-guy came walking along the ridge, calling out to his partner, looking for him in the dark. He began descending the slope and Finley stepped out from his cover behind the rock, stuffed the muzzle of the Glock into his back and told him to put his hands up.

He complied quickly.

Finley relieved him of his gun and radio and then marched him down the hill to join his partner. Foster duct taped him and they made the two men sit back-to-back and then taped their ankles together and wound a few lengths of tape around their chests to tie them together.

"We just subdued a pair of camo-guys up near the top of the ridge line, took their guns and radios and wrapped them up with duct tape." Finley narrated as he and Foster climbed up farther to the road at the top to go and borrow the white Cherokee parked there with its motor running. "They left their Jeep idling on the road while one of them went off to relieve himself. They're now taped together in the bushes and we're on our way down the hill toward the air base at Groom Lake with their car."

As they walked up to the Jeep, Foster began to get into the passenger seat but Finley stopped him, "You drive, John."

"Me?"

"I know the way up to the top of the ridge, but I've never been beyond here. You know the way from here much better than me. You've been down there."

"I suppose that makes sense. Okay." Foster walked around the front of the car, got into the driver's seat and buckled up his seat belt.

"There must be an access road along here somewhere that they used to get up here. Must lead down to the base."

"The trick is getting across the airfield," Foster explained. "The base is on the other side."

"Hell, we're driving one of their cars. We're one of them now — right?"

"I suppose. That's really our only hope."

"Nobody's ever done this before, John. We're making this up as we go along."

"You ain't kidding."

Foster pulled the Jeep out from where it was parked and back onto the dirt road along the top of the ridge and turned north. They eventually came upon a listening station set up on the side of the road, pointed down the eastern slopes toward the fence where intruders would often venture out from. On the western side of the road was an intersecting dirt road that led down the slope to the flat desert plane below and the dry lakebed.

It took them nearly an hour to get to the foot of the Freedom Ridge slopes and out toward the long runway that once hosted top secret test flights of U-2 spy planes and SR-71 Blackbirds over the years. The road they came to paralleled the runway on its eastern side from end to end. Foster turned right — north — to go around the end of the runway and hopefully get to the road that rounded Papoose Mountain on the western side of the base without having to actually go through the base itself.

As Foster drove, Finley narrated. His constant talk was somewhat distracting and the presumptions that he made about what he saw were almost more than Foster could allow without blurting out corrections, but he kept his tongue and focused on his driving.

When they got to a road that crossed the long runway, they drove to the other side where they came upon a long north-south service road. They turned south and drove a short distance until they came upon a right hand turn. "This must be it," Foster commented. "I think this will connect with the road that goes around the mountain."

"Are we lost?"

"I'm not lost," Foster quipped. "I can't speak for you, of course."

"Funny guy."

The road was fairly short and when they got to the intersection, they came upon another white Jeep on patrol coming south, having just rounded the end of the mountain ridge. Foster began to roll his window down.

"What are you doing?" Finley asked.

"We're all comrades in this — or so we're supposed to appear — right?"

"I guess."

Foster reached his hand out and waved to the oncoming Jeep. As it passed, the driver blinked his headlights quickly to high beam and back to low beam in greeting.

And then drove on without a pause. Finley quipped, "Hmph — just one big happy, eh?"

With just the illumination of their headlights and the moonlight on the narrow, dirt road, Foster and Finley drove around the northern end of Papoose Mountain and then turned south down the other side of the ridge. They continued along the foot of its western slopes toward the dry Papoose lakebed located just off of its southwestern point. Foster had ridden on that road numerous times in a shuttle bus and was expecting the time that it would take but Finley was anxious and would occasionally ask if they were getting near or if, in fact, they'd already passed it.

Finally, as the hour was nearing three o'clock, Foster recognized certain familiar rock formations alongside the road. "We're nearly there. Should be coming up on our left."

From the passenger seat, Finley kept an eye out, peering into the darkness. The moon, setting in the west, backlit various rock formations and undulations of the desert floor showing strange silhouettes and shadows stretched across the ground along the way. Both were expecting to see a glow of floodlights ahead from the Facility's entrance, fences, gates, guards and the paved parking area in front of the tunnel into the mountain.

Suddenly, Foster slammed on the brakes and the Jeep slid to a stop on the gravel road.

Finley quickly reached his hand out to brace himself against the dashboard. "What's wrong?"

Foster looked out to his left and announced with a tone of astonishment, "We're here."

"You sure? It's all dark."

"Yeah, I'm sure. I recognize the place," Foster replied quietly. "It looks abandoned, though."

From where they sat in the Jeep out in front of what had once been the busy entrance gate that led into the outside parking area, he looked over the scene in amazement. The guard shack at the mouth of the driveway was gone along with the red and white striped gates. The chain link fencing and all of the coiled razor wire that had encircled the parking area were gone. The asphalt of the lot inside was covered in wind-blown desert dust with small, dry weeds protruding from numerous cracks.

He slowly turned the car into the driveway and rolled into the parking area. At the back, against the mountainside, their headlights lit up the concrete archway that protruded from the rocks that still stood as the entrance to the long tunnel that led inside and into the labs. The metal plates with the extending steel teeth that prevented entrance to the tunnel were gone, too. The overhead fixtures in the tunnel were still hanging there but were dark.

The pair sat and studied the bizarre scene for several minutes.

"What d'you think?" Finley asked.

"I didn't think we'd be able to get any closer than the road back there, no way they'd let us inside, not without arresting us anyway. Sure wasn't expecting this. Well, we've come this far — how many felonies have we already committed? May as well keep going."

"Yeah, may as well."

Finley continued his narration, describing the deserted scene that they'd encountered and then, once Foster put the Jeep into drive and rolled slowly into the tunnel, described all that their headlights illuminated beyond.

It all looked familiar to Foster, even though he was then only seeing just what the Jeep's own lights showed as they drove through. The tunnel took a slight curve and emptied out into another, much larger parking area inside the mountain where the shuttle busses had once dropped him and his colleagues off.

When they pulled in from the tunnel, he stopped the car in the middle of the space so that their lights would shine on the back wall. To their right was the row of loading docks. The massive blast door that had led to the hallway into the labs had once been to their left. But the big roll-up doors at the loading docks were gone as was the blast door leaving gaping, dark openings along the length of the wall.

There wasn't a single vehicle or sign of any sort of life, not even desert fauna who might have set up housekeeping inside. The walls were bare, any signage that was once there were gone as well.

"This is amazing," he whispered.

Finley, narrating for his radio show, said, "Well, we're here. But 'here' doesn't seem to be here anymore. We just drove through the tunnel into the mountain and are now parked in a large, open space where semi-trucks once made deliveries at a number of loading docks. Security vehicles were once parked here in rows, out from the hot desert sun. Area Fifty-One transports would drop off and pick up scientists and administrators who worked here in busses that made regular runs between here and the base on the other side of the mountain. It's all gone now. It's all dark. There's nobody here and everything is gone. Even the doors and the signs on the walls are all gone."

Foster pulled the Jeep around to the left to aim its headlights through the open doorway and down the long hallway to give them at least a little bit of illumination for their quest. Leaving the engine idling, he then got out and walked around to the back of the car and opened up the hatch to retrieve the two big flashlights.

"Where you going?" Finley asked as he climbed out of the passenger side and walked around to join him at the tailgate.

"You wanted a tour? I'll give you a tour."

"You sure you want to go in there?"

"Never so sure of anything in my life — where are the guns?"

"The guns?"

"Yeah, the ones you took off of the two camo-guys back there?"

"Oh, I tossed them out the window."

"Why the hell would you do that?!"

"Because if we get busted in here and they see we're armed, they're likely to shoot first and ask questions later."

"Hmph, alright — I guess. Do you still have the radios at least?"

"I do," Finley unclipped one of them from his belt and handed it to Foster.

He turned it on but only got static issuing from its small speaker. He tried adjusting the knobs and pushing the buttons for the various pre-programmed frequencies, but it only produced more static.

"I guess there's no reception inside the mountain," Finley mused.

"We'll take them anyway. This may just be a dead spot."

"Yeah, maybe."

They clipped the two radios to each of their respective belts and put on their backpacks. They each grabbed one of the lanterns and then walked toward the opening to stand at the entrance to the long hallway that penetrated deep inside the mountain. Foster shone his light around the walls inside and explained, "As the corridor extended deeper and deeper into the mountain, the level of security clearance required increased. Out here in the front was the green zone, the lowest level of security. Partway down the hallway would be a desk manned by a pair of armed guards in black where the zone changed from green to yellow. Another guard station down farther where the red zone began and then one more nearly at the end of this hall where the highest security level began, the black zone. That's where the hangars and the morgue are."

"Let's start there," Finley said. "You lead — and don't forget to narrate."

"Narrate. Right." Foster began walking into the dark corridor. He shone his flashlight around. The colored stripes on the walls were gone, sandblasted off of the concrete blocks leaving bare masonry where they once were. Tan asphalt tiles were still on the floor and the ceiling of exposed steel rafters, ducts and conduits was still visible above them. All of the doors were gone as were any of the signs and keypads to unlock them.

As they walked past the gaping open, dark and empty offices, he shined his light into a few of them and announced each that he knew. "That was Dr. Hidleman's office," he noted as they walked past it. "This was still the green zone. These other doors were various other administrative offices, that one was the infirmary."

As they walked through the yellow zone, he pointed out the rest rooms, "Each security zone had its own rest rooms so that people wouldn't have to venture into areas that they didn't have clearance for to do their personal business."

They walked into the former men's room. The door, like all of the others, had been removed from its hinges. Inside, evidence of plumbing protruding from the walls and the floor were all that was left. All of the fixtures — sinks, toilets, partitions, towel racks, mirrors — were gone.

"Even the bathrooms," Finley quipped.

"They're nothing if not thorough," Foster commented as they walked back out to the hallway.

When they walked into the red zone, Foster paused for a moment and pointed his flashlight's beam at a spot on the floor, "This is where the security desk from the yellow zone was to enter the red zone. That's where I worked. Every day we'd each have to stop here, show our identification badges — they all had a colored stripe on them coinciding with our level of security clearance. They'd search briefcases, women's purses and pass a metal detecting wand over us before allowing us to go by."

"That's pretty involved. They did that every day? They didn't get to recognize people after a while?"

"Oh, they'd recognize us. They'd call us by name and they were totally courteous, but they had their job to do and, yes, they did it to every one of us every day."

"Wow. Must have been pretty intense, working under those conditions."

"Believe it or not, one gets the hang of it after awhile. It was much the same where I worked before — not as involved or intense there — but a routine you just sort of got used to."

"I guess."

Foster started walking farther down the corridor. To his right was the open doorway to the lounge. It, too, was stripped bare. He shined his light inside but didn't comment. A little farther down the hall, on the left, was what had been the particle lab. "This is where I worked," he announced and then led Finley inside.

He shone his light around the empty room and pointed out where his desk and the others were once located, where the various work tables and counters had been and rattled off a list of sophisticated test equipment that was once set up all around the room. As he swiped his light around the room, the beam caught something small and shiny in the middle of the floor, "What's that?" he asked quietly.

He walked over to the center of the floor with his light trained on whatever it was that had glinted from it until he bent down and picked it up. "Well, I'll be darned," he whispered.

"What is it?" Finley asked.

"It's my ID badge," Foster explained as he stood up again.

"Seriously? Somebody's playing with you, man," Finley warned.

"They knew we were coming?"

"How could they?"

"Your trailer could be bugged," Foster speculated.

"Bugged? Come on, I think I'd know it."

"I've seen things out here, 'Mike.' Trust me, they have ways."

"Well, let's get back to the hangars while we still can and get the hell out of here."

"Alright. Anything else I'll point out on the way back." Foster slipped the laminated badge into his shirt pocket and the pair left the lab space and walked quickly toward the back of the facility where the hallway ended at the intersection of a perpendicular hallway that extended from the left and across to the right. All along the opposite wall were a number of gaping, vacant doorways, all of which missing their heavy, radiation-sealing doors.

"Alright, these are the hangars," he turned right at the intersection and then led Finley into the first door they came to on the left wall. As they walked inside the cavernous space, he explained, "This was hangar number two. This was the first look I got at two of the alien craft that they had here."

The huge space was empty and echoed with their voices and footsteps. The gray and red electrical boxes around on the gray walls were still there with their corresponding high-voltage warning signs, but all of the other signs were gone. All of the radiation exposure warnings, even the black-and-yellow striped lines on the smooth concrete floor were gone. Everything else was bare.

Again, using his flashlight as a pointer, Foster indicated where he had seen the crashed remains of the saucer from Roswell that was recovered in 1947 and then, in the opposite corner, the fully intact craft that had been surrounded by scaffolding, various machines and technicians.

"Is that the one that you saw fly?" Finley asked.

"No, that one was in the next hangar, hangar three."

"I'm sure it's not there anymore, either."

"Yeah, I'm sure." Foster turned and walked back out to the hallway. On the other side of the corridor was a large, steel-framed window. He pointed to it with his flashlight, "Come on."

They walked up to the window and looked inside, then walked around into the dark, empty room through a doorless frame just to its right. "This was the morgue," he explained.

"This is where you saw them doing an autopsy?"

"There were three tables in a row in the middle of the room. That wall along the back was lined with metal refrigerator doors. All that's left now are the tiles on the floor."

"It's amazing that they were able to strip this whole place bare like this so quickly."

"It's been about a year."

"Still, considering the inefficiency of the government, it's pretty amazing that they got all of this done so fast."

"I suppose — maybe they had help."

"So, you saw them cutting open an alien on one of those tables?"

"Yeah. I guess he was one of the lucky ones."

"Lucky?"

"He was already dead."

"Oh — *Oh?*" ■

CHAPTER FORTY

Busted

Foster and Finley stood looking around inside the empty space that once housed the Facility R-Four-Seven morgue with their flashlights when, suddenly, Foster got very quiet and snapped his head around to look out through the open doorway into the empty, dark hallway.

"What's the matter?" Finley asked.

Foster put his finger up to his lips, "Shhh," he said, then quietly added, "I think I heard something."

Finley stood still for a moment and listened intently and then nodded in agreement. He turned off his flashlight and Foster did likewise.

They were in a large, open room, there was no place to hide. All they could do was stand there still and silent as church-mice and hope that nobody would notice them.

The sound of approaching feet grew louder, echoing down the bare masonry walls of the long corridor. They could see the beams of flashlights and red lasers projected onto the walls of the hallway outside growing larger and brighter as their pursuers neared the intersection that would turn and lead to the hangars and past the room where they stood.

Listening closely, they could hear hurried footfalls spreading out to check each of the three hangars and then, as they swarmed past the former morgue, one of them stopped in his tracks and turned his light into the room. "In here!" he shouted to his comrades.

Within seconds, a dozen men in menacing black SWAT gear poured into the room carrying M-16s with bright lights and lasers fixed on them, their beams all converging on the pair standing in the center of the room who quickly raised their hands high into the air, still clutching their flashlights.

Finley began narrating, "Busted. They found us. Black-suited stormtroopers are now encircling us with their weapons trained on us. Our hands are raised in surrender — will they honor that? Or will they just gun us down for daring to intrude into this abandoned, secret laboratory to seek out the truth of Area Fifty-One?"

"What the hell are you doing?" Foster asked.

"We're still on the air, man."

"Are you out of your mind?"

"This is *great* radio — I can't waste this!"

"Shut up, you two," a man in black riot gear ordered as he entered the room. Apparently, he was the one in charge though he wore no rank or any other insignia on his uniform. None of them did. "Identification — both of you — *now!*"

"Uh, sure," Foster reached into his back pocket with one hand — keeping the other raised in clear view — and removed his wallet. Finley did the same. He slid his driver's license out of its clear plastic sleeve and handed it to the man. He gathered Finley's as well and then studied them under the beam of his flashlight.

"Michael Casey and Harrison Blake. You both live in Rachel?"

"We do," Finley replied. "We're all neighbors."

The man glanced up at him, not responding to his lame attempt at familiarity. He returned their licenses and allowed them to put them back into their wallets and replace them into their respective back pockets before ordering two of his men to handcuff them both.

The pair were each frisked, their wrists shackled behind their backs and then black hoods were draped over both of their heads. The soldiers then led them out of the morgue, carrying their backpacks and lanterns with them. A couple of the men held the pair by their arms to steer them along in the dark. They led them back down the corridor to the large, open parking area inside the entrance where they had left the car they had commandeered on the mountain ridge. Also parked in the broad space were several more identical white, unmarked Jeep Cherokees and a few desert-tan Humvees all positioned with their lights glaring at them as they emerged.

With the black hoods on their heads, neither could see any of what was happening around them.

Foster was put into the back seat of one of the Jeeps, his backpack and lantern were set into the cargo space at the back and a soldier in black sat beside him. Finley was likewise inserted into another Jeep along with his backpack of transmitting equipment which, unbeknownst to their captors, was still broadcasting, the microphone still on, recording everything on the computers back at the Extraterrestrial Resource and Research Center trailer.

One of the Humvees led the two Jeeps out through the tunnel with a soldier protruding from an opening in its roof, his hands steadying a fifty-caliber machine gun mounted at its rim. They were followed by another Humvee likewise armed and ready to repel any intrusions — or prevent the pair of them from escaping their captivity.

Foster had never been handcuffed before and spending an hour in the back seat of the Jeep with his hands shackled behind him pressed into the seat cushion and riding along that uneven and often bumpy dirt road back to the Groom Lake air base, became torturously uncomfortable in short order.

When they finally rolled onto the campus of buildings behind the hangars that lined the runways at the base, they drove past the Village where he had lived during his time working there. A few buildings beyond, they turned and pulled into a large, open garage. Inside, the convoy parked side by side, the two Jeeps beside one another with the two Humvees parked at either side of them. They waited inside the vehicles until the overhead door was rolled closed behind them to prevent their escape when the car doors were opened. The soldiers then climbed out of the Jeeps and brought out their captors with their backpacks.

They were guided down a short hallway, still hooded and braced by soldiers keeping a grip on each of them. They were separated and brought into two adjacent interrogation rooms.

Once securely inside, the black hood was yanked off of Foster's head, He found himself sitting in a chair at a metal table in a stark, concrete-walled room painted a glossy, institutional gray. A pair of similar metal chairs sat empty across the table from him and a large mirror facing him on the opposite wall gave whomever was behind it a panoramic view of the entire space.

It took his eyes a moment to adjust to the bright light in the room. He squinted and forcefully blinked his eyes for a little while until he could see clearly with minimal, diminishing glare.

The soldier who had escorted him in from the car stood guard just behind him with his machine gun hung in front of himself, his hands resting on it at the ready. Foster could see him clearly in the mirror.

"Hey," Foster said to him, "are these handcuffs really necessary? I'm a scientist for cryin' out loud. I'm no threat."

The soldier just stood there stoically looking at him through the reflection in the mirror without responding.

The door opened and two men walked into the room, one dressed in a black suit and another older, balding man in a dark gray suit and loud, colorful tie. He'd seen them both before, but he recognized the man in the black suit immediately as he stepped through the door. His face instantly flushed red and he began to leap to his feet, "Steele, *you bastard!*"

The soldier reached out with one hand, clamped it onto his shoulder and shoved him back down into the chair.

"Now I know why I'm wearing handcuffs — I promised you that the next time I saw you, *I'd kill you!*"

He sat there seething, snarling at Steele as he and the man in the loud tie cooly walked up to the opposite side of the table.

Steele looked down at the papers he had in his hand, dismissing Foster's outburst, and began, "Harrison Blake, is that right? And you live in Rachel, Nevada? Hmmm, not too far from here. Is that correct?" He acted as though he didn't know who Foster actually was, his violent outburst was seemingly no sort of evidence. The full beard and long hair that he sported since moving to the tiny town in the desert and taking on that new persona shouldn't have concealed his identity all that much to someone like Steele.

"Stand up, Mr. Blake, and empty your pockets onto the table," he ordered.

He hesitated but the soldier grabbed his arm and tugged him upward. The handcuffs were removed and reluctantly, he complied. He reached into his pockets and removed his wallet from his back pocket, a few dollars and pocket change from another pocket and a Swiss Army knife from a third.

"Is that everything?"

"That's everything."

Steele looked up at the soldier and patted his own breast pocket. The man then reached around Foster from behind and yanked the Facility R-Four-Seven identification badge out of his shirt pocket and tossed it onto the table with everything else.

"No, *that's* everything." Steele corrected. "Sit down, sir."

"I'll stand, thanks."

"Sit down, Mr. Blake."

Foster refused. The soldier again placed his hand on his shoulder but Foster spun around, batting his arm away and shoving the soldier back, catching him off guard and knocking him momentarily off balance.

The soldier instantly raised his weapon and aimed it at Foster's face at point-blank range, its red laser dot dancing across his forehead.

"Go ahead! *Go ahead, dammit!*" Foster shouted. "You've taken everything else. Why the hell not?! *Finish it, Steele!* I've got nothing left to lose! Go ahead! *Finish it!*"

"Let's calm down here!" the man in the loud tie called out. "Stand down, soldier. I don't think Mr. Blake poses any sort of real threat now."

The soldier held his threatening posture for a few seconds and then eased back and stepped away, lowering his weapon as he did.

"Please, Mr. Blake, have a seat," the man continued, pulling one of the chairs out from the table on the other side and seating himself down. "No need for any of that sort of drama."

Foster turned back around and looked down on the man seated across the table from him. He'd seen the man before. He was hovering in Hidleman's office when he was accused of attacking his co-worker and ultimately fired. He was never introduced, he didn't know the man's name.

Without a word, he stood his chair back up on its legs and sat down to face him at the table.

"Look, Mr. Blake, you were caught on a high-security government installation — trespassing. There are signs all around this place saying 'keep out' and warning that deadly force is authorized. You could have been shot. Didn't you see any of them?"

"Your signs are actually rather famous," Foster grumbled. "You know they sell replicas in the gift shops around here."

"A source of continual bemusement, I'll have to admit. I have one in my garage, actually. Nevertheless, you made it all the way around to the other side of Papoose Mountain somehow and wandered into an abandoned nuclear waste dump. I can't recall anyone ever being so brazen to have penetrated this facility quite so far."

"I had help, and it's not a nuclear waste dump — we both know that."

"Help, yes, your conspiracy theory friend — the pirate radio host. Frankly, this isn't the first time that he'd been caught inside the fence, but it will be his last."

"His last? What are you going to do to him?"

"We're not going to take him out into the desert and shoot him, if that's what you're worried about. He'll have a trial before a military tribunal and probably end up in solitary confinement at Leavenworth for the rest of his life so that he can't prattle on to anyone about aliens, flying saucers and Area Fifty-One anymore."

"This is your first offense," Steele added. "If you answer our questions, we'll let you off with a warning — which you had best seriously heed — and then cut you loose. You'll be red-flagged after this, like your friend, and if you're caught in here again you may well be shot down like a rabid dog and just left for the buzzards and coyotes."

"So what the hell do you want from me?" Foster slouched in his chair. "What do you want to know that you don't already?"

Steele set a small tape recorder into the center of the table and switched it on. For the next few hours he and Weisz (the man in the loud tie who never introduced himself) asked a barrage of questions about Foster's life, his employment and other, extracurricular activities. They asked about his associations, friends, relatives and co-workers. All the while asking questions of Harrison Blake, not Dennis Foster, ignoring his true identity and connection with the abandoned Facility R-Four-Seven where he had been caught — even though they both knew otherwise.

Most of the answers that he'd offered were made up on the fly. They were asking questions of a fictitious person so he gave them fictitious answers. It was surreal. He couldn't understand why they were doing what they were doing but, if it meant being released and not being charged with a felony and/or spending the rest of his life in prison — or worse — he'd play along.

It was a bizarre theatrical performance by all involved.

The fatigue eventually took its toll as the interrogation dragged on. Someone kept bringing fresh cups of coffee into the room for all three men. Foster, having been up since the previous morning, having had no sleep for nearly thirty-two hours and having actually scaled a small mountain in the interim, was more than spent.

Finally, Steele announced that they were through. He opened the folder that he had brought into to the room at the outset and removed a form and laid it on the table top. He laid a pen down on top of the paper and then slid it across to Foster, "Here, sign this."

"Sign what? Another form? What is this?"

"It's a nondisclosure agreement. Under penalty of arrest and imprisonment, you agree not to divulge anything that you had seen here today or anything that we'd talked about."

"And what if I refuse to sign it?"

"Then we will have no choice but to detain you indefinitely — or until you do."

"And then you'll let me go?"

"Yes, then we'll let you go."

"And I should believe that?"

"I assure you, Mr. Blake. We will drive you off the base and let you go."

"Hmph, we both know that your assurances mean next to nothing — you tried to kill me, I'll never forget that."

Steel stood without replying to Foster's accusation, his face registering no acknowledgement.

"Alright." Foster picked up the pen, poised it over the blank line at the bottom of the form and hesitated. "Which name would you like me to sign?"

"Your own name, of course. Harrison Blake."

Foster shook his head in annoyed disbelief. He still couldn't figure out what was going on but nevertheless, if it meant being set free, he'd comply. After signing the form, he slid it and the pen back across the table.

Steele put the document back into the folder while Weisz stood up and waved to an unseen person on the other side of the large mirror behind him. In a few minutes, a pair of men in camouflage walked into the room and Weisz directed Foster, "Stand up, Mr. Blake."

He sat up in his chair, then pushed it back and got to his feet. One of the two camo-guys walked up to him with a pair of handcuffs in his hands, "Is that really necessary?" he asked.

"Do you want to get out of here?" Steele interjected.

Foster just heaved a sigh of resignation and put his hands behind his back to allow the man to handcuff him.

"In front," Weisz corrected. "I think we can afford that much of a concession. And don't make them any too tight."

Foster then reached out his two arms toward the man who then clamped the metal restraints onto his wrists.

"Alright, Mr. Blake. I honestly hope that I never see you again," Steele commented as the camo-guy led him around from behind the table toward the door.

"Believe me, Steele, the feeling is more than mutual."

The other camo-guy gathered up all of Foster's personal effects and placed them into a zip-locked plastic bag, all but the Facility-R-Four-Seven identification badge. Steele scooped that up, commenting, "No souvenirs."

Foster watched as the only shred of physical proof of his story was snatched away and disappeared into the folder to join with the form he'd just signed.

Just before the door was opened, a loose-fitting black fabric hood was once again draped over his head. He didn't protest, For want of that episode to be finished and to be set free back into the real world, he just stood still and allowed one more indignity.

He thought that he should never have allowed his dubious former neighbor to have talked him into such a risky adventure in the first place. ∎

CHAPTER FORTY-ONE

Fifteen Minutes

With his hands shackled, gripping the plastic bag containing his wallet and other personal effects, and with a black hood draped over his head, Foster was led out of the interrogation room and back out through the labyrinth of hallways to the garage where he'd come in from. He was put into the back seat of one of the white Jeeps with one of the armed camo-guys beside him and driven out from the air base and east through the desert for nearly two hours. The sun was up by then shining its bright morning light in through the windshield but he couldn't see any of it with the hood covering his face.

After what seemed like an eternity of being jostled around, riding in the back seat of the Jeep on a rugged, gravel desert roadway, they finally came to a stop and the driver got out. After a few minutes of waiting quietly, the door beside him opened while the man seated next to him pushed his own door open and got out. The two camo-guys helped Foster out of the car and onto his feet.

"Are we there yet?" Foster sarcastically asked.

The humorless soldiers didn't reply. They just led him blindly along a short distance of dirt road toward the north gate. They kept their hands clasped firmly on his upper arms in case he should stumble on the uneven surface of the dirt road, not being able to see where he was going.

He could hear voices, young voices mostly, both male and female. They were getting closer or perhaps he was getting closer to them. The chatter and laughter sounded like he was being led to some sort of a cocktail party. Eventually he could make out some of what they were saying. They were pointing out the white Jeep and the two camouflage-clad men leading a man in handcuffs out toward the gate. Their voices got quiet as they speculated about just who it might be that was being escorted out of Area Fifty-One on foot.

As Foster and his attendants neared the gate, it rose up just enough for the three of them to walk under it to the short remaining segment of dirt road where a second gate was raised to let them out to the paved shoulder of a more substantial gravel road that led off into the desert and, ultimately, to the Extraterrestrial Highway. He could hear a number of young voices ahead of them. Once there, the voices became still as one of the men instructed Foster to hold out his manacled wrists. He could feel the man manipulating the handcuffs — presumably unlocking them — and in a moment his hands were free.

The other man then yanked the hood off of his head and the pair of them then just turned and silently walked back under the gate and up the road, back to the car.

Foster turned and saw the Jeep parked about fifty yards back from where he was standing. It was parked on the dirt road in front of a small, corrugated metal building. In front of him was a red and white striped gate with a stop sign attached at its center extending across the road and a second identical gate was located inside, just behind where the Jeep was parked.

Ten foot tall chain-link fencing topped with coils of razor wire lined both sides of the dusty road from the inner gate where the Jeep was parked to the outer gate where he stood and then extended out from there in both directions — to his left and to his right — as far as the eye could see. On the steel fence posts were fixed numerous warning signs threatening imprisonment and deadly force for anyone who dared to venture inside without authorization.

The two camo-guys got back into the Jeep, turned around and drove away, disappearing back into the vast, empty desert.

He just stood there and watched them leave, knowing that eyes from inside the tinted windows of the small building were watching him intently.

"Hey, man," one of the young tourists loitering around by the gate addressed him with curious excitement. "You get caught in there?"

"You up on Freedom Ridge, dude?" another asked.

About a dozen people were standing around at the mouth of the road into the base taking pictures of each other posing in front of the sinister warning signs, the guard station inside the fencing and the signs ironically prohibiting photography. They stopped their almost celebratory revelries when he was led out and dumped off outside the gate, photographing the entire event.

He just looked at them for a moment. Young, starry-eyed and completely clueless.

They all seemed to think that the whole UFO/alien culture that they were engrossed with was just so much fun, some sort of pop-culture game engineered for its entertainment value. He had heard about people like that and seen plenty of them passing through town since he'd moved to Rachel but never cared to actually interact with any of them.

"Yeah, I got caught inside," he reluctantly answered as he opened up the plastic bag and began returning the items inside to their respective pockets. "We climbed up Freedom Ridge, stole a Jeep and drove down into the base."

"You did? Dude! *That's awesome!*"

"'We?' Who was with you? How come they just brought you out? Alone?"

"The guy I was with is headed to prison — probably for the rest of his life. They're gonna make him disappear."

"That's heavy, man. Who is he?"

"You ever listen to the broadcasts from the Extraterrestrial Resource and Research Center here in Rachel?"

"Yeah, man — you were with Mike Casey?"

"They busted the both of us. He's still being held in there."

"They gonna do experiments on him?"

"Look, you people think this is all for fun — believe me, you have no idea what you're messin' around with here." He turned and waved his hands toward the array of warning signs, "These aren't here for decoration, these people mean business! You walk in there and you may never be seen or heard from again."

"They can *do* that?"

"They can — and they do."

"*Cool!*"

Foster just shook his head.

"Your voice sounds familiar," a young woman wearing a beaded gift shop Indian headband and a tank top with a green cartoon face of an alien printed across her chest said. "Didn't I hear you on Casey's radio show?"

"Yeah, now that you mention it, you *do* sound familiar," the young man who stood by her added. "He interviewed you, didn't he?"

"He's Smith," another young man added. "I recognized him, too."

The young woman's eyes widened, "*You're John Smith?!* I heard those interviews, saw you on TV!"

Foster looked around himself in disbelief. Somehow he had become famous — the very last thing he wanted to have happen. "Yeah," he reluctantly admitted. "I'm afraid that's me — or at least it used to be."

"Can I get a picture with you?" the young woman in the tank top asked.

"Huh? Seriously?"

"My brother won't believe that I actually met John Smith at Area Fifty-One! Can we stand over here by the signs?"

"Uh...okay."

Foster followed his newfound groupie to one of the fence posts to pose for a photo. He quickly brushed his hair back with his hands, straightened his glasses and brushed his shirt down while she pressed herself up against him and wrapped one arm around his back. He wrapped his arm around her and the two of them then held up peace signs with their free hands and smiled for the photo.

"Me next!" another voice called out.

Before long, almost every one of the group of conspiracy-theory-nerds-turned-groupies posed with "John Smith" — one by one and in various combinations — in front of the threatening Area Fifty-One warning signs in the hot, dusty desert.

When they were finally satisfied, and asked all of the questions of him that they could think of, he asked if anyone would be willing to give him a lift back into town.

"I can give you a ride!" one man volunteered.

As if to outdo the offer, another announced, "I got cold beer in the cooler!"

Foster smiled, "Thanks, I think I could use one about now."

He turned and waved to the rest of them like some sort of rock star getting into a limo after a concert as he climbed into the back seat of a blue Honda Accord with the young man driving and his girlfriend riding next to him up front.

"Cooler's on the floor back there," the driver explained. "Help yourself!"

"Thanks."

"Where to?"

Foster removed a wet, dripping bottle of cold brew from the cooler, took off his glasses and began rolling it across his forehead to cool off. "You know where the Research Center is?"

"Yeah, we stopped there," the girl responded. "It was closed so we came out here."

"I've got the key. You can drop me there. I left my car there last night."

"Cool! Can we get a tour?!"

"Uh, sure, I guess so. Not much to see but I don't imagine it would hurt anything now. I can show you around."

"This is *so awesome!*" the driver exclaimed.

The weather-beaten trailer that was the Extraterrestrial Resource and Research Center was about halfway between the north gate road and the cluster of buildings and cross streets that made up the tiny village of Rachel along the Extraterrestrial Highway. He was continually asked question after question along the way which he did his best to answer. When they got there, the driver pulled off the road and parked on the dirt patch in front.

"That your car, dude?" the driver asked when he saw the old Dodge Dart with the bullet holes in it parked in front near the propane tank.

"Yeah, that's it."

"Not much of a car for a guy like you."

Foster smiled, "You don't need much out here — especially when you're trying to stay under the radar."

"Hmmm, smart. I like it."

"Can we get that tour now?" the girl effervescently asked, bouncing up and down in the passenger seat clutching her Instamatic camera in her hand.

"Sure, come on." Foster got out of the car and the three of them stood off to the side of the trailer. He pointed out to them the satellite dishes, the air-condishioned shipping container filled with transmitter equipment with the various antennae and smaller dishes on its roof. He showed them the mast behind the trailer with the broadcast antenna mounted at its top. The girl snapped photo after photo and got Foster to pose with them in front of the sign near the road.

He then walked up to the front door, reached up to the metal framework of the fiberglas canopy over the porch and retrieved a spare key that was kept hidden there. He unlocked the door and pulled it open, then led the two groupies inside.

The space was cramped and only took a few minutes to point out most of the relevant features. For the most part, it was kind of disappointing but the radio studio that took up the front half of the trailer was a great source of fascination for the couple. They took photos of themselves both at the host's microphone and as guests across the counter. They even got Foster to sit in for a few.

Foster found a few brochures in a box promoting the Research Center and encouraging donations to the cause. He handed them a handful as they were leaving and told them to share them with the rest of their friends.

"Thanks, Mr. Smith!" the girl gushed, and then kissed him on the cheek before they got back into their car and drove away.

Fifteen minutes of fame, so he thought. Doesn't everyone supposedly get those fifteen minutes? It was kind of fun but, in reality, he really just wanted to disappear into the desert there and be left alone. Hopefully, it was over.

Knowing that Finley wouldn't likely be back anytime soon — if ever — he rummaged around to see if there was anything that he should take with him to preserve from the looters, vandals and souvenir hunters who would inevitably ravage the place in his absence. Finley would know where to find him if he would ever return to collect it up.

He couldn't save the broadcast equipment, there was just too much of it and it was too big to move and store. He knew, however, that microphones were pretty expensive so he plucked each one out of their mounts around the table, wrapped them in layers of paper towels from the kitchen to protect them, and put them into a plastic storage tub that he found in the bedroom having dumped out the clothing that it contained onto the bed.

In a cabinet behind the radio host's chair, he found a wooden box filled with cassette tapes. Recordings of every episode of the Mike Casey radio show for the past couple of years, including, he presumed, his own interviews.

He also found some loose-leaf binders filled with maps and various notes and then, finally, grabbed a few of the brochures that he'd given to the young tourists and tossed them, too, into the plastic tub with everything else.

After one last look around, he stepped out the door, locking it behind himself and replacing the key into its hiding place overhead.

He carried the tub back to his car and set it into the trunk, noticing as he did the bullet hole in the lid as he shut it — a continual reminder of just why he was living in Rachel in the first place and why following Mike Casey into Area Fifty-One the night before was such a bad idea.

A familiar song came on the radio once he'd started the car, one of his favorites. He turned up the volume a little bit to hear the music over the wind blowing through the open windows once he'd be on his way.

He backed the car around and then pulled out to the end of the driveway — pausing to check for traffic — then turned left and began to drive away, back toward Rachel.

With the Research Center receding behind him, he got momentarily lost in the song on the radio.

Then, just as he turned out onto the road, instantly, the trailer was thoroughly destroyed in a massive explosion, a huge ball of fire, the shockwave and radiating heat slammed into his car from behind.

The car was rocked by an unseen jolt. Thinking for half a second that he'd been struck by a vehicle that he didn't notice when he'd pulled out onto the road, he realized that all of his mirrors were illuminated by a bright, angry, yellow-orange flash, his ears were stabbed by the deafening sound.

He slammed on the brakes and quickly spun his head around to look out of his window just in time to see the trailer that had been the Extraterrestrial Resource and Research Center engulfed in a fireball that had reduced it to an airborne scattering of twisted metal and flaming wreckage that was still flying out in every direction, some of which in fiery arcs that shot out like bullets from the smoke and flames and littered across the roadway and into the desert beyond.

Instinctively, he ducked down for cover until the sound of the blast had diminished to a rumble and roar accompanied by the crackling sound of whatever was left being incinerated in the resulting flaming heap. Bits of debris landed on his car, he could hear things falling onto the sheet metal — mostly small, insignificant bits but also a few alarmingly large chunks that slammed into the car with a resounding crash.

He put the car in park and got out. Trepidously, he flicked a few charred bits of rubble off of his thigh that had blown in through the open window. Then, standing next to the open driver's door he felt that he had to do something but once the initial explosion had subsided — a matter of seconds — all he could see was the mutilated chassis of the trailer with mangled bits of the aluminum walls still attached to parts of it, sitting in the middle of a black, scorched patch of dirt. The force of the blast was so powerful that the wall of the steel shipping container behind the trailer had been caved in and the doors thrown open in the twisted framework. He quickly realized there was nothing to be done, nothing left to be saved.

The sign out by the road, its posts bent and standing at a skewed angle with some black carbon along the charred edges that faced toward the blast, was the only thing left that suggested that the flaming, smoldering pile of rubble was once the Extraterrestrial Resource and Research Center.

Like a man staring into the eyes of a snake that he'd come upon unexpectedly, he just stood and stared at the scene, frozen. He knew who did it, or at least, who was responsible.

He began to get back into his car when he noticed that the roof of it was scattered with small dents and bits of charred debris. A large, ragged and charred piece of wood with some of the trailer's aluminum skin still attached to it laid across the trunk thankfully having missed hitting the window. He was going to brush it all off but thought it might still be too hot to touch so he'd just drive off and let the wind do the job for him as he went.

They wanted Mike Casey to be as thoroughly erased from the public eye and the planet as possible. It was clear that Finley — or Ted, as he'd first known him — would never be seen or heard from again.

Ever. ∎

PHASE 8
THE PRIZE

CHAPTER FORTY-TWO

Something Special

Foster stood just outside of the circle of whitewashed stones that rimmed the flower bed around the flagpole at the entrance to the Shady Acres Mobile Home Park with a garden hose in his hand, liberally watering the greenery and flowers within the confines of the decorative edging. It was fairly late in the afternoon, as was his habit. It was cooler out in the sun than it would have been at the apex of the day. By watering the plants late in the day, the heat of the sun wouldn't be as likely to cause all of it to quickly evaporate, giving a chance for the water to seep down into the soil overnight to the plants' roots.

It had been about six weeks since his excursion inside the fence with Finley and that brutal morning when the Extraterrestrial Resource and Research Center had been blown to smithereens. Nobody in town said a word to him about it other than to include him in on their own conversations of lamenting how unfortunate it was that the trailer out on the edge of town had blown up like that — even if the guy who lived in it was a conspiracy theory crackpot that they all shunned.

The fire department, when they'd arrived on the scene even as quickly as they did, could do nothing. There wasn't anything left to save by then. They saw the twisted remains of the propane tank about fifty feet away from the mangled remains of the trailer's chassis and presumed that it was the cause of the explosion — clearly, there must have been a gas leak inside the trailer, something sparked it and the whole place blew up. Thankfully, no one was home at the time and nobody was hurt.

Foster, of course, had been inside the trailer just minutes before and hadn't smelled even a hint of gas, but he kept that to himself. He knew better.

For the ensuing weeks, life was quiet for him in the tiny town of Rachel. Certainly, some of the people who lived there had heard the Mike Casey interviews with him, but nobody had put two and two together to realize that the "John Smith" they'd heard on the radio was, in actuality, the man they knew as Harry Blake. It was just as well, he thought. He'd had his fifteen minutes of fame and it nearly killed him. He much preferred the quiet life out in the anonymous netherworld of the lonely Nevada desert.

As he stood there with hose in hand, he noticed an older minivan with California plates roll slowly past on the road outside the entrance. Unusually slowly, as though the driver were looking for something. Not much for anyone to be looking for out there, he mused, especially on such a side road. If whomever it was in the minivan was a tourist looking for UFO attractions, they were far off of the beaten path, a fair distance removed from the famous Extraterrestrial Highway.

The vehicle rolled past and then picked up a little bit of speed after it went by. He continued soaking down the greenery and nearly forgot about it until it returned from the opposite direction and slowed again as it approached the entrance to the trailer park, then turned into the driveway and rolled past him into the labyrinth of narrow streets between the rows of mobile homes.

Obviously, it was someone who was looking for an address. Whoever it was, he reasoned, they were lost — whether they realized it or not. He just continued at his task watering the flowers and paid no more mind. He had become well-practiced at minding his own business since living in that isolated, miniscule berg.

After a short, unnoticed while, he was nearly finished with his watering chores and began coiling up the hose when he noticed that the minivan was coming back out from the criss-crossing roads and toward him still standing by the flagpole flower bed. The vehicle slowed to a stop and the driver began rolling down the window. Foster put the coil of hose down, sensing that the person at the wheel might be stopping to ask for directions. He waited until the minivan came to a full stop and an attractive woman seated behind the wheel turned to look at him and called out, "Sir? Can you help me?"

He walked up to the side of the minivan and looked at the woman behind the open window. He couldn't believe his eyes, "Oh my word!"

He stood there in shock. "Livvy? Livvy — *is that you?*"

She sat frozen for a moment, then asked, "I'm sorry sir, do I know you?" His voice sounded oddly familiar to her but she couldn't place the face.

"*Hell yeah!* I mean, yes, you know me. You're *married* to me — or at least you used to be."

"I don't..." She cut herself off as she looked more intently at the scruffy, bearded man with the long hair and floppy hat that stood outside her door. "Denny? Is that you?"

"Yeah, Livvy, it's me!" He quickly grabbed his hat and lifted it up off of his head so she could see him better.

"Oh, my goodness!" she threw the door open, nearly clipping him in the face with it, and then ran up to him and embraced him.

She then froze and quickly stepped back from him, "I'm so sorry, I shouldn't have done that — it was presumptuous. Sorry. It's just that it's *so good* to see you! I've been looking for you for *so long!*"

Foster was stunned, but still, he couldn't help but smile, "It's okay. I'm really glad to see you, too, Livvy — I *really am!* I can't believe it — I've missed you *so much.*"

She stepped back away from him. He didn't think he'd ever see her face again and then all of a sudden— out of the blue, in the middle of nowhere — there she was.

Livvy stood awkwardly without saying anything for a moment and then quickly looked around behind them at the rows of trailers, "Do you live here?"

"Uh, yeah, I do."

"I thought so. Someone told me that I could find you here."

"Nobody knows I live here — or at least, nobody knows that Dennis Foster lives here. Who told you?"

"Ted. He called me a few days ago."

"A few *days* ago? From prison?"

"Prison? No, I don't think so. I could hear noise in the background like he was in a big office somewhere. Lots of voices, people typing, phones ringing, that sort of thing."

"Son of a bitch," Foster grumbled. "Played me again."

"What do you mean?"

Foster grinned broadly and offered, "Oh, it doesn't matter — are you hungry?"

"Hungry? Uh, yeah, I suppose I could eat. I've been on the road from Vegas for most of the day trying to find this place."

"Great. Let's go back to my trailer so I can clean up and we'll go get a bite."

"You mean, like a date?" She coyly smiled.

"Uh, okay. Yeah, like a date. Unless you have a problem with that idea, then let's just call it dinner."

"No, I actually like the idea. A *second* first date."

"'A second first date'," he smiled again. He couldn't recall the last time he'd been so spontaneously inspired to grin so broadly.

"Hop in. You can navigate me through this maze."

Foster jogged around to the passenger side of the minivan and climbed in. He directed her to drive back into the park to find his trailer and then invited her in. She sat down in his obsessively neat and orderly — albeit tiny — living room while he scurried to the back bathroom and bedroom to wash up and put on a clean pair of pants and a clean dress shirt (though he chose to casually leave it untucked).

As he came back up the hallway, she asked, "I didn't see any restaurants in town when I drove through."

"Well, technically, there aren't any. But there's the diner at the Little A'Le'Inn."

"I saw that place. Didn't look like much. I thought it was just a gift shop for tourists."

"It's that, too, but the food's great — comfort food, ya' know. And the people are really nice."

"I wouldn't care if they weren't."

Foster got quiet and leaned up against the end of the kitchen counter, his face changing to a more serious expression, "Uh, before we go, I need to say something," he took a breath and sheepishly looked down at the floor. "Umm, I've had an awful lot of time to think about this — about us. In fact, aside from trying to just stay alive, it's really all I've been thinking about for the past couple of years or so. Sweetie, I was an ass, I know. They manipulated me and got me to believe all sorts of things about you that I never should have. I should have known better. I hate myself for what happened between us," he sighed and looked up at her. "I should never have doubted you and I should *never* have lied to you. I wish I could somehow take it all back." He looked up from the floor, "I should have just walked away from it all right at the beginning."

Her face flushed as he spoke and her eyes began to well up. He reached back behind himself and tore off a few paper towels from the roll hanging above the sink and handed them to her to wipe away her tears.

"I don't want this momentary euphoria to be riding on a dark foundation that could just collapse out from under us for good, I'm not sure I could handle that." He continued. "I want to get this out in the open before we go any farther. No more lies." He took another breath. "Can you forgive me?"

His plea caused her to smile for a brief moment. "They manipulated me, too, Denny. I should have trusted you. I knew there were things that you couldn't tell me. I remember your days at Cyberdine when you couldn't tell me stuff. I knew I married a rocket scientist and a lot of what he worked on were government secrets. I should have known better, too. But when things started happening with our finances, the IRS, creepy guys in black hanging around and then that phone call from that woman, my mind was overwhelmed, I just couldn't take it anymore. So much bad happening so fast and when they took everything we had left and we had to leave the house, it seemed the best thing to do then to just walk away." She wiped her eyes and then looked up at him with a faint smile, "I've regretted that day ever since. But then I saw the interview on television."

"You did? I just did the one interview with that local station in Las Vegas. How did you see it?"

"The national networks aired it. They explained that you had walked in off the street in Las Vegas to tell all about Area Fifty-One and the whole secret alien laboratory story. As you talked, even though they hid your face and made your voice sound weird, the things you said began to ring true to me. I could remember when you'd come home and hint at some of it from time to time. And then when you talked about what happened at the end, how that woman set you up and they fired you, I knew it was you."

"I should have known I couldn't fool you, even with the hat."

"I got a Las Vegas phone book and started looking for your number. I found it — at least I *thought* it was you — but when I called, it was disconnected. So I drove out to see if I could find you. I didn't know where to begin. I looked in the casinos, the hotels, finally ended up in a diner and asked if anyone had seen you and showed your picture around. They told me there that you had actually worked there as a cook for a while but then, one day, you just didn't show up for work and they'd never seen you again. The owner seemed to be pretty ticked off about it all."

"Yeah, I kinda feel bad about that, but I had to just disappear. I couldn't take the risk to give notice or even say good-bye. They had shot at me the night before as I drove home from work — I've got bullet holes in my car! They knew where I was, where I lived, where I worked. I was running for my life and didn't want to give them a second chance."

"I figured it was something like that." She stood up from the chair and took a step toward Foster. "I've been trying so hard to find you, Denny. I now know the truth, I know it was all a lie. I should have seen right through it back then. I've been looking for you to ask if you would forgive *me*."

"It's been a really rough road, sweetie, but I've never stopped loving you. Ever. Living out here in the desert is safe, but painfully lonely. Still, I couldn't dare hope that this moment would ever happen."

She thought for a moment and then hesitantly asked, "Did you ever find another girlfriend?"

Foster laughed, "Ha, ha! A nerd like me? Seriously?"

"Some girls are attracted to nerds like you. This one is."

"Well, no, there was never anyone else. Even when I was convinced that we could never be together again. There was only ever one girl for me, I just wasn't interested. You?"

"No. Never."

"I can't believe a girl like you — sexy and beautiful and so smart — didn't have a long line of wannabe suitors."

"Well, if I did, I never noticed. I had my guy — out there, somewhere. I couldn't believe it when Ted called me, I don't know how he got my phone number. By the time he did, I'd already moved a couple of times."

"I know how he got it."

"You do?"

"Yeah. He's one of *them*, part of that whole government machine."

"Ted?"

"That's not his real name. He went by Mike Casey here in Rachel, did a UFO radio show from a studio in a trailer out on the outskirts of town. He told me that his real name was Tom Finley — but I'd be skeptical of even that."

"And his girlfriend?"

"Bambi?! Ha, ha! She was one of them, too. She was also Dr. Kimber's assistant Melissa Lopez in St. Louis and then Dr. Jennifer Teller at the lab."

"The one who called me?"

"One and the same."

"Oh, Denny, I had no clue."

"I know, me either. But that was apparently the idea all along."

"What about the aliens, the space ships you saw, that new element you discovered there? Was that all fake, too?"

"The readings on the test machines I was working with can't lie. That much was real, I know. I have to think that, if element 115 was real, then the saucers that I saw and the autopsy were just as real."

"Why all the theatrics, then?"

"To get me to do the work that I did for them and then, when they got out of me what they wanted, to have an easy way to get rid of me, discredit me and keep me quiet. I got them to a point where they would be able to go ahead and synthesize the element, that's all they wanted from me."

"My goodness," she whispered. "That's amazing — the lengths that they went to."

"I honestly believe that I don't even know the half of it. There's probably so much more that I never even got a glimpse of."

"Doesn't that make you angry?"

"Hmph — you know, it did — at first, anyway. For a long time I was really angry. They were relentless, wouldn't let up and then, finally, losing you. But then I realized how pointless it was. 'You can't fight city hall,' right? After that, all I wanted to do was disappear so maybe they'd leave me alone and, if they didn't think that I was a threat to them anymore, maybe they'd leave you alone, too."

"So you ended up here in the middle of nowhere?"

"I tried to make it in Vegas but I found out that they had somehow gotten my degrees to evaporate, too. When I applied for a job, the guy who interviewed me accused me of fraud and threatened to report me to the FBI. I figured I'd find something to do there to pay the bills while I tried to straighten that out and found a job as a short-order cook at that diner. Thought I was far enough under the radar that I could just take it easy — until they tried to kill me."

"That's when you did the interview."

"That's right, on my way out of town."

"So, now what?"

"Now what? What do you mean?"

"I mean, you know — us," she added hesitantly. "What about us? Do you think we could ever pick up where we left off? Where we were before all of this?"

"Well, I don't see any need to forgive you, even though you asked me to. In my mind, there's nothing to forgive. If you can forgive me, we can go out for that second first date and see where it leads us."

"Funny, I feel the same way. I know now what happened and, no, there isn't anything to have to forgive you for, either. I think the only fault in either of us is that we trusted and believed people who couldn't be trusted and chronically lied to both of us. They engineered all of this."

"So — 'where we'd left off'? Certainly a little older and a lot wiser though, I'm sure," Foster mused. "I think it was Mark Twain who said that 'the best revenge is success'." He smiled at her.

"I was in church last year…" She began.

"Church? You got religion since I last saw you?"

"Or it got me, I'm not sure which. I was alone. Every time I looked down at the ring on my finger, I felt a pang of fear. I just sort of wandered into a church in the neighborhood where I was living at the time — just to listen."

"And that helped?"

"A little. At least I felt like I had somewhere I could go and wasn't so alone anymore. But something the pastor said one Sunday changed everything. He was teaching out of Second Corinthians. I'll never forget what he said: 'We are troubled on every side, yet not distressed. We are perplexed, but not in despair. We are persecuted, but not forsaken, cast down but not destroyed'."

Foster stood there for a long, silent moment as he absorbed his wife's words. "That's powerful stuff," he said quietly. "It's as if whoever wrote it was talking to us."

"You said that the best revenge is success. How do we define that? Getting our lives back? Our home? Your job? I don't think so. We — you and me — together, we two are success. Putting us back together, for richer or poorer, in sickness and in health, till death do us part. That's success." She walked up to him and put her arms around him and looked him in the eye, "I'm game if you are."

"I can't go back to California," he warned.

"I don't care. This place looks kinda cozy."

"You could live out here in the desert? The middle of literally nowhere, as you observed? There isn't a mall for a hundred miles or more."

"That doesn't matter. I'd be here with you. It's peaceful here, quiet. I think I could get used to it."

He glanced around the inside of the trailer and then chuckled, "Okay, okay. Look, I've been thinking lately, what about this idea — tell me if you think it's a stupid idea — but maybe, with you back, we could make it happen. I really liked Boston when I was going to school there. I have a little money saved up. What if we moved there, far away from Area Fifty-One and these men in black. What if we opened up a bakery or a deli or something? It turns out I seem to have a talent for working in a kitchen. Who knew?"

"I don't think it's a stupid idea at all. I could bake things and we could sell floofy coffee." She pulled herself up close to him and kissed him.

"Hmph, hey, not so fast, young lady," he joked. "I don't kiss on the first date."

"That's not what I heard."

"Oh?"

"How about that second first date? Then maybe we drive to Boston in the morning."

"Ha, ha, ha! Temptress." He smiled a mischievous, broad grin, "Just one more question first."

"What's that?"

"Uhh...are you wearing any underwear?"

She chuckled, "Something special, lacy — black — just in case," she smiled seductively. "But that's for dessert." ∎

CHAPTER FORTY-THREE

You've Been Served

The Atomic Bakery & Deli on the corner of Berkeley and Stuart Streets in Boston had become a popular spot for the people working in the innumerable offices and businesses all around that part of the city, and in particular, the towering John Hancock building nearby. Early mornings, fresh pastries came out of the ovens and paired up with freshly-brewed coffees of various configurations and juices to begin the work days for hundreds of well-dressed customers wearing suits, ties and, on casual Fridays, polo shirts and neatly-pressed blue jeans.

In the warm weather months, they'd have small tables and chairs set up on the sidewalk out in front of the bakery. At midday, customers would often order sandwiches to bring them out there or bring them to nearby Copley Square to eat their lunches in the warm sunlight.

Denny and Livvy Foster had opened the shop after having fled the southwest desert and, they'd hoped, all of the complexities and pains that they'd left behind there. They made a new home for themselves in Brookline, a suburb on the green line, just outside of the city proper.

The decor inside the shop included photos and posters of the space race of the sixties and seventies. Images of Mercury, Gemini and Apollo spacecraft which included the cherished photo of Foster posing with astronaut Michael Collins from his days at Cyberdine Technologies. None of their customers ever asked any questions about the photos.

No one ever asked, either, about a large, metal sign on the wall just inside the door warning that it was a restricted government facility, that entry could result in arrest and imprisonment and deadly force was authorized. A few recognized it for what it was, a souvenir replica of the warning signs at Area Fifty-One and just chuckled when they saw it. It was just another element of the thematic decor.

Considering the name of the shop, customers just took for granted that all of the memorabilia on the walls was just part of that theme — part of the quirky ambiance of the place. Some of the more curious would take a few moments now and again to take a closer look and a few thought they recognized the young man in the photo with the astronaut as the same gray-haired guy behind the counter making coffee and serving them pastries and ham sandwiches.

In their late sixties by the time that calendars began to reach into the second decade of the twenty-first century, they had no intention of slowing down or — God forbid — retire. They had made a good life for themselves in Boston. As a married couple, they'd been tried in the fires that most would never in their wildest dreams ever have to endure or expect to survive and yet, somehow, they'd persevered. They'd been able to jettison any baggage from those most desperate days and move on with their lives.

They'd found a local church to be a part of and got involved in some local civic groups, using their business as a means to do some good, charitable work in the city. They'd been fortunate to find a few really good employees who'd by then been with them for several years.

Life was good. They were at peace. They seemed to have finally found their own personal "happily-ever-after."

Early one morning in the middle of the week, in the usual busyness of that hour, a young woman in a gray skirt suit stood in line, queued up along with innumerable regulars waiting patiently for their turn to step up to the counter and place their orders. She looked no different than any of those in the line wearing smart office attire and blended in as just one of the many faces queued up for their morning fix of caffeine and sugar.

Livvy stood behind the counter taking down each order for their two employees working alongside her to fulfill, pouring coffee and bagging up sweet morsels for breakfast noshing at countless desks throughout the city. They had a routine, a well-choreographed process that got customers in and out and on their way to work with minimal waiting.

One by one, each customer stepped up, greeted with a cheerful smile and was served. With their morning nosh in hand, they'd voice their thanks and walk back past the line to the door on the way to their respective offices. Finally, the woman in the gray suit stepped up for her turn at the counter and asked if Dennis Foster was in.

Livvy smiled and called out, "Denny?" without turning around, knowing he was busy at the back counter right behind her.

Before she could ask why the woman was asking for him, he'd heard his wife's voice as he was refilling the coffee grounds in one of the Bunn machines and turned to where she was standing at the counter and told the young woman, "Hi, I'm Dennis Foster. How may I help you?"

The woman reached out with a plain, unmarked white envelope and handed it to him. Once his fingers touched it, she humorlessly announced, "Dennis Foster, you've been served."

"Served?" His demeanor completely changed, "*What the hell is this?*"

"You've been invited to testify at the Senate Judiciary hearing on unidentified aerial phenomenon in Washington next week."

"What?!"

"Why can't you people just leave us alone?!" Livvy snapped.

"Are you *Mrs.* Foster?" the woman asked.

"Yeah, I am. So what?"

"Your name is on the subpoena, too. Have a nice day." The woman then turned on her heel and walked back across the shop, past the waiting line of waiting patrons, and out the door.

As Foster opened the envelope and he and Livvy looked over the papers inside in disbelief, the next person in line stepped up to the counter having overheard what had just happened and remarked, "I've heard about these hearings on the news. They want to examine all of the information about UFOs and aliens and Area Fifty-One and Roswell including the Air Force's Project Blue Book and the Robertson Panel. Everything the government has ever investigated — including themselves. They want to talk to you two?"

"Yeah," Foster replied. "Guess we just can't get far enough away from these people."

"You were involved in all of this stuff?"

"Involved? Yeah, you could say that."

"And now you run a bakery in Boston. That's so cool."

"Well, we certainly *thought* so. Until just now, that is."

"You need a lawyer?"

"A lawyer?"

Livvy looked up at her husband, "Might not be a bad idea, dear."

"You know someone?"

The man reached into his pocket and produced a business card, "As a matter of fact, yeah — me. I'd love to represent you."

Foster took the card and looked at the face of it. The man was Saul Rabinowitz, one of the partners at Rabinowitz, Rabinowitz and Rabinowitz, one of the most powerful and respected law firms in the city. He looked up at him and replied, "We don't have much money. The plane tickets and the hotel in Washington alone — we'll barely be able to cover those expenses. That is, I suppose, as long as we don't eat while we're down there."

"Pro bono, Mr. Foster. I'd be honored to stand up for you and your wife and my firm will cover any travel expenses."

"Why would you do that?" Livvy asked.

"This is the sort of case that law firms like mine hope would come along one day, the sort of thing that makes a real impact — maybe even historical. Besides, I've been coming here for a few years now and I see how you two are. If you don't mind me saying, there's a lot of love in this place. If anyone ever deserved someone like me to stand up for them, it's you two."

Just then, one of the young women who worked behind the counter with the Fosters reached around them with a large, empty coffee can and set it down where everyone in the place could see it, then reached into her pocket and peeled off a few bills and dropped them in. The other waitress stepped up beside her, tossed in a few dollars and then held the can up and called out to the rest of the people waiting in line, "Save the Fosters!"

Word spread quickly. As customers — regulars and others who had heard about what was happening through word of mouth — frequented the Atomic Bakery & Deli over the next week, they'd walk up to the counter to place their orders and dig deep to add to the collection in the tin can along with their change from each order.

With a broad smile on her face, Livvy began to cry. ∎

Epilogue

In the smoky, rowdy environs of Callahan's Irish Pub on Commercial Street in the north end of Boston, a small crowd was gathered for the second day of televised testimony from local heroes Dennis and Livvy Foster at the Senate hearing in Washington. The spectacle was showing simultaneously on all of the television screens at the bar and around the room with the volume turned up loud enough for everyone in the place to clearly see and hear every probing question and edged reply over the raucous din as the Fosters told their incredible story. The screens, normally tuned to some sort of sporting event — especially if the Red Sox or Patriots were playing — were all set to CSPAN to watch gavel-to-gavel coverage of what had become known as the "UFO Hearings."

The same scene was being replicated in pubs, bars, restaurants, appliance stores and even in the Atomic Bakery and Deli on Berkeley Street across town — anywhere a television screen could be set up to follow the drama, people were gathered around it. The various newspaper offices, television and radio newsrooms were gathered with most of their employees — some reporters, some just pulling for the "little guy" — engrossed in the proceedings with rapt fascination. People watched intently all over the city, listening to every word as Dennis Foster detailed his experiences at the secret Facility R-Four-Seven laboratories, what he saw at Groom Lake and Area Fifty-One, the insidious Ramos Project, the powerful new and still undefined ununpentium and the potential for a devastating new nuclear weapon. He detailed, too, how the government then tried to thoroughly destroy him when they were through with him — including the attempts on his life.

In Callahan's Pub, loud, rousing cheers and snarling jeers could be heard out into the busy street in response to certain parts of the tale as they were related, especially following some of Dennis Foster's barbed commentaries and the caustic back-and-forth jousting with some of the senators on the dais. As the proceedings continued and sequential pints were consumed, the crowds grew increasingly raucous and incrementally louder — as though they were watching the Dublin football team playing against Manchester for the World Cup.

The two waitresses who had been given charge of the Fosters' bakery while they were in Washington had brought in a large, flat-screen television and set it up on top of the glass bakery case so that everyone who came in for their daily coffees, pastries and sandwiches could stay updated on the store's beloved owners who'd been suddenly and unexpectedly thrust into the limelight as they stood up to the heavy-handed oppressions of their own government. It wasn't lost on anyone that, if they could do all that to such nice people as the Fosters, they could do it to anyone. Anyone at all.

It was a genuine "David and Goliath" sort of scenario and everyone was enthusiastically — and vociferously — rooting for "David."

Many of the bakery's patrons who had come in for their regular coffees, pastries and sandwiches each of those two days, lingered in the shop for as long as they could to watch and hear a bit of the testimony before having to return to their respective offices but would continue to follow the drama on their smartphones or stream it on their desktop computers throughout the rest of the day. They continued to generously add money to the tin can on the counter wanting to show their support, knowing that the hearings and all the legal fees and logistics associated with them were costing money that small business owners like them could ill-afford.

The city of Boston was once again feeling caught up in that same rebellious spark that a couple of centuries before had inspired the infamous "Tea Party" and the skirmish at nearby Lexington and Concord that began the struggle for independence from an oppressive and intrusive government in earnest. The complacent trust that people had thoughtlessly placed in their government at every level from local municipal leaders all the way up to the White House itself — and the vast network of black operatives that were gradually being exposed in the Fosters' testimony — was quickly evaporating.

The Phoenix and the Boston Globe had each run human-interest articles on the Fosters over the previous week putting a face on their local heroes. That, and enthusiastic word of mouth, had alerted the entire populace to the spectacle and anyone who could, made certain that they would not miss a moment of it. In the articles, a photo of the couple posed in front of the Atomic Bakery and Deli appeared along with the address in the accompanying stories. Though it was great publicity for the shop — and it's said that there is no such thing as bad publicity — the Fosters would have been just as happy without it.

The shop had become a sort of pilgrimage destination for well-wishers from all around the city. Someone began leaving flowers and other things on the sidewalk in front of the shop's big front window the night before the hearing was to begin, propped up against the wall. Some left notes of encouragement, small teddie bears and a few big-eyed, green-faced stuffed aliens that were added over the next several days, even after the hearing would end until the Fosters' return to the city.

A large paper banner hung in the front window of the bakery that said in bold, hand-painted blue letters, "Save The Fosters!" The tin souvenir Area Fifty-One warning sign mounted on the wall by the front door had suddenly taken on new significance to those who walked into the place and some — like the UFO groupies in the desert — paused to take selfies beside it.

As the broadcast ended on the first day of the hearing and dusk gathered over the city, people began to add candles to the growing collection on the sidewalk in front of the shop and many people gathered there to show support and talk about the day's events. Members of the couple's church came to pray for the them in an all-night vigil, bringing snacks and hot coffee for anyone gathered there after the shop had closed.

Finally, nearing the end of the second of two long days of testimony, the Fosters had related all that they had come to say. Senator Chow pounded his gavel on the dais and sternly looked across at Dennis seated at the witness table before him. "Mr. Foster, the esteemed members of this panel have sat here for two days, enduring your interminable, ponderous relating of a story that I can only characterize as a dubious flight of science fiction and conspiracy fantasy. I haven't heard such a fairy tale since reading bedtime stories to my grandchildren."

"You've wasted an enormous amount of this panel's time and taxpayers' money," Senator McDermott chimed in.

Rabinowitz leaned forward toward his microphone to respond on his client's behalf, but Foster reached out and placed his hand on his lawyer's shoulder, "Thanks, Saul, but I got this."

Rabinowitz cupped his hand over the microphone in front of him and replied, "You sure, Denny?"

"Oh, yeah. I'm sure. Remember what you said to me? This isn't for their benefit, it isn't even for us, this is for America. This is for all those people out there watching and listening to this circus who are suddenly realizing that they could just as easily become the next victims of such overreaching government manipulations. Yeah, Saul, I got this."

"Okay," Rabinowitz sat back in his chair and grinned, waving his hand toward the dais. "They're all yours."

Foster turned back toward his own microphone, looked up at the senator and smiled a sly smile. "Senator Chow, I have spent these two days patiently telling you nothing but the unvarnished truth. I've held nothing back. I've answered your ridiculous battery of insipid questions and responded to each ignorant accusation with complete honesty. I have no physical proof, no photos, no documentation — you and your people have made certain of that. Believe me or don't believe me. Frankly, Senator, I don't give a damn one way or another."

"Are you accusing me of having orchestrated the things that you allege were done to you?" Chow retorted.

Foster stood up and began pointing out faces seated behind the panelists, "The man in the black suit sitting behind Senator McDermott — his name is Dwayne Steele, the boogie man himself. He's one of the black operatives that I talked about — an inhuman, soulless creature. He's the man who did all the dirty work for them, the man who tore my life apart, split up my marriage — the man who tried to kill me. Now he's sitting smugly behind the dais as an advisor to a Senate investigative panel. And behind you, Senator Chow, that scowling, balding, tired-looking old man with the loud tie, he's the puppetmaster. He's the one who calls the shots, Steele's boss. Even more soulless and inhuman — keeping himself hidden the whole time in the shadows. And he's sitting back there whispering in your ear!"

Chow banged his gavel to get Foster to stop talking but he would not be intimidated.

Foster leaned in and continued, "I see a number of other familiar faces back there, too — people who were there at Facility R-Four-Seven, at the Groom Lake air base and even at the airports. Can you explain that, Senator?! Tell me that you have had nothing to do with any of this! Tell me this isn't a bona-fide government conspiracy! Tell me your hands are clean!" His face was becoming flushed with rage, "Go ahead — I dare you — lie to me again!"

The crowd at Callahan's cheered wildly as Foster verbally assaulted the senators on the panel.

A loud murmur of voices erupted behind him in the hearing room gallery as Chow again pounded his gavel and shouted out, "Order! Order!"

Livvy reached out and grabbed her husband's arm. He looked over at her to see her smiling up at him and nodding her approval.

"Mr. Foster, lying at a Senate investigative hearing is a felony — are you aware of that? You are dangerously flirting with contempt!"

Foster slapped his hand on the table top and barked back, "Contempt?! Contempt?! Senator, you don't know the half of it! Before all of this, I was a hardened patriot. I worked with thousands of others who had put men on the moon and beat out the Russians. We built orbiting satellites, space laboratories and the shuttles. I was proud of what we had accomplished and proud of my country. I can't describe how much it pains me to realize that arrogant, power-drunk, sniveling sociopaths like you are now at the helm of this great nation! People like you who look down on people like me with such disdain that you wouldn't think twice about squashing us like a bug to accomplish your political ends. We're nothing to you! Disposable! We're just collateral damage — all in the name of 'national *freakin'* security'!"

Chow violently pounded his gavel with a flaming red face, purple veins protruded from his forehead as he once again warned Foster, "You are in contempt! Stop now or else I'll have you behind bars!" He waved his gavel to a couple of marshals in the room to have them close in on the ranting Foster in preparation to handcuff him and take him away.

"How dare you, Senator? How dare you?! You're supposed to be a servant of the people — the only 'people' you serve is yourself — you narcissistic, self-righteous, sick son-of-a-bitch! Go ahead, throw me in jail! That won't make anything that I said any less true! In fact, that would just prove that every bit of it was undeniably true and you can't bear to have it revealed to the American people! So, go ahead!" He turned to the marshals and held out his wrists, "*Go ahead!*"

Chow continued pounding his gavel while Foster spoke, interrupting and shouting over him, "Shut up, Mr. Foster! Dammit, stop talking! Stop talking now!"

"You put on these hearings, broadcast all over the country, photographers from magazines and newspapers snapping away for that money shot to put on their front covers. This whole thing is just another political dog-and-pony show. 'Let's investigate the whole unidentified aerial phenomena thing once and for all.' All to manufacture the illusion that you give a damn, to make you look good and help ensure your reelection. But what is your report going to show? Nothing — 'inconclusive' — as usual. Why put on this show and then shut down someone who dares to lay open the truth? What are you afraid of?" Finally, Foster stopped and took a long breath. He lowered his hands, standing with his fingertips resting on the tabletop and the red flush was beginning to drain from his face. He looked up at Chow and calmly added, "Are we done, here?"

"Done?! No, Mr. Foster, we're not done until I say we're done!"

"I'm sorry, Senator," Foster replied in a sedate, measured tone. "That was a rhetorical question," He reached down and wrapped his hand around Livvy's arm, urging her to stand up from her seat. "We're done." He turned to his wife and said, "Come on, sweetie, let's go home."

She stood up, smiling, and gave him a quick peck on the cheek. Camera strobes flashed furiously all around them to capture the moment — the so-called money shot — the real story behind the story not lost on the public. It wasn't really about UFOs and aliens, it was all about a couple who had persevered through the morass, whose bond was too strong for the government machine to tear apart. What God had joined, try as they might, the government's darkest elements could not pull asunder.

Gatherings all over Boston cheered and erupted in applause as they watched the Fosters on television, computer and cell phone screens throughout the city.

Followed by their attorney — who had clearly been caught by surprise, scurrying to pack up his briefcase and keep up with them — they turned their backs on the senators and defiantly walked away from the witness table, down the center aisle toward the doors through a gauntlet of cheers and applause punctuated by the piercing sound of Chow's gavel violently pommeling on the receding dais behind them.

When they neared the doors, a pair of Secret Service agents stepped in front of them, blocking their way with grim expressions. The Fosters fully expected to be stopped in their tracks, maybe even arrested.

They kept walking without a pause. As soon as they approached the doors however, the agents each reached across and grabbed one of the handles from either side of the aisle and pulled the doors open wide to allow the Fosters their hard-fought freedom.

The crowd gathered at the Atomic Bakery & Deli exploded again in applause. A small group that had gathered outside on the sidewalk waiting for news or watching the CSPAN broadcast on smartphones and tablets, yelled and cheered and banged on the window, waving to the waitresses inside — who were themselves jumping up and down and cheering wildly — showing thumbs up and beaming smiles. Some began to weep with joy and call out their thanks to God through bright, tearful smiles.

Photographers from the Globe and the Herald posted at the corner of Berkeley and Stuart Streets awaiting the reactions of the gathered crowd, snapped photos of the celebration while television news reporters with microphones in hand stood along the sidewalk in front of the shop with cameramen facing them with the celebratory crowd behind them to report the event for the evening news and streaming reports on their respective websites. Some ventured inside to get comments from the bakery's waitresses and customers gathered around the television screen toasting the Fosters with cups of freshly-made espresso.

Television studio vans were double-parked along the curbs on either side of the streets and any remaining clear roadway was throughly blocked with other vehicles and crowds of Bostonians waving homemade signs and cheering loudly for Denny and Livvy and their victory.

They'd tilted at the government windmill and prevailed.

The Fosters walked through a gathering of cheering people in the hallway just outside of the hearing chamber's doors. Rabinowitz walked ahead of the couple, trying to clear a path for the three of them to pass through as they were being mobbed by well-wishers and reporters reaching microphones and digital recording devices out into their faces. Dennis and Livvy kept their heads down as much as they could. The small, previously disinterested gathering that had been in that hallway when they'd first arrived the morning before had since more than doubled. Security guards and velvet ropes kept them corralled within that segment of the hallway just outside of the hearing room's doors.

Finally, they made their way through the crowd, beyond the ropes and out to the expansive, echoing lobby while Rabinowitz and security guards successfully kept the last of the pursuing media at bay.

Outside the glass lobby doors to Constitution Avenue where a livery car was waiting to take them back to the hotel, was another swarming mass of even more hungry media. Outside of the building they were unrestrained — television cameras, innumerable reporters with microphones and digital recorders once again poised to be extended out into their faces. They watched like hungry predators through the glass, waiting for the Fosters' approach.

When the hearings were first announced, the news media at large paid little attention. UFOs and Area Fifty-One were the stuff of science fiction movies and paperback novels. There was other "real" news to be focused on. But then the Fosters began their sensational testimony and all of that attention turned and focused on them.

The curbing on either side of the street was lined with vans emblazoned with the logos and channel numbers of a dozen or more local television and news agencies with their satellite dishes and antennae extended high into the air. News reporters' cameras, some photographers standing on step ladders, waited to follow them from the doors to the curb and get photos of them over the swarm of media.

Without passes to be inside the building, the Fosters were protected from them for the time being.

The trio stopped in the middle of the open lobby, relatively devoid of other people, just a few who passed by them attending to their own business within the government building and paying little mind to the three of them standing there catching their collective breaths. They were safe there, away from the seething media. Livvy looked out across the lobby's expanse, past the metal detecting arches and out through the glass doors to the street at the roiling mob of media that were gathered outside waiting for them and sighed, "We have to walk through that now?"

"Apparently — you two have suddenly become national heroes," Rabinowitz commented, surveying the scene with her.

"I never wanted to be a hero," Foster commented. "I just wanted them to leave me alone — to leave us alone."

"Dennis Foster?" a man's voice echoed from behind them in the open, marble-walled space.

Foster turned and saw two men walking toward them. One, a middle-aged man of color with short, curly hair. He was tall and wearing a dark blue sport coat over a pink polo shirt, pressed blue jeans and white deck shoes. The other man was much shorter, thin, with a mustache and receding hairline. He wore round wire-rimmed glasses and dressed in a tweed suit replete with plaid bow-tie. The pair couldn't have appeared to be any more incongruent.

As they neared, the man in the polo shirt — the more extroverted of the pair — reached out his hand to him, "Mr. Foster, a word, please?"

Foster reluctantly reached out and shook the man's hand then turned and shook hands with the man in tweed, "Who are you two?"

"We are opportunity come knocking, Dennis — may I call you Dennis?"

"I suppose — it is my name afterall. So," Foster asked with an edge of suspicion, "what do you mean by 'opportunity'?"

"Let me introduce myself. My name is Jackson Braun. I'm with Parker and Ford Productions in Hollywood. My colleague here is Mr. Myron Krebbs with the Fifth Avenue Publishing Company in Boston. We want to tell your story."

"What? Tell our story? What are you talking about?"

"A movie, Dennis! A big-budget Hollywood production and a best-selling novel."

"Seriously?"

"Yes," Krebbs soberly replied. "Seriously."

"The nation has always had a fascination with UFOs and aliens. Hundreds of movies and I don't know how many books have captured people's imagination. Mostly they've been the product of someone else's imagination — pure fiction, vapid entertainment. Your story, well, your story is different. There's substance to it, real meat that people can get their teeth into. Everyone — I don't care about their politics, race, religion, finances — everyone feels that the government has screwed them over somehow or other. Whether they believe you or not, they won't be able to keep from being drawn into it, talk about it, debate with one another — even argue about it. They can relate. The little guy standing up to the big, bad, oppressive government. Abused, crushed, deceived — he stands up, shakes his fist in defiance and shouts back 'Im not gonna take it anymore!' He's not just a number, he's not nobody, he's a man — with no less dignity and no less import. Everyone loves to cheer for the underdog. It's classic, it's huge!"

Foster couldn't help but be taken by the man's unbridled enthusiasm, he was undoubtedly a practiced and polished pitchman. He looked at his wife for a moment who just shrugged her shoulders with a faint smile. He thought for a moment, then his expression melted and he turned back to Braun, "Naah, I don't buy it. You two are with them in there. You're just baiting me, taking another stab at me to get back for what I said."

"I assure you, Mr. Foster," Krebbs pleaded, "we're in earnest." He reached into his jacket pocket and produced a business card. Braun did likewise and they handed them to Foster.

He looked at the two cards in his hand for a quick moment and then handed them to Rabinowitz, "You know, I can have business cards made up at any print shop in Boston that can say anything on them that I like. Those don't necessarily mean anything — might not even be your real names."

"Well," Braun responded as he reached into a pocket inside his jacket and removed an envelope with the production company's logo printed in the corner and Foster's name hand-written across its face, "I can appreciate how all of this could make a man so jaded, but maybe this will be more convincing."

Foster took the envelope from him, it was thin and flimsy, containing just a single piece of paper. The flap wasn't sealed so he flipped it up and slid out the contents. His eyes widened in astonishment as he quickly tried to catch his breath. He turned and showed it to Livvy, "Oh, my word..." she stumbled as she looked at it.

He closed the envelope up again and looked back at Braun, "That's a lot of zeroes. Is this for real?"

"You can cash it anywhere."

"Once you sign the contracts, of course," Krebbs qualified.

"This is for my story? To use it for your movie and for your book?"

"No, Dennis, this is just the retainer, to option your story. Krebbs has a check, too — a couple less zeroes — for the rights to your story for the book."

"Then the royalties, box office and various other residuals after that — action figures, flying saucer toys, little white Matchbox Jeeps, DVDs and videos, the movie soundtrack," Krebbs added. "That's the real money."

"This isn't 'real' money?" Foster asked as he handed the envelope off to Rabinowitz to take a look.

"Is there a quiet place where the four of us can sit and talk about this?"

"Uhh, five of us."

"Five?"

"Mr. Rabinowitz is our attorney. He'll be representing us. We won't sign anything until he's had a chance to review it and ask any questions he might have."

"We were hoping to keep this simple."

"You've heard my testimony, I assume you've seen the Vegas interviews on TV, you know what I've been through. I'm sure you can understand why we have trust issues."

Braun chuckled, "Of course." He reached out his hand and shook with the lawyer, "Mr. Rabinowitz."

"How about the restaurant at our hotel?"

"Sure, I think that would work just fine."

"One thing," Livvy interjected.

"What's that, Mrs. Foster?"

"In the movie — can we have Johnny Depp play Denny?"

"Johnny Depp? Ha, ha! Well, Mrs. Foster, I can't make any promises but I'll have my people call his people and see if we can't make that happen." ∎

END

Thank Yous, Acknowledgements, and Endorsements

Dana Pierce for suggesting the story being
bracketed with a contentious Senate hearing.

The Mount Mansfield Scale Modeling Association,
the on-line Grumpy Scale Modeler's Group
and Starship Modeling Society
for inspirations and encouragements in the construction
and photography of models used for illustrations.

The Smithsonian Institute Air & Space exhibits.

Dr. James Dobson.

The family of brothers and sisters and long-time friends of
Union Baptist Church of Waterford, Vermont
and Crossroads Church of Littleton, New Hampshire.

My wife of thirty-four years (so far), Stephanie.

About the Author

Bob Pierce was born and raised in southern Connecticut and has lived in New England all of his life (so far, anyway),

currently residing in northern Vermont in which many of his novels are set, particularly those featuring the character of Jack Walsh. He's been a graphic designer for almost all of his adult life and has written numerous articles for periodicals and promotional copy for clients. This is his fourteenth novel.

Other artistic pursuits include painting, photography and illustrating. His paintings have shown in galleries all over the east coast and reside in collections across the country. He also works on a freelance basis for publications, marketing and promotional companies both as a writer and designer. He coaches other independent authors and has an instructional video series on YouTube called "From the Studio" to help them complete their projects and self-publish them.

He is married to Stephanie, has three married sons and five beautiful granddaughters.

On his mother's side, Bob has a rich Irish heritage and his wife's parents were first-generation immigrants from Ukraine and Czechoslovakia. He has a deep interest in both his and his wife's respective heritages and draws heavily from each for the cultures and histories woven into many of his books.

Contact him at BobsAwesomeBooks@gmail.com and keep up with the writing process of his future projects by following his "Bob's Awesome Books" Facebook page and online at www.BobsAwesomeBooks.com.

Other Titles by Bob Pierce

One Kill: Hunting Lilith

She was alluring and deadly, credited with dozens of brutal contract killings. He was a celebrated writer and a social neanderthal who found his fellow man to be an annoyance. Their worlds collide when she recruits him to write her biography. He is captivated and finds himself relating with her scarred humanity. She was a black widow — but still he couldn't resist a self-destructive attraction. Hunted by an obsessed FBI agent for over two decades when they realize they can follow the writer to find the assassin and once she'd been eliminated, he would be next to keep her secrets from being published.

Blood on the Moskva
A Murder of No Consequence.

She was a beautiful young woman of privilege, the only daughter of a powerful minister of the Russian Duma. Murdered in her suite at an exclusive resort and suspicions immediately fall upon a Russian mobster boss. Detective Yuri Rozanov and his FSB Vory Section team are called to Moscow to arrest him. But Rozanov senses a face-saving political media event when he's shown no real evidence to support the government's case and so launches his own investigation. Frustrated by the Kremlin's road blocks, his team is immersed into the notoriously depraved Moscow nightclub scene in the thick of ruthless mobsters and international espionage as they work to unravel the complicated case. They face threats to their lives and careers both from within and without, side-stepping political entanglements as they dig deeper to ultimately find the truth.

Soldiers Statesmen Thieves & Spies
The Legend of Vanished Confederate Gold.

When the Confederate capital of Richmond fell at the end of the war, President Jefferson Davis and what was left of his government fled the city bringing with them the entire Confederate treasury. In the next couple of weeks the war would end, Davis was arrested and the treasury had vanished.

Recruited for one last spy mission by Abraham Lincoln's spymaster and with the aid of Moses Jones and old friend Samuel Clemens, James Butler "Wild Bill" Hickok orchestrates the secret destination of a legendary cache of gold and silver.

Perilous that it already was, nothing and no one, it seems, turned out to be quite what they may have appeared.

Made in the USA
Middletown, DE
03 June 2022

66462435R00250